ALONE NO MORE

Also by Marvin Noe

ALONE

ALONE AGAIN

ALONE IN THE COLLINS HOUSE

ALONE NO MORE

MARVIN NOE

ISBN 978-1-5142-4407-4

Printed in the United States of America

To contact the author write to:
Marvin Noe
2311 West 16th Avenue
Spokane, Washington 99224

Or email:
marvinnoe@msn.com

ACKNOWLEDGEMENTS

This book again is dedicated to Roger Van Voorhees
and my wife Sandy Noe for their help editing
Alone No More.

CHAPTER 1

Twenty seven year old multimillionaire, Brad Collins, grew tired of sitting in his office with his sixty year old office manager yacking at him about him needing to be at the Oregon Beach with his family. "Lighten up Wendy. I'll be joining my family soon as I complete the purchase of the medical building. I'm so close to completing this deal I can't give up now."

"What is more important, acquiring more work, work you don't need, or your family?" Brad glared at Wendy. Wendy Olsen had been his faithful secretary for many years. "It is an easy question. Why aren't you answering me?" Still he remained silent. "Are you even listening to me?"

"Of course I'm listening to you. You know my wife's brother Ray Richards recently joined our group as our apartment manager. As of now he is the least paid employee we have. Marie and I are aware he will not be comfortable very long at his current pay level. I doubt you would sit around two years waiting for a pay raise while we build more apartments. If we can complete the purchase deal on the medical buildings, Junior could instantly earn more income. Once he is in a position to earn additional income Marie and I would feel much better about him being with our organization for many years to come."

"I still think you should be at the beach with your family and friends."

At the beach the Collins best friends from Seattle, Sam Anderson and Judy Anderson, were putting doubt in Brad's wife, Marie's mind. "Something is wrong, are you and Brad having marital problems we don't know about?"

"We are not having marital problems. Our marriage is fine. I'll call Brad again. Hopefully he won't be tied up in a meeting where I can't get him."

Marie's call went straight through. Brad answered her call on the third ring. "Hello Mrs. Collins how is my favorite person this fine day, are you and the boys having fun at the beach?"

"The children are having a blast. Emily and Laura, our nannies, are enjoying themselves. Sam and Judy are enjoying every minute of their

1

time here. That leaves me, I'm bummed out. I'm wondering if you are coming to the beach at all. Sam called the City Treasures Office in Vegas and was told there was no auction scheduled for Monday like you said. Do you mind telling me what is really going on?"

"Tell Sam he is full of shit, and to mind his own frigging business. On Monday the properties go on the auction schedule. I never said the properties were being auctioned off on Monday. Somebody wasn't listening to what I was saying. I told you the medical buildings have an eighty thousand dollar tax lien against them. I managed to track down why there were two different figures on the tax lien. One was the original tax lien. The second is the interest and penalties incurred. The problem I'm now having is the tax lien was filed by a lumber yard that sold one year ago. The new owner claims the money goes to him, and the old owner claims the money goes to him. It's a frigging mess. Al Claymore is now working on trying to find out if we pay the current owner would it clear the tax lien. That would allow the previous owner to sue the current owner if he thinks the money should be his. We may be a fraction away from getting the tax lien cleared so we can acquire the properties. I'm confident we are within hours of owning the property."

"Level with me, is this tax lien business on the up and up, or an excuse so you don't have to come to the beach. Are you avoiding the Anderson's?"

"Geez Marie, weren't you listening to me? Clean out your ears. I just explained what was going on. Why are you asking if I invented this tax lien to keep from going to the beach with my family?"

"Answer me. Did you invent the tax lien? I want to know the truth."

"I didn't make this shit up! Who in the hell do you think I am?" He shouted back. "Stay where you are, I'll call you right back." Brad ended the call long enough to search the archives of his phone for Al Claymore's number. He immediately called his wife back. "Do you have something to write on?"

"I do have pen and paper, what am I writing down."

He gave Al Claymore, their attorney's phone number to his wife. "That number belongs to Al Claymore, call him and chew his ass for a while. I've had enough ass chewing for one damn day. Tell that asshole Sam to mind his own business. Once a property is placed on the auction list, it cannot be bought off without paying the extra auction fee. The cost of the medical buildings would be twenty percent higher. On two million dollars that is two hundred thousand dollar increase." Brad hung up.

Tears streamed down Marie's cheeks as she turned to see Sam and Judy walk in. "Brad is furious at me for questioning him. He gave me our attorney's phone number and told me to chew on our attorney's ass a while. Brad hung up on me after saying he had enough of my accusations. I'll try to collect myself enough to call Al Claymore."

Marie wiped her tears away as she dialed Claymore's number. "Good afternoon Mrs. Collins. I haven't had the pleasure of hearing your charming voice for some time. What may I do for you?"

"I have a question for you. Are you working with my husband on some type of tax lien on the medical buildings we are trying to purchase?"

"Oh heavens yes, Mrs. Collins, didn't he tell you. Your husband is upset with me, and irritated with everyone involved. The progress I'm making is slow. I'm working as hard as I can to clear this matter. We all know the medical buildings are a buy of a lifetime. To get a clear title to the property we need this tax mess cleared up. Brad told me the delay in purchasing the property is creating havoc with his family life. Working these multi-party deals is always hard. Too many fingers all trying to grab as much money as they can. I feel we are so close we might be able to end this charade tomorrow. I'm starting to feel like your husband, I'm starting to bark at everyone."

"Thank you for your information, Mr. Claymore, and do the best you can to clear away our problems." Marie ended the call shaking her head. "Am I ever in trouble, I accused Brad of making this tax lien business up. According to Al Claymore, our attorney, the tax lien is very real and irritating to everyone. If it weren't for disappointing the boys, I would grab my belonging and dash home to apologize to Brad. He is furious at me."

"Marie, you are not at fault for doubting Brad, this is our fault. Sam and I are to blame. Our questioning you got you in trouble. Sam or I had better call Brad, and explain what we did to cause her to question him." Sam failed to move so Judy grabbed the phone. Being angry Brad refused to answer her call. "Sam you try calling with your cell phone, we must contact him immediately. It's up to you and me to straighten out this mess we caused."

Seeing the ID caller's name Brad again refused to answer. In his current state of anger it was best not to speak with Marie, Judy, or Sam. Being observant, Wendy saw him brooding. "Okay Brad out with it, what is bothering you now?"

"Marie, Sam, and Judy all have what I call, Wendy syndrome. Like you they believe I'm dragging this frigging tax lean business out to avoid going to the beach. Everyone has Marie not believing me when I say this delay isn't my fault. What a damn mess."

"If that is all you are brooding about, stop brooding. I know the tax lien is real I can call Marie and straighten her out. Don't be too upset at Marie. She isn't totally wrong. I happen to think you should be at the beach. You can handle the tax lien next week. I realize it will be harder and more expensive to handle the tax lean next week. Your family is important too. Think what it would be like without your family. In the name of money you are risking your family."

"It won't do me any good to tell you not to call Marie, so call if you want. Don't expect me to speak with any of those people until I cool off. No telling how long it might be before I cool off. It may be snowing in Las Vegas before I cool off. People around me should know I despise my word being questioned by anybody. I'm out of here."

Seeing the office number on her phone Marie's eyes lit up. "This must be Brad calling now, wish me luck, hi Honey!"

"Hi Marie, it's me Wendy."

"Oh hi Wendy, I was hoping this was Brad calling. I goofed big-time and made him furious at me. I tried calling him back, but he won't take my calls. Do you have any idea where he might be?"

"Brad was here in the office waiting a call from Robin or Al Claymore. He made it clear he wasn't talking to anyone until he cools off. Then he stormed out the door. I'm not sure he will cool off anytime soon. He was spitting fire when he left here."

"I can be such an idiot at times. This beach trip was supposed to be a mini vacation for us, a place where we could relax and be a normal family. It may not help much, but if you see him give him a hug for me. Tell him I'm sorry, and I love him."

"As I said he just dashed out as I called you. I have no idea where he went, or if he will be back. I don't recall ever seeing him this angry. His anger scares me. One thing I do know, he should not be driving when he is so angry."

"I know, I should never have challenged his word. I knew better, but I did it anyway. Now I feel horrible."

Brad went over to Robin Tilly's reality office. He barged straight in. "Good morning Robin. These medical building, are money makers. We need them to generate additional income so we can pay young Ray more money. We want him to have the opportunity to work with us a very long time. The stress of putting this deal together is killing my relationship with my family. These medical building people are pissing me off."

"Don't kill yourself trying to do things you can't get done. Ray Junior is happy where he is now. He can see a brighter future as the second apartment complex is being built."

"Yes but what happens when he gets married. His office secretary is my first wife's sister. Junior has taken a shine to her. She is a wonderful gal. He isn't making enough money to support a family in a manner he would like. Robin, you know well as I do, money is king. I'm willing to take a chance on a long shot. I'm writing two eighty thousand dollar checks. Offer the lumber yard combatants eighty thousand dollars each to release their lien on the property. Maybe with them out of the picture we can complete the purchase of the medical buildings."

"Wow Brad, are you sure about this?" He nodded yes. "Alright, your offer should grease the wheels and get things moving."

"Thank you. I'll get out of your hair now. Have a good day."

Having no desire to go home to an empty house, Brad drove down to a casino. One huge advantage living in Las Vegas provided there was always a place to get away. The lounge he chose to get a beer was void of customers. The tall young brunette bartender greeted him with a smile. "How may I brighten your day?"

"Your pretty smile has already brightened my day." He read her name tag. "Nikki, I'll have a light beer. I'm not fussy. Whatever beer you have on tap is fine."

"I love easy customers." She stated patting his hand. She filled the chilled glass without spilling a drop or foam running down the outside of the glass. "There you go. You look sad this afternoon. What is bothering you?"

"Life is bothering me."

Nikki busted out laughing. She touched his hand again. "Until now I thought I had heard everything." She gently rubbed the back of his hand. "I'm a good listener if you care to explain how life is bothering you." Brad sat silent for a few seconds. "If you are worried about a secret of some kind, I'm good at keeping secrets."

"It would take months to tell you about my life. Then you might hate me much as everyone else does."

"Hate is a strong word. I highly doubt people hate you. They might get irritated at you but hate you, I don't think so. Give me the condensed version of your life."

"When I was five years old my parents abandoned me. I was left in the care of nannies as I grew up. I seldom saw my parents. I didn't realize it at the time but they were quite wealthy. For fear I could be kidnapped, and held ransom, they basically hid me away. I was never allowed to go outside and play. I couldn't have friends over to the house. Outside of school, I had no friends. I hated being alone and hated my parents more for abandoning me."

Nikki squeezed his hand tighter. "Under those conditions everyone would feel alone."

"My parents traveled all over the world for business. As the years slipped by I grew determined to prove how wrong my parents were to chase all over the world to gain wealth, in place of taking on the responsibility of raising me. Working here in Vegas, financially I've done well. With the death of my parents, I turned my attention to gaining the family and friends, I always wanted. Now it's as if I'm standing with one foot about to fall in the hole my parents fell into. My family is vacationing at the Oregon Beach with friends of ours, while I'm here in Vegas waiting to sign paperwork on a new purchase. A purchase that is too good to pass up. The seller is dragging his feet as he tugs at me for an extra nickel. My family and friends are screaming at me to be at the beach. My business managers, my friends, and most of all, my wife, are all gripping at me to join them at the beach. Everyone is pulling on me from all directions. They don't believe what I'm telling them what the holdup on the purchase is."

Nikki frowned. "Your wife doesn't believe you?"

"Not for a second does Marie believe a tax lien is holding up the completion of the sale. People not believing me is nothing new. I've always been straight forward with people. Why they don't believe me I don't know."

"I can tell by the way you are looking at your beer, you are not a big drinker. Be happy you are not a huge drinker. If you were a big drinker depressed as you are you would soon be falling off the stool. The average man coming in here would have been on their second drink by now."

"Tell me this, how can you, a person who just met me, know me so well and believe me yet my wife doesn't? We have been married over four years. We have two delightful children. When does complete unconditional love kick in?"

"I don't know. I'm a bartender not a therapist."

"You are better than a therapist. At least you are listening to me." Brad paused as he took a sip of beer. Nikki used her index finger to wipe a tiny bit of foam from his lips before licking her finger clean. "This property I'm trying hard to acquire would be additional property for my wife's brother to manager for us. The business will easily support doubling his income. Marie and I have all the money we need. My goal now is to keep family and friends close enough to us my children never experience the loneness I experienced growing up."

Nikki moved out from behind the bar to massage his shoulders and neck. "People in all walks of life experience stress. The trick is how we handle the stress. Others can't tell us what to do to reduce the stress in our lives."

"I have twelve to fifteen people all tugging at me without counting attorneys and accountants. I'm on mental overload. I have so many things going at once I have little time to concentrate on anything."

Nikki moved back behind the bar as a second customer entered the bar. "Don't run off."

Brad watched as the sexy bartender fixed the man a mixed drink. After getting his drink the customer walked back out into the gaming area. "Our drinks are stronger in here than the free drinks out on the floor. Now back to our conversation. There is an old saying that goes something like this. Those who have the money make the rules. You need to take a deep breath, and then decide what is best for you and your immediate family. That is priority one. Others come after that."

"You see me as a weak person!"

"In this instance, on this acquisition, yes you are taking a weak position. In general I doubt you are a weak individual. You are describing a marriage in decline. Both you and your wife must take bold steps to save your relationship, if it's worth saving. Only you and she can determine your future."

Brad took the last sip of his beer. Again Nikki wiped his lips with her finger before licking it clean. "With such an important decision to make, you don't need a second beer. May I offer you water?"

"Water would be nice." Brad called Al Claymore for a progress report.

The boring little man again stated progress was slow. "We should know the outcome tomorrow or the next day." It was the same answer he received two days ago.

Nikki returned with his water. "By the look on your face, I know your call didn't give you the answer you wanted. I'm sorry."

"Everybody is dragging their feet. Business should be a simple yes or no. This carrot dangling in my face is upsetting me more each hour. I don't need another sleepless night."

"Have you eaten anything today?"

"I had a piece of toast with my morning coffee."

Nikki grabbed the bar menu. "We have these items available night and day. May I recommend the combination plate? You need nourishment."

"I'm not overly hungry. I could sit here for a short while, and nibble on my food like a rabbit. While I decide how much harassment from my friends and family I can take." Nikki quickly placed the food order. "I'm surprised so few people are here in the lounge."

"This is the mid-afternoon slump. I have two slow hours each afternoon. Around four things will pick up here in the bar. My shift starts at eleven, and I work until seven this evening."

"I noticed your wedding ring, what does your husband do?"

Nikki tapped on her ring with her opposite index finger. "This ring is a phony, I'm not married. I wear the ring to keep the drunks from hitting on me. Some people can get out of hand very easy. No woman wants to be groped in public. In private with the right caring guy, little gentle touches can develop into something interesting."

Brad smiled. "You make a valid point."

His food order arrived. Being hungry he ate more food than he expected. "This combination plate is good. It's time I moved on and let you prepare for the evening customers. Thank you for listening to my complaints. I think our talk helped."

"We had a nice conversation. Don't be a stranger. Come back and see me again sometime. Good luck with your property purchase. Give your wife and children an extra hug when you see them. Sometimes hugs are better than words."

Back in his private office Brad made a decision to withdraw his offer to purchase the medical buildings. He sent an e-mail to the parties involved notifying them he was tired of playing games, and he was moving his business interests in a different direction.

Come morning at the beach Marie woke to the smell of coffee. She instantly knew someone was up and went straight to the kitchen. "Good morning Laura, Sam and Judy will be along in a couple minutes I heard them stirring. It's such a beautiful morning do you mind serving our coffee on the veranda, you and Laura should join us."

Marie's words put a pleasant smile on Laura's face. "Having our coffee and breakfast rolls on the veranda sounds nice. I'll take five cups out right away."

Marie started off to tell Judy the plan of having their morning coffee on the veranda when she heard Laura let out a blood curdling scream, along with the sound of breaking glass. Thinking Laura had burned herself she ran straight to the veranda. "Laura are you, Brad!!! When did you get here?"

"I arrived about 3:00 am this morning. Sorry about scaring you Laura. I had no key to get in the house. Had I gotten in the house I would have had no clue what room Marie was in. I didn't want to disturb anyone, so I kicked back in a lounge chair out here. I'm here to tell you it is a bit damp and chilly, sleeping out here."

By now Sam, Judy, and Emily arrived on the scene. Sam looked the most shocked. "It's you, good morning. It's nice to see you Brad. By the sound we heard, and now seeing the mess I think you scared the hell out of poor Laura. You could have given the woman a heart attack."

Marie snuggled in tight against her husband's body as he spoke. "It wasn't my intention to scare anyone. I thought staying out here until I heard some stirring inside would be my best entrance. My plan didn't work smooth as I thought." Brad shook his head. "You all know me. I'm highly capable of doing stupid things."

As Laura's heart began to settle down she could speak. "I wasn't expecting to find a man sleeping on our veranda. You shocked me, but I'm okay now. I better clean this mess up before the barefoot children wake up."

Marie continued to hug her husband. "I'm just happy you were able to finish up our purchase of the medical buildings so you could join us. How late did you have to work to close the purchase of the medical building?" Marie asked with excitement in here voice.

"We did not get the medical building. I withdrew our offer, and came straight here." Everyone looked at him in stunned silence. "Oh come on people, I'm here. Isn't that what everyone wanted?"

Marie looked rather sheepish. "We did want you here, but nobody expected you to give up on our business deal to come here."

"That sure as hell wasn't the feeling I was getting yesterday."

"I'm sorry about yesterday. I should have kept my nose out of the deal. I can tell you are disappointed."

"Of course I'm disappointed to say the least. When it came down to it, my family was more important than acquiring the buildings. Those medical buildings were the sweetest deal I ever saw. Too bad now, deals come and go. This deal is dead." Brad pulled his cell phone out and opened it to show Marie. "Look at that twenty three missed calls since last night, and early this morning. That number is our attorney's phone number. He must have been up all night after I notified him to rescind our offer. This other number is the kid's attorney's number. Last we have the kid trying desperately to contact me. Canceling our offer really shook these boys up. Too bad for them, they should have been more cooperative. They had ever opportunity to work this deal out. Somebody in the chain dropped the ball."

Marie gave him a startled look. "Don't you think you should return these calls? Maybe you can still purchase the properties." Brad shook his head no.

Sam and Judy were quick to side with Marie. They too encourage him to return the calls. Before further conversation could occur four little people begin attacking Brad. He loved the attention the four urchins poured on him. Judy grabbed the camera. "Marie, get behind Brad. You may as well be in the picture with them."

"Better yet, Laura you take the picture and we can all be in the picture. Come on Judy, Sam, get in the picture." Marie suggested.

She looked down at the blinking phone lying beside her husband. "Your phone is ringing. You are getting call number twenty four. You should answer this call, it could be very important."

"Twenty five will be next call. I say to hell with those people. I tried dealing in good faith, and nobody cooperating with me. They can kiss my backside. The kid created the poisonous atmosphere not me. Trying to hurry here, I missed dinner last night. What is on the menu for breakfast?"

"That is Mr. Claymore's number you better take his call. You never know his call may be important. Why else would he keep trying to call you?" Marie insisted. "Go ahead and answer his call."

Sam placed a hand on Brad's shoulder. "Judy and I sort of feel responsible for pressuring Marie into urging you to hurry up and get here. Please take the call, we don't want to be responsible for you not being able to purchase the property. "Please answer your attorney's call."

"I don't understand you people. First you get upset when I don't drop business, and come racing here to the beach. Now that I'm here you want me to continue working on a dead deal." Brad scratched his head. "I'll call Claymore after we finish eating breakfast. Then I'm going to the beach with the children. I want to see the sand castle the kids built. I'm told the sand castle is very nice. I may want to buy it."

After finishing his muffin and coffee, Brad decided to call his attorney. Everyone sat quiet but remained gathered around Brad as he called Al Claymore. He put his phone on speaker. "Good morning Al, it's a beautiful morning here at the beach. What is on your mind my friend?"

"No wonder I couldn't contact you, and give you the good news. The tax lien was cleared late yesterday. The kid accepted your offer. You will get the property."

Those surrounding Brad showed their pleasure. "Hold on Al, you are an attorney. You must realize this deal is a no go. I rescinded our offer last night around nine thirty. The kid can't accept an offer he doesn't have. Didn't you explain the law to the little pissant?" Three shocked faces stared at Brad.

"Hold on a second Brad. I'm getting a call from the kid's attorney on the other line." Brad sat tapping his fingers on the table as he waited for Claymore to get back on the line. "I'm back Brad, are you still with me?"

"I'm here Al, and I'm listening. Why I'm listening, I have no idea. I dealt in good faith, the kid wouldn't. Life goes on."

"The kid's attorney is asking you to reinstate your offer. He is ready to deal." Marie's face was glowing with excitement as was Sam and Judy. "The kid's attorney, a Mr. Jones asked if you are willing to resubmit your offer. They have agreed to all your terms. All you need to do is resubmit your offer and the medical buildings are yours. May I resubmit your offer?"

"Hell no, I'm not resubmitting our offer." Brad shouted.

"Did I hear you right, you said no?"

"Yes, I said no. These people irritate me. Yesterday things could have been worked out. Today I'm on vacation at the Oregon Beach with my family. I'm not returning to Vegas or Seattle until Monday or later. The kid can kiss my ass. Tell him to deal with someone else." Three shocked faces stared at Brad in disbelief.

"Exactly where are you in Oregon?"

"We are at Pacific Beach Rental Cottages, unit number three. What the hell difference does it make where I am, I'm not leaving here. Tell the kid to blow it out his ear. I'm through dealing with them."

"Now hold on Brad. If I can put this deal back together, and bring all parties involved to you for the paperwork signing, would we have a go?"

"Hell no Al, every day is different." Marie's jaw dropped even further. "I'm not in the same generous mood I was in yesterday. This jackass kid needs to sell the property more than we need to buy the property. My current thought is I'll wait until these properties come up for auction. At that time I may put a low-ball bid on each of the properties, in hopes of getting one. I see no value in my resubmitting our same offer, at this late point. I'll not lose another night of sleep trying to deal with a frigging idiot, I'm finished. The kid and his representative have been pulling my chain far too long. Send them a text message saying no, I'm no longer interested."

"Didn't you hear me Mr. Collins? The property is yours at your price if you allow me to resubmit your current offer. I'm almost certain I can get all the parties involved to drive out to your location."

"I heard you. I responded by saying there is no value in resubmitting the same offer. This little shit pissed me off. He caused me severe family problems, my wife and friends are angry as hell at me. You know me. I'm not a forgiving person. My wife will vouch for that." Marie was using hand gestures to urge him to go ahead with the deal. "I need to discuss our options with my wife before committing to any numbers. I may call you back, but don't hold your breath."

After ending the call he asked Marie for a pen and paper. As the others silently watching he wrote the names Robin, Bob, Rusty, Carol, Wendy, Susan, Ray Sr., Ray Jr., Darcy, Sam, Judy, Carrie and Kristy. "Let's see that is thirteen people, thirteen is unlucky, I better round our list of names to fifteen."

He promptly called Claymore back. "Okay Al, here is the deal. Drop our offer by one hundred fifty thousand dollars. There should be a penalty for their unwarranted delay in completing the deal. Don't bother to call me back. If they want the deal, just bring them here. If they don't accept my offer, so be it."

"Oh geez I don't know Brad, this may put a kink in the purchase of the property."

"What the hell are you talking about? The kid caused the kink in purchasing the property these past few days, I didn't. Marie and I are willing to take our chances at the auction. Here is the address where we are vacationing if you can put the deal together again at the lower price, bring the paperwork to us. As I said don't bother calling. Marie and I are not chasing that damn kid all over the country to sign any paperwork."

"I'll try but it's going to be tough, no guarantees Brad."

"If you don't wimp out on me we will get the medical buildings. I'm getting ready to head down to the beach with my family now. Remember, don't call me back. If they go for my new deal and you get the paperwork finished bring it to me. Otherwise forget it." Brad ended the call without further discussion. "Okay people my day is free."

Marie smile before kissing her husband. "I'm stunned, I just saw you put your family before business. This is a first, it may be an expensive first. Just the same, I'm proud of you."

"What can I say, I love my family."

"I hope I'm smart enough to never challenge a business decision of yours again."

"For me every day is a new experience, and family is very important to me. Family and friends both, are important to me. Come along people let's go to the beach."

Sam extended a hand for a shake. "Ladies, I believe we saw a master at work this morning. Tell me if I'm wrong, you put your phone on speaker so we would be quiet and listen careful." Brad nodded an affirmative nod. "By allowing us to hear your complete conversation we automatically leaned to your side as we realized others caused your delay getting to the beach. What I am confused about is the names you wrote down on the paper, were you simply stalling for time?"

"You are partially right Sam. I wanted you on speaker phone with me. Unless I'm totally crazy, Al Claymore had a three way conversation going himself. I bet the kid's attorney was on the phone with us. By ending the call, I broke the cycle. By calling back I was only talking with Claymore. The thirteen names on the list I made, I saw as unlucky, so I added two more names in my mind. I had my mind made up what I was planning to do before I ended the first call. There was no reason to waste time writing the last two names down. If you are curious about the last two names, I added were Emily and Laura's names to the list." Brad pointed at Marie. "Look at her smile, she knows what I'm doing. These people

I'm trying to do business with caused undue stress on everyone I named on my outsider list. Marie and our boys are not outsiders so I left them off the list. I think people should be compensated for their undue stress. By cutting our offer one hundred fifty thousand dollars we can give every person on our stress list ten thousand dollars if the deal comes together."

Sam blinked his eyes. "Are you flipping serious?"

"I'm dead serious. If the deal goes through each person on that list will receive ten thousand dollars. The money will be paid to you out of the saving we won't be paying the kid to acquire the medical buildings. Sam, look around now and see who wants this deal to go through?" Brad grinned. "Marie and I are not the only people to lose if the deal doesn't go through. If you want to call me controlling, go ahead it won't change the facts. Now you will be worrying if we get the deal completed or not right along with me."

Judy immediately voiced her objection as she grabbed Brad's shoulder to turn him towards her more. "We have caused you nothing but problems. True friends wouldn't act the way we acted. I'm totally embarrassed by our actions. We don't deserve any money if the deal goes through."

Sam nodded his head. "Judy's right. I'm the true culprit, the person at fault. Go ahead and chastise me all you want, I deserve it."

"I realize giving you money won't change your opinion of me. The opinion you have of me is part my fault, I am who I am. I'm not always open enough to allow people to know exactly what I'm doing. Listen careful, no deal, means no money. Now would someone mind leading me down to see the sand castle I've been hearing so much about?" His voice still contained a hint of irritation.

Marie grabbed her husband's hand and pulled him to his feet. "Our precious little ones moved their sand castle building further away from the water's edge so it wasn't washed away each night. This is the third day of adding to the children's sand castle. I think you will be impressed with their work. By week's end the kids hope to leave a sand castle other visitors can enjoy after we are gone."

"I know it's still early in the day, but show me the sand castle quickly. I want to return to the cottage for a nap, I'm exhausted and fading fast."

"If you can hold out until after lunch we can all nap at the same time?"

"Honey, I'll try to hold out until noon. I can't promise anything. I better use the restroom before I go inspect the kid's sand castle."

As he returned to join the others Judy was apologizing to Marie for her and Sam's actions. "I pray your deal on the medical building goes through. Not because we stand to gain financially, but because if it doesn't go through, Brad will never forgive Sam and me. Our interference caused him to back away from a deal just as he was about to complete it. I am so sorry. I feel Sam and I are totally responsible for the medical building deal going sour."

Brad remained in the hall listening to the ladies talking. "Maybe this acquisition wasn't meant to be. I wanted the medical building more for my brother's sake than Brad and my sake. If the deal doesn't work for us, maybe something else will come along we can acquire."

"Alright guys, I'm ready to go."

The four youngsters lead him down to the sand castle. The sand castle impressed Brad. "Geez guys this is great, I'm proud of you. I doubt I could make a castle this nice."

"We did work hard." Kristy stated with pride.

"I can see that Sweetie." Brad picked her up to give her a hug. "We need pictures of you guys working on your sand castle."

"Mama took lots of pictures as we slaved away. I think she took the pictures to get out of helping us build the sand castle. Daddy helped us, but mama didn't help much."

Brad sat the young tyke back down and kneeled to hug the other children. "I'm proud to see how well the four of you work together. Life is all about teamwork. Although it's only been a few weeks, it seems like ages since I walked on a beach. I forgot how it feels to walk on the warm sand with my bare feet. "

"Father, we are going down and play in the waves now. After lunch we can build on our sand castle more. Will you play in the water with us, Uncle Brad?"

Brad turned to Marie. "Don't look to me to save you. We are all getting in the waves. The water will help keep you awake until after lunch."

"Dang, I'm out numbered. Give me a chance to make one call and I will join you." Marie waited beside him as he called Junior. "Hello Junior, I called to give you an update on the medical buildings. Completing the purchase is proving to be difficult. We are dealing with idiots who cheat and lie, as they use every tactic they can think of to gain an advantage. As a result I'm no longer certain we can complete the purchase of the medical buildings. With each passing hour the odds of acquiring the medical buildings grow slimmer. By morning we should have a final answer one way or the other. I'm sorry, Junior, I thought I could pull this off. I think the deal passed me by. Keep the faith, another deal will come along eventually."

"Darn the luck, Darcy and I were looking forward to the challenge. Sometimes bad things happen. You are the business people, we are the puppets meaning you know more than we do. Thanks for the heads up brother-in-law."

Marie appeared to be shocked as he ended the call. "You really think the deal is dead?"

"I'm about ninety five percent certain the deal is dead. Our next shot at acquiring the medical building will be at the auction. I lowered our offer because I know how Claymore operates. If he was willing to bring everyone here for us to sign the papers he will bill you and me later for the plane tickets to get everyone here."

"What about giving the money to the names you listed?" She inquired.

Brad looked around to be certain Sam or Judy was not close to them. "The hundred fifty thousand dollars split among them was to distract the people around us. If I stood and argued with Claymore over a hundred fifty thousand where Sam and Judy couldn't hear me, they would think I was cheap and useless. I cut them in. Now they think I'm the good guy, and hopefully they should stay out of our business in the future."

"I'm sure you meant that to be an informative moment, but you lost me."

"Honey had Sam and Judy kept their thoughts to themselves as they should have, you would not have called and gave me hell causing me to race up here in the middle of the night. This morning the medical buildings would have been ours."

"You are blaming Sam and Judy for not getting the medical buildings?"

"Who would you point a finger at if not them?" He paused for a second. "Let's go join the gang in the water. It is plenty warm to get wet."

His words left her confused. If he blamed Sam and Judy for the business deal falling through. He also must blame her because she made the call that triggered him to cancel the offer.

CHAPTER 2

Brad's phone rang giving everyone false hope. "Excuse me, Junior is calling. I do need to take this call."

"Brad, I hate to bother you. I have a question. How do you feel about employees dating employees?"

"Junior, who our employees date, is none of our business. If you are talking about yourself, and there is someone in our organization you want to ask out. Go for it. Would Darcy happen to be the person you are thinking of asking out? Brad inquired.

"Yes, I want to ask Darcy out for a nice dinner."

"You have made a great choice Junior, she comes from a fine family. Junior, let me tell you a little about business 101. If you spend a small portion of your dinner time discussing business, you are entitled to use your company credit card to pay for dinner."

"Thank you Brad, Darcy and I will be praying for a miracle so you can acquire the medical buildings. We'll keep our fingers crossed for you."

"It might take more than a miracle to get the medical buildings, but I appreciate the thought. I do have all night until I know the fate of the deal. Junior, life is like a card game. You play the cards dealt to you. Sometimes you win sometimes you lose, in the meantime its best not to worry about it. Marie and I will be in touch when we learn something. Keep up the good work and give Darcy a special hug. She is doing a great job and so are you."

"Goodbye Brad." Junior walked straight over to Darcy. "Brad wanted me to give you a hug, for doing such a great job." His quick hug came as a surprise causing her pretty eyes to blink. He then pulled her to a standing position for a more generous hug and a kiss to the cheek. "That hug was from me, I also appreciate your hard work."

"Thank you. I appreciate you noticing my work effort. If you think about it we make a very great team. We are making great progress getting this office in order. In a couple weeks we should be caught up."

"Your pretty smile goes a long way with me. You never fail to brighten my day. I know it is only Thursday, but I will ask you anyway. Would you care to join me for dinner this evening?"

She flashed her pretty smile. "You mean dinner like a business dinner, or a date?"

"We'll have a genuine date. Complete with a good night kiss for a beautiful lady. Tell me where you live, and I will pick you up. Please keep in mind this is a social dinner. We may talk business until our food order comes. We are not allowed to discuss business as we eat."

"You will have time to tell me all about yourself." Darcy quickly wrote her address and phone number on a piece of paper. "This is where I live."

Ray studied the address she gave him. "You live in the apartments over on Flamingo Road, that's not far from here. Do you have a special place you like to eat?"

"I'm not fussy, I eat most anything. I'll let you to choose where we shall eat. I'm up for anything. I never turn down a free meal."

"Dress casual, we will be eating in a normal everyday restaurant. I want good food but nothing all that fancy. Financially, I'm not in the same league as my brother-in-law."

"Mother and I ate twice at the Mongolian Grill. We found the food enjoyable. The prices very reasonable, for average working people like mother and me. We could eat there if you like Mongolian food."

"Does the Mongolian Grill serve Red Wine?"

"I believe they do serve wine."

"Eating at the Mongolian Grill is probably a fast place to eat. We need a glass of Red Wine to stretch out our dinner thus stretching our evening together. Otherwise we won't have time to tell our life stories. Being a Thursday evening the restaurant should be quiet enough we can sit and talk long as we want." Darcy saw nothing but joy on Junior's face. "Don't let me forget I have an appointment with the yard care people at eight in the morning."

"I'll make a note for your appointment. What time should I be ready for our date this evening?"

"Six thirty, now I have a couple quick errands to run today so I will see you at six thirty this evening." Ray leaned over close as if he was going to kiss her, but changed his mind at the last second as he turned away. "I'll see you later at your apartment."

Back at the beach the kids played in the shallow water while Brad made a second call. He called Banister Construction indicating he was ready to start phase two of the apartment project. Feeling the medical building deal was dead the only way he could keep Junior secure with the money he was making, was by showing him more money would soon come his way. He looked up to see Marie motion for him to come and join the others. "I'm coming Honey." He yelled back.

That evening Ray and Darcy sat enjoying their inexpensive dinner while Brad sat nervously waiting for a late evening phone call. His uneasiness showed by his constantly checking the time. In the kitchen area Marie whispered in Judy's ear. "I hate this waiting as much as Brad does. Had I not mouthed off to him on the phone yesterday we would now own the medical buildings. We would be toasting our successful purchase with a glass of wine."

Marie grabbed a beer from the refrigerator. "Maybe this will help him relax." She took the beer straight to her husband. "I brought you a beer to help you relax. I hate seeing you stressed this way."

"No thank you, Honey, I never drink when I'm working. Maybe Sam would like the beer, give it to him."

"Brad, you are not working now, its evening. You should be relaxing."

"Are you blind, woman, I've been praying for hours. I really have no desire to go against others at an auction to acquire the medical buildings. People sometimes go crazy bidding at an auction. Inexperienced bidders often pay more than something is worth. No doubt they would auction all four properties separately making it harder than ever to buy all four properties. Massive advertising could draw in a multitude of out of state bidders or even foreign bidders bidding on line for the buildings. I'm going for a walk Honey. Would you care to join me?"

She quickly grabbed his hand. "Let's go." She tossed the beer to Sam.

"Shall we see if the boys want to go with us?"

"The boys are busy playing with Carrie and Kristy." Marie stated.

"Maybe all four of the kids would like to go hiking with us?" He suggested.

"I would rather just the two of us went walking this late in the evening. We could use some much needed alone time on the quiet beach."

Brad and Marie no more than stepped out the door when Sam turned to his wife. "What a frigging ding-bat, she has no clue how to help her husband relax. A good bedroom tussle would serve him much better than a long walk this time of the evening. At least it would be a good start."

"You think a bedroom tussle is the answer for everything. I doubt you realize how much time and effort Brad put into trying to acquire the medical buildings. Now because of our interference it appears his efforts were all for nothing. In case you haven't noticed Brad is not used to failing at anything. There may be repercussions coming our way in the future, and I wouldn't blame him one bit."

"Ah, hell, Honey he needs to grow up, and join the real world. Adults don't always get their way. Didn't Marie say some things are just not meant to be? This medical building takeover he was trying to pull off may be one of those deals. He will figure out another way to expand their holdings. He is a mover and a shaker. That is bar talk for a greedy bastard."

"For someone who has a stake in his success, you have a strange outlook towards him that I don't understand. I think you are getting pleasure thinking his efforts to get the medical buildings will fail. What I can't understand, is why you are the way you are. It makes no sense to me."

"I'm not taking full blame for his failure. You heard the attorney clearly state all he needed was to resubmit his offer. By now the deal would be signed."

"Resubmitting his offer would have meant him and Marie flying straight back to Vegas or Seattle. If by some last minute miracle they are able to acquire the medical buildings we are not accepting the money he mentioned we would get."

"Now hold on, you don't have full say if we accept that money or not. You are talking about forty thousand dollars. I want my daughters going to college and we will need money for their education. Given the opportunity we are accepting the money and that is final. I don't want to hear any more about it." While Brad and Marie were walking Sam and Judy continued to argue about upsetting Brad.

In Vegas, things were different. Ray Jr. was introduced to Darcy's mother. "Hey, you are the lady from the restaurant out on the old highway. I eat there sometimes. Nice to officially meet you Mrs. Burns, I love the food you serve in the restaurant."

"Thank you, it's nice to meet you too. Darcy has been telling me what a pleasure it is working with you. I've never seen her enjoy a job more than she has now. I think you may be spoiling her."

"Your daughter has been a welcome addition to my office. Without her help I would be in deep trouble." Ray glanced at his watch. He remained nervous as they talked. "I wanted to ask your daughter out the first day we met, but I wasn't sure Brad and Marie, they are our bosses, would approve of our dating. Different employers have different ideas about employees, dating other employees. I asked Brad if it was okay to ask your daughter out, before I actually asked her out. I need Brad and Marie more than they need me."

Later Junior and Darcy's dinner conversation proved interesting. "I'm sad to say I goofed off in the military more than I should have. Further education did not enter my mind during those years. Brad and Marie offering me this job rescued me from poverty. When I left the military my plan was to come here and visit mom, dad, Sis, and Brad. I had no clue what I was going to do. I couldn't believe my ears when Sis called and offered me the job I have. As you know I do not make great money with only stage one of the apartment complexes complete. Once the other two stages are completed my income will increase. I was so hoping Brad could complete the purchase of the medical buildings, and give me an instant pay raise. Apparently it wasn't meant to be. His earlier call was to say the purchase wasn't going well. You are eating dinner with a pauper."

"Oh come now you shouldn't put yourself down. There is no shame in working a normal steady job. Plus your job comes with a promising future. You should see the house I grew up in. Brad described our house as tiny, but filled with love when he first saw our home in Montana. Someone as tall as you could almost touch the ceiling scratching your head. As a family we knew we were short on money. Somehow we managed to get the things we needed to get by. Your Brother-in-law's generosity is what brought mother and me to Vegas. My uneducated advice to you is stick by him and Marie. They value family. Even though the medical building deal may have collapsed eventually something will come up later where you may well benefit."

Ray reached over and gently patted the back of her hand. "I believe you a hundred percent. My parents are living proof. They did well since moving to Vegas and working near Brad and Marie. I'm not going anywhere anytime soon. I'm flexible, whatever they want me to do I'll do"

For Junior, and Darcy, their first date couldn't have gone better. Conversation flowed with ease. Their evening ended with a wonderful kiss, and a promise of a second date Saturday evening.

At the beach when Brad and Marie returned from their walk, she was more than happy to sit and rest. He continued to pace around in the lower rooms of the cottage. Sam watched until he couldn't stand it anymore. In hopes of distracting his constant worry about the medical buildings, he decided to try changing the subject. "Sit down and have a beer, I have a question. Have you considered Ray might not be happy working for you no matter what you try to do for him?"

"Anything is possible. I grew up with no family and being alone was a horrible thing. I wouldn't wish that on any person. Junior is his own man, same as you are. People are free to come and go any time he wants, same as you are. Personally I think Junior enjoys being near family, and wants to be near family. Naturally, we hope he will stay and work with us. At the same time we must be realistic. We can't be certain he will stay working with us. What we can do is try to do right by him financially so he can make the choices that are best for him. In the process I want our boys to know their uncle." Marie slipped around behind her husband to begin massaging his shoulders. "Honey that feels great, you have fabulous hands."

"My hands will get tired after ten minutes. If you will slip down and sit on the floor I can round up four volunteer helpers to massage you at no charge."

Of course small children have big ears, they heard Marie's word's and came running. In a matter of seconds eight little hands pulled him to the floor. From Marie's vantage point it was hard to tell if he was getting a massage or being mugged. Being a good sport he played along with their scuffling hoping they would wear themselves out. His twenty minute massage seemed like two hours. He tired out long before the children did. Seeking help he looked up at Laura smiling down at him. "Do we have any ice cream left?"

In one split second eight tiny feet raced for the freezer. Marie replaced the children on the floor next to her husband. "That was sneaky, you tricked those kids."

"I was in a danger zone, and nobody was trying to help me. Wish I had remembered the ice cream sooner. I had to save my own life. Sam, where were you? You could have been the hero of the day by saving me."

Taking his cue from Brad, Sam pulled Judy to the floor so he could snuggle and cuddle with her. As the two couple's horseplay escalated in front of the fireplace they eventually bumped one another. Their bumping seemed innocent to everyone except Brad. Bumping Judy sent a twinge of guilt racing through his body. To end the two couples intermixed horseplay Brad faked a leg cramp. His effort to end the session made things worse as three people quickly began massaging his left leg. "Stop, stop, I need to stand up, you are killing me."

"You need more fluids. I'll get you some water." Judy was gone in a flash to retrieve the water. "Drink it all if you don't replenish your fluids the cramp will return later when you are in bed. You need to rehydrate your body."

Being helpful Laura brought him a sports drink. "This is what you should be drinking not water or beer. You can dilute the sports drink with water if you like a milder drink. A fifty-fifty mix isn't bad."

"Geez people, how much can I drink without spending the night dashing to and from the restroom?"

"Get in the hot tub and sip your sport drink while you relax, we can all join you and relax together." Marie suggested. "A little relaxation will be good for everyone."

"I don't know about getting in the hot tub. If my cramp comes back while I'm in the hot tub, I might kick someone trying to straighten out my leg. Someone could be injured. I better drink my sports drink and head off to bed."

Marie, Judy, and Sam insisted he get in the hot tub. "I'll get your swim trunks for you to put on. I'll get us each of us a beer. You might like a beer better than a sports drink. I've never been a fan of sports drinks."

As Brad started to his room to change Judy grabbed his arm, and held him back to whisper. "I hate seeing you this up tight. I'm not the business person you are but maybe you are asking too much of these people. That was a stiff ultimatum you gave your attorney this morning. Maybe you should think about giving them additional time."

He glared at her. "Be assured they won't get more time from me. These jackals have been jerking my chain long enough. I don't knuckle down for anyone. They can play, or pass at this point. I can easily turn my site in a different direction."

"Don't get upset at me it was only a suggestion." She stated in a simplistic manner.

"I know you meant well, Judy. Go change, and we'll talk more as we soak away our tight muscles." Once everyone assembled in the hot tub he felt obligated to explain his situation. "Judy asked me a few minutes ago if

I should call our attorney, and give them more time to put the offer back together or up my offer. The way I feel these people are jousting with me, it's as if we are in a high stakes poker game. The kid and I both want next month's rent from these medical office tenants. These buildings are one hundred percent occupancy. We are talking about a lot of money. This idiot kid should have been straight with me from the get go, and we could have worked out a deal. He withheld crucial facts stalling for time. Now if he allows the property to be auctioned off he gets nothing, zero, zilch nothing. Hopefully by morning the little dipstick comes to his senses, and does the right thing before he loses complete control of everything."

"This person you keep calling a kid, doesn't he have a name?" Sam asked.

"Yes he has a name, but I don't respect him enough to call him by his name. To me he is a flipping spoiled little kid. Any money he gets would probably be spent on drugs."

After thirty minutes of light conversation Marie announced she was ready for bed. "Are you coming with me?" He nodded he was ready for bed. Once in the privacy of their room Marie again apologized. "I'm sorry I was such a baby, and put pressure on you to get here. I'll never again interfere in your business."

"Don't fret Honey maybe I wasn't making the progress I thought I was. I was so sure I was within hours of completing the deal on the medical buildings. I never should have allowed them to string me along. All afternoon I wanted to kick myself. This could have been a magnificent acquisition for us. What I need now is for people to stop apologizing to me. It's over, let's forget the whole event and move on."

"Mr. Claymore said you were close to completing the deal. That must mean something to you." She began enthusiastically running her hands over his body.

"The old fart was probably stringing me along waiting for me to up my offer. Eventually I came to my senses and told him I wasn't willing to gamble on losing my family over a dead business deal. It's not worth it. I love you guys too much to risk losing you."

Marie leaned around enough to kiss him. "Promise me you won't get mad if I tell you something?" He motioned for her to keep talking. "Sam and Judy are embarrassed because they were thinking you were avoiding them."

"They shouldn't be embarrassed. Who knows, they may be right. Subconsciously I may have been avoiding them. I'm a little uneasy being near Judy. She isn't exactly some old ugly barfly walking down the street, I'll never see again. She is and has been your best friend for a long time."

"No she isn't an old hag. In fact Judy hasn't aged a day since college. I forgave you and her for what you did. Now it's time for you to forgive yourself for not including me in your decision to donate sperm to Judy so they could have the children they wanted."

"I love you, Honey, partially because you make life sound so easy." He rolled over and pulled Marie tight to his chest to kiss her good night. "It is well after midnight we better get some sleep before the boys get up. Those two will be on top of us tugging at our covers come daylight. I never realized how much energy children have. Those kids are like the energizer bunny. They just keep going and going."

"I doubt you will see any of the kids before eleven tomorrow. They were exhausted when they went to bed after their baths."

"With any luck we can also sleep in tomorrow morning. Lord knows I need a mountain of rest."

CHAPTER 3

Marie's summation the night before, about the boys sleeping in late was dead wrong. As the darkness of the night gave way to the dawning gray of the morning light tiny hands were tapping on his cheeks. "Get up dad or you will miss the sunrise." There was no discouraging the boys, as two little girls stood in the shadow of the hall. "Come on mom help us get dad up before we miss the sunrise."

Marie kissed her husband. "It's no use mister. We may as well get up."

"I'm not getting up until I get a kiss and a hug from each of the children, including the girls peeking in our room from out in the hall."

With squeals and laughter soon all four children pounced on the bed smothering Brad and Marie with love, and kisses. "Okay people, enough loving we are awake. Scoot along and we will get dressed and watch the sunrise with you."

"Go wake Sam and Judy, if I'm getting up so are Sam and Judy." Brad insisted.

"Is that a promise, mom?"

"Yes Sweetheart. Now scoot on out of our room, and close the door as you go so we can get dressed." Marie made a quick dash for the shower.

Judy poked her head in as the kids darted out. "We heard a commotion from way down the hall. What on earth is going on in this room?"

"Four urchins summoned us to get dressed and see the sunrise. I bet you and Sam would also enjoy a good sunrise. If you need help getting Sam up take the little people with you, they can do the job getting him up."

Judy blinked her eyes as she shook her sleepy looking head. "I'll try. I can't promise anything. I'll start the coffee. Emily and Laura are not up yet."

"Hey Judy, you might want to brush your hair you look a little on the evil side this morning." Brad stated with a snickering grin. "You look pretty, but evil."

"What a brilliant determination, from a man who doesn't look too sharp himself. Go join Marie in the shower."

"I'm only kidding Judy, you look great. Go get that man of yours up, or he will miss all the fun."

The distinct sound of laughter of young children ended Judy and Brad's kidding as they pulled Sam down the hall. "We got him up, mom. He needs coffee, dad's eye lids keep drooping."

With his one free hand Sam rubbed his eyes. "I'm up, why are we up? No one on vacation should be up this early. It's anti-American." The commotion in the house might wake Emily and Laura.

"It's very simple Sam. Our four little angels decided we needed to watch the sunrise. Brad and I were just talking. We figure the sun won't rise for another hour so we all have time to shower and dress before going out on the upper deck. Should I shower first or do you want the shower first?"

Again Sam rubbed his eyes. "I better shower first, or I might fall asleep again."

"Okay Sam, you shower first. I'll try corralling the kids before they wake Emily or Laura."

"You are too late Honey. Our little pests are in their room now. In a few minutes the whole house will be awake, grumpy but awake."

Sam turned and left the room. "I should go lay out his clothes." Judy indicated she should leave but remained standing where she was looking at Brad.

Brad rose from the bed, took the time to slip his robe on and then stood silent facing Judy as if his eyes were asking permission to step forward to wrap his arms around her. He couldn't resist touching her. At arm's length he touched both her shoulders causing her delicate body to quiver. "You better go lay out Sam's clothes." She turned and left as he stood watching her walk away.

"Okay Brad it's your turn in the shower." He turned to see Marie watching him. How long she had been watching was anybody's guess. "You did right sending Judy away. I know it's not easy being around her, but it will get better with time. The daylight is getting brighter. You better hurry if you want a shower before dressing. Johnnie and the crew will be back in a few minutes to get us."

Despite the confusing rude awakening, they all made it out to the deck in time to see a perfect view of the sunrise. Carrie led the cheers as the first glimpse of the sun appeared. "It looks like a fire starting. The world is coming alive again, isn't the sunrise beautiful?"

Judy leaned around to kiss Carrie's cheek. "Yes Honey the sunrise is beautiful. Thank you for waking us."

Brad sat in dazed silence as he thought back to when he was young. Not once had he experienced watching a sunrise with his parents. Watching the sunrise put a smile on all their little faces. It turned out to be a magic moment in time. The fun experience left him feeling awkward. He wanted to talk about his childhood but couldn't. Sam would think he was feeling sorry for himself again. He remained quiet with a somber look on his face.

"Brad, you are rather quiet this morning. Are you feeling okay?" Marie asked.

"I'm fine, Honey. A little lost sleep is a small price to pay, to see the smile on the kid's faces as the sun peeked over the horizon. I'm glad they woke me. Next on my list today is get my two hours of lost sleep back. I've had a lot of sleepless nights lately. I need my rest. I may have a light breakfast before I lay back down."

Marie smiled and quickly kissed him. "I'll take the children down to the water so they can hunt sea shells, and not bother you."

Judy changed Marie's plan. "Better yet let Sam and I take control of the little people. You can rest with Brad." She winked at Marie. "We better feed the troops first."

Sam turned and touched one of Brad's shoulders. "I agree with Marie. You are very quiet this morning, are you sure you are okay?"

"I'm a little out of it. I was hoping to wake up this beautiful morning and find a van full of people sitting out front with a handful of papers to sign. Doesn't appear that is going to happen. People, I bid you good night again. Boys you mind Uncle Sam and Aunt Judy. Stay near your group."

"Yes father, Jimmy and I will mind Aunt Judy. We get an extra cookie if we are good. Homemade cookies Emily brought from her house."

"Then eat fast and use the restroom before you leave."

"We will use the restroom father. Laura says nobody can pee on the beach. She makes us come back to the cottage when we need to pee. I think they need to put a restroom down near the beach."

"They can't have restroom too close to the beach. A winter storms, could wash the restroom away in no time. Just like your first sand castle washed away."

"I wouldn't want to be in the restroom when it washed away. I might drown." Jimmy looked worried.

"An angry, powerful, winter storm can do amazing damage. People seldom get near the beach during severe storms, the giant waves could wash them out to sea the same as it will anything close to the shoreline."

"At ten AM Brad and Marie were woke a second time by Emily calling out from the doorway."Mr. Collins, come quick. There is a van stopped in our driveway with several people sitting in it. Hurry, get up."

"They may be the men I've been waiting for, thank you Emily. Serve them coffee on the veranda. Tell them I'll be out soon as I dress." Brad motioned her away with his hand. "I better shower again." After giving Marie a quick kiss, he urged her to get dressed too. She would need to sign the paperwork along with his signature. "Come on Honey get up." He turned her to sit up on the edge of the bed.

Like Emily, Sam and Judy were surprised to see all the people on the veranda as they returned from the beach. Sam snuggled Judy tight against his body. "If that is the men Brad hoped would come here, he has to be the luckiest bastard alive."

Entering the kitchen area Emily surprised Sam by giving him a giant hug and a kiss on the cheek. "I think Mr. Collins did it, the kid as Brad calls him conceded to Brad's demands. I've been eavesdropping on their conversation." She whispered before giving Judy a hug equal to the hug, Sam received. "We are about to get the ten thousand dollars each. It's like a magical moment in time. I've never had ten thousand dollars at one time in my life. I'm ready to dance and sing in the kitchen."

"Let's not get carried away Emily, we get a ten thousand dollar penance from a billionaire, big deal." Sam said. "It's pocket change to him."

Emily couldn't help but shove him away. "Call it what you want, to me ten thousand is a big deal. Being a nanny do you realize how long it takes me to earn ten thousand dollars?"

Judy looked at her husband in anger. "You need to quiet down before they hear you spouting nonsense, and jeopardize everyone's unexpected windfall. I can't believe how you think."

Marie came walking through as she went out to join the veranda group. "I hope the negotiating part is over, so all I need to do is sign on the bottom line. Spending huge chunks of money all at once like this scares me." Upon Marie's appearance she was met with a round of smiles from the three men as they stood to greet her. "Good morning, gentlemen."

In minutes the medical building purchase was completed. "Thank you gentlemen, Marie and I appreciate you coming out here to complete our deal. We postponed this beach trip long as we could. I had no choice to come here at this time, or lose my family. As you can see my beautiful wife and my boys mean a lot to me, business comes second in my life now."

After further thought the forty thousand dollars his family stood to gain began to excite Sam. He waited until the van carrying the businessmen was out of sight before turning to Brad. "My hats off to you old buddy you are one hell of a businessman." Using his left hand Sam patted him on the back and congratulated him by rubbing his shoulder. "What you did was an óverwhelming accomplishment, and beneficial to all of us." He then extended his other hand for a shake.

"Sam my man, don't get carried away, I have a tendency to change my mind from time to time and this is one of those times." Thinking he had heard part of Sam's ranting earlier Judy's heart sank. "I spoke to our attorney last night. I've decided not to write the ten thousand dollar checks I promised each of you yesterday." Now Sam's chin dropped as Emily and Laura looked surprised. "I've decided Marie should write the checks for you." He pulled a pen from his pocket and flipped it towards Marie who caught the pen in mid-air. The check book was tossed in the same manner. You do the honors Honey. One small change Honey, make each check for thirteen thousand then, IRS has upped the legal gift requirements."

She shook her head. "Will you stop teasing people? You may be precious to me, but you have a mean streak running through you a mile wide. Why torture these people with a practical joke, you know you love these people to death."

By now everyone was laughing except Marie. "I know I'm being mean, but I can't help it. The devil made me do it." He answered with a grin. "Everyone has a little devil in them. You must admit even our four youngsters can be little devils at times. If I upset you, I'm sorry."

Judy stopped Marie's hand as she started to write. "Sam and I do not deserve any money. We almost blew this medical building purchase for you. Drop our names from Brad's list."

Brad pulled Judy's hand away so Marie could continue to write the checks. "Nonsense Judy, many people think I didn't deserve the money my father left me. I thought about their words for a long time. Then I realized the people giving me the money thought I was deserving of the money. We think you are deserving of the money. Marie and I wish to give you the money more for what you do every single day, than this one event. Please accept the money and use it wisely." He sealed his words with a slight massage on her back. "You guys are great friends."

Marie wrote six checks for those who were present. Minutes later a joyous celebration broke out. The four little ones didn't quite understand what had happened, but were more than willing to join in the celebrating. They danced with anyone willing to dance. "Emily and I are fixing tuna sandwiches for lunch. We will have them ready in ten minutes, wash up kids."

"You heard the lady, wash-up for lunch. Sam, Judy, you two be sure and take a good nap after we eat. Driving here yesterday, I drove past a Small Pub with a sign in the window that read live music and dancing Friday nights. Today is Friday and I feel like dancing. We need to take our wives dancing and celebrate our successful business deal tonight. Besides I haven't taken Marie out in a long time."

The girl's eyes lit up as Marie gave him a quick kiss. "Dancing will be fun. You are right. We haven't gone dancing in ages. Judy and I both brought our denim skirts in case we went out for a nice dinner but we didn't expect to go dancing."

"The same goes for us, Honey. We need to rest after lunch because we may be out late tonight." Brad explained their plans to Emily and Laura. "See if you can keep our little angels up an extra couple hours, so we can all sleep in tomorrow morning."

"Taking your wives dancing is a fine idea Mr. Collins. Emily and I will have no problem keeping the kids up later this evening; they can nap longer than usual and thank you again for the nice check, I can use the money." In her excitement Emily extended a hand for a shake.

"You are welcome." He pushed her hand away. "I'll settle for a hug not a handshake." Being Emily, he gave her a soft gentle hug. Without a doubt giving money to the two nannies had made an impact on everyone's happiness. "Thank you so much."

After lunch everyone welcomed their naps. The sunrise excursion earlier that morning had taken its toll on everyone including the kids. While the adults napped a good two hours the kids managed to sleep three full hours before Jimmy woke the others. If he was finished napping, so were the rest of the kids. Typical kids, the first to wake, wakes the others.

Come time to go dancing, Marie emerged wearing her short denim skirt and a white lacy blouse. Her method of dress accented her beautiful legs. "Oh my, Honey, you are gorgeous, absolutely stunning. You look so sharp you might stir up the locals."

"Wait until you see Judy, we may look like twins. She is wearing a similar denim skirt and a light blue top. You and Sam will be dancing with the prettiest women in the pub this evening."

He kissed his wife as Sam and Judy came to join them. "Both you gals look super sharp. If you are ready let's tell the kids goodbye, and be on our way. People, it's time to party."

Carrie had her own idea about dancing. "Play music here in the cottage, so we all can dance with you. We can dress up in the best clothes we brought."

"Not tonight Honey just the adults are going dancing this evening. Daddy and I can dance with you another night. If you ask real nice Emily and Laura might let you practice dancing with them this evening." Carrie's face showed her disappointment.

CHAPTER 4

The crowd at the Sweet Spot Pub surprised the four tourists. There were several people dressed in biker type clothing. Marie showed her uneasiness by whispering to the others. "Do we really want to be dancing in here, they look a little rough."

"Relax Honey. These people could be doctors and lawyer, up from California. If people become unruly later we can quietly slip out." As the two couples danced they drew lots of attention. When the waitress came to take their order for a second round of beer Brad inquired about the crowd. "Are these your normal local patrons?"

"This biker crowd is from San Francisco. Towards midnight they can get juiced up enough to argue among themselves. Seldom do they bother outsiders." Donna the waitress leaned down closer. "See the tall brunette with the blue bandana tied around her head. She belongs to Big Charlie at least he thinks she belongs to him. Occasionally she dances with other men when Charlie goes outside. Her flirtatious actions are not appreciated by him. He can get mean and nasty in a hurry. I'll be right back with your beers."

Brad grabbed the waitress' hand as she started to leave. "I see several people going in and out. Do you have any idea what they do during the break outside?" He held her hand. "My wife is a little uneasy, are we safe staying here?"

Donna scanned everyone at the table before answering his question. "They could be doing drugs outside. I've never looked outside to see what goes on out there." She turned and walked away.

Sam touched Brad's arm. "Maybe we should duck out while we still can."

"Relax Sam; we'll duck out in a few minutes. If we go now after ordering more drinks it will look funny. We don't want to draw a lot of attention, and show these clowns we are afraid of them. We should dance a few more times then use the restroom and leave." Brad's plan took a sudden curve as the band took a half hour break at the end of the song. The bikers retreated to the parking lot for their quick drug fix. Brad leaned near the others. "Listen carefully, when ninety percent of the bikers return inside it's time for us to leave. Here are the keys to our car, Honey. Marie you start the car and drive us away quickly as you can. I'll be the watchdog and the last to get in the car. As you drive us away go the opposite direction we came. After a few blocks we can loop around and double back towards our cottage." Marie, Judy and Sam all nodded okay. "Sip your beer and we will soon be out of here."

After a seemingly long wait the band begin to play again. The music started drawing the bikers, one by one back inside. Brad started counting the bikers straggling in. He estimated there were thirty or more bikers in the Pub earlier. Somewhere between twenty five and twenty seven needed to be inside before they attempted to leave. At twenty six he patted Marie's hand. "It's time we moved on if we are going to meet the others in our group." He stated in a loud voice as a cover. Everyone was anxious to leave. "Walk out casual, smile and go straight to the car. Try not to speak to any of the bikers."

Marie breathed a sigh of relief as she stepped into the fresh air. Just outside they met one straggling biker walking towards the entrance. "Hey, where in the hell are you going, get back inside. I want to dance with your lady."

Remaining calm Brad turned towards the biker. "Excuse me sir, did you say something to us?"

"I said get your ass back inside. I'm dancing with your old lady." The ugly biker barely had the words out of his mouth when Brad stomped his right foot and gave him a sideways karate chop to the Adam's Apple. The big man dropped to his knees instantly grabbing his neck as he fell over sideways.

Brad turned to make a dash for the car only to bump into Sam and the girls. They hadn't gone on to the car as they had been instructed. He gave Sam a huge push. "Go, get in the car." Two other bikers appeared from nowhere. Brad pointed back towards the entrance. "There is a fight over there." Twenty feet later he was in the car. "Go but don't speed."

Marie drove several blocks before circling around through the neighborhood to work her way back towards the beach cottage. Her passengers remained dead quiet as they looked about for motorcycles cruising around. Safely back at the beach cottage Sam patted Brad on the shoulder. "You were great back there. I couldn't believe how quick you disposed of that big ugly-ass biker. That son-of-a-bitch was huge and he looked mean as hell. You dropped him like a rock."

Marie stated she needed a comforting hug. "Honey you are shaking like a leaf. You are safe; I wouldn't let some little old bad dude biker get to you. A man must protect his lady."

"Stop being so modest, you were great. I agree with Sam, that guy was big."

"Oh Honey he was fat. Besides he was drunk or high on something. He had the reactions of an elephant. I wasn't worried about him because he was no real threat to anyone. My fear other would try stopping us from leaving."

Hearing voices Carrie came charging out to see what was going on. "Mommy, mommy, you came back to dance with us, yea!"

"Yes we did Sweetheart, turn up the music and let's have some fun."

"Jimmy isn't a very good dancer can you help him learn to keep step with the music, he is really bad. I don't like dancing with Johnnie either he won't let me lead."

"Sweetheart, boys are supposed to lead the girl when you dance with them." Carrie frowned at her mother. "That's life Honey, you dance with daddy and I will dance with Johnnie a couple of times and we can trade dance partners later. Johnnie is your size."

Sam was in the kitchen getting a beer when Emily and Laura inquired why they were back so early. "Bikers invaded the bar. For our own good we felt a sudden urge to leave. Even then Brad had to whip one guy's butt on the way to the car. You should have seen him. He dropped the guy with a quick blow. The Biker couldn't have dropped any faster if he had been shot in the head. The guy never laid a hand on Brad."

Emily immediately showed concern. "Was the guy okay when you left?"

"Good Lord no child. I just told you he was down for the count. That ugly buzzard won't be challenging anyone again tonight. He was totally out of it, flat on the ground face down, when we left. When a man goes face down he isn't getting up any time soon. Brad did a number on him."

Emily continued to show concern. "Was the guy alive?"

"Oh heck yes, he was rolling on the ground gasping for air. Why would you be concerned about the biker?" Sam couldn't understand Laura's concern.

"I heard Brad killed a guy once with his bare hands."Emily whispered. "He should not have been fighting with anyone, not now, not ever. He could get in a lot of trouble if the guy was badly injured. Leaving was okay, but you should have called to police so someone checked on the guy."

Emily's words startled Laura and momentarily froze Sam. "Shit, now that you mention it. I heard a rumor to that effect once. I don't remember the details. I did hear he killed a guy once during some kind of altercation."

Emily glanced around to see if Brad or Marie were near. "Supposedly Brad killed an intruder. I don't know for sure, anyway he kicked the guy in the Adam s Apple to cut off his breathing. According to the rumor I heard, the man died in seconds."

"Holly shit, Brad hit this guy in the throat area. You girls keep him busy while I call 911 and report a fight at the Sweet Spot Pub. The biker may need medical help." While Sam made his call, Judy watched Brad dance with Marie. Sam's call was unnecessary, medical help had already been summoned to the pub. "Do you know if anyone was seriously injured?"

"Sir we don't have the type of information you are requesting. If we had the information, we would not be able to give the information out. I'm sorry I can't help you with the information you are requesting."

"No, I guess you wouldn't know, thank you anyway." He rejoined the others for some down home dancing. Carrie and Kristy were only too happy to take their turns standing on their father's feet as they danced with him. Sam danced with Judy before dancing with Emily to whisper in her ear. "Medical people were summoned to the Pub before I called so the guy will be okay."

"At least we know the man was getting medical care."

In time Brad danced with Marie, Emily, Laura, Carrie, and Kristy, but avoided dancing with Judy. Marie pointed out his reluctance to dance with Judy. "She knows you are not acting normal towards her. If you don't dance with Judy, Sam may soon join her with the same thought. I danced a couple times with Sam." Brad looked at his wife without responding. "I'll get you a beer while you dance with her?"

"No thank you Honey, I've had enough beer for one night. If you think I should dance with Judy, I will." He walked directly over to her. "May I have this dance?"

She smiled at him. "I was wondering if you were going to ask me to dance, or not. You have been extremely distant since joining us here at the cottage." She whispered.

"You asked, I hold my emotions in check. I wasn't sure if I should ask you to dance until Marie nudged me to ask you. She thought it looked odd for everyone, but you and I to exchange dance partners." He felt extremely awkward dancing with her as his wife watched their every move. He kept sneaking glances at his wife. Her reaction to his dancing with Judy seemed normal. It was as if nothing had ever happened between him and Judy. Unfortunately Brad's mind drifted elsewhere as he fantasized about the extramarital sex they once shared, and his desire to enjoy those times again.

Judy could feel the tightness in his body as he held her tight keeping time with the seductive music. "You need to relax, everything is fine." She whispered. "Marie understands why you helped me have children. Sam will never know, we are home free, and our sins have been forgiven." Her tender words failed to affect his emotional well-being. He remained nervous as his desire to kiss her grew stronger. He wanted to say thank you for the dance. Although he nodded his head slightly words failed to escape his lips.

Lost in thought he returned to Marie's side. "Now that wasn't so hard. Sam saw you dancing with his wife, and paid no attention. He was busy dancing with Carrie and Kristy. Those two little girls love their father to no end. It's getting late Honey. I think I'll turn in."

"It's only eleven, if it weren't for the bikers at the bar we would still be dancing at the Pub. Have another beer. I'm not ready for bed. I feel like dancing longer."

"I've had three beers tonight that is enough. I may be up half the night urinating as it is. Another beer is the last thing I need." His nerves clearly showed.

Marie checked her watch. "How about we dance until midnight, put the kids down and then we can sleep in come morning?"

"Alright Honey, you win midnight it is." They immediately began dancing again.

On their second dance Sam cut in asking to dance with Marie. "Hey buddy let me give your wife a twirl while you dance with my wife. Don't forget Kristy and Carrie expects a dance from you too." Brad bypassed Judy and started dancing with Kristy. "What is wrong with Brad this evening, he seems distant?" Sam questioned. "Is he upset about the incident at the Pub?"

"The altercation at the Pub did upset him. He doesn't like violence."

"For someone who doesn't like violence he is pretty damn good at fighting. He came out a winner in a matter of seconds without scratch one. He should feel great." Sam stated in an envious way.

"Brad doesn't work out at a gym nor does he do physical labor. He isn't a physically strong person. What he has going for him is fast hand eye coordination from years of computer work, and game playing on the computer. He reacts fast and direct. Fighting upsets him. If he is right or wrong doesn't matter, confrontation upsets him."

"Thank you for the dance Marie, you are a great dancer. Maybe the next time Judy and I are in Vegas the four of us can go out dancing at a nice high end club where Biker riff-raff won't be part of the clientele? If we could find a grand ballroom we guys could wear Tuxedos and you ladies could wear Formals."

"We would enjoy going dancing with you and Judy somewhere nice. Next time we are together in Vegas, we'll do it. I suspect the grand ballroom dance you are visualizing would only happen on New Year's Eve."

Judy surprised Brad by asking him for one last dance before calling it a night. He glanced at Marie before agreeing to her request. "It's been an unusual evening, but I've enjoyed it once we returned to the cottage."

"I wish we had stayed here. Carrie and Kristy are having a blast." He remarked.

"Your boys were hesitant about dancing at first. Emily, Laura, and Marie worked with them now they are having fun. Look at the smiles on their cute little faces."

"Give yourself some credit you helped Johnnie and Jimmy get the hang of the rhythm. I'll tell you something else, I happen to agree with my boys. They told me you were a good dancer."

A sudden thought flashed through her mind. "I miss our closeness." The song came to an end. "I think it's time to put the little one's down before they topple over. They are looking mighty tired."

The four little people fell asleep soon as their heads hit the pillow. It had been a long tiring day for them. Who would have guessed dancing would wear them out when running in the sand didn't. It may have been a combination of both that caused them to crash so fast. In the privacy of their bedroom Sam cornered Judy. "Listen Honey, this is important, what do you think about Brad hitting the biker dude at the Pub?"

"I wasn't close enough to hear what the guy actually said to him. He must have said something not too nice for Brad to react as he did."

"Emily and Laura asked me in the kitchen why we came back so early. When I explained what had happened Emily became concerned. She mentioned Brad had killed a guy once with his bare hands. I heard a rumor to that effect long ago, but never gave it much thought until she brought it up. I hope the Biker is okay. I must say he is one hell of a no-nonsense fighter."

"The incident Emily was referring to was different. Brad was only seventeen when an intruder broke into his house. They scuffled and the intruder died in the short exchange. I saw the incident on security video. Brad was not at fault. Self-defense is not a crime then, or today."

"I don't see what he did tonight as self-defense. The guy never tried to strike him that I know of. He only said something. I'm thinking Brad panicked."

"Give him a break. You don't know what the guy said. It's any man's instinct to protect women. The guy probably made some unkind remark about us. Brad decked him. The guy will sober up in the morning and be okay."

"I saw the guy walking towards him. He appeared to be no different than any other guy walking by. For all I know the guy may have said nothing at all. Maybe Brad struck out in fear?"

"Oh for heaven's sake Sam, go to sleep. I'm sure the guy is fine and the incident is over. We have no reason to discuss this matter any further."

Brad felt the need for a shower before turning in. With closed eyes he was enjoying the soothing warm water cascading down his tight neck and back muscles. A sudden chill of cooler air caused him to pop his eyes open as Marie pulled the shower door open to join him under the cascading water. "Is there room for one more?" Words failed him as he drew her tight against his body. His actions while comforting were less than she expected. The normal increased passion created by them showering together failed to materialize. "Why does it bother you to be near Judy after all this time?"

"She may be part of my depressed state. What is really bothering me is the altercation with the biker dude at the Pub. The guy went down so quickly. I should have stayed around long enough to see if he was going to be okay. With so many bikers I felt the need to grab you girls, and escape while we could. I should have stayed."

"Getting out of there was the right choice. Had you stayed and waited for the police to come his thirty some buddies may have killed you, and rode off in the night. It would have been dangerous to stay there. The bikers all dressed alike, they were gang members. Anyone harming you, or any of us for that matter could never be easily identified one person out of the group. We needed to leave when we had the chance to leave. You did the right thing."

"Maybe, but what if the biker I hit isn't okay?" Marie looked him straight in the eye as if she was about to question his words. "The man could be dead like the intruder years ago for all we know. He went down so quickly. I should have tried walking away from him."

"Stop beating yourself up. The guy was drunk, of course he went down quick."

"If only I knew he was okay, I could sleep easier."

"Don't be silly he isn't dead. You never hit him but once. That looked more of a slap towards his face than a punch. I tell you the guy went down so easy because he was drunk. It's not like you stomped the guy when he was down. You walked away."

"If the guy isn't okay, I could be in trouble for leaving a crime scene. They could have our altercation on parking lot security cameras."

"I'm sure the guy is fine. If it will make you feel better we can check on his condition tomorrow." Marie reached around and turned off the water. "Let's dry off and get a good night of sleep, morning will come fast."

Brad lay wide awake much of the night watching his wife's beautiful chest rise and fall with her every breath. Towards sunrise he dosed off. Around noon the four innocent children piled in bed with him and Marie. "Wake up, breakfast is ready. Emily said to get you up." Carrie's words were followed by hugs and kisses from four little people."

Brad blew bubbles on their necks as he threatened to eat them, if he and Marie were not allowed to get up and dress for breakfast. Jimmy was the last to scurry from the bed. "Some alarm clock this place has. I'm thinking kids should be caged at night. After lying awake much of the night thinking about that biker, I didn't get a lot of sleep. When I finally got to sleep, I was sleeping soundly, until we had early morning visitors."

"Be a sport sleepyhead. It's no longer night, get up. Our darling children are ready to play. This is our last day here at the beach, and it's half gone. This is your chance to get down and dirty with our boys one final time. Please don't force me to go get the kids again."

"I'm with you Honey, I love getting dirty." Brad mocked.

Being concerned about the biker's health, Brad sat quietly as he ate. Sam noticed his quietness. "Hey buddy why the long face this morning. You are on vacation with family and friends and you completed the deal of a lifetime, what could be better?"

"I have some unfinished business. I should have taken care of yesterday. I'm thinking about how best to deal with my concerns."

"Let the business go until you get home. We are running out of time for this trip. Last night I saw a sign for Horseback Riding. I'm thinking none of our kids ever rode a horse before. We should go check this Horseback Riding out and forget about your business for one more day. Acquiring the medical buildings is enough business for this trip. You are successful beyond belief. It's time you learn to relax, and enjoy your family."

"I'm sure the kids would enjoy Horseback Riding. Why don't you, Judy, Laura and Emily take the kids on their pony ride?" He suggested. "Marie and I can check on my business and we'll meet you back here later this afternoon?"

"Brad's right, Laura and Emily can help watch the boys." Marie added. "I want to be at Brad's side when he conducts business today." Although not commenting on her actual words Judy gave her a funny look. "Our business may not take long. You guys go have fun."

Marie went to finish dressing while Brad walked out on the veranda and stood staring off into space. Judy quietly slipped out to join him. "Isn't the ocean beautiful this morning?"

He glanced around to look at her. "Yes the waves are beautiful this morning, and so are you. The sunlight makes you hair glow."

"You weren't looking at the ocean when I walked out. Does our being together bother you that much?" Judy asked with concern. "You seem to worry more with each passing moment."

"Being near you may be part of my problem. Then again why shouldn't I have warm feeling towards you? We both enjoyed our adulterous affair. I fall in love with women faster than most guys. I'm not a love them, and leave them type of guy."

"You need to learn to love me without intimate contact so our families can enjoy one another much as possible. I'm thinking if our families were together more it might help you settle down and be more comfortable around me. I'm not asking you to disavow your affection for me. I'm asking you to control your affection for the benefit of everyone. There is no reason we can't be close in every way except being intimate. As friends we can enjoy our lives much better."

Sam joined them on the veranda ending their private conversation. "What a beautiful day it is. The kids are ready to go ride a horse. We packed a few snacks and they are anxious to go see the horses."

Brad pulled a wad of money from his front pocket. That should cover the horseback riding. Thanks for taking the boys along, and keeping an eye on them for us. Marie and I need to check on the biker this morning."

"I knew something has been bothering you. Checking on the biker is the right thing for you to do. I doubt you will find out anything about him. Those bikers probably moved on early today."

In town they learned the biker he hit in the throat the night before had in fact died. The thirty year old biker suffocated from lack of air. Brad and Marie hung out at the local coffee shop trying to learn everything they could. Listening to the patrons they learned the bikers had come to the area many times causing various disturbances. This was the first time anything has turned deadly. One crusty old gentleman had his view on the biker dying. "These clowns came up here from San Francisco once a month when the weather is nice causing more trouble each time they come. It was only a matter of time until someone came up injured or killed. Authorities speculate this was a killing among the bikers themselves over drugs or women, possibly both. They have no suspect at this time. I doubt anyone will be held accountable for the killing."

Brad sat quietly listening to the waitress respond to the old gentleman talking about the killing. After she moved away he indicated they should be leaving. In the car Marie pointed out he should be safe if they think the killing was among the Bikers themselves. "I'm not so sure Honey. If Sam finds out about the guy died, I'm dead meat. He would never keep quiet. Judy might remain quiet, but not Sam. I should go talk to the police."

"Wait, we should talk to Sam and Judy before you talk to the police."

"Sam will get a certain pleasure out of my being in hot water. You three were ahead of me. You couldn't hear anything said between the biker and me. Your testimony will be of little help in clearing me. I may need to retain an attorney before saying much of anything to the police."

The horseback ride for the children turned out to be a big hit, and as a result they rode longer than expected. The group did not return to the empty cottage until late evening. "I wonder where Brad and Marie are. She didn't think their business would take long."

"Their business was to check on the biker Brad clobbered last night. I hear someone coming now. That might be Brad and Marie returning now." The car Sam heard passed by driving on to another house nearby.

"I hope they never ran into any of the bikers, and get in any trouble."

The four kids took a late nap, and were sleeping when the Collins' returned. "Hi people how did the horseback riding go?"

Sam's chest expanded with pride. "My idea was a big hit. Unfortunately come Christmas they may ask Santa for a horse. We rode their normal trail ride twice because the kids enjoyed themselves so much. Even Laura enjoyed herself. For Emily it wasn't so much fun she remained nervous. She expected her horse to run away with her any given moment. She only rode the trail once with us."

Brad broke the Pub news to them. "The biker died. I met today with a local attorney. "This guy being a local small town attorney isn't who I want representing me in this unfortunate incident. When we get back to Vegas, I'll nose around until I find the attorney I want. The firm I hire can work with this local attorney if they want. I need to know I'm getting the best representation I can get."

"Why would you need an attorney, you didn't do anything wrong." Judy protested. "The guy threatened you. That is self-defense. The police can't charge you with anything."

"I don't think I did anything wrong. Not being a fighter, I didn't stand around and argue. I struck the first blow. This local attorney isn't sure self-defense will stand up as a defense since I went on the attack. Had the guy hit me, or others heard what he said then I might have a chance at self-defense. As things stand he isn't sure."

"You said the guy was getting ready to force us back inside against our will. That would be kidnapping. Any man would fight against being kidnapped, if he were a man at all." Judy insisted. "I wish we had heard what he said."

"We didn't hear what the guy said." Sam pointed out. "Brad may be right our testimony may do more harm than good. We were not all that far ahead of Brad."

The words Marie was hearing from Sam Anderson proved Brad was right. Sam would never tolerate a cover up of any kind. She rubbed her forehead. "We'll have to wait until we retain the services of a good attorney before seeing how we should come forward."

Sam and Judy went off to bed leaving Brad and Marie in the kitchen area. "You were right about that brazen idiot not defending you. I'm wondering what this will mean in court with him going against us?"

"Only time will tell. I would love to be a little bird, and hear what he is saying in private to Judy. His words might prove helpful in making my decision. Whatever the case, Sam will be of little help to me."

"Why don't I wonder down the hall and check on our kids. If I get lucky, I might hear a word or two as I passed their door." Before Brad could respond to his wife's words she dashed off down the hall. Pausing at Anderson's door it became clear there was an argument ensuing inside. Trying to hear better Marie leaned her ear close to the door.

"All I'm saying is, the dumb shit shouldn't have struck the first blow. He has a great business head, but lacks common sense when it comes to dealing with people. He doesn't know how to resolve a situation, he goes berserk."

"We should tell the authorities there was a heated exchange of words, and the guy appeared as if he was about to take a swing at Brad. We can say Brad was lucky enough to avoid the attack, and swing back."

"Honey telling the police there was an argument, and the guy struck at Brad would be a blatant lie. We could all be in trouble. I'm not sticking my neck in that noose."

Judy was shocked at her husband's reaction. "No it wouldn't be a lie, the guy argued with Brad about forcing us back inside. The fact we never heard the biker's words doesn't change anything. I believe what Brad told us is true. You can't honestly think Brad reacted that fast without cause. He doesn't go around beating people up."

"I'm dead certain Brad knew what he was doing. Now he wants to shift the focus to self-defense. This complete mess was created by his doing. He over reacted because he doesn't believe anyone is brave enough to repudiate his words. I don't care what you say Honey, Brad has issues. He needs to take anger management classes so he can learn to think before he reacts."

Marie came rushing back down the hall. "The evidence against you just became worse. Sam will not testify in your best interest. He is being an asshole. He and Judy are arguing about what happened now. That man is something else. There will come a day, Judy will dump him."

"I expected as much from Sam. The only thing I can do is put my faith in the hands of a competent attorney. There is nothing we can do tonight. I'll speak to Sam and the others in the morning."

"Sam is starting to irritate me. We have done a lot for him and Judy. I would like to kick him in the groin." Marie stated with great anger. Her anger appeared to be increasing.

"That won't help Honey. I consider him a weak person. For Sam to tell anything but the truth as he knows it, could prove devastating. If any good detective or prosecuting attorney were to cross examine him he could break under the pressure. It's best if Sam stands on his ignorance. He knows nothing about the exchange of words between the guy and me. His testimony means nothing."

Thinking her husband could be charged with a crime Marie slept very little. Come morning she was the first to rise. She had coffee waiting for the others. Judy and Sam came walking in to the kitchen together to dark circles under Marie's eyes. "Did you sleep at all last night?"

"How could I sleep thinking my husband could be charged with a crime and sent to prison for many years? If he is charged with a crime, it will be a shame."

Judy gave her friend a huge hug. "I'm certain Brad was only defending us. Try not to worry he won't be convicted and sent to prison."

"I know he is innocent, but who else is going to believe he is innocent. He has no witnesses." She glared at Sam. "If you know something I don't, please tell me."

Brad came in temporarily ending the conversation. "I don't want anyone trying to cover for me. Stick to the truth, as you know it. Speak out when asked to do so, and tell what you know. Don't make up any lies. A good detective or prosecuting attorney will rip you to pieces if you say anything untrue. My defense strategy is uncertain at this time." He paused briefly. "Do we still have cereal and milk, I'm hungry."

"We have plenty of cereal. Have a seat. I'll get it for you."

"Thank you Honey, I'm starved." Judy paced the floor trying to think of a way to help him. "Isn't anyone going to join me for breakfast?"

Judy looked at Sam before stating she needed something from her room. He read her look. "Why don't I help you Honey." Together they disappeared down the hall. In the privacy of their room he gave her a sheepish look. "What is it you want me to do?"

"Sam if you, I, and Marie, all say the guy was trying to force us back into the Pub. Brad would be off the hook, and we all go about our business."

"We don't know the guy was actually serious about trying to force us anywhere. I didn't see a weapon of any kind, did you?" Judy shook her head no. "Then why would anyone believe we were about to be forced back inside. There were four of us and the biker was alone."

"We could say he had one hand in his pocket as if he had a weapon of some kind. We can't let Brad go to prison."

"Your idea would never work. Mr. Big Shot rejects most ideas given to him anyway. You heard him say not to lie for him. Being a first time conviction, he may get off with few as ninety days in prison and placed on parole for three years. He won't get a harsh sentence."

"You stupid fool if he is charged and convicted because we fail to testify in a favorable manner, it will mean the end of them working with us forever. Think about what an economic downturn for us. We need to do this good deed and continue to be rewarded. He has done a lot for us. Now is our turn to do something for him."

"Judy, don't yell at me. This seemed like the perfect way for us to vacation and it was going good until Brad showed up. We should have stayed home, or vacationed somewhere else with just our family. There is a term for those people who vacation at home. They are calling these people *staycationers*."

"What is wrong with you, after all Brad has done for us you should feel obligation to him. I don't understand you. You can be the most selfish person at times'."

"I feel no obligation to lie, and get myself in trouble over his stupid actions. This isn't like he may be charged with urinating in public, he killed a man. If we lie, we could all wind up in jail. Our personal success is earned through our own responsible hard work. We are not totally relying on dumb-ass Brad and his enhancing system. I bet we could enhance most of our videos ourselves. We are intelligent experienced people. We know what makes a house sell, and what doesn't."

"You can't get in any trouble if we simply tell the local police the guy was trying to kidnap us, and Brad hit him once and we left not realizing the guy was injured to the extent of needing medical help."

"Maybe you have a point Honey. A simple story like that might work. No, it can't work. Nobody is going to believe one man was trying to kidnap four people."

"Of course it will work. The local police are not big city detectives. I wouldn't be in favor of this except I believe Brad is telling the truth. He never killed the biker on purpose. The guy died as a result of his own drunken actions."

"Alright let's play it your way. Tell Brad we will save his ass this time."

"When Emily and Laura take the kids to the beach is when we should have our talk with Brad. The others need not know anything about this screwed up mess." Judy and Sam marched back to the kitchen area to find Marie and Brad each holding two little ones. "Look at what we have here, the whole world is up. Are you girls pestering Aunt Marie and Uncle Brad?" Carrie and Kristy simultaneously shook their heads no. "What kind of cereal do you girls want for breakfast?"

"Emily promised to make turtle pancakes for us this morning. She isn't awake yet. Uncle Brad won't let us wake her, but we are hungry."

"How would it be if Aunt Marie and I make turtle pancakes?"

"No thank you mother, it wouldn't be the same. Emma makes better pancakes."

Using one hand Brad spun Carrie's head around to face him. "How about Uncle Brad, and your father, make your turtle pancakes, would that work?"

Carrie looked at the other kids as she smiled, and threw her hands in the air. "You and dad can cook. Johnnie and Jimmy can help them." The smiles disappeared from the faces of Johnnie and Jimmy.

Brad saw their disappointment. "Come on boys we can do this. You two can be the official testers before we feed the girls."

"Hey, that's not fair." Carrie protested as Laura entered the room. "We want Emily to cook our turtle pancakes and we don't need them tested."

"Alright girls have it your way. If you people will excuse me I need to call Junior. I neglected to call him yesterday. He needs to be told the medical building takeover went through. Do you want to call him Marie, or should I make the call?"

"I would be happy to call my brother."

"You have better cell reception out on the veranda than in here. Tell Junior we will be flying home tomorrow. Ask to keep the next day open because we need to contact all the businesses in our four buildings soon as possible. Plus you might remind him acquiring the medical buildings will generate great revenue and benefit us all. We can work out the details of his raise later."

Marie went out to the veranda while Brad reminded the others his business interests were in order. I may be tied up with attorneys in the coming months. The Ad Palace will operate fine without me being there. None of you people should be affected in any way."

Judy instantly responded to his statement. "While Emily and Laura have the kids at the beach today Sam and I would like to drive into town with you. We can help you clear up this personal matter clouding your thoughts."

Brad smiled but was uncertain how to respond. No telling what she had in mind. With the kids and nannies in the room, this was not the time to discuss anything. "How are your pancakes kids?"

"Emily makes wonderful pancakes." Johnnie stated. "Look dad, I ate the head off my turtle first so he can't bite me as I eat him. Would you like one of her pancakes?"

"If she has enough batter I'll have a pancake." Carrie raced off to tell Emily to make Uncle Brad a pancake.

"I'll have a heart-shaped pancake, because I love each and every one of you kids." He shouted as the tyke ran away.

Emily caught Carrie as she raced to her. "Your wish is my command Sweetheart. Anyone else want a heart-shaped pancake?" Judy and Sam each raised their hand. "Coming right up, I'll cook four heart-shaped pancakes in case Marie wants one too."

Marie returned all smiles. "Ray was thrilled. By the sound in the background Darcy was dancing around the office as he spoke to me. Hey, heart-shaped pancakes. How sweet of you Emily, thank you very much." Marie actually hugged her.

"Honey, Judy thinks we need to drive into town while the kids go play on the beach. She has some kind of errand for us. The kids are getting ready to leave soon. They plan on making a giant sand turtle today. Emily's turtle pancakes gave Jimmy the idea. He wants the sand turtle big enough for all four kids to sit on."

Soon as the kids were gone Judy turned her attention to Brad. "If you trust me to do the talking we can brush off the biker incident with ease. Sam has agreed to follow my lead, what do you say?"

Brad sat rubbing his face, and chin, as he thought over her words. Sam placed one hand on his shoulder. "If we don't put this to bed, before leaving here we may be dragged back several times for questioning. At first I thought her idea was risky. After thinking about it, I believe it may work."

Marie leaned in and kissed her husband's cheek. "Let's give their idea a chance."

"Needless to say I'm nervous. If we are going to do this, let's do it before I chicken out and most of all let's pray this doesn't make matters worse for me."

It was a quiet ride into town. Brad parked directly in front of the police station and drew in a deep breath. "I'll explain why we are here before you guys say anything."

Judy touched his shoulder. "After you talk let me speak for the rest of us."

Brad led the way in. "Excuse me Miss, is there an officer we may speak with?"

"Officer Greenfield is in his office. Have a seat. I'll notify him you are here."

Sitting silently in the waiting room Brad's nerves grew tense. "Is there a drinking fountain around here my throat is dry?" He asked the receptionist.

Officer Greenfield emerged before he received an answer to his question. "Good afternoon people how may I be of help?"

Brad quickly stood up. "We have been staying at a cottage out on the beach front this past week. Today while starting to get supplies, we noticed the paper from yesterday with a front page article about the biker dying out at the Sweet Spot Pub. I have information pertaining to that event. We were there dancing in the Pub when all these creepy looking bikers came in. They started drinking and as you might expect we became fearful and opted to leave. Walking across the parking lot on our way to the car I was accosted by one of the bikers. He tried to force us back inside. I lashed out at him before dashing to our car. I saw the biker go down, but never realized he wouldn't get up. Seeing the paper a few minutes ago startled me. The dead biker may be the guy I hit."

"You can relax Mister; your story makes perfect sense. Approximately a month ago we had a similar incident at the Pub. Two young women claimed to be forced back inside."

"That would be kidnapping, a criminal offence."

"You are quite correct again. The problem was the bikers claimed the girls went in of their own free will. There were far more bikers than girls to testify the girls entered the bar of their own free will. In addition the bikers claimed they were willing sex partners. There was no way we could charge any of the individuals with the crime of rape. Come into my office and I will type up your statement. Soon as you sign the statement you can be on your way." Officer Greenfield wrote up a simpler version of Brad's words indicating the biker had tried to kidnap the four individuals, two men and two women. The officer further indicated there was no direct evidence to support Brad was involved in the biker's death. "Read it carefully. If everything meets with your approval the four of you sign the paper, and you are off to the beach again. You ladies were lucky." Officer Greenfield declared. "The other girls claimed they were raped repeatedly by the bikers. The women didn't go straight to the hospital. They should have taken a rape test to collect D&A. We had no witnesses siding with the women, and no D&A evidence of semen and bruising on their bodies, we were unable to charge the bikers with any crimes." Officer Greenfield thanked them for coming in. "Most people would have left town, and never said a word about being at the Pub that night. We appreciate you coming forward. This report should give me the leverage with the city council to post undercover officers in the Pub the next time the biker return. I'll give you one more piece of information before you leave. When our first officer arrived on the scene he took a switchblade knife form the man's hand. The knife had not been opened. The way the knife was positioned in his hand it left little doubt he was ready to open it."

In the car Brad breathed a sigh of relief. "That went better than I expected. Our next vacation we won't be dancing out in the middle of nowhere. We can choose a better place to go dancing in the future. We'll go dancing from home. There are many wonderful places in Las Vegas or Seattle to go dancing."

Judy reached up and patted Brads shoulder as he drove away. "It's Marie and I who owe you. We heard Officer Greenfield say the bikers were accused of raping two girls during the other incident. I can't think of anything worse than being raped. Had you not acted quickly, he may have opened his knife and stabbed you."

"I'm just thrilled someone finally believed what I said without question. Maybe these small time city policemen take their job serious, and actually do a good job."

CHAPTER 5

Driving back to the cottage Brad continued to express his gratitude toward the police. "I didn't think anyone would believe me about what the biker said. I was awake much of the night visualizing what it would be like going through a trial. I could see thirty bikers at my trial waiting for a verdict. Even if I were acquitted I might lose my life, and leave my family in disarray."

"You are okay now." Judy declared. "We need to celebrate!"

"I'll pass on celebrating today. Let's save our celebrating until someone's birthday when celebrating is appropriate. We shouldn't celebrate the end of an ugly incident. It needs to be forgotten."

Arriving at the cottage Brad went straight to the veranda to stretch out in one of the lounge chairs. Marie followed him out. "Would you like a beer or a snack?"

"No, thank you Honey, I don't need beer or food. I'm out here soaking up my freedom. It will take major rest to revive me."

"If you don't mind, while you nap I'm going down to the beach, and sunbathe near the boys. If we are not back yet when you wake up, come join us. I'll take snacks for the kids so they will be content to remain at the water's edge longer. Nap and rest long as you want."

"You go right ahead Honey. Keep our brood busy, and I will rest better. Be sure and check on their sand turtle. If the boys get good at construction maybe they can build apartments for us some day."

Marie, Judy, and Sam, all went to see how the sand turtle was coming along. Judy put her arm around her friend. "Brad leads such a stressing life as it is, he didn't need anything like the Pub incident. I feel badly for him. He looks so tired and stressed. I hope his rest relaxes him. It might have been better if he had gone back to bed in place of napping on the veranda. Had he done so I'm certain he could have slept for a longer period of time?"

"I happen to agree with you Judy, but when he wanted to rest on the veranda I felt it best not to argue with him. He said he was enjoying his freedom being out on the veranda. Brad and I need more time away from the city."

The group soon came upon the sand turtle. "Guys your turtle looks great."

"Mom where is dad, he needs to see our sand turtle, it's really neat. It's big enough we can all sit on our turtle at the same time."

"Honey, your father is resting. He can see your turtle later this evening. He may come down at sunset with us. You can also show him the sun sinking in the water one final time before we go home tomorrow."

"Mom, we like the beach. We don't want to go home."

"Your father and I must return to work so we can earn money to come back to the beach next year."

"Can Carrie and Kristy come to the beach with us next year?"

"Yes Sweetheart, I think we can all vacation at the beach again next year."

Their well appreciated snacks only lasted so long. In addition the kids needed the restroom. "Mom can we go back to the cottage, we are hungry and Johnnie needs the restroom."

Marie knew there was no way of delaying the youngsters returning to the cottage nor would they be quiet when they arrived at the cottage. The best she could do was to instruct the kids to avoid the veranda. "Mom, what is a veranda?"

Marie hugged Jimmy. "Honey a veranda is a porch on the lower deck. Don't ask me why a porch has so many names. I have no idea. Come along and we can find you something to eat. You kids need to be quiet as you can, and let your father sleep. He hasn't been here resting long as we have."

Inside the cottage people scurried about getting their snacks while Judy stood looking out the French Doors leading to the veranda. Her eyes were locked on Brad as he slept. She had heard the story about how Brad's life was a mess, after he killed the intruder many years before. She wondered if the biker's death would affect him in the same manner. If he were her husband she would be comforting him in their room. By now they would have been sleeping peacefully together.

After eating a cookie Sam walked up behind her. "Looking at the waves Honey?"

Judy turned enough to whisper to him. "I was watching Brad, he needs rest but he shouldn't be alone. The night he showed Marie and me the security video of his intruder incident he changed before our eyes. I remember it was several days, before he calmed enough to be anything close to what he was. Communicating with him was difficult. He didn't appear to understand the simplest question anyone asked him. His mind was elsewhere."

Sam motioned for Judy to follow him out a different door. "Since you saw Brad's condition before, you need to speak with him, alone soon as you can. Try and get him to open up, and talk about the incident if he feels the need to do so. Sleeping this long today he may be up late tonight. After Marie turns in this evening you might have a chance to check his condition. You could be right he may need help."

Judy appreciated her husband's kind words towards Brad. Where Brad was concerned, Sam seldom mentioned any kind words. "I'll try talking to Marie first, so she knows I will be talking to her husband. Hopefully Brad will be okay by the time we talk later today. Let's hope I won't need a private conversation with him."

"Do what you think is best. He is different than anyone I've ever known, my talking to him probably wouldn't help. He and I are on different wave lengths most of the time. My trying to discuss anything with him may make things worse."

Marie walked out looking for Sam and Judy. "Did you get all the kids fed?"

"Feeding a kid is a temporarily event." Sam declared. "In two hours they will be searching for more food. All four of the youngsters are growing like weeds."

"How well I know. I see Brad is still sleeping peacefully. I have no idea how long to let him sleep. I know he needs rest. When we get home tomorrow our workload will be extreme for a few days. We have hundreds of new tenants in the medical buildings to contact. I have little doubt he will want to set up an automatic electronic billing system to track all the payments easier."

"Keeping his mind busy with financial thoughts should be good for him, tiring but good for him. He needs to think of things besides the biker incident at the Pub. Of all things to happen the biker incident was the last thing he needed to be involved with." Our boys want to show their father the sand turtle, and see the sun set in the ocean one more time before we leave tomorrow. Tonight is their last chance to show him. I'm wondering if I should wake Brad or not. He has been sleeping four hours. The sun won't be setting for a couple more hours. I'm thinking I should wake him in about an hour in case he wants something to eat, before going down on the beach. I know he would enjoy seeing the kids' faces as they watch the sun disappear into the water."

"Sam and I will leave the decision to wake him or not to you. You know him better than we do. If it is any comfort to you he does love watching the kids enjoying themselves, we all know that. If you don't wake him he might be disappointed at not getting to see the joy on their little faces."

"I'll give him another hour of sleep before checking on him. With any luck he may wake on his own before long. If need be, I bet I could get four little helpers to wake him if I asked."

Marie's voiced her idea too loud and Carrie overheard the conversation about waking her Uncle Brad. She quickly rounded up her gang before charging towards the veranda. Judy put the brakes on the kids plan. "Whoa, where are you four going?"

"Aunt Marie said to wake Uncle Brad."

"Honey, she didn't mean right now. Aunt Marie was talking about waking him in one hour. Your uncle needs his rest. He has been working very hard. When you do wake him be very gentle."

Carrie wrinkled up her nose. "Mom you always kill our fun."

"Little lady, straighten that face out. You better straighten up and listen to me. Do not bother your uncle until Aunt Marie tells you specifically it is okay to wake him."

"Yes mother." Again the little girl frowned. "Mom what does specifically mean?"

"Specifically means Aunt Marie will tell you when to wake your Uncle Brad, now go play. An hour is too long to wait out here."

"Nobody has taken us for a walk out to the highway and back today. We love to go hiking almost much as we enjoy horseback riding."

Marie volunteered to take the four children for a walk to keep them from bothering Brad until it became time to wake him. Sam went to the bedroom for a nap. Emily and Laura were already napping.

Brad spoiled everyone's plan by waking on his own. Judy was looking out as he started in. "Welcome to the living world. We were starting to take bets on when you would wake. I was thinking it might be tomorrow."

"I'm sorry to disappoint you. I need to be up some or I might not sleep tonight."

"Actually it's the little people who you will disappoint. They have been itching to be unleashed for the past two hours. They wanted the pleasure of waking you up."

"In that case I'll slip back out, and pretend to be sleeping. You can have them wake me. I'll be waiting and surprise them. Give me a minute to get set."

"Hold on, the kids are not here. Marie took the kids for a walk."

"I may as well go back and rest until they come back to wake me. I'll act surprised when they wake me. On second thought, I'm hungry. What do we have left around here to eat?"

"Sit down at the table. I'll fix you a sandwich. Do you want a whole sandwich or a half a sandwich?"

"I'll have a whole sandwich with the works, lunch meat, cheese, pickles, lettuce, mustard, and tomato."

Judy checked the refrigerator. "Sorry, all we have left to make a sandwich out of is peanut butter. Our darling little children ate everything else."

"A peanut butter sandwich is fine." He managed to eat half his sandwich before seeing Marie and the children walking up the driveway. "I'm going back out to the veranda send the kids to wake me when they get here."

When the kids returned, they made a dash to wake Brad. "Come on dad, get up we are going to see our sand turtle and watch the sun set into the water. You can hear the sun sizzle when it goes in the water. It's like a giant fireball sinking in the water."

"Okay, I'll get up. Lead the way guys, I'm right behind you. First I need a water bottle." Walking inside to get his water he grabbed the second half of his sandwich.

Brad walked hand in hand with Marie as they walked to the water's edge. Jimmy grabbed his leg urging his father to pick him up. Once the boy was in his father's arms Marie turned and kissed both Jimmy and Brad. "I love it here at the beach. I wish we could stay longer."

"So do Jimmy and me, but I'm sure Junior wants us home. He must be anxious to hear how big a pay increase he will get and to be truthful I haven't given his raise much thought. Have you thought about his increase?"

"Good heavens no, we need to crunch some numbers first. Then we need to assess how well he and Darcy are working together. She will be more valuable to him now than before. I'm thinking she may rate a pay increase as well. Darcy's raise will be less increase than Junior's pay increase of course. If they are getting along okay she will get a pay increase."

With the sun setting darkness crept in fast. Jimmy informed his father he didn't like the dark, and was ready to go back up to the cottage where the sea monsters couldn't get him. "I doubt there are any sea monsters nearby."

"Carrie and Johnnie said there were sea monsters on the beach at night." Jimmy insisted. "They said the sea monsters are big and creepy."

"I think they were funning with you. Sea monsters are not native to this area. A whale might come by once in a while, but not a sea monster. Whales are fun to watch."

"What about sharks, I know there are sharks in the ocean?"

"Carrie, you and Jimmy need to stop putting scary ideas in Jimmy's head. To answer your question, Jimmy, sharks do not come up on land. You are safe walking or playing on the beach."

"Yes they do. Johnnie and I heard you talking to our neighbor back home. You were talking about land sharks."

Brad couldn't help but laugh. "Mr. Brown and I were talking about loan sharks. Loan sharks are entirely a different thing. People who loan other people money at enormous interest rates are called loan sharks. Son, I will never allow anyone or anything to bother you."

The remainder of the evening was spent eating and relaxing. First the kids were put to bed. Sometime later one by one the adults complained about being tired and soon retreated to their room leaving Brad and Marie alone. "After sleeping much of the day you may not be tired but I am. Do you mind if I turn in?" Marie asked.

"You go ahead Honey. I'll be along in a couple hours." They kissed good night as Marie parted and went off to bed alone. Brad soon changed his mind and joined his wife in bed. They snuggled tight before drifting off into a deep sleep. Sleep came easier than Brad expected. He was at peace with himself.

Judy's opportunity to speak with Brad privately slipped away. Oh well she thought, maybe it's for the best. Proper sleep will do him more good, than talking half the night.

By the time Brad and Marie arrived home the following evening they were exhausted. "Dragging luggage around wears me out." Marie proclaimed. "Laura can you put the boys to bed for me, I'm beat?"

"I would be happy to put the boys to bed, come along guys."

"Thank you Laura, we'll see you in the morning." Brad and Marie showered together before going to bed. "Our vacation was wonderful, but it tires me out lugging everything back home. Except for the medical buildings takeover I could sleep for a week."

"Honey, seeing our tenants soon as possible is important. Why don't you sleep in tomorrow while I lay out our schedule and meet me at noon in Junior's office?" Brad suggested. "The four of us can have lunch together before contacting our first tenants. We need a plan of attack before dashing out like a bunch of wild idiots."

"Bless your heart, sleeping in sounds wonderful, my body needs recovery time. Morning will come too soon as it is."

Come morning, Brad's first stop was at the Ad Palace. "Good morning people. I don't see a pile of videos to be worked on. How are things moving along?"

"With Judy and Sam vacationing sales are down, but we are doing okay. Robin Tilly is a different story. I've never seen a woman work as efficiently as she does. She must maximize every minute of her day. Her sales, even in this housing decline, are excellent. According to the news, Las Vegas in general is a tough area to sell houses at this time. They claim the credit crunch put the brakes on new buildings. I think the key to Robin's success is she doesn't limit herself to any single type of house. She sells from the top to bottom of the price range. Bob converted two large homes he built into duplexes and they sold. He is an amazing builder."

"Robin and Bob are good people, I was lucky to find them. Marie and I did manage to acquire the medical buildings. She and I, starting this afternoon, will be busy working in that area for a few days as we meet our new tenants. You guys are doing such a great job here you may not miss us. If something comes up don't hesitate to call me." Before leaving the office Brad wrote five thirteen thousand dollar checks. One thirteen thousand dollar check each for Wendy, Rusty, Carol, Bob Tilly, and Robin Tilly. In unison the office staff asked what the checks were for. "Your checks are a tax free gift for putting up with me. Call it a celebration of Marie and me completing the deal on the medical buildings."

"I don't understand. This is very generous of you. We did nothing to help acquire the medical buildings. We earn bonuses on our work here not on work you do in other areas. You puzzle me. If I live to be a hundred years old I'll never understand how you think."

"Oh but you did help. You did a magnificent job in this office so I could concentrate on the medical building deal. You earned your checks. Now I've got to run. Keep up the good work."

He went straight to Robin Tilly's office to drop off her and Bob's check. He handed Robin her and Bob's checks. "Here is a little non-tax bonus for you and Bob for being such good friends."

"Hold on, get back here. What may I ask are these checks for?"

"Those are small gifts for you and Bob for all the little things you do for Marie and me. Use the money for a vacation or anything you want. Keep in mind gift money not exceeding thirteen thousand dollars is tax free. We appreciate your efforts on our behalf. You and Bob are a huge part of Marie and my business success. Without you two, I may not own anything in Vegas."

"I must tell you Mr. Collins, you and Marie are full of surprises. Bob and I certainly thank you. For everything we do for you we are rewarded many times over. It's a pleasure working with your organization."

"You and Bob are a valuable part of our team. Keep up the good work." He took the opportunity to pat her back. "You are doing a great job. I need to run over to the apartment complex office and do some work there. Have a good day Robin and thank you for your help on the medical building deal."

Moving on to Junior's office Brad found Darcy alone. Ray was out checking with the gardening staff. "Are you busy Darcy, or do you have time to help me draw up a form for us to use as we tour our medical buildings?" Always in a hurry Brad never waited for an answer. "I want us to start meeting and welcoming our tenants starting this afternoon."

"I would be happy to help you. Tell me what you need."

"How would it be if we create two letters? We need one letter that introduces us as the new owners of the medical buildings, and a second letter more of a form to check the condition of the building itself? We need to take a quick look at the general condition of the building. We need a quick visual inspection of the flooring, and how clean the paint on the walls is. In the introductory letter make it plain we are not intending to make any changes. For our tenants it will be business as usual."

Darcy was instantly on board with his ideas. In minutes she created two wonderful letters.

Ninety minutes later Junior returned to the office. "Hello Brad." Junior was all smiles. "I can see by the dark circles under your eyes the medical buildings takeover took a toll on you. I think you need to go to bed, and stay there a full week."

"Going to bed sounds great but we have tons of work to do. Marie will be joining us for lunch today in a few minutes. After lunch we can go out and introduce ourselves as the new owners of the buildings. Darcy drew up a beautiful letter of introduction we can leave with each tenant. The letter contains all the pertinent information about Collins Enterprises. Our office hours, phone numbers, fax numbers and e-mail address. Help us out Junior, look the letter over and see if we missed anything. The second letter is a form for our benefit. We'll take a quick peek at the general condition of things like the flooring. I'm guessing the buildings were not all built at the same time. At some point we need to get on a schedule of how we should be looking at general building maintenance of these buildings to keep them in top shape."

"This letter looks perfect to me. You are the boss my friend, Darcy and I will follow your lead."

"I haven't come up with a formula as to how to figure your pay increase, but I won't forget you. As of now you are paying Darcy twelve dollars an hour and I think we need to boost her pay to twenty dollars an hour."

Darcy's eyes sparkled as Junior grinned at her. "Consider your pay increase effective immediately."

Marie soon joined them. "Hello people are we ready for lunch?"

"Not quite Honey, we have a little business to take care of first. You need to write the last two checks, before we forget to do so."

"Oh yes of course." Marie wrote Junior and Darcy each their thirteen thousand dollar checks. "These checks are a gift for all the things you do for us." Darcy and Junior were speechless. "Gifts not exceeding thirteen thousand dollars are tax free. Call it vacation money or whatever."

In a split second Darcy hugged Both Marie and Brad. "I'm not sure I deserve this, but thank you." Junior followed Darcy's lead and hugged his sister and shook Brad's hand. Words escaped him as he let his smile do his talking.

"Let's go eat lunch." Minutes later the four were off to lunch. While eating Brad brought Marie up to speed on what had been done, and what they were expecting to accomplish in the afternoon. "Let's all go in the first office together, and see what kind of a reception we get before we split up into pairs."

The first tenant in the office they choose belonged to an attorney, John Berry. "Good afternoon, Miss. I'm Brad Collins representing Collins Enterprises. We are the new owners of this medical building. Our purpose for stopping by today is to introduce ourselves along with giving out the pertinent information on our company."

"Mr. Collins, wait right here. I think Mr. Berry will want to speak with you personally."

Mr. Berry came stomping out to meet them. "Please come to my office he barked. Brad, Marie, Junior, and Darcy, all followed him to his private office. "This new annual lease increase is unacceptable. I'm looking for a new location to move our office. We will not be a tenant in this building for long."

Brad stuck out both hands in a stopping motion. "Whoa, hold on Mr. Berry. We do not have any lease increase that I know about. Tell me what you think is going on."

"According to the letter we received last week all leases were being doubled. Here look at the letter." Mr. Berry jerked his desk drawer open to grab the letter he was referring to. "It's signed by Steven Avery, Tom Avery's son who took over the buildings after his father died."

"Mr. Berry, my wife and I, purchased these medical buildings from Steven Avery five days ago. We did not make this purchase based on these inflated tenant leases this letter indicates. That increase means nothing because the kid no longer owns the buildings. Collins Enterprises will use last year's lease as our starting base. Naturally each year we will reassess the profit line along with the building needs and adjustments will be made only on an as needed basis. I can assure you no lease will ever be doubled on anyone."

Mr. Berry sat quiet for a few seconds before responding. "In that case, I'm glad you stopped by today. Last year's lease will be fine. We were thinking we would be moving. Moving would be a huge expense for us."

"Believe me we are glad we came when we did, and we appreciate you seeing us in a timely manner. Our company information was left with your receptionist. Unless you have further questions we'll be on our way, and allow you to return to your work. Please keep in mind we are only a phone call away if any problems crop up."

Out in the main foyer Darcy reminded Brad he never covered the second letter with Mr. Berry. "I know, Stephen Avery messed things up for us by making our tenants upset. There is no reason to discuss maintenance with mad tenants. We need to calm everyone down and worry about maintenance whenever. I think we better return to your office and regroup."

"I agree." Junior voiced. "We need to change our letter indicating we are rolling back the leases to last year's level so we can send out e-mails to all tenants before we start darting through the offices making personal connections. I still want to drop off letters fast as possible tomorrow. In about a month we can follow up with a longer personal visit. We need to squash this lease increase business before we lose all our tenants."

"Steve Avery was trying to pull a fast one on us. He doubled the rent in hopes of collecting another larger month's rent before selling the medical buildings to Marie and me. He didn't care if part of our tenants moved out. I knew that kid was trying to pull a fast one on us. We need to kill his rate increases before we actually lose tenants. I hate dishonest people."

Back at Junior's office he was quick to ask why an attorney was located in a medical building. "I took one of Mr. Berry's business cards." Brad handed it Junior. "Our Mr. Berry is a personal injury lawyer. He apparently wants to be near the action."

Everyone had a good laugh. Darcy started drawing up a new introductory letter.

"You don't need four people to draw up a new letter." Marie commented. "I should go help Wendy in our other office the rest of the afternoon. By the time you draw up the letter and send out the e-mails the afternoon may be gone."

"I may as well leave too. I wasn't able to finish checking all my people." Junior added. "I'll go finish up so tomorrow my morning is free."

Darcy laughed as Marie and Junior darted out. "You scared those two." She commented. "They want to keep busy elsewhere."

"What are you talking about, how did I scare them. I never said one harsh word to either of them."

"You didn't have to say anything your reputation spoke for you. You are a very energetic business person compared to those around you, me included. We want to keep busy in your presence."

"Dang, that's not right. I don't want to scare people into working harder. All I ask of people to work efficient so they are productive. Maybe I should leave so you can relax as you draft our new introductory letter."

She quickly grabbed his arm. "Oh no, don't go, I may need help drafting your new letter. You helped draft our first letter. Help me again. You and I work well together. Don't let me down now. Roll Ray's chair over here next to me so you can see the computer screen."

"You just said I make people nervous. If I make you nervous wouldn't it be better for me disappear so you could relax, and do your work? I'll go hang out somewhere else."

"Please stay. Yes, I'm nervous around you, but I want to learn from you. Junior says you are a brilliant business person who he admires. He thinks he and I can learn from watching how you operate."

"Much of my success comes from money my father left me. Another equally huge chunk of my success comes from the fine people working with us. If someone approaches me with a bargain they can't afford, I give their suggestion serious thought. In some instances Marie and I move forward with a project such as these medical buildings. It never hurts to move forward with a low-ball offer. Cash money talks, if someone needs to sell a business more than we need to buy a business, we have an opportunity to make a nice deal. Right now the only growth I'm interested in is projects that fit our current employees. We need people like you and Junior in these slow economic times to have the opportunity to increase your income."

"I don't care how much money you were left by your parents, I still think you and Marie are brilliant business people."

"Calling Marie and I brilliant would be wrong, calling us opportunists would be correct. The only thing we are smart enough to do is value our excellent employees. We believe by keeping people happy we will all profit."

"I think you are spoofing me, you are as sly as a fox. You have large ears and your eyes are always open looking for a business opportunity. Junior claims most people who inherit money usually do little, but live off the interest. He tells me you started out by buying and operating a hamburger joint and now look at you."

Brad laughed as he put one arm around Darcy for a gentle hug. "When Junior agreed to work with Marie and me. He said he wouldn't mind working with us for the next fifteen to eighteen years. He thought by then our sons would be old enough to join the family business. He reasoned he would be out of a job by then and need to move on. Marie and I do not plan to let that happen. In order to retain his services as long as he wants to work with us, we needed to expand. I grew up alone, no family and few friends. I want Marie and my children to be surrounded by family. My vision is for all of us to be equally successful so everyone can live a good life. Sometime I'll take you and Junior to lunch at the Burger Palace. That's the burger joint I once owned. You can see my humble beginnings." He released his grip on her. "We are not getting our letter written."

"Do you want to try salvaging this letter or start over?"

"Throw that letter away and start over. Say something like welcome. Collins Enterprises has purchased the medical buildings. Under new ownership the lease fees will remain as they were the past two years. The rumor of fee increases is a false rumor. Then put in all the mush-mush things like we are looking forward to working with them to create a profitable business venture for all businesses involved. Make it sound nice, simple but nice. Once your letter is proof read, e-mail it to all our tenants."

Darcy's computer skills impressed him. In a matter of a couple minutes she completed the letter. "Proof read our letter to see if it meets with your approval or if we need more changes."

Brad scanned the letter before winking at her. "Good work Darcy. Send the letter out as e-mails to all tenants. Then make enough copies of the letter so we can hand deliver a copy to every business. Some medical operations contract with billing services so we don't know where the leases are paid from. We need to cover all of our bases." Darcy smiled with pride because he approved her work. "Now it's time for me to skip out and let you finish your work. With any luck we can get at least part of the letters delivered tomorrow."

"I'll have all of the letters finished for tomorrow. Before you leave today I want to thank you again for the generous check you gave me." Her words were accompanied by a tender hug. "It is nice to be appreciated."

"You are welcome. Keep in mind no one expects you to kill yourself getting these letters ready." As he left the office he touched Darcy's hair gently and leaned down for a second quick hug. The fresh smell of her hair reminded him of Alice, her sister, his first wife who died in an automobile crash. "Your hair smells like Alice's hair used to smell. I'll call you towards evening, and see how you are progressing with the letter."

"Bye and thank you for your help." Noticing him smelling her hair aroused her curiosity. She couldn't help but give him a sexy smile. "Did you just smell my hair?"

"I did smell your hair, and you smell nice. Do you know every woman smells slightly different?" She starred at him in a questioning way. "It's true. You can put the same perfume on two different women, but because of her natural smell mixed with the perfume you will have different smelling women."

"I suppose that makes sense. I hadn't thought about it nor do I go around smelling other women."

"Sometime when you are out shopping with a girlfriend, stop by a perfume counter and put perfume on the underside of your wrist. Use the same perfume as your friend and then an hour later, do the smell test. You will actually notice a difference."

Marie was surprised to see Brad walk into the Ad Palace office. "I thought you were busy working with Darcy on the letter for Collins Enterprises?"

"That girl is competent. She doesn't need my help to make a simple letter. I'm in the way over there. How are things going here, anything we need to catch up on?"

"Since Sam and Judy ended their vacation they sent several extra videos to us for enhancement. We are presently working through the stack of videos as we speak. Both Rusty and Carol have become very proficient at enhancing videos. Things are going magnificently here. We soon will have a stockpile of videos for the Anderson Agency like we have for the Tilly Agency."

"All our employees are doing so well, I may wind up bagging groceries at the super market to keep busy. According to Darcy, I make employees nervous when I'm working near them. She is probably right. I don't mean to make anyone nervous. All I really want from an employee is for them to work efficiently. I'm convinced an employee working efficiently will be less apt to make a mistake."

"Two things come to mind." Wendy stated. "Somehow I can't visualize you bagging groceries. As far as making your employees nervous, all bosses make their employees nervous, welcome to the club."

"As a young teenager, I bagged groceries three days at the market near our house. That means I'm experienced, and could easily get a job in any store."

Rusty couldn't help but make fun of him. "You worked the whole sum of three days. What happened did you get fired?"

"One of my father's business associates from the Import-Export Store saw me working, and called my father. My job ended that day. My father lived in fear I would get kidnapped. I was sent home, and told to stay there in no uncertain terms. There was no discussion at all, home I went."

"You had a tough father."

"I never truly knew the man claiming to be my father. He never had time for me. I saw him once or twice a year. Never once did he take me anywhere. Seldom did I get an answer to any of my questions. I guarantee you my children will know who I am. Marie and I will do things that will include our boys every chance we get."

"Let's get back to business." Marie suggested. "May I be so bold as to suggest we consider taking on one or two more Real Estate Agents?"

"Hold on, Marie, this office will not be growing any larger than it is now. The truth is, had I realized how fast other business opportunities would come around I may not have ever, started enhancing house videos subliminally."

Wendy looked surprised. "Why would you say such a thing? This business makes us bundles of money."

"I worry about getting sued. If anyone ever learned what we are doing they could easily take advantage of the knowledge by suing us big-time, claiming we forced them to purchase something they did not want. In reality we are doing just the opposite. Not one house we enhanced has been foreclosed on. Our process matches buyers to houses the buyers like, and the buyers to houses they can afford. Speaking of houses and buyers, why is it Rusty or Carol hasn't bought a house?"

Both Rusty and Carol sat quiet. "I'm a big believer in marriage and family. Playing house the way you two are doing is dangerous. It may leave you alone one day, alone with nothing more than a few pieces of unmatched furniture. It's time you looked to the future and decide, do you want to be together, or do you want to date other people, is your choice. I urge you to make your choice before life passes you by."

Marie interrupted his lecture. "Rusty and Carol don't need you telling them how to live their lives."

"The divorce rate is so high, marriage is risky Carol added. "Look at mother, who would have expected her and daddy to get a divorce?"

"I doubt you asked your mother if she ever regretted marrying your father. Your mother loves you, and she put your health as a priority when you needed care. She sacrificed time with your father while you were healing. Your father mistakenly accepted what your doctors were saying about you not getting better. He couldn't cope with the stress of your situation. He opted to continue being out on the road with his truck much as possible. Being weak he took comfort where he found it. Had he stopped driving truck, and worked a local job. He could have spent more time with your mother and you. Had he done so, he would still have his family today. Your mother loves you with all her heart. Had she not married your father she wouldn't have you. I doubt she will ever regret marrying your father. I'm sure she wished he had been a stronger person."

"Are you saying my condition caused their divorce?"

"No, I'm not saying that at all. Your father's reaction to your condition caused their divorce. I'm saying if you and Rusty don't make some kind of a commitment to work together towards a common goal, your relationship will likely end one day as you drift apart." Brad paused long enough to take a drink of water. "Only with total commitment can you or any other couple weather the rough times everyone has in their lives. All relationships have ups, and downs, but working together you can survive. Your father tried to go it alone and look what happened to him. He lost everything of value to him, you, his wife, and his business. He lost everything. All he has is his truck, and it may soon wear out leaving him with even less."Carol dropped her head. "You miss your father. It's normal to miss your father, you love him. It's okay to love him. You can love your father, and at the same time hate what he did."

Marie reached over and touched Brad's arm. "Brad, ease up on Carol. She is an adult. She is entitled to make her own decisions. She doesn't need your help."

"Marie is right. I'm sorry Carol. I don't mean to lecture you. Everyone knows I have weird ideas about life. I see people who live together as they are failing to make a decision. Don't feel bad most people would disagree with me. I place great value on not being alone."

At home, Marie further admonished her husband for speaking to Carol and Rusty as he did. "We need these people. Why are you trying to upset them? That office runs smooth. Leave them alone."

"Lighten up Honey I know you are right. Sometimes I say things without thinking I'm not sure this is one of those times. I will apologize to Carol and Rusty again first thing in the morning. You need to write the last two checks for your mother and father before we forget to do so."

"What do I do if my parents won't accept the checks?"

"Explain how the checks came about, and who all received the gift. We want them to have the same gift as the others. If that doesn't work tell them they may get a visit from your crazy husband if they don't accept them."

"You and the boys walk over to their house with me? I may need moral support. Giving my parents money may not be easy." As a family they trudged next door to deliver the checks.

Knowing Ray and Susan couldn't turn them down; Marie had the boys give their grandparents the checks. "You have checks for us. Thank you boys but why are we getting checks?"

"I don't know, it's a gift from mamma and daddy. Johnnie and I didn't get a check form mommy and daddy." Jimmy gave his father a sad look. The boys did not appreciate being left out when the checks were passed out.

Brad smiled as he touched Jimmy's head. "Jimmy, you and Johnnie don't need checks. You are getting your share. Your mother and I contribute to your bank account each month. Your bank accounts increase every month."

"Dad, what does contribute mean?"

"Contribute means we give you money each month. We put money directly in the bank for you, in your name."

"That's not the same as getting a check. Look how happy grandma and grandpa are. They got a check and we didn't. I don't think that's fair, we like to smile too."

"Son, I think we need to discuss your financial situation later at home."

CHAPTER 6

The following morning, Brad dashed by the Ad Palace on his way to the apartment office. Entering the office he expected to see three people working. What he found was Carol working alone. "Good morning Carol where is everyone?" He asked with a sly grin.

"Mother dashed to the Post Office. She has some packages to ship, and Rusty had a dental appointment this morning. He should be in our office by ten. He is having two laser fillings. They shouldn't take long to fix his teeth. The best part of laser fillings, he shouldn't have any after effects. We will still have a productive day."

"Just my luck to have Rusty not here this morning, I wanted to apologize to the two of you. I had no business spouting off about the two of you living together. I was totally out of line. Marie was right. She scolded me properly at home. I am sorry, please except my sincere apology. I'll watch my tongue better in the future."

Carol smiled. "Rusty and I talked about what you said. We see wisdom in your words. We too wonder about our future. We are making good money. If we completely combined our resources we could live quite well. Unfortunately, both Rusty's parents, and my parents are divorced. We are hesitant to make the final commitment. I watched mother go through her divorce, it was an ugly process. It was terrible to watch."

"When any relationship, married or not, breaks up, it is ugly to go through. Extremely painful for those who are going through the incident. I'll let you and Rusty work out your concerns. Personally, I wouldn't trade my marriage, or my boys for the world. Everyone knows children need two loving parents to have the best chance in life."

"What about your gir...." Carol caught her words before she finished her question.

". . . my girls, you were going to ask if I love my girls. The answer to your question is yes. I do love my girls, and Marie loves my girls. I'm the luckiest man on earth because she stuck with me after learning what I had done with Judy. I was young and stupid thinking I was in a position where I could help everyone, and I wanted to help everyone. I had one goal. I wanted to prove I could make money without chasing all over the world like my parents did. Luck was with me when Carrie's bone marrow turned out to be the match that ultimately saved Johnnie's life. Johnnie surviving is what saved me and our marriage was spared. Sometimes luck goes a long way."

"I have a question I'm curious about. I maybe shouldn't ask, but do you believe Sam would stay with Judy if he knew you were the girl's biological father?"

"That is a tough question. I can't speak for Sam. There is little doubt he would be upset. How he would react is anybody's guess. Judy and I both have a subliminal message CD made to play for him in case he ever finds out. One or both of us could zap him enough to hopefully calm him down enough he wouldn't become irrational, and react in complete anger. It's been almost six years now so I think we are fairly safe with our secret. You should see Sam with the girls. He loves his family dearly." Brad paused briefly before saying more. "I'm meeting Marie in a few minutes at our other office. Our medical building takeover hit a roadblock yesterday. We had to pull back and regroup. Hopefully we can do a better job of meeting our tenants today. I bid you goodbye. I'm off to sooth ruffled feathers today. I can honestly say this time the ruffled feathers are not of my doing. This is an inherited problem."

Rusty joined Carol a few minutes after Brad left. "Good morning again Honey. What is our plan, any certain video I should start with?"

"The stack on your left came in first so work on any of those videos. So far I accomplished very little this morning. Brad stopped by to apologize this morning for the comments he made about us yesterday. He stayed and talked a mile a minute. After he left I thought about our conversation. It wasn't so much the words he said as the tone of the words. This office generates a lot of money for him, yet he shows more emotion when he talks about the office over at Collins Enterprises. Add that to him urging you and me to marry. He wants us to pool our money so we can work as one. I'm wondering if he may someday close this office. He could easily step away from the Ad Agency altogether like he did with the Burger Palace."

"Now you are scaring me. I hope this office doesn't close. We need these jobs."

"Yes we need our jobs. The problem I see is he gets bored with a business easy. We need the money we make but he doesn't necessarily need the money we make."

Rusty shook his head no. "We generate far too much money for him to close this office completely. His problem is he loves new challenges. The money we make allow him to take on these new challenges. He does things for pleasure more than money. He loved chopping the Avery kid down on the medical building purchase while he didn't care about the money he saved. Why else would he share his ill-begotten riches with fifteen people?"

"I wouldn't call a good business deal, ill-begotten gains. You know as well as I do, Brad wants those he works with to prosper when he prospers. With the bonus' we can earn, he expects us to grow our own wealth same as he wants to grow his wealth."

"Maybe, sometimes I'm not so sure." Rusty commented. "I heard Marie say Darcy is Brad's former sister-in-law. She is the secretary working in the office at Collins Enterprises office. She looks almost identical to Brad's first wife, his first love. Considering what he and Judy Anderson did, I would think a bell should be going off in Marie's head. I'm certain he wouldn't hesitate to jump this new girl's bones, if given the chance. I believe his chance may come fairly soon. To him it would be like reliving his first love. If that isn't a danger sign, what is?"

"I hadn't thought about why he is spending so much time at the other office. I hope you are wrong."

"Marie is too nice a woman for him to treat her the way he does. His actions with Marie's best friend tell us what type of man he is. Here is the kicker, now he wants to tell us what we should do and how we should live. You heard me say good old Brad, likes new challenges. In my mind Darcy would be a new challenge for him. He lives on the edge of danger. Excitement fuels his body like nobody I've ever known before. He is one of a kind."

"That really isn't a fair statement. You have no idea how Brad acts around Darcy. You better never let anyone besides me hear you make a remark like you just made. If he ever heard what you are saying about him, he would chew you up, and spit you out in little pieces before stomping you flat. You know he has a huge temper. We better mind our own business and get to work. Mother should be returning any minute so get to work."

Over at the Collin's Enterprises office Darcy smiled as Brad walked into her office. "I thought you would be coming along soon. Bad news though, Marie called saying Jimmy wasn't feeling well so she won't be joining our team today."

"Poor little guy. I wondered if he was getting sick last night, he wasn't his normal rambunctious self. I feel bad when one of the boys gets sick. In most cases there is so little a person can do to make them feel better. Their sickness needs to run its course."

"Problem number two, is Ray. He also is under the weather this morning. That leaves just you and me to distribute our letters so we are going to be extremely busy today."

"Wow two strikes against us before we start. We have a list of our clients. You sent out the e-mails. Our tenants have the information we needed to get out fast. We need to remain calm and follow up as we planned, even if it takes a week or longer so be it. We'll do the best we can and use whatever time we have available?"

"I hope you realize this office will suffer."

"We can't help this office at the minute. You and I can only do so much. When we get the letters distributed, to our new tenants we'll decide how best to catch up on the work here in this office."

Darcy's preparation for their personal visits impressed him. She made their work easy. "Would you care for a bite of lunch before we tackle our first building?"

"I doubt we could catch many people during the lunch hour so we may as well eat lunch." She said with a smile. "I'm always up for a free lunch, lead the way."

"There is a little sandwich shop nearby over on the next block. We can grab a bite to eat there. Ann's Diner has pretty good food. I noticed the diner when I was driving around looking at the medical buildings."

"I have a better idea. How far is it to the Burger Palace? I would love to see your humble beginning, if we have time to go that far?"

Brad glanced at his watch as he wondered how he could resist her pretty smile. "You are in luck. I believe we can accommodate your request. Come along my dear. I shall enlighten you, as I show you my humble beginnings."

Carol had the same idea. She wanted food from the Burger Palace and sent Rusty to retrieve their lunch. As Rusty left the Burger Palace he witnessed Brad and Darcy arriving. He circled around in the parking lot so he could see how they were acting, or if they were alone or meeting others for lunch. Brad and Darcy were in an exceptionally happy mood. Rusty couldn't wait to tell Carol what he witnessed. He returned charging into the office. "I saw them together. It looks like I'm right after all. His zipper is bulging again."

"What in the devil are you talking about, who did you see together?" Carol asked.

"I saw our anointed boss and his new sexy playmate, Darcy big-chest Burns. You never saw two happier people to be having lunch together. They were going in the Burger Palace as I left. For a brief second, I thought they were going to kiss before going inside to eat."

"Having lunch together doesn't mean anything." Carol insisted. "Were they hugging, kissing, or pawing, at one another clothes?"

"Well no but....."

".....was Ray and Marie with them?"

"They were alone, and no, he wasn't exactly pawing at her clothes. They were in public, but you know he has wondering eyes. This certainly explains why he is over at the other office more than he is here. The dipstick got off so easy on infidelity before so now he is willing to risk getting caught again. I don't understand why men with money think anytime they get an itch between their legs, they can do as they please?"

"Don't go spouting off too loudly, you really don't have any idea what was going on. Maybe there is a logical explanation for them being at the Burger Palace. You said they weren't hugging, kissing, or pawing one another?"

"They were alone and extremely happy. If that isn't the basic seeds for future illicit activities, I don't know what is? They left little doubt in my mind they were thrilled to be dining together. Of course you may be right there could be a logical explanation, like they didn't have time to get a motel." He snickered at his own words.

"Keep your thoughts to yourself. I see mother returning from lunch. Don't say anything about seeing them together around her. You can't be sure what, if anything is going on."

Unable to convince Carol anything was going on, he shook his head in disgust. "Yea right and pigs can fly. Only when things blow up will you believe I'm right about our philandering boss."

Darcy was amazed at the size of the Burger Palace. "So this was your start and you built it from the ground up?" She nodded her approval. "I like it."

"I didn't exactly build it from the ground up, the shell of the building was here. With the help of people like Pam Tilly, Bob Tilly, Ernie Meadows the current owner, and Wendy, we build up a great business. Once I had taken the business as far as we could, it was time for me to move on to bigger and better things. Wendy and I started the ad business in the office upstairs. Two months later we realized we were cramped for space. We set out to locate a new office. Again I hooked up with Robin Tilly to share the building we are in, the rest is history."

"My food is excellent, and the prices are reasonable. I'm bringing Junior here to eat before long. He would enjoy eating here, and seeing your former business."

"It's a long, ugly story, with lots of growing pains, as to how I came up with a burger joint as my first business. Believe me we don't have time to go into that story today. I'm thinking my complete story might be better left in my dark past, and never mentioned again. There are a lot of unpleasant memories associated with starting this place. Of course I was a young, inexperienced, kid in those days."

Darcy cocked her head slightly to the left as she spoke. "Maybe you should talk about your story. I can tell by the tone of you voice the incident still bothers you. Talking things out sometimes helps cleanse the soul."

"If I live to be a hundred years old, I'll never forget the incident. My business career was almost over before it started. I often think how differently things would be today if Alice were alive. She was mature beyond her years. She would have been able to keep me on the straight and narrow. I have little doubt she would have kept me from making all the stupid mistakes I made as I went into business. Your sister was one of the most intelligent people I've ever met. She was wise beyond her years."

"All lessons in life are meant to teach each of us to lead a better life. Had it not been for your brass comments, I may have still been in Montana with that loser military guy. By now I may have had a couple kids with rags on our backs while I slung food in a dingy restaurant to earn a dollar."

"You are too smart to hook up with the likes of a bad guy for long. I hope with all my heart if Junior isn't the right guy for you, the two of you together will recognize the fact, and remain friends, while moving on with your lives."

"Junior and I get along well, but we have known one another such a short time we hesitate to move forward too fast. He wants to be married, and I want to be married. All things said this still may not be the right time for us to move forward with our relationship. Time is on our side. We'll play it slow and see where we go."

"It's the right time if you enjoy being together more than being apart. Take right now for instance. I can tell you are enjoying lunch with me, but you mentioned bringing Junior here during our conversation. Your words tell me you think about him even when you are not together. In case you don't know it when a person does this, it's an expression of love for the person dominating your thoughts. Junior may be the right guy for you."

"You make life sound so easy. What about other temptation like when a girl sees another guy she enjoys spending time talking to?" Without actually saying it she was talking about Brad.

"There is an old saying. I don't know who said, it but it goes like this: no man, or woman, is an island. I believe what the person was referring to is, as we go about our daily lives we will be required to interact with many different people. Some of the people will be of the opposite gender. These encounters cannot be avoided. Among these encounters there will be people we like more than others. People we like we spend more time with. Like now for instance we finished eating thirty minutes ago, but we are remaining here enjoying our conversation. The best part, there is not one thing wrong with working and enjoying good conversation with others. Life is all about enjoyment. Never shy away from enjoyment."

Darcy glanced at her watch. "Good heavens we have been here a long time. If we expect to cover any offices today, we better get our tails moving."

Driving across town Brad's phone rang. "That is Marie's number I wonder of Jimmy is feeling better, and she is coming to join us?" He put the phone on speaker. "Hi Honey, what's up?"

"I was wondering how you are feeling?"

"I'm fine Honey. In fact for just two of us Darcy and I are moving along with our work quite well today." To make Marie feel better he fibbed about accomplishing anything.

"Good because I hope you don't need me any time soon. Everyone here is sick. Mom, dad, Ray, Laura, Johnnie, Jimmy and I are all sick as dogs. Call me before you come home tonight."

"Will do Honey, if you need anything before then call me. Drink lots of fluids and I will see you this evening, bye."

Marie hung up the phone before saying goodbye. "Marie said everyone there was ill. I hope we don't get sick before we finish distributing these letters. If you talk to Junior encourage him to stay out of the office until he is completely well. There is no reason for him to come back too soon and spread germs to you. It appears you and I will be delivering the letters. We'll do the best we can long as we can. I told Marie we were doing fine so she wouldn't worry about business. Business is the last thing she needs to worry about when she is sick."

They left the last office in the first building at five thirty. "Wow Brad, what an afternoon my fanny is dragging, and you look as tired as I feel. I shouldn't complain, we made great progress today."

"It has been a busy day, and same as you I am tired. Do you mind if I swing by the Ad Palace on our way back to the office. I have a couple things to check on?"

"I don't mind, my guy is not feeling well. I have nothing to do this evening. While you are checking on your things I will call Junior." Together they went inside.

Brad caught Wendy just as she was about to leave the office. "Did the builder call and say if he was able to get our permits for stage two of apartments?"

"Karl Banister did call and he did get the permits. Ground breaking can be next week. I knew you were busy so I called Bob for you. He is willing to work with you same as he did on your other apartment building if you need him."

"Wendy you are good, thank you. I won't bother you anymore today. Run along and enjoy your evening." Brad turned to Rusty and Carol. "I'm surprised to see you guys working this late. Don't wear yourselves out so you get this horrible flu bug everyone is getting. I'm the lone exception in my family. Everyone else is sick. I better call Marie, and see if she needs anything before I go home. I'll call from the private office so I don't disturb you guys." Being careless he never closed the door tight. Then again he didn't need total privacy.

It took Marie several rings before she answered her phone. He quickly learned everybody at home was still major sick. "Geez Honey, I almost hate to come home tonight. We have at least one more day of hard work before I can afford to get sick. It's very important we complete our personnel office contacts."

"Then get a motel room for the night. If you come home it is certain you will get sick. Getting those letters out to our tenants is important. We have everything we need for tonight."

"Alright Honey I'll call and see if I can get my old suite back at Caesars. Promise me you will call me if you need anything."

Unknown to Brad, Rusty walked in behind him as he called Caesars. "Hi, Brad Collins here, I would like to get a suite for tonight if you have a suite available." Rusty ducked out before Brad saw him. With his suite reservation made Brad rejoined the others in the outer office. "Darcy, if you are ready to go, we better be on our way. How is Junior doing this evening?"

"Not real good, he sounds awful. He won't be helping us tomorrow. I called mother also, she is not feeling up to par and plans to go straight to bed this evening."

"This flu traveling around is something else. We handled things today just fine. I guess we can again tomorrow if we don't get sick. I'll be eating my evening dinner at Caesars' Buffet, would you care to join me for dinner this evening?" Brad asked. "They do have a fantastic buffet."

"Dinner sounds wonderful. A good balanced dinner might help ward off the flu another day, and allow us to get more of our letters before we get sick. It may be hard for us to avoid getting the flu all together but maybe we can ward it off for a short time."

"Then it's settled, we are off." At the door Brad looked back long enough to say good night to Carol and Rusty. Don't you guys get yourselves run down to the point you get the flu. If you do get the flu don't come to the office until you are completely over the flu."

Rusty waited only a few seconds to spout off. "Do you believe the nerve of that arrogant bastard?" Rusty shook his head. "When I walked in the other office, I heard him making a room reservation at Caesars for a suite. Then in this office right in front of you and me, he invites Darcy to join him for dinner at Caesars. The same place he has a suite for the night. Now try telling me nothing is going on between the two of them?"

"I don't know what to think. I heard Darcy talking to her mother earlier. She is not feeling well either. I do know whatever is going on is none of our business. There could be a simple explanation as to what it is."

"I can't believe you Carol. You would have to catch them naked on a bed going at it. Before you would believe what I'm saying is true. How about this, I dare you to go with me to Caesars. We can observe how they are acting as they eat. It might be interesting to see where they go after they finish eating."

"Use your brain Rusty, you can't spy on Brad. He would spot us in a heartbeat."

"Not if I wore a ball cap and shaded glasses. You could put your hair up in a bun and wear a dress. He would be so content entertaining his cute little playmate he would never notice us. His mind will be occupied elsewhere. Darcy is a cute little thing with a magnificent chest. What do you say, shall we do it?"

"What you are proposing is dangerous. Getting caught could end our employment here at the Ad Palace." She warned. "Besides it's not any of our business."

"Stop being a coward, we won't get caught. Come on, let's go, they may not be eating long, we'll dash by the apartment so you can change into a dress. The buffet is a public place to eat. We have as much a right to eat there as they do. If they spot us it's no big deal."

The Buffet at Caesars impressed Darcy. "Junior told me you lived at Caesars for several months. How did you keep from gaining weight with food available like this?"

"Portion control was my secret I allowed myself two bites of anything I wanted. Eating like a horse may be fun but it can make a person miserable and it is easy to gain weight."

"I may try your two bite theory, everything looks so inviting how can I not try everything?" She asked. "Sitting at my desk all day is not a lot of exercise. I'm also amazed how clean everything is."

"You can always come back another time. Marie loves to eat here. I would expect Junior might also enjoy eating here. The four of us should come here and eat together some time."

Rusty and Carol did a quick change at their apartment before dashing off to Caesars. "This is stupid. We may never see them in the large crowd even if they are there."

"All we need to do is sit near the elevators to the suites and they will be hot footing it by on their way to an evening of illicit passion. They will be so wrapped up in anxiety they will never notice us."

Brad enjoyed eating with his evening dinner guest along with the pleasant conversation. "With Marie suggesting I not come home tonight. I made reservation for my old suite tonight. Right here at the buffet is where I will be eating breakfast in the morning. She knows the importance of getting our letters delivered tomorrow." Darcy sat momentarily stunned. "Why are you looking at me so funny, I can't afford to become ill? I'll take my chances tomorrow night when I go home."

She looked at him in a questioning manor. "Are you planning to drive me back to my car later?"

"Of course, I need to go out and buy a change of clothes for tomorrow anyway. I'll drop you off at your car on my way shopping."

"My food is excellent. I hope you realize you are spoiling me buying lunch and now dinner. I feel guilty enjoying myself while Junior is sick. I'm selfish, I can't help but enjoying myself. This is my first time in a glamorous casino. I bet the rooms are plush and nice."

"Every room in the hotel is nice. I always stay in a suite. Suites are the more lavish rooms with great views. Are we ready to move on?"

"I need to use the ladies room and then I'll be ready to move on."

"You could use the restroom in my suite, and see how I spoil myself." Darcy hesitated. "We can be there in a couple minutes. The elevators are back over this way." Again Darcy hesitated. "Are you afraid someone will see us going up to my suite?"

"Sort of I guess. If someone happened to see us going up to the suites what would they think?" She questioned. After a brief silence she nodded yes. "Actually I would like to see your suite."

"I see your point. We are in Caesars with thousands of other guests. We are not going up there to get in trouble. All you want is to use the restroom and peek at my suite. What is the big deal?"

"I am curious. I do want to see your suite." She reached over and patted the back of his hand. "Let's do it, before I turn coward and change my mind. Marie told me when you first married you lived in a suite here."

"Indeed we did. It was like a honeymoon every night."

Rusty and Carol arrived at the suite elevators seconds ahead of Brad and Darcy. "Let's wait over by that pillar. You can watch one way, and I'll watch the other. If we spot them we can hide behind the pillar."

"This is the silliest thing I've ever let anyone talk me into. How long are we planning to hide? Standing here watching people eat you know, I'll get hungry. Oh my word I think that may be Brad and Darcy coming this way now."

"Oh yes." Rusty pulled her around behind the pillar. "Now what were you saying about this being a silly idea." As the elevators doors closed on

Brad and Darcy, Rusty turned to face Carol. "Have you seen enough or do you want to knock on their door?"

"I've seen enough. Please keep in mind it's still none of our business, they are adults. Come on let's get out of here." She coaxed. "We should eat somewhere else."

"Why the big hurry, we should hang around long enough to see if they settle in for the night or if this is a quick rendezvous. Look at all the good food."

"Geez Rusty you are begging to get caught spying on our boss."

"This is a public place we can eat at the Buffet if we want. If we grab the corner table across there we can watch the elevators. You go in and get the table while I keep watch. Soon as you get the table in the corner, I'll come in and join you. From the table we can take turns filling our plates so we don't miss them if they come out."

"Call me stupid for going along with you, but I'm hungry so I'll eat here." Carol shook her head as she started off to the Buffet line.

As Brad popped the door open Darcy's eyes grew huge. "Oh my word what a luxurious intimate setting this is. This is unbelievable, absolutely astonishing. I've never seen anything like it." She was admiring everything in the suite.

"You can use the restroom through there. I'll go use the restroom in the other half of the suite."

Before leaving Darcy explored the suite from end to end. "This is unbelievable, your suite looks like something I would see in a movie. After the day we've had the Jacuzzi in the bath area looks ever so tempting."

"You can bet your bottom dollar when I return with my new clothes for tomorrow I will be unwinding in the Jacuzzi. After our intruder incident years ago Alice and I stayed in a unit similar to this set up. Not as luxurious but the same basic layout. She had her side of the unit and I had my side. Very unusual for a nanny and the punk kid she took care of. We got along well by respecting one another's space and survived quite nicely."

"Alice told me about the two of you staying in a suite. Somehow I never expected anything like this. Do you mind if I stretch out on the bed real quick, so I can experience what luxury feels like?"

"Be my guest but don't get too comfortable, I need to go get my clothes for tomorrow before I crash some place. I'm choosy about the clothes I wear, so I need all the time I can get to pick what clothes I need for the next couple days."

"I really should be moving on too. I'm sure if mother is awake she is wondering why I'm not home by now." Darcy rose from the bed. "I could get use to this bed in a very short time."

"I'll tell you what, when the time comes for you to get married. Marie and I will purchase you a bed just like this as a wedding present for you. So if you want a bed like this, start husband shopping."

"Do we get just the bed, or do we get the complete bedroom set?"

"You pick out a bedroom set, Marie and I will pay for it. I can pull a few strings and get you the exact queen mattress, and box springs set as you were lying on. I'll purchase it direct from Caesars. Somewhere they have extras in case someone damages a mattress set."

Darcy extended her right hand. "It's a deal, take me to my car."

Eagle-eye Rusty spotted them the instant the elevator door opened. "Look who surfaced for the time being. Notice her hair is slightly ruffled. That is pillow hair if I ever saw pillow hair." As a result of lying on the bed to test it Darcy's hair was slightly pushed up in back. "I believe that is our friendly boss stepping out of the elevator on his way home to mamma. I'll give him credit he is very neat, his pants are zipped up anyway."

Carol slapped at him. "I've seen enough. Can we dash out of here and go home now? I do not want to be seen by him."

"Sit tight Carol. We'll wait five minutes to be certain they are gone before we leave. It may take the lovers a few minutes to say goodbye outside."

Long before Rusty was willing to leave the Buffet area, Brad stopped at the office next to Darcy's car. "I'll meet you here at ten tomorrow. That will give you time to be certain you don't have something needing your immediate attention."

Brad started making his medical office rounds at eight the following morning. At a quarter to ten he called Darcy. "Good morning, how is your day going?"

"Our gardener at the apartment complex was in an accident this morning. I understand he wasn't injured, but the pickup may be totaled."

"I'm glad he wasn't hurt. Check on him personally, so he knows we care about him. If he is in fact okay, take him down to the dealership and buy him another pickup."

"You want me to buy him a pickup, what do I know about pickups?"

"Find something similar to the pickup he had. You have the check book. I'll continue visiting medical offices. Good Luck and have fun."

Late in the day, Brad called Darcy a second time. She quickly informed him they did buy a pickup. "It's been a strange stressful day."

"I know how those days go. I have an idea, why don't you sleep in come morning, and arrive at the office after lunch."

"What about the medical office visits we are supposed to be doing together?"

"I'll keep plugging along. I have yet to meet an upset tenant. We both have had a couple tiring days. Extra rest will do you good, and might make the difference in you getting that horrible flu or not. I need you as healthy as possible. It would never do for everyone to be out at the same time,"

"Thank you Brad, you are one considerate boss, sleeping in tomorrow sounds wonderful to me. I'll call you when I get to work."

After a quick phone call to Marie for a grocery list he made a stop at the store. Arriving home Marie and the boys were feeling better, but still weak. Laura had recovered slightly better. She could perform her duties, and care for the others. "I suppose now it's my turn to get sick?"

"I wouldn't wish this flu on anyone. My advice is the same advice you gave me. Drink plenty of fluids, and get extra rest. You look exhausted. Vitamin C might help along with the rest." Marie further advised. "I'll get the vitamin C for you."

Midmorning the following day Brad walked into the Ad Palace, Rusty and Carol failed to look up at him as he said good morning. Wendy returned his greeting. "Is Marie getting over the flu?"

"My complete family is getting better, including Laura, and Marie's parents. Junior is still a little under the weather. If he follows the same pattern as Marie and the boys, tomorrow he should be starting to feel better. So far I've avoided getting the flu." He reached over and tapped on the wood desk for continued luck.

"If you get the flu don't come to the office. Bob Tilly called a few minutes before you walked in. He never said what he wanted. You maybe should call him he seemed disappointed you were not here."

"Thank you Wendy, I'll call Bob now." He went to the private office to place his call to Bob. Bob wanted a meeting at the construction site. "I can be there in half an hour."

Brad met a stern faced Bob standing beside a gentleman he didn't recognize at the construction site. He soon learned Karl Banister of

Banister Construction had been hospitalized with heart problems. "Karl never set up a second man to be in charge of a project in the event he fell ill."

"This isn't good news. It's hard to work without a leader. Where do we stand, is there office personnel somewhere to do payroll if we let the workers continue?"

"Karl's wife does his accounting so payroll is not a problem. The on-site construction foreman is the missing person. Young Evan Thomas here was suggested by Mrs. Banister to be the construction foreman. I felt we needed to discuss options with you before moving forward."

Brad gave Evan a serious look. "How long have you been working with Banister Construction?" He asked.

"I started working for Karl fourteen months ago. Before that I worked with smaller construction firms, and bounced around working several different smaller jobs."

"What you are telling me is you are short on experience. Why Mrs. Banister chose you to be construction foreman I don't know. Karl Banister and I have a contract that could easily be broken because of his absence. What do you think Bob? Can we get quality construction done under the circumstances Mrs. Banister is proposing?"

Evan interrupted before Bob could answer. "Mr. Collins I can ramrod this construction project, and keep the time frame Bill set. With the help of Mrs. Banister, I can also keep this project within the allotted budget."

Brad glanced at Bob who shrugged his shoulders. "I don't know what to say Mr. Collins, it's your call. I would hate to say one way or the other. My thoughts parallel your thoughts, this is a huge concern."

"Alright, Mr. Thomas, I think we should proceed. I feel the need to warn you. Bob, Junior, and I, will be watching you closely. You can count on us asking questions and requesting updates. I also feel you should be man enough that if you get in over your head to step forward, and say you need help. This being your first job as the head man the inspectors will automatically keep a closer eye on you than normal."

"Fair enough Mr. Collins. You watch my every move. I will make a believer out of you, and I promise you won't be sorry."

"Let it be known, while Junior doesn't know a lot about construction he does know when a crew is slacking off. My suggestion is you have a talk with the different crew leaders under you. Explain how important it is for them to continue doing quality work, and stay within the budget. I would hate to stop construction in the middle of a project, but I'm not a patient man. Giving second chances is not my normal nature."

"I understand, Mr. Collins." Evan extended a hand for a handshake. "I know of nothing else we need to discuss at this time. I think we covered everything quite well. Thank you for coming over and discussing this concern. It's time for me to get to work."

"Then I'll continue my office checking, and make it a short day. Marie and the boys have been sick and I haven't spent enough time with them lately."

"I'll call you with updates each day."

"Thanks Bob."

CHAPTER 7

In the apartment complex he found Darcy working alone. "I thought maybe your sidekick Junior might be here. I heard he was starting to feel better."

"Our landscape man showed up drunk today and Ray is down delivering a letter of warning to him. This is Ramon's first written warning. Ray did talk to him one time because a tenant complained, but this is his first official written warning."

"I don't want to interfere with Junior's business, but you would do us all a favor by encouraging him to dismiss this intoxicated grounds keeper before he hurts himself or crashes our pickup again. He may have been drinking when he crashed our pickup before. There is no room in our organization for a worker of this caliber."

"Labor and Industry has guidelines to follow in these matters. Steps must be taken before you can dismiss anyone."

"Steps my ass. This is his second warning. He cannot drive our pickup if he has one beer. Tell Junior to ride his ass about everything. Arriving late or leaving early from work, he is gone. Get a new landscape man soon as possible." Brad demanded.

Junior returned a few minutes after Brad left. "You just missed your brother-in-law. He seemed tense when he arrived. When I explained what you were doing, he grew angry. He made it clear Ramon should be fired."

"Brad is right. I if I had any backbone Ramon would be gone by now. I've never fired anyone before. Do you know he has five kids to feed?" Darcy remained quiet. "I know his family doesn't enter into my decision to fire him. I kept the pickup and sent him home in a cab. I better call Ramon and tell him we no longer need his services, we will mail his check to him."

"Do you want to write his check or shall I write it?" Junior nodded yes. Darcy wrote the check sealed it in the envelope with Ramon's check inside. "If you want I can drop the check in the mail on my way home this evening. You shouldn't feel badly about dismissing Ramon. This won't be the last shoddy worker you will need to deal with in this job. Few people would take pleasure in firing people. I read a book on leadership once. In the book I learned when a person fires an employee they often feel inadequate as a boss. Eliminating someone from their position is part of being the boss. Nobody ever said being the boss would be easy."

"Sweet-child, if you are trying to make me feel better you are failing."

"The only way you will feel better is to replace Ramon, and move on. When your next employee does a better job you will feel much better. The reason Brad came over was to tell you there would be a new foreman on the apartment complex project. He wants you to keep a sharp eye on anything done differently, and report to him immediately. Evan Thomas is the on-site foreman until Karl Banister is up and around at full speed again. Whenever that might be is anybody's guess. Evan assured Brad he was highly capable of running the construction site."

"Not a problem for me, if Brad thinks he is the right man. I'm tired and going home. Tomorrow will be soon enough to advertise for a new landscape man. I may have a beer when I get home tonight. If I'm lucky I won't see Brad this evening."

Brad had a similar idea, and went home early. Marie met her husband at the door. "This is a nice surprise, you are home early."

"It was still a bear of a day. It's time to kick back, and relax so I can recuperate enough to start over tomorrow. I'm certain tomorrow will go much better than today."

"Take a quick shower now, and we can get in the Jacuzzi together later." During his shower Marie came in to talk with him. "Tell me about your day, what office upset you?"

"Maybe it was just me. I was still tired from my two days of hustling from one office to the other trying to calm our tenants. Had they already signed leases with other buildings, we were screwed. I saved all but five Tenants. I didn't think that was too bad. I made a quick stop at the Ad Palace. Carol and Rusty were acting odd, no telling what the hell is going on with them. I have a lot going on, I can't be in the Ad Office helping them as much as I used to help. Time and again I told them to pace themselves so they won't burn out. Then when I went over to the apartment office your brother was playing patty cake with our drunken landscaper. He should have fired his ass on the spot. As you might suspect Darcy made excuses for your brother."

"What did you say to Junior about the landscaper being drunk?"

"Nothing, I came home to cool off before talking with Junior. I have more important things going on, than dealing with a drunk landscaper. This is the time Junior needs to be a man. Kick the guy in the gutter, and move on with life. We are not in the alcohol addiction rehab business. Making money is our business."

"You were smart not to speak with Ray when you were angry. He is trying hard to do the job we hired him for. With the addition of the medical buildings his workload has increased as has everyone's. At the same time we all understand in time our lives will settle down."

"That's exactly what I'm talking about. He doesn't have time to deal with a drunk. Although Darcy making excuses for Junior is bad, I understand why she makes excuses for her man. You heard me more than once tell him if his workload increased beyond what he could do, let us know. We can look for options if necessary. All options are open, we can add additional people where needed. Junior knows our landscape guy should have plenty of time to circulate among our holdings, and see how the garden contractors are doing. What could be easier, if the man could stay sober?"

"The job sounds easy but it's hot in the afternoon."

"Screw the heat. Our landscape person should work from four in the morning until twelve noon if that is what it takes. Either that or check the outside plants in the morning, and the corridor plants in the afternoon. There are options if the person has half a frigging brain."

"You are starting to wrinkle it's time for you to get out of the shower. We can continue our talk again later when we get in the Jacuzzi. Our boys are in the play room if you need to wrestle someone."

Unfortunately Brad's energy level crashed after eating, the flu nailed him. It was straight to bed for five miserable days. Marie did her best to keep him abreast of the business operations. During the five day siege he lost twelve pounds leaving him extremely weak as he began to circulate. His first thought was to get to the apartment complex office to check numbers on the new construction. After showering and getting dressed he settled for the leather chair in the living room. "Honey I can't make it to the office today. I just don't have the strength."

"Be smart and don't over tax your body until your strength comes back. Rest a while before calling the office to check in. Rest again and then make another call. Ray, Bob, and Evan all say the construction site is progressing as expected. I wouldn't worry about getting there today if I were you."

"How many construction workers are on site?"

"When I was at the construction site yesterday with Junior, I never saw a huge amount of employees, twenty maybe. I'm not sure how many construction workers there should there be. Nothing looked out of the ordinary. I'm sure everything is going along on schedule just as the boys are saying. You look pale. Your job is to continue resting until you are a hundred percent well."

"For the foundation work twenty sounds about right. Maybe this Evan kid is okay after all. He is so young and inexperienced. I can't help but worry about his ability. The kid has all the confidence in the world but sometimes that isn't enough."

"Your eyes are drooping, lay back and rest. I will corral the boys so they don't bother you. Maybe between Laura and me, we can keep the boys quiet until they head off to school."

"I can't believe how fast our little devils are growing up. To me it seems like only yesterday Jimmy was a baby and now he is in the second grade."

Calling Wendy, she filled him in on how things were at the Ad Palace. "Don't you dare come to the office until you are one hundred percent over the flu; we don't need anyone here to be laid up five days."

"I must admit it has been a long five days. I wouldn't wish this flu on anyone. Trust me I won't be coming to the office any time soon. I will be calling though. Keep up the good work, Wendy."

After the call, Wendy turned to Carol and Rusty. "You may have guessed that was Brad. He is feeling better, but sounded weak on the phone. He promised not to come to the office for another week. We don't need to catch the flu."

"It didn't surprise me Mr. Collins got the flu. No man can burn the candle on both ends the way he does, and stay healthy very long. In my opinion he walks a thin line every day. The man doesn't know how to relieve stress from his life, without creating more stress."

Wendy looked at Rusty as if she didn't understand his words. Carol felt the urge to run interference, between Rusty and her mother. "What Rusty means is he takes on too many projects all at the same time. No man has that type of energy."

"He is a busy man. Things can get out of control very fast. It's up to the people like us surrounding him to try and ease some of the stress in his life. I'm making a quick trip to the Post Office is there anything we need while I'm gone?" Wendy announced.

"Not that I can think of." Carol answered fast hoping her mother would leave immediately. She continued working on a video without concentrating on what she was doing, until Wendy was well out in the parking lot. "What the devil is the matter with you Rusty, why are you hinting that Brad doesn't know how to relieve stress?"

"I'm saying if he becomes stressed in this office, it could be he would turn to you for stress relief." Smack, Carol backhanded him across the face. "What was that for?"

"I didn't like what you were referring. Keep your thoughts to yourself." Carol thought back to after her rape when she begged Brad to make love to her to test her sexual ability. He had done the right thing at the right time by refusing her request to help her get over her fear of men. "Brad has done well by us, and he deserves our respect. You have nothing but suspicions. Suspicions are not facts."

"Oh give me a break. If I led the life Brad lives you would kill me. I don't understand why you stick up for a louse like Brad, and his wicked ways? Too many women are willing to overlook a man's faults, if he has money. These types of men abuse their power over adoring women."

"As I said, all you have is suspicion, no concrete facts at all. There could be some logical explanation of some kind we don't know about. We saw actions we are uncertain about. You need to shut your mouth before you cost us our jobs."

"Somewhere in your gene pool there must have been an ostrich, your head is buried in sand. Wake up and see the light girl. Brad has a thing going on with Darcy and you know it. You saw them together going to and from a hotel room, but you won't admit anything is going on. That is wishful thinking. You would like to believe nothing is going on. "

"All I'm saying is if you keep flapping your jaws you are going to ruin a good thing for all of us. So I will ask you one more time to keep your thoughts to yourself. This job is our meal ticket. We earn our bread and butter working here. This is the key to our future. Why do you want to kill our future?"

"I have no desire to ruin anything for anybody. I will tell you this. If he ever sets his sights on you, that is a game changer. I'm not just standing by, and letting him use you."

"You can relax. I'm a big girl and I can fend for myself."

After recovering a full extra week from his flu Brad's workload returned to normal. He spent his days circulating between the offices and the construction site. He saw Junior every day, and kept in touched with Bob either in person or by phone. All their reports remained positive. At home one evening, Marie noticed his depression. "Is there anything going on you and I need to talk about?"

"I don't know Honey. Remember how well things continued working when I was sick with the flu. Everyone did their jobs excellent without me. Now I'm back, but all I'm doing is making people nervous. I'm a control freak wanting to know every little detail of everything. I'm not helping people, and in most cases I'm hindering their production."

"You are blowing things out of proportion. These are people you hired and trained to do various jobs. They follow your orders well. It's called harmony in the work place. Everyone is happy and doing fine. You are worrying over nothing."

"Our so called happy employees, as you call them, resent my stopping by to see them. If you don't believe me spend the day with me tomorrow. Walk beside me, and see if you experience what I feel. How about it Honey, do you want to be my shadow for a day?"

"If it will help clear your mind, I will be happy to accompany you to work any day you choose. It can be early as tomorrow if you want." He nodded yes. "Then tomorrow we'll make your rounds together. It will be fun working together."

The following morning after the boys were off to school Brad and Marie started their rounds to visit essential employees. In the Ad Palace office, Marie immediately felt the uneasiness her husband spoke of the night before. Wendy appeared normal while Rusty and Carol remained quiet, never once did they look up or smile at her or Brad. Marie picked up on what he was talking about. As they continued on their journey she was quick to remind him about the lecture he gave Carol and Rusty about getting married a few weeks before. "I supposed you could be right, but that was weeks ago."

"Ignoring advice is human nature. Everyone does it to some degree. Maybe apologizing to them again would help. If nothing else, it can't hurt."

"How many damn times am I supposed to apologize for one incident?" He fired back at her. "I did apologize twice, that's enough. I did everything, but get on my knees and beg for forgiveness. Rusty wasn't there when I apologized, but Carol seemed to understand." Brad's next stop was at the apartment office. "Watch how Darcy reacts to me. I think you will notice she has no problem with me. Junior is a different story he resents my questioning him. The way I see it we are risking big bucks. Millions of dollars in fact on this new construction project, we have every right to know every detail of what is happening. Our Construction foreman is very inexperienced, and this is his first big project. How could we not be somewhat concerned?"

"Hold on a second. Is Ray aware this is Evan's first big construction project he is ram-rodding?"

"I assume he does, I thought he did, but I'm not certain. I told Evan at the beginning he would be under more scrutiny because of his lack of experience. He didn't seem to complain when I told him Bob, Junior, and I, would all be asking more questions than normal."

"How would it be if I took Junior to lunch, and you stayed and talk to Darcy. He might open up, and talk to me more about his thoughts if you weren't with us when we talk."

"Whatever you think might help is fine by me. If Junior isn't at the office you can track him down by phone, and hook up for lunch. Take long as you need for your talk. I'll see what I can do to help Darcy. If you get busy and can't get back to pick me up, call me. I can taxi home."

"Be careful what you say in the office. I don't want you making Darcy mad. You might try explaining to her very carefully why you and she are excluded from Junior and my lunch. We don't need her mad at us. Ray said she is doing a magnificent job in his office."

"I'll stop at the pizza place by the filling station. You can track Junior down while I get lunch for Darcy and me." Marie soon learned Junior was over at the construction site. "That is perfect Honey, are you meeting him there?"

"Yes, but you should call Darcy, and make certain she knows you are bringing pizza to the office for you to share. It's possible she has noon-time errands to run, and won't be there. You really need to check her plans."

"Good idea, Honey." Brad called Darcy, she sounded thrilled to hear he was bringing pizza by for lunch.

With their plans set Marie dropped Brad off at the apartment complex office before moving on to meet Ray. Darcy smiled as he entered. She was pleased to have company who brought lunch for them. "This is a pleasant surprise. I never expected a nice looking gentleman to bring me lunch today. This must be my lucky day."

"Luck had nothing to do with my eating with you today. It was Marie's idea to ditch me here with you so she could have lunch with her brother. She wants to speak with him without me being there. That leaves you babysitting me." Darcy seemed confused by Brad's words. "Something isn't right, Junior seems nervous around me. I have no idea why. Every project we have is operating well, but I get the feeling people are annoyed by my asking questions." Darcy's silence told him he was correct in his thinking. He paused to serve the pizza. "If you know Junior is upset with me, tell me why he is upset with me."

"First you must promise you won't get upset with me." Brad nodded. "It is really very simple, with you checking on Junior so often he thinks you don't trust him."

"Marie and I are spending millions of dollars on this construction project. We have an inexperienced construction foreman on his first big project. It's Evan Thomas I can't afford to have screwing up. I thought I made my position clear when we began this project. I told Evan, Junior, and Bob, that the building inspectors and I would be watching him closer than ever because of his inexperience. I'm not dissatisfied with Junior any way shape or form. He is doing a fine job."

"Unfortunately he thinks you are dissatisfied about something. I keep trying to tell him you are fine with his work. He is tired, and edgy from working the extra hours. We come in an hour early, and work two hours late in the evening here in the office. We are trying and catch up on the paperwork. Because the new construction is moving along at a rapid pace we are not gaining on the paperwork."

"Oh good heavens, Darcy, what did I tell you and Junior?"

"You said get extra help if we needed help. We may not need help after the apartment construction is completed and things settle down."

"Darcy, Darcy, Darcy, what am I going to do with you and Junior. You need help, get your help now. As we move more towards completion of the apartments, the bills will roll in faster than they are currently coming in. If you need help now think what will it be like later?"

"We haven't thought about later. I'll speak to Junior, and see if we can work out something to get additional help in the office. We do need to relieve my workload to prevent us from working these endless hours we have been putting in."

"Tell Junior help is just a phone call away. We can get you a temporary until you decide if you need permanent help. We do need to get this office in order fast as we can. At the end of each week decide if you have gained enough or if extra additional help is needed."

Marie and Junior come to a similar decision as Brad was thinking. Help was needed in the apartment office. "You can get temporarily help in the office. You and Darcy can't keep putting in the hours you are trying to put in forever."

"Sis, I have an idea. Could you get Brad to help Darcy in our office? If you could convince him to help her, it would keep him away from the other people. Thus relieve pressure on the other workers. He and Darcy work fairly well together. It would be easier for everyone to work without him constantly looking over our shoulder."

Marie touched her brother's hand. "You better allow me to suggest he help Darcy with her paperwork. Brad may not take kindly to you telling him to stay away."

"Be my guest, Sis. All I care about is for Brad to keep busy for a while. He may still circulate among the job sites, but he won't stay as long. He asks the same question fourteen different ways. He puts unnecessary pressure on all the workers, me included."

Come evening, Brad stepped straight into Marie's plan. "That brother of yours is a hard-headed character. Poor Darcy is getting worked to death. I gave him strict instructions, if they were having trouble keeping up on the office work, he was to let us know. We need to work out something to get the office work finished in a timely manner. You should see the paperwork stacking up on the poor girl's desk. You know your brother better than I do. How do I get him to take the leadership role, and hire the help she needs?"

Marie held one finger up as though she just thought of an idea. "You could help Darcy for a while. She doesn't appear nervous when you are in her office. In fact if you were to hang around helping Darcy, Junior might realize eventually she needs help, and talk to you about increasing his office staff?"

"That my Dear is one terrific idea, are you sure I should offer to help Darcy? I don't want to step on Junior's toes."

"For the next month Junior will be extremely busy at the construction site. If he sees you putting in several hours a day to help her, he would have to realize she needs help. You could swing by the Ad Palace first thing in the morning and drive by the construction site for a visual check. Then hustle on over to help Darcy. Keep in mind Junior is under a lot of pressure. I doubt he notices how she needs help. Given time, he will notice. My brother isn't totally stupid."

"You may be right, Honey. I'll try helping Darcy tomorrow. I'm going to go find our boys. I feel like playing catch with them. My father never took the time to teach me to throw, or catch a stupid baseball. I was watching our boys, and your brother toss a ball around this past weekend. I'm no expert, but our boys could use help in the throwing and catching department. They need encouragement and practice. I wonder if I should hire an older boy in the neighborhood, to teach our sons the basics of playing baseball."

"Can't you and Junior teach the boys?"

"Junior does not have a lot of free time to help Johnnie and Jimmy. If I'm honest I could find time to help the boys. My problem is I don't have the knowledge to teach the boys baseball. Down at the intersection, I see a young boy once in a while who looks to be about fifteen wearing a baseball uniform. He might be the kid. We need to help me instruct the boys."

"I don't know what you should do. Why don't you talk to the young man, and see what he says. Outdoor exercise is good for the boys, but there is more to life than sports. Not everyone can become professional athletes."

"Honey, being on a team is not all about sports. It's about building friendships, and learning about competition in the world. People compete throughout their lives. I have very few friends, I developed on my own. Most of the friends I now have were developed through other people. Take you for example; you became my friend through Karen. In turn this allowed me to become friends with your friends and family. Just walking out and shaking hands, I've developed very few friends on my own. Only two people come to mind, Wendy and Ernie Meadows. Their quest for employment may have been the only reason why they hung around me."

"What you are saying is partially right. Everyone gains friends through other friends. Darcy is my friend through you and then there is Bob and Robin Tilly. You knew them before I met them."

"Darcy became my friend through her sister Alice. I met the Tilly's through Karen. Think about it Honey, I seldom initiate friendships on my own. If our boys could learn, and enjoy recreational baseball, they could play on little league teams interacting with more kids their age. Friendships would bloom as our boys come, and go, playing on different teams. You and I might benefit from our boys playing baseball. We might develop friendships with other parents."

"I said it was okay for you to get a young baseball trainer for the boys. We bought our house for security reasons so be careful who you allow in, and make it plain they cannot bring others to our house without prior permission. Why don't I send the boys in so you can discuss your plan with them? It is possible baseball does not interest them."

"Let me talk to the older boy first, to see if he is interested in helping train our boys. I'll drive down to the corner now, and see if the young man is around."

Brad soon learned the boy he was looking for wasn't in sight. He stopped in front of the house he had seen the boy at several times. The boy's mother answered the door. Brad introduced himself as he studied the boy's mother Mrs. Ramirez. He explained he was looking for her son. "Is Juan in trouble of some kind?"

"No Mrs. Ramirez, your son is not in any trouble. Fact is I don't know your son. I saw him, and another boy, tossing a baseball around quite often. I was wondering if he might be interested in a job that might be fun for him. My wife and I have two young boys that could use some coaching in the basics of baseball. If your son has a couple extra hours a week, and would like to make a few dollars have him give me a phone call. My cell number is on my card here."

"Are you the Mr. Collins, from Collins' Enterprises?" She asked with a heavy Mexican accent.

"You are correct Mrs. Ramirez, my wife and I do own Collins Enterprises."

"My husband, Manuel, is working at your construction sight. He is helping make new apartments for you. He says your buildings are good, you like class. My Manuel is proud to be working on your building. He is a good worker. My son will be glad to help your boys with their baseball training."

"I'm sure your husband is a good worker, and he is correct we do want nice apartments built. Thank you for your time, and have your son call me if he is interested in helping our boys. We live about a half mile down the street. He could ride his bike to our house and back."

"My son has a car, he needs gas money. I'll make him help your sons."

Not more than an hour later young Juan was at the house meeting Brad and Marie's shy boys. Practice time was set for twice a week. Each practice would consist of one hour. They didn't want Jimmy and Johnnie becoming tired, and bored before given the chance to learn the game of baseball.

CHAPTER 8

The following day Brad helped Darcy in her office most of the day. Even though Junior told her why he would be helping her, she was appreciative of Brad's help. It was her job to keep him away from the construction workers, so they could work more efficiently. In reality she welcomed his help. Even more surprising to her, Brad went to work immediately proving to be valuable in making great strides in their pile of paperwork needing posted. Near the end of the work day she walked past him on her way to the supply room. She paused behind him long enough to massage his shoulders. "It is so nice of you to notice I needed help, and are willing to help me. Junior has so much on his mind, he doesn't need a backlog here in the office to mess things up further."

"I don't mind helping you. I enjoy working with you. Intelligent people are always of interest to me. I must be honest with you though, I think my being here is a human made conspiracy cooked up by Junior, and his sneaky sister. They want to keep me away from the construction site."

"If you helping me is a conspiracy, I'm all for it. I'll welcome help from anyone." She stated with a grin. "I'm working hard as I can, and my work load is getting bigger every day. Why do you think you being here is a conspiracy?"

"I'm thinking my darling wife and her sneaky brother concocted my helping you. According to my Marie, Junior thinks I don't trust him. She claims my asking so many questions makes people nervous, and leads them to believe I don't trust anyone. To keep peace in the family, I'll play along for a while, and help you. In doing so I can check some of the bills, and where they come from. I can follow the construction progress without Junior or Marie, knowing I'm keeping an eye on every little thing." Darcy busted out laughing. "What is it you find so funny?"

She leaned forward and gave his cheek a huge kiss. "You are dead right, as usual. Marie and Junior thought they could outsmart a sly fox like you. They should have known better. How long are you planning to pretend not to know want they are up too?" Brad shrugged his shoulders. "You must have some idea." All the while Darcy was talking she was working away.

"I'm not sure, I suppose my decision rests in your hands much as anything. If you are a good actress we could play along quite a while and see what happens."

"I'm probably not the greatest actress, but I can and will keep a secret. I will welcome any and all help I can get. So far Junior isn't convinced I will need a full-time helper. I suggested we get a halftime helper, but let the person work all day until we were caught up. We could see what happens from there. Before I could find a person to help me they decided to stash you here for a while. I don't mind you being here, you never make me nervous. Working together today we accomplished quite a bit. I may continue working my two extra hours for a short while."

"I'll leave that decision to you, but please don't overwork yourself. Nag Junior until he gets you the help you need. I'm hoping his little stunt backfires on him, and my working with you will make him be more observant to your needs. I enjoy working with you. I can probably play along with this little game a month, but eventually you will need someone more reliable than me to help you."

"Thank you Brad, I appreciate you giving Junior the time he needs to realize I need help." Darcy checked her watch. "It's time for you to scoot home to your family."

"You are so right I have two little boys waiting for me tonight. We are going shopping at the South Mall for baseball gloves. I hired a young boy to coach my sons so they have a chance to learn the game of baseball. When I was their age I never had the luxury of tossing a ball around with anyone. To my knowledge, I never owned a ball of any kind." Darcy gave him a sad look. "My computer was my entertainment. Father was so fearful of my getting abducted, I was kept in a cocoon. Seldom was I allowed outside, and never was I allowed outside without my nanny until I was age twelve. Even then I couldn't be out near the street where I could see other young individuals playing."

"I can't imagine growing up the way you did, it's bizarre. It was as if you were in a cage. I can understand you not being real fond of your parents."

"You want to hear something funny. Marie caught the boys peeing out behind the garage the other day and went ballistic. I laughed at her before explaining our back yard has total privacy. Long as they were out behind the garage they were out of sight from both our house, and their grandparent's house, I didn't care if they peed out there. They weren't hurting anything. I didn't say anything to Marie but maybe the older boy I hired pees out there too. Growing up I was never outside without a nanny keeping an eye on me, so never urinated outside ever. My boys are doing many things, I wasn't allowed to do. I think it is neat. I may let the boys see me pee out there some time."

"You never peed outside, that's strange. I thought all boys peed outside some time or other. Growing up in Montana we had an older neighbor boy who wrote his name in the dust when he urinated. His name was Tom. Saying you might let your boys see you urinate out behind the garage may be a good idea. Your boys need to realize they are different than girl. Long as they are not in public, it's natural for guys to pee outside when they need to go."

"Did you watch this urine writing neighbor boy of yours write his name?"

"I was a tomboy when I was young. Being around guys I peeked a time or two. I can't imagine having a sheltered childhood like you had. What kind of things did you and your friends do?"

"I saw kids at school. Never were any kids allowed at our house, or I allowed at their house." Brad smiled at Darcy. "I must say for a tomboy you filled out quite nice. It's time for me to go home, I'll see you in the morning."

Two little boys were anxiously waiting on the step for their father's arrival. "Can we have Juan help pick out our new baseball gloves?" Johnnie asked. "He knows a lot about baseball."

"If Juan is available this evening, it would be fine for him to join us to help select your baseball equipment. Give Juan a call and see if he is busy this evening."

A quick trip to the sporting goods store at the mall provided the baseball equipment the boys needed along with a new baseball glove for Juan. Back at the house reality set in as to what Juan had gotten himself into. "Mr. Collins, pardon me for saying this. I thought all boys had more basic skills in baseball than your boys have. This is going to be a bigger job than I thought. Would you mind if I brought a friend of mine along to help me work with your boys. Ruben is a nice kid. He and I have played baseball together for several years on various teams."

"I'm a busy neglectful parent. I will yield to your judgment. Ruben may help you if he wants. I will pay him same as I'm paying you."

By late evening Marie gave her husband a big hug. How was your day working with Darcy?" She inquired with a smile.

"We were so busy we had very little time for personal conversation. I never got around to calling the Ad Palace, or Junior. I was thinking if I'm going to be of more use in Darcy's office, it would be helpful if you did part of my public relation calls. I haven't talked to Sam, Judy, or Robin, for a couple weeks. While you are at it you might call Wendy a couple times a week, or stop in when you get a chance. We need to keep everyone happy by remaining in contact. I don't need them thinking I'm in a rehab center again."

"If you think I should contact these people, I see no reason why I can't make a few calls for you each day. It sounds like an easy job to me."

At the time Marie agreed to make calls for her husband, she didn't realize the time it takes to make these phone calls, and personal contacts. Much of her time became keeping everyone filled in on the growth of Collins Enterprises. With her calling in place of Brad, she sensed people felt their roll in Brad and Marie's lives might be diminishing. There seemed to be an underlying feeling there could soon be an effect future business operations. Wendy feared he might be considering closing down the Ad Palace. Judy was quick to point out their families had not been together for some time. "When are you and Brad bringing the boys to visit us?"

"I would love to come tomorrow, but we are so busy. I doubt I could break Brad away at this time." Marie went on to explain he was working in Darcy's office to help catch up on some of his daily duties. Marie admitted she didn't realize how much actual work, Brad did in a day. Jockeying money around keeping our various accounts at the desired levels is a stressing task. I thought he had easy carefree days. Judy, I've got another call coming in from my brother. I better get this. Ray never calls during the day this could be important."

Marie's call back to her brother proved interesting. Evan had screwed up and poured a concrete floor before all the base work was completed in one section. "Sis this is also my error. I saw the forms set before they poured the concrete. I should have caught the problem. This is an expensive screw up. Brad will blow a gasket, and I don't blame him. The sooner I face him the better. Evan thinks he will get fired. I am at the construction site working with Evan trying to figure out the best, least costly way, to redo this area to correct our error before we move on. I can't face Brad without a plan."

"Stay there I'm coming to the construction site. Don't do anything until I get there. I need to make one quick stop at the Ad Palace, and I will be right there."

As if she didn't have enough problems, there was another problem waiting at the Ad Palace. Rusty had spilled coffee on one of the computers, and killed it instantly. Wendy had gone and purchased a new computer. She was unable to match Brad's setup. One subliminal message station was dead.

Sweat was pouring off Rusty's head in fear of what Brad would say. "You are right Rusty, he may be upset. If you continue working at the two remaining computer stations in service he will be less furious. Slowing progress is one thing; stopping work all together is something else, keep busy. We better let Brad set up the new computer."

While Marie continued on to the construction site Rusty spouted off about Brad spending all his time in Darcy's office cozying up to her. Wendy immediately questioned why he cared where Brad was, or what he was doing. "Darcy needs help. He is helping her so what's the big deal, it's only temporary. What he does or doesn't do, shouldn't concern you one way or the other."

Rusty bristled up. "Yea right, Carol do you want to tell your mother what we saw or shall I?"

"I think you have already said enough. Rusty thinks we saw a lot while I'm not so sure what we saw." Carol went on to tell her mother what they had seen Brad and Darcy do, and why they had followed him to Caesars. I keep telling Rusty not to spew accusations when we can't be sure."

"Oh come on Carol the fine virtues of Mr. Collins fast zipper, is well known. Marie beat the living crap out of him when she learned of his first affair. You do remember the affair he had with her best friend Judy, and how that turned out. Marie is a fine looking woman. Most men could easily remain faithful to her. Not Bad Brad though. He has wandering eyes."

"Hold on you two. Stop arguing we have other problems right now. We need to call Brad, and tell him about our problem. He and Marie's personal relationship may be a never ending problem. What they do is their problem we should not get involved one way or the other."

"See that Carol, your mother, agrees with me. She hasn't seen them together, but she thinks he could be on the prowl same as he was before. A leopard can't change his spots. The man is as guilty as sin, and you should realize it."

"I didn't say I agreed with anybody." Wendy voiced. "My concern is getting control of this office again. That means forgetting about what our boss may, or may not be doing. When you get to be my age you learn to prioritize your thoughts so you don't create dramatic shake ups. If Brad finds out you are talking about him behind his back, you will be history."

"Mother is telling you to shut up, and stay quiet. We need to call Brad so he can resynchronize the new computer. Marie told us he is trying to control his emotions towards his employees. Destroying one of our computers will upset him. Let's just worry about the computer for now, and keep our mouths shut about everything else."

"Alright ladies, I will keep my mouth shut. If I'm right, things will blow up soon enough without my help. Then you will know I was right."

At the construction site Marie listened to the explanation of how the construction error occurred, and what needed to be done about it. All three agreed there was no way to hide the error. It was time to fess up, and level with Brad. He should be the person to decide if he wanted a cheap fix, or step back and rip things out enough to do the job over in a proper manner. Doing the job over would mean a hundred thousand dollar loss and a week delay. Marie cleared her throat before speaking. "I better go tell my husband the bad news while you two brace your feet. He won't be happy about this. You likely will be hearing from him very soon. Regardless of how irate he becomes focus on what he tells you to do."

Marie's visit to the apartment office came as a surprise. "Hi Honey, did you stop by to bring us a treat, or just to kiss me?"

"Neither actually, I came by to discuss a couple problems you need to be aware of. Problem number one, coffee was spilled on one of the computers in the Ad Palace Office."

"Oh shit, let me guess. Butterfingers Rusty was the culprit. I've warned him time and again not to drink his coffee near his computer. I swear the man is an idiot. When he gets his coffee he reaches over with his right hand picks up the cup, and brings it across his computer to set it on the other side. If the coffee is hot he transfers the cup to his left hand during the process. I've told him more than once not to get any liquid near our computers. How many computers were destroyed?"

"Just one computer was damaged. Rusty offered to pay for the new computer they bought. The real problem is they cannot get the new computer synchronized so it will work proper."

"First, Rusty isn't paying for the new computer. Second, he isn't supposed to be able to just drop a new computer in line, and go to work as if nothing happened. I have a safeguard built in so when someone tinkers with our system they can't operate the system. The new computer will automatically lead them astray. Call Rusty and tell him point blank, to stop tinkering with the new computer. I'll stop by their office on my way home this evening after they are gone and restart the computer. If he keeps screwing around he could damage all three computers."

While Marie called Rusty, Brad went back to separating bills to enter in the computer. "Okay, I told Rusty to leave the computer alone." Marie paused for a deep breath. "Now comes the hard part. We have a huge problem at the construction site. Evan and Ray overlooked one step, and poured concrete before the electrical tubes for the electricity lines were put in place. At least part of the concrete needs sawed out so the tubing can be installed. Evan thinks the floor can be patched smooth. Junior thinks the floor could become rough over the years if it were patched. They are undecided as to what they should do."

Without further comment Brad voiced his opinion. "I vote with Junior we don't want a patched floor. Tell Junior, he is right. Remove the floor, and do it right. Who wants an apartment with a huge crack across the floor?"

"Cutting the floor out will cost you and me, a hundred thousand dollars, and a week of time loss."

"We need our building to be right from the get go. Let this be a lesson to those young bucks. When I was checking on them, and asking questions mistakes were not made. You tell them if they want me staying away from the construction site they better get things right the first time. One more serious error and I'll be down there with spurs on riding their ass all day."

"Maybe you should call and talk to Evan and Junior personally?"

"No Honey, you are their boss now. I'll let you make the call. Is there anything else I should know about?"

"Not that I know of, I think that's enough anyway. I can call Junior from my car." Brad took her bad news better than she expected. He seemed temporarily satisfied.

"Honey, before you go, Darcy accepts volunteers, if you care to stay and help."

"Not today, I'm going back to the construction site. There are a couple nervous men over there awaiting my report. I think it best if I go see them personally. Junior said Evan expects to be fired."

"Nobody is getting fired. For some reason people think all I do is run around making people nervous." Marie looked a little sheepish. "I'm doing what everyone wants and leaving them alone. You took over my job. You go deal with the guys, and get them back on track. Make sure you scold them enough they check each step more carefully."

Marie spoke directly to Junior and Evan as she relayed Brad's message to them. "He said if you want to keep him away from the construction project, don't screw up again. If need be, he is willing to come down here personally with spurs, on and ride your butts." Evan was quick to point out there would be no more errors made.

Darcy quietly worked in the office until break time. She looked at Brad with a mischievous twinkle in her eye. She finally stood up and walked over next to him. Standing just to his right she rubbed his shoulder blades. "Are you really taking Evan and Junior's hundred thousand dollar screw up this easy?" She asked smiling down at him. "This isn't like you."

He swiveled his head around enough to look up at her. "Did I tell you how nice you look in your scalloped neck, print dress today?"

She shook her head no. "That wasn't my question."

"Listen to me carefully. I'm not happy about a hundred thousand dollar mistake. At the same time it was a mistake. The important thing is they never tried to hide their mistake. These boys were honest with me. I appreciate that, I want the best building I can get. Mark my words this unfortunate incident should build character, and make stronger men of these two individuals."

"It's very refreshing to know you understand, and forgive them. Do you really think my simple print dress looks nice?" She asked with a smile.

"I do like your dress. Too few women wear dresses today." He paused and smiled to enjoy her glow from his compliment. "You said it was refreshing that I understand someone making an error. This might be a good time for me to emphasize basic business fundamentals to you. No man is an island, and there is no such thing as individual wealth. We need an equitable balance of people working together. I can't build the apartment building. I'll also add, you are as important to this project as those men working on the construction site. Keeping the paperwork straight is a huge part of our team. Life is all about teamwork. If it weren't for everyone's teamwork I might be working alone in an espresso hut."

"What an interesting way of putting things. This is a hectic job sorting these bills. I never thought about me being part of a team before. I like how you look at things." She leaned down and gave him a hug and a kiss on the cheek. "Oops, I shouldn't have kissed you."

"Kissing a person on the job is called sexual harassment. Do you realize I can sue you, and collect millions from the company you work for, if you continue this unacceptable practice?"

Darcy laughed. "You wouldn't get much from me personally, and I see little to gain by suing yourself." She hugged him again. "I have an idea. Why don't you call Marie and invite her to join you for lunch. I think you and she can break away long enough to have lunch together today."

He picked up on Darcy's hint. "I may just do that, provided you call Junior and have lunch with him. He might like a breath of fresh air too." Darcy smiled. "Do we have a deal?" She quickly nodded yes.

In the Ad Palace office a different scenario was developing. Rusty was nervous about seeing Brad. "I can't stand this waiting until he comes this evening to fix the computer. I'm going over to the apartment office, and talk with him personally. The longer I wait to see him, the angrier he may be. I'll pop in right at the end of his lunch hour so I don't disturb his lunch."

Carol looked irritated. "If you must go, go. Be careful what you say."

Wendy looked at Carol before saying anything. "I agree with Carol. If you feel it is necessary to speak with Brad face to face go ahead. I have some errands I can run today. Use my computer in my absence until you leave."

Rusty's timing wasn't the best for a suspicious person. As he walked up to the office he glanced through the window, and saw a Brad hugging and kissing who he thought to be Darcy. He darted back to his car, and went straight back to the Ad Palace. "That didn't take long, what did Brad say?"

"I didn't speak to him. He was busy, busy necking with Darcy. You should have seen them their kisses were filled with passion."

"You actually saw Brad and Darcy kissing."

"I was walking up to the entrance when I happened to glance through the window. I saw them embracing like two hot lovers. He was kissing her with one hand wrapped behind her back, and the other hand appeared to be massaging her breast. Their relationship is getting hotter by the minute. How long do you think it will be before Marie walks in on them, like I almost did a few minutes ago?"

"Did Brad see you?" Carol asked with her heart racing.

"Bad-boy Brad was busy, he never saw me. He had his back to me so I split before he turned around where he could have seen me. Are you still a naysayer Mrs. Olsen?"

"Seeing them kissing is hard to deny. I'm still not sure we should do anything. We may not like what Brad does, but we can do nothing about it. People have the right to make their own choices."

"I bet he is cheating with any woman who will have him." Rusty paused to glance at both women. "You can't deny what I'm saying. Has he ever hit on either of you?"

Wendy slapped at Rusty. "He most certainly has not hit on us. There are other things to think about here. What if you are right, what if Marie knows he cheats and is willing to tolerate his actions?"

Her question created total silence. "Rusty if you don't keep your mouth shut, we may all become unemployed. Stay out of Brad's business. There is no reason to stir up more trouble."

Rusty wasn't about to agree with Wendy. "Marie should strangle him. What woman wants her man continually chasing other women?"

"Rusty, money is power. Marie came from a middle class family. In one giant step she elevated herself to a wealthy woman. She can have all she ever wanted when she wants it for her complete family. Her Father, mother, brother, and her boys, they can have it all. I doubt she would ruin everyone's lives over Brad having a lady friend. Long as he is reasonably discreet she may not care."

"No way Wendy, tell me another one. Mrs. Olsen you are telling me if I married Carol, and had a girlfriend on the side it would be okay with you?"

"You don't have enough money to live the life he lives, so I would kill you."

"About the time I think I have women figured out, I learn differently. I doubt any man has women figured out."

"You don't learn because men never listen. If I had a broomstick to rap you up the side of your head before telling you anything you might learn faster." Wendy was clearly irritated. "Mind your own business. Brad's money will draw women to him. He will have more temptation from women than most men. Butt-out it's none of your business."

"Temptation overload, now I've heard of everything. You are making excuses for him. Why do you keep making excuses for our philandering boss?"

Carol had her fill of her mother and Rusty arguing. "Will the two of you stop with the arguing? I need to get some work done. Otherwise our paychecks may be rather small at week's end?" Wendy left the office to run her errands. As one might expect, Rusty failed to quiet down. "You better lighten up, and let this go before you cost us our jobs. Now let's get to work." Even then he was slow to quiet down.

On his way home Brad stopped off at the Ad Palace to activate the new computer to the current system. He barely completed his task when Carol walked in looking sad. "Hi Carol, what brings you back here this late of an evening?"

"I was hoping you have a few minutes to talk."

"Is there a problem of some kind?"

"It's Rusty he can't keep his mouth shut about your personal life. I'm afraid he will mouth off, and mess up mother and my jobs."

"My personal life is pretty much an open book. I would prefer people didn't talk about my misguided past. I've turned a new leaf. I'm a different person today than I was before. Some individuals may find that hard to believe but it's true."

Carol fidgeted around. "I don't know how to say this. Rusty found out about your involvement with Darcy. He won't keep his mouth shut."

Brad nodded. "My working with Darcy is not a big secret. I was sort of stashed there by my other employees. It shouldn't be anything to Rusty. So far it's cost me a hundred thousand dollars at the construction site, and a new computer here. I have the new computer working now. It's time for me to go home now."

"I wasn't talking about your business relationship with Darcy. It's the personal relationship that Rusty found out about. You and Darcy were seen together a couple times. In Rusty's mind there is little doubt you are having an affair with her."

Brad smiled when he wanted to laugh. "I think you are serious. Let me assure you there is nothing going on improper between Darcy and me. You are a poor misguided individual. Whatever eagle-eye Rusty thinks he saw is wrong."

"I keep telling Rusty what you do in your personal life is none of our business, but he won't keep quiet. He is jealous of your success. I fear he may call Marie. Mother and I tell him not to interfere. We all benefit from the money generated by your businesses. Mother and I understand it's easy for you to have an affair. Money draws women."

"Carol, I'm not having an affair with Darcy, or any other woman. I've changed. Maturing is probably a better word to use to describe me."

"When Rusty went over to apologize to you for ruining the computer, he saw you through the office window. You were kissing Darcy today." Brad frowned. When Marie was sick Rusty overheard you making plans to have dinner with Darcy. He talked me into following you because I didn't believe him."

"So you spied on me. People have dinner with friends all the time. Again I don't see any reason for great concern."

"I was with Rusty. We went there to eat. We both saw you and Darcy get in the elevator that goes up to the suites."

"As amateur detectives you are not very good. This is something we need to talk about more. I certainly don't want anyone spreading wild rumors of this type about me. When did Rusty allegedly see me kissing with Darcy?"

"He saw you today, right at the end of lunch hour. Around one o'clock when he went over to apologize to you for destroying the computer. He clearly saw you."

"I see, poor misguided Rusty is all screwed up. You mentioned the word jealous earlier. Jealous is the word that scares me. I'll have a talk with him. There is no emotional, or physical entanglement, going on between Darcy and me. How are you and Rusty's relationship moving along in general?"

"Our relationship is sluggish at best. After your lecture on marriage the other day, he pooh-poohs our getting married any time soon. He claims marriage means nothing anymore, because people never marry for life. Then he goes on and uses your affairs as an example."

"This is nothing we can deal with this evening. I'll set up some kind of meeting tomorrow. It's time to clear the air. I do appreciate you tipping me off to a potential problem."

In Seattle a far different conversation was going on. "Judy, I've been thinking about our beach vacation with the Collins'. I don't think we should vacation with them anymore. Brad is too volatile. Hanging around him, we may be drawn into trouble we don't need. He has money to hire the best attorneys in the world. We could be innocent bystanders and be charged as accessories to a crime he was involved in."

"Sam, you are being ridiculous. You are talking about friends of our, good friends. Protecting us the way he did does not make him a bad person. Our children love to play together. We are going to Hawaii with them someday."

"His quick actions combined with his anger are a dangerous combination."

"I disagree with you. Our friendship means a lot to me and our girls. Your jealousy scares me more than Bard ever has. Have you forgotten all he and Marie have done for us? We can't just turn our back and walk away. You are talking pure nonsense."

CHAPTER 9

The following day Brad seemed nervous while working in the apartment office. Darcy knew something was amiss. She was hesitant to say anything. Eventually curiosity got the best of her. "Anything going on you care to talk about this morning?"

Brad glanced her way. "You young lady are very observant. I do have something on my mind. I'm running different scenarios through my mind as how best to handle the situation."

"Do you mind telling me what you are talking about?" He remained quiet. "Has someone screwed up again at the construction site?" He shook his head no. "If we keep wasting time by me guessing what is wrong, we may not get any work done at all today."

"What I'm concerned about concerns you, but it's not you. I hate pulling people off their jobs to help me solve a personal problem, that I should be able to snap my finger, and take care of. I'm thinking over my options. Considering few people believe me, I can't think of another way to handle this problem. I have no choice but to pull others off their work schedule."

"I'm a good listener, talking things out might help." Brad sat quiet as he looked at her. "Is Junior your problem?" Even now he was slow to respond. "Let me guess you gave Ray a big raise, and now his performance isn't what you would like?"

"You shouldn't guess at my problem. Junior is not my problem. It's that butt-head Rusty, in the other office spreading rumors. He needs to be gone from our organization, but how do I replace him?" He paused briefly. "The vile man has a loose tongue. I can't ignore what he is saying."

"You should use your own advice. You stated Junior needed to deal with his gardener-landscaper guy, and get it over with. Take your own advice. Do what you have to do with Rusty, and get on with business."

"You are right. Call Junior and have him meet us for lunch while I call Marie and ask her to join us. See if Junior can spare a few minutes after lunch. I need to borrow him. Tell him it is vitally important. I need to leave for a short while. I'll be back before we go to lunch."

Brad made a surprise visit to the Ad Palace. While there he proceeded to readjust the new computer. "This computer is very sensitive. I'm not sure I have it set properly." While fiddling around checking various settings Brad installed different videos in and out of the system. Using slight-of-hand he created a subliminal message for Rusty. The message was for Rusty to forget what he knew about subliminal messages and how to create them. In addition he set up a secondary message for Rusty to argue and irritate Wendy to the point she would eventually fire him. "That is the best I can do for now. I may stop by this evening and check the computer again. I have a lunch date today. I've got to be moving on."

Rusty waited until Brad drove away before. "There goes our resident playboy, off to see his lady friend again for a noontime rendezvous."

"Shut up Rusty."

At lunchtime, as the four proceeded to eat Marie, Darcy, and Junior, couldn't help but wonder what Brad had on his mind. He hadn't called them together for nothing. "How long are you planning to keep us in suspense?" Junior asked.

"Dear brother-in-law you are quite right. I do have other things on my mind. For starters, I'm thinking about the apartment construction project. Unless my math numbers are totally goofy we are at this stage two hundred thousand dollars under budget."

"I would agree we are coming in under budget. Doing so should make you happy."

"Happiness is a state of mind. The figures I see include the hundred thousand dollar error, when the concrete floor was removed and redone. A red flag pops up in my head. Normally when a person builds in stages as we are, stage two comes in budget wise slightly higher than the previous budget. I allocated for a five percent increase hoping to hold the cost down much as possible. With this reverse, I'm wondering if other things were missed during the various building stages."

Junior smiled. "I'm pleased you noticed we were well under budget. The reason for being under budget is Evan and I are buying on bid rather than getting everything through one main source like they did on the first building. He estimated in the beginning to save around five hundred thousand dollars utilizing the bidding system. Then we goofed and lost a hundred thousand on the concrete floor removal. We dropped our current estimate to four hundred thousand."

"Marie and I love saving money. I urge you to use caution. Don't skimp on anything trying to make your project look good on paper. In the end we want quality construction."

"Quality wise we are exactly where we were on the first apartment complex. We are not sacrificing quality anywhere." Brad could hear pride in Junior's voice.

"Then everything is cool at the construction site. Concern number two is a red haired hot-head idiot named Rusty at the Ad Palace. Finish up eating and the four of us all will pay Rusty a quick visit."

After eating, Junior thanked Brad for the dinner along with saying he needed to return to work. "Whoa, hold on, I need you a little longer. We are all going to see Rusty. Meet us at the Ad Palace office." All three lunch guests were confused because Junior had nothing to do with the Ad Palace. "Trust me, you might find this amusing. Rusty needs a few facts tossed in his face to set him straight."

Marie and Junior arrived at the Ad Palace seconds before Brad and Darcy drove in. Junior became concerned. "I don't get it Marie, why am I needed at this office. I'm not part of the Ad Palace business. I have work of my own needing my attention. If Brad thinks I need to see him rip into Rusty he is wrong. I've seen Brad become upset before. Once is enough."

"I'm clueless why we are here, too. I doubt he is using this event to threaten you. If Brad has a problem with you he wouldn't beat around the bush. He would deal with you direct. We better go inside and listen to his words carefully."

Inside the Ad Palace office you never saw three more surprised people in your life than Wendy, Carol, and Rusty. "Good afternoon people." Brad announced. "Stop what you are doing we have business to conduct this fine day." In a split second Brad spun Rusty's chair around shoving it against the wall. "Okay hot-shot you are in the witness chair." Brad pointed to Marie, Darcy, and Junior. "These three people are jurors. Tell them in a convincing way, what you think you saw me doing yesterday." Rusty remained quiet as tiny beads of sweat began to form on his forehead. "What's the matter big boy, cat got your tongue?" Still he failed to speak. "Oh come on Mr. Jerk. What time of day did this alleged incident take place on Tuesday?"

Finally Rusty drew in a deep breath. "It was at the end of lunch hour, around one o'clock."

"That wasn't so hard, please tell our jury more." Again Brad pointed to his lunch guests. "Don't keep these fine people waiting. They are dying to hear your wild accusations against me, so they can return to work. "What did you see, and how did you happen to see it?"

Rusty gave everyone a nervous glance before speaking. "As I said, it was right after lunch. I went over to the apartment office to apologize to you for ruining a computer. As I walked up to the office, I glanced in the window. I saw you kissing Darcy. One arm was wrapped around her and your other arm appears to be touching her breast." His words caused Darcy to blush.

Marie smiled causing Brad to point at her. "It seems Mrs. Collins finds your story amusing. Suppose she and her two friends were to call you a blatant stupid-ass liar, or a confused idiot what would you think?" Rusty looked panicky. "Oh come on Rusty, we are waiting to hear what you have to say."

"I'm only telling what I saw." Rusty stated looking at the floor.

"Don't stare at the floor when you are talking to me. Look me in the eye. Marie, tell this young misguided individual what you think of his story."

"Rusty, you are so mistaken. Brad had lunch with me on Tuesday."

"Tell the man what time we were together Honey. He might find our time frame interesting as well. On the other hand, maybe I should slap him up the side of his head so we have his attention first."

Marie touched Brad's shoulder. "I think you have his attention. Getting back to what we were talking about, I didn't check my watch. I picked Brad up somewhere near a quarter to twelve and dropped him back off at the office around one thirty."

"Junior my friend, do you have anything you would like to add to this conversation?"

"Only that I had lunch with Darcy in her office on Tuesday. It was me you saw kissing Darcy. She is a great little kisser." Junior's words amused Darcy, but cause her to blush even more. "I left the office at one twenty."

Rusty's eyes were now huge. "Okay Red, what the hell made you jump to the conclusion Darcy and I were having an affair?" Rusty fidgeted in his chair as he worked his fingers. "Oh come on, we all have work to do. Don't keep us waiting. I heard there was more gossip coming from your mouth."

"There was the hotel incident." He quietly stated.

"Oh yes the hotel incident. Carol did tell me a little about that incident too. Why don't you tell my lovely wife, her brother, and Darcy your accusations on that occasion. We all should be up to speed on the event you saw." Rusty looked at everyone in the office as if he were seeking help. "Oh, come now, we all know you have a loose tongue, don't keep us waiting."

He cleared his throat before speaking. "Everyone here knows about you and Judy's past."

"If everyone here knows my past, skip to the recent events. You are wasting time. I keep telling you we all have important work to do. We cannot dink around all afternoon prying information out of you."

"I overheard you making a room reservation at Caesars."

"Don't bullshit us." Brad voice in anger. "You can do better, date and time please."

"I'm not sure of the date, but it was Tuesday before last. It was late in the day."

"Do you recall anything about that date Marie?"

"I remember week before last very well. Everyone at the house was sick with the flu. You called me late in the day to see if I needed anything from the store. You had been working with Darcy delivering tenant letters that day. If you had come home you were certain to get sick. I suggested you get a room for the night, and stay away until the tenant letters were delivered."

"Okay Rusty, back to you. You heard me making my room reservation. I might have guessed, please continue with your story Rusty. I like this next part, it's really sneaky. Be a nice witness. Hold your chin up high and look these people in the eye when you talk to them. Tell them what you talked Carol into doing with you."

"I heard you make the room reservation and invite Darcy to eat at Caesars' Buffet. We followed you and Darcy to Caesars."

"Darcy this is where you come in. What can you add to this story?"

"I had spoken to my mother on the phone probably about the time you were talking to Marie. Mother said she wasn't feeling well, and going straight to bed when she got home. You and I talked about your entire family being sick. Then you said something about eating at the buffet. I mentioned your dinner sounded better than the soup I was planning have. You asked why I didn't stop by the buffet at Caesars and eat with you so I did."

"Do you recall any of our conversation that evening?"

"We talked about so many things. We talked about my life in Montana, your marriage to my sister, and about Junior and my relationship. Then there was Marie and you, we talked about how the two of you met. We spoke about how fast you were married, and the fact you lived in a suite in the very Casino we were eating at. When you told me about living at a casino, I found it hard to believe. I remember thinking it was funny the two of you living as newlyweds in a hotel even if it was a suite. I made fun of you to the point you showed me the suite, it was awesome. A country girl like me had never seen anything like that suite, luxury beyond belief."

"The two of you were up there a long time." Rusty blurted out.

Darcy turned to face Rusty. "I have no idea how long, I toured the suite. Brad laughed at my innocence. Admittedly I was acting like a kid in a Candy Store. I stood looking at the in room Jacuzzi wondering what it would be like relaxing in the soothing water after a strenuous day."

Brad interrupted Darcy's words. "Marie can answer that question for you. We have a Jacuzzi in our home now, because of our time in the suite. What else happened in the suite while we were there?"

"Ah let's see, oh I know, I stretched out on the bed. That bed was sent straight from heaven."

"What did I tell you about the bed?"

Darcy blushed. "You said if Junior and I get married someday, you and Marie would buy us a complete bedroom set. You went on to say you would buy a new queen mattress and box spring set from the casino because you knew they kept extras mattresses and box springs in storage somewhere. They had to keep extras in case a mattress was damaged some way."

"Very good Darcy, you have a perfect memory. Is there anything else you want to tell Rusty?"

"We each used the restroom, the suite had two restrooms. Then we walked out together, and you took me back to my car. We most certainly never embraced in any way or kissed good night. You were in a hurry to go purchase clothes to wear the next day to work."

"Rusty, do you have anything to add?"

"No Sir."

"Then I suggest we all return to work."

"Do I still have a job?" He inquired.

"Ask Wendy, she is the office manager. I would never second guess her decision. If I'm reading her right you are walking on thin ice. You might be wise to put on a life jacket in case you go under. At best, you will need to prove your worth to our organization. If I were you I wouldn't drag my feet."

Out in the parking lot Marie admonished Brad. "A few words of warning might have helped make things more comfortable for everyone."

"There was no real reason for me to say anything. People have a hard time believing me. I felt it best if Rusty talked directly to each of you. I knew his ridiculous accusations would be uncomfortable for you. Hell they were uncomfortable for me when I heard them. Rather than speak with each of you privately, I felt it best he tell you his idiotic concerns. Now we all have the same information as close to the source as possible. I admit it was a crude way of handling a situation. Personally I would love to have tied him up, and beat him over the head with a frigging club."

"You should have told me Rusty was spreading rumor, about you. I would have believed you."

"My concern was if information was fed to you a little at a time, it would be like throwing mud at a house. Some mud would eventually stick to the house."

Back in the apartment office Darcy remained quiet for over an hour. Brad felt compelled to say something. "I can tell by your quietness Rusty's accusations still bother you. My scenario about throwing mud at a house, and some of the mud eventually sticking to the house is true. What concerns me now is if one tiny iota of Rusty's words stuck in Junior or Marie's head, it could be a seed for future doubt. Tomorrow we will start looking for you a permanent helper. I will soon fade off into the sunset, and get out of your hair."

"That's not fair." Darcy protested. "We are doing great working together. To allow Rusty to force you out of this office is ridiculous. Nobody in their right mind would believe one word of what he was saying."

"Darcy, wake up and smell the roses, this is life. There is always someone willing to believe gossip. Anyone who knows anything about me can become jealous, and cause trouble for me, or those around me in many different ways."

In the Ad Palace Carol and Wendy were furious at Rusty as they wondered about their future. "Oh grow up ladies, he can't do without us. We generate more money than any three people working for him. You are worrying over nothing."

"Rusty you are forgetting one large detail. Brad does not need money. He needs friends, and family. Until now we were considered among his friends. Being an idiot you may have changed the friendship status for all of us."

Like everyone else Marie and Junior were discussing the situation also. "Brad and I had conversations about people not believing him before we married. I never realized how disrupting lies and rumors can be for him. At the time we talked, I thought he was exaggerating his concerns. Now I see what he sees. Did you notice not one word said in the Ad Palace Office changed Rusty's opinion. In his mind Brad and Darcy are guilty."

"I got the same impression as you did. If I understood Brad correct, he expects Wendy to fire Rusty. Considering Rusty is Carol's live in boyfriend Wendy is in an awkward position."

"I haven't the slightest idea what is going on in Brad's mind now, except he is doing a good job of controlling his anger. I will have a long discussion with him this evening."

The apartment office continued to be a silent place most of the day. Come closing time Darcy walked over to Brad and placed a hand on his shoulder. "I hate what happened. Our close friendship has been shaken. You may not believe this but watching you work these few days, I've learned to be more efficient. We both realize you can't work in this office permanently. I was hoping you would help me long enough to learn much as I could from you. You seem to have a special talent for making money. I was hoping some of your advice might rub off on me."

Brad reached up and rubbed his neck. "I knew my working with you wasn't the best situation. I expected we would be okay for a month or six weeks before, I needed to fade off into the sunset. Try and get a good read on Junior these next few days. I'll listen intently to Marie and evaluate her comments. Maybe together we can find out the urgency of my leaving this office. Either way we do need to start interviewing people to permanently help you. Scoot on home, and I'll work a little longer today and come in later tomorrow. By jockeying our hours a little we may distract a few onlookers. You can almost bet Rusty will be sneaking around somewhere watching our every move."

Darcy shook her head, but left the office without comment. A few minutes later he heard someone outside the door. Thinking it was Darcy coming back he continued working without looking up. "Did you forget something?"

"It's me, your loving wife."

"Oh hi Honey, I thought Darcy forgot something, and come back to get it. What are you up to?"

"I was passing by and saw your car still here, and wondered why you were still working. By now I know you made up the work you missed during our meeting at the Ad Palace."

"I'm still working for several reasons. We have lots of work needing done. Secondly I don't want Darcy working overtime, and burning out on us. My third reason for still being here is I thought if she and I staggered our hours a little, people like Rusty wouldn't see us coming and going at the same time."

"Of course you know more than I do, but I would think staggering your hours is unnecessary. I doubt Rusty will be spreading any more rumors. You put him in his place today. If he has any smarts at all he will be busy trying to save his job. By reading Wendy's face he is in hot water with her."

Brad laughed. "Don't think for one minute, I changed Rusty's mind. I would be surprised if he didn't continue spreading rumors. Tomorrow Darcy and I will start a search for a permanent helper for her, so I can get out of this office completely."

"Junior and Evan will be disappointed if you leave this office so soon. I think they are enjoying you being busy, they seem more relaxed."

"I have things to do besides seeing them to keep me busy. You and I need to make a trip to Seattle. We haven't been there for considerable time." As Marie started to talk he held one hand up. "When I go to Seattle you and the boys are going with me."

"What about my communicating with Junior, Evan and the various office people? Who will cover for me if we both leave for a few days."

"Our employees will need to buckle down and do their own jobs. I'm not sure how long we'll be in Seattle. I'm guessing three days minimum. We could be there longer."

"Spending time in Seattle for any reason sounds good to me. May I call Judy and tell them we will be going to Seattle and visit soon?"

"Call Judy if you want. I'm thinking it might be a week before we can go to Seattle. I need time to be certain Darcy's finds a new helper, and then educate the gal so she knows what she is doing without slowing Darcy's work."

"You work on getting her the helper, and we'll see how it goes. I better run along and let you work. Please don't work all night."

"Give me a kiss before you go. Tonight is baseball night for the boys. Since the boys are busy I may work longer this evening than I originally planned."

"Juan and Rubin are good with the boys, but you still need to spend time with them. You of all people know kids need their father. This minute I would like to kick Rusty in the butt."

"I would like to kick Rusty myself, but not in the butt. I know what you mean about Rusty. Soon as we get this current situation behind us, I will spend more time with the boys. Don't forget, when we go see the Anderson's the boys are going with us. One day we are going to the zoo."

"What about Laura, will she be going with us to visit the Andersons?"

"How about letting Laura decide if she wants to go with us, or not. She might like a few days off to go visit her family. She hasn't had a true vacation in a long time."

"For a guy you have great ideas. Bye, I'll see you later."

Near eleven PM Brad arrived home. "I was beginning to wonder if you were coming home or if you fell asleep at the office. What took you so long? You missed seeing the boys altogether."

"I was working and thinking. I've made up my mind, Rusty needs to go and I was thinking how best to get rid of him. I could drop the ax or boot him out slow. I prefer he leave fast, yet it might look better to our other employees if he left over time."

"You look tired, sit down, and I'll fix you something to eat. Laura is in bed for the night, and so should you and I be in bed. Rusty or no Rusty, I hope you are not planning to work this late every night."

"I won't be working this late every night." Marie scurried around wearing her pink satin pajamas as she fixed him a Taco Salad. "I love seeing you dressed in your pink satin pajamas. You look very sexy Honey."

"Hurry up and eat your salad before I drag you off to bed." Brad smiled at her. "Junior was here about an hour ago, and wanted to speak with you. He and I both think this plan for you to alternate hours at the office is ridiculous. Why let rumors destroy your work schedule?"

"My goofy hours will only be for a week or two, and then I'll regain control of my life again." Simultaneously they leaned together to share a kiss. "I mean it, Honey, you do look fantastic. Your gown reminds me of the glamorous bridal lingerie you wore the night we were married."

Brad hurried to eat his late night dinner before taking his beautiful wife to the bedroom. Near the Jacuzzi he eased the silk robe off her shoulders. Slow and lovingly they relaxed in the soothing water. A half hour later he was drying her body while she was drying his. Eventually they kissed and maneuvered themselves towards the bed. Her body trembled at his touch. Ten magical fingers ignited a flame in her beautiful body. Shock waves rippled through her body as they made incredible love. It was well after midnight when Brad and Marie drifted off to sleep."

Although Brad woke at nine he was in no hurry going to the office. Darcy became concerned thinking he might not come at all. She called Junior asking if he had seen Brad, he hadn't. She fought off the urge to call the Ad Palace. Recalling Brad's words she called the Unemployment Agency to inquire about secretarial help. In a matter of minutes she set up interview times for the following day. Six interviews were spaced one hour apart. Brad walked in at eleven. "Good morning big guy, you are late."

"Good morning to you too. I told you yesterday I would come in late, and work late after you leave."

"I know, but this is ridiculous. Junior told me he went over to your house last night around ten and you were still working. If you want us coming and going at different times a simple fifteen minute shift would be enough. He also told me he and Marie talked a long time yesterday before he and I talked. We all know Rusty is a flipping idiot." Brad sat down in Junior's office chair. "I took the liberty of setting up interviews for my office assistant tomorrow. May I count on you to help interview these people?"

"I shouldn't be helping you hire anyone. The person you hire must realize you are the boss in this office. Whoever you hire will work for you, not me. They need to know you are their boss from day one."

"Can you at least be here, while I interview my applicants?"

"I can be here working, but I'm not helping you conduct interviews. You won't have any problem hiring someone you think you can work with."

"It's somewhat terrifying for me to think about hiring anyone." Darcy rolled her office chair over next to him. "I don't want to go through all my interviews forgetting to ask an important question. If you could at least listen in you would know if I forgot to ask something. You could tell me between interviews, so I don't continue to make the same mistakes during my interview process. I'm not as courageous as you think."

"If you are looking for advice I would say draw up an outline so you ask your questions in a certain order. End your interview asking if they have any questions for you. What people tell you may only be a reflection of what you said. You won't have a problem knowing if they are telling you the truth, or they are telling you a bunch of BS."

"Thank you for your advice. I'll make a simple outline while I eat lunch today." She rolled her chair back to her work area. "Promise me you won't work until eleven tonight. Come Monday, I may have my new assistant hired. Then with both you and her helping me we can catch up on our back log of work in a few days." Brad failed to respond to her statement as he plugged away at the stack of receipts on his desk. "This may be a long boring day if you never talk to me."

"I'm sorry, I was lost in thought. I have business concerns needing tended to elsewhere. There is a mountain of work here on this desk. Had I been doing my job weeks ago, I would not have let this office get this far behind. I have a bad habit of setting up an office, and then neglecting the everyday operation. Then there is Rusty. I should have realized Rusty was not happy, and would eventually cause trouble. I let down on my job in many areas. Step by step I need to take better control of my life. Family time is something else I need more of. I'm feeling the weight of the world on my shoulders."

"You worked half the night yesterday. What you are feeling is lack of proper rest. You need to relax. The trouble Rusty caused has been put to rest. This backlog in this office will soon be straightened out."

"Rusty's car was at the Ad Palace this morning. I doubt Wendy will have the strength or courage to deal with Rusty. It may take time for that weight to fall off my shoulders. Be assured I'll be checking things in that office this evening after everyone working there has gone home. I'll check their work from top to bottom. Sitting here I would venture to guess he is a weak link. I doubt he is worth the money Marie and I pay his royal fanny. I think he needs to get in his rust-bucket Chevy and cruise on down the road. We can't have Rusty running around like a loose cannon mouthing off about things that are none of his business."

The tone of Brad's voice left no doubt he was extremely angry at Rusty. "If you need to go over to the Ad Palace, why not go now when you can go over the facts with the employees? End his employment today. Why wait for Wendy to make up her mind as to when Rusty should be gone?"

"I want all my facts straight when I speak to Rusty. If you are somewhat certain you will have a helper soon I should scoot over and have a talk with Robin Tilly. Ultimately what happens in the Ad Palace may affect her office."

"With your mind being preoccupied you won't be much help here today. Go see Robin. You may want to call first to be sure she is in her office."

Brad immediately left the office leaving Darcy concerned about him. She called Marie. "Hi Marie, I'm glad I caught you. Brad was here a few minutes and then left to go see Robin Tilly. He said he wasn't feeling well and he is in a strange mood. A mood I've never seen before. He left no doubt he is still furious at Rusty."

"We all know he is sensitive about being judged, and gets furious every time someone doesn't believe him. He blows off steam in all direction. The main thing is to not further irritate him. Let him vent any way he wants to vent, and then when he calms down a little give him a shoulder massage if you see him. If he comes home first I'll give him the shoulder massage. I realize this current situation is slightly different in the fact he didn't come to any of us. He actually believes Junior, and I, might not have believed there was nothing going on between him and you. "

"That's unfortunate. I hope Junior believes what I tell him."

"Of course Ray would believe you."

CHAPTER 10

In Robin's office Brad explained he wasn't sure she needed the Ad Palace as much as she was using the agency. "I feel your people are creating excellent videos and if you learn to narrate your videos as we do for you. You may not need our services as much."

"I must say this is a complete turnaround on your part. Suggesting we enhance our own videos would hurt your business." Brad smiled at her. "You really think we could learn to do what is done in your officer."

"I know you could do part of what we do. How much you can do is the question. Our office isn't running as smooth as I would like. When I make the necessary adjustment our enhancing ability will diminish some. This might be a good time for you to test what you can do on your own. Long as you read your client's ability to choose a house they can easily afford, I don't see how you can lose."

"I appreciate your honesty. You really caught me off guard. How large a test would you suggest I try enhancing on our own?"

"Thirty percent might be a fair number since we will be short one worker in the very near future. By the way don't say anything about our losing one employee. It's not official yet. What I'm looking at is if we need to replace the person, or can we work with two employees in our office. I have no intention of pulling the plug on the Ad Palace, but it is time to reassess our value to you, and the Anderson Agency."

"In that case my lips are sealed. I appreciate you tipping me off before dismissing one of your employees. I'll implement the necessary changes here to test our ability to pick up the slack. I can easily do weekly checks on our cutback, within one month we should have our answer."

"I'll run along and let you get back to work. We'll talk again soon, I promise."

From Robin's office Brad went directly back to sort receipts in the apartment office. "You came back. Did you accomplish what you hoped to get done?"

"I only set the stage, now it's waiting time." Darcy slipped around behind him to begin massaging his shoulders. "Oh my, you have great hands." He momentarily closed his eyes. "You better stop though we are not getting any work accomplished."

"Just relax. Our work can wait a few minutes." She whispered in his ear. "I spoke to Marie on the phone. She suggested I give you a shoulder massage if you returned. I'm a good listener if you care to share your thoughts with me. I can also keep secrets if you don't want others to know what we discussed."

"I'm angry at myself for reading Rusty wrong. I thought he was a team player. If he had concerns, he should have come and talked to me rather than spreading rumors. Even if it were true he should have come to me first. Had he been any kind of a man he would have come to me."

Darcy moved around in front of him as she looked him straight in the face. She touched his left temple. "Try thinking about the situation from his point of view, where would someone like Rusty get the courage to ask you what was going on?"

"Power shouldn't mean anything to a guy, men are supposed to be tough."

"Rusty is far from tough, and far from a leader. He sniveled around telling others what he suspected in hopes they would take the lead, and talk to you. It's the old safety in numbers theory."

Using his index finger he gently touched Darcy's nose. "You are right about Rusty's weakness. You are also correct when you say you are a good listener. Unfortunately I can't tell you everything going on in my mind. Certain things are private. I just feel tough today."

"You can trust me enough to tell me everything." She ran her soft hands up his chest. "Try finding it in your heart to forgive Rusty. He is human and we all know humans make mistakes. Think about my words before you act."

"Darcy you are barking up the wrong tree. Rusty is in hot water with me. The Ad Palace is going to change. Week after next Marie and I will be going to Seattle, to have the same talk with the Anderson Agency I had with Robin Tilly today. If they accept what I have to say well as I think Robin did, the Ad Palace won't need Rusty."

"You lost me, I don't understand."

"It's really very simple I don't want people around who constantly remind people of my checkered past. I will not tolerate my past being tossed in my face time and time again. Rusty uses my past as an excuse to keep accusing me of things I'm not guilty of."

"Rusty made a mistake, who among us is perfect?" She put her hands on his cheeks as she leaned forward but stopped before kissing him. "On the tip of your tongue are words you want to tell me. I can almost hear those words."

He leaned forward enough to touch the tip of her nose causing Darcy's eyes to pop wide open. He checked his watch. "We may not have time for my complete story today but bring your chair over. No reason to stand bent over."

He paused long enough for Darcy to get her chair. "You may be aware of certain parts of my story." Brad went on to tell about his lonely life growing up along with him killing the intruder so many years before. He explained how the incident sent him and Alice to live in a hotel suite where they grew close as two people could get without crossing the line of moral character. "I'm stronger than people give me credit for."

"Alice told me all the things you are saying."

He went on to tell about how he desired to create friendships, but didn't have the slightest idea how. "One day while watching a movie about a man who had the ability to control people's minds caught my interest. I instantly wished I had the ability to control people. The movie combined with the intruder incident when the police didn't believe me, became the driving force to develop computers to match music, and voice, to subliminally feed messages to unsuspecting people. I wanted to control people's action so they would believe me.

Darcy smiled thinking he was pulling her leg. "Are you kidding me?"

"I was about eight when I became a computer geek. My computer was my only friend. The movie reignited my early desire to be liked. I told Alice I may never perfect my idea, but I would never give up on my attempt to control people. I also wanted to prove to my father I didn't have to fly all over the world to make money the way he did. I wanted a family someday, and I wanted my family to know who I was. Chasing all over the world gathering dollars isn't for me."

"There is nothing unusual about a man wanting family. Everyone needs family. You are no different. Furthermore nobody taking time to know you believes you are different than other people. I have a theory about why you helped Judy have her children." Brad rotated his hand encouraging her to keep talking. "You were aware how lonely Judy would have been without a husband and children."

"I like your theory. No way could I sell your theory to any other person. At this point in my life it doesn't matter. I can't change history. I can only deal with now. During my lonely years I had what I thought was limited success with my subliminal messages, but my experiments couldn't be repeated enough to be certain of my success. During my third year of college I decided to buy a small business for my testing ground."

Now she was looking at him rather serious. "You bought the Burger Place."

"Unfortunately I was no business person, and too stupid to hire business people." He continued with his story about how he almost was sued for sexual harassment before straightening up his act. "I finally hired good people to operate the Burger Palace so I could repeat subliminal advertising experiments."

"You recognized your error and corrected it. I call that being smart."

"I've wasted your day. It's time for you to leave, and time for me to go investigate things at the Ad Palace. Maybe we can finish up my story tomorrow between your interviews."

"Is that a promise, I do want to hear the rest of your story very soon, and I won't take no for an answer. I have one other request. Get proper rest tonight. Don't stay here late."

With Darcy gone for the day he hustled over to the Ad Palace to create a second stronger subliminal message for Rusty. Rusty needed to be kept in line. There could be no more of his unfounded accusations. From there he went straight home to his family. Johnnie and Jimmy instantly pulled their father outside to show off their baseball skills. "You guys have been working hard you are getting good at tossing, and catching the ball."

"Dad it's throwing and catching the ball, not tossing and catching."

"Oh, excuse me. I'm a little weak on baseball knowledge. You guys know more about baseball than I do."

"Juan said we could be on a team next year if we continued to work hard. Dad, we are not very good batters yet, Jimmy swings a bat like a girl."

"Honey, Jimmy is younger than you. Give him time and he will learn to hit the ball. I better go in and say hello to your mother before she comes to get me. Its hot today don't you guys play outside too long, and get overheated."

"Dad, don't call me Honey, when I'm playing baseball with the guys?"

"You got it buddy, I'll remember next time."

Marie welcomed her husband with a kiss. "You look tired, why don't you kick back in your chair until dinner is ready, you have plenty of time for a nap if you want a nap?"

"I better shower first it's so hot out today, I must smell to high heaven. Before I forget did you call Judy and tell her we were planning a visit soon?" Brad rubbed his head. "I have the worst headache ever. My whole body feels weak."

"You need rest. I did call and she is thrilled to hear we will be visiting them soon. She can't wait for us to get there. I could hear the girls squealing in the background, yelling Johnnie and Jimmy were coming, bless the girl's little hearts."

"Great, that makes three out of four family members happy we are going to visit them. I hope when we get there Sam is in a good mood. I do have some business to discuss with them. Business he may not like."

"Please don't tell me their videos getting bad again?"

"Their videos are great, every bit nice as the Tilly Agency. Seeing the quality of their videos started me thinking if they still needed our full services as much as they once did. I spoke to Robin and she is going to back off thirty percent, and try selling more houses without our services to check our value. The Anderson Agency should do the same. I have no desire to take money from people if we are not earning it."

Marie looked shocked as she studied his face. "If they don't need our services what would become of the Ad Agency, and the people working there?"

"Rusty is worthless, Wendy may be retiring soon. We may only have Carol left. We might be able to work her into our organization somewhere else. Until we know our true value of the Ad Palace, we can't make any final decision about the Ad Office. There is an old saying I've read many times, it goes like this. All good things must come to an end."

"Are Rusty's accusations what started you questioning the value of our Ad Palace?"

"I supposed it was him. He upset Carol so I know they are not getting along well. Unless I miss my guess Rusty will become odd man out very quickly. At that time we need to decide if we rebuild the Ad Palace staff or maybe gear it down." Marie gave him a questioning look. "Don't look at me like that. You had to know this Rusty incident would upset me. Reevaluating the Ad Palace is going to happen. In the long run, refocusing our direction at the Ad Palace should be good for everyone."

"I realize you have little tolerance for people like Rusty. In all fairness, he made a butt of himself more than anyone else. I was hoping it wouldn't upset you this much. Of course I don't know anything about Carol and Rusty's relationship. Wouldn't you think this dust up will blow over?"

"Rusty won't change. If you don't believe they are having trouble call Wendy. She can give you her thoughts on the subject. She knows their relationship is fading because he is jealous of our money. We can't cure his jealousy."

"I don't need to call Wendy. If you say they are having problems I believe you."

"No, really, go ahead and call her, I don't mind. Try not to worry about the future of the Ad Palace. We will do fine with, or without the business. My only concern is Carol and Wendy. Closing the office could disrupt their lives in the short run. As I said at this point who knows what is best. Wendy may retire soon. This problem with Rusty may be the first in a series of problems surrounding the Ad Palace."

"I haven't paid a lot of attention to business as I should have. I assumed everything was going fine. Only when you mentioned you were bothering workers, and suggested I make your rounds while you helped Darcy, did I know anything was wrong. I also learned you do far more than any of us expected you do in a day."

"None of this is your fault, it's me. When we decide we want something, I want it too fast, and put undue pressure on those around me. What I don't understand is how can I be so stupid as to not recognize my problem, and not know how to control my actions?"

Marie grinned from ear to ear. "You are making a mountain out of a mole hill. Once the new apartments are completed, and the Ad Palace settles down as I know it will, you will be fine. After that we can take a nice relaxing family vacation." Brad applied pressure to his chest as he belched.

The following morning Darcy showed her nervousness by pacing the floor waiting for her first interview to arrive. "Sit down and relax. I can't work with you pacing around the office as you are. Draw in a few deep breaths and relax."

"I'm sorry I don't mean to distract you." She eased down in her office chair. "My first interview should be here in ten minutes." Showing nerves again she twirled completely around in her chair.

"Would you like for me to leave?"

"No way, you stay right here. After my first interview I want you to be honest with me. Tell me how I did, and make suggestions on how I can improve my interviewing skills. I want to be certain I hire the best applicant. I've never interviewed anyone before."

"I suspect you interviewed yourself, when Junior hired you. Suck in a few deep breaths before anyone gets here. I see someone is coming up the sidewalk now, show me what you got. If it's any consolation, your first applicant dresses nice, perfect attire for an office."

Brad busied himself while Darcy conducted her interview. As any true professional she methodically went through her questions in a timely manner, making notes as she went. Once the applicant left Darcy grabbed the back of Brad's chair and spun him towards her. "How did I do?"

"Except for roughing me up, you did fine." She quickly hugged him. "Whoa girl, don't choke me."

"Joke time is over. Be honest with me, how did I really do?"

He placed one hand under her chin as he lifted slightly. "I am being honest, you did great. Now I would suggest you stop hugging me and get ready for your next interview. This lady is early if it is her coming up the sidewalk. We don't need this lady peeking in like Rusty did, and actually seeing you hugging me."

All three interviews the first day went well. Darcy was pleased with her work, but exhausted. "Darcy, I have a question for you. I've been working in your office for more than a week. Junior hasn't been by except to have lunch with you that one day when dumb-ass Rusty saw him kiss you. This is his office, he should check in now and then."

"After Evan's concrete error, Junior is afraid to leave the construction site in fear of a second error happening. They both know you won't tolerate additional screw ups."

"Are you sure about what you are saying, or is it he doesn't come by to see you because I'm here?"

"That might be part of Junior not coming by I'm not sure. He also thinks you and I can handle the office without his help. We are not the only people in your organization to be busy. He does have a lot of things going on right now."

"I have high hopes for your relationship, but with both of you working this hard finding time for dating must be difficult. We both know that's not good. Love can't grow if you never see your guy. I happen to believe you have more love to give a guy than any single girl I know. You need to have a gentle conversation with Junior and explain he needs to readjust his schedule, and give you some of his time."

"I can't demand more of Junior's time. He is doing the best he can."

"Have it your way, it's your relationship. Be as patient as you want to be. Now let's talk business. My being here has helped catch up a good portion of the backlog of work. Looking ahead, once you get your new employee trained, this office should catch up on posting information in our computer. At that time I expect you to take some vacation time. I also see no reason Junior couldn't take the same time off if you want time off together. Perhaps you can spend some quality time together."

"I'm willing to take some time off. Convincing Junior to take time off might be more difficult. Trying to impress you, he is becoming a workaholic. The under budget numbers they were projecting is slipping away. Half of the four hundred thousand they hope to impress you with is gone."

"The boys are beginning to see the real world. This is why watching the budget from day one is important. Money only goes so far. I never scrimp on a budget. I expect more of the under budget money will disappear as the construction is winding to a close. Why don't I have a mild discussion with Junior, I can threaten to get his sister after him if he doesn't slow down and take a little time off." His comment put a smile on Darcy's face.

On day two of Darcy's interviews, one applicant stood out among the others. She was a wheelchair bound twenty four year old black woman named Sharon Abrams. She was a college graduate who partied too hard one night, and fell from a balcony injuring her spinal cord. The young woman was a business graduate with excellent computer skills. As the interview came to an end Darcy seemed to be at a loss for words causing Brad to enter the conversation. "Miss Abrams, Darcy and I are somewhat at a loss here. We are inexperienced at hiring office help. What type of changes would be required for you, if you worked in this office?"

Sharon looked around the room as she wheeled her chair over to the file cabinets. "New file cabinets would help, they make a two drawer side style file cabinet that I could use easier than these tall cabinets. Your restroom would need handicap bars with a wheelchair type sink and this desk is about four inches too high. Other than those changes I think things are set up very well. The room is plenty large enough to accommodate the needed changes." Sharon indicated the desk height with her hands.

"Thank you for your information. We will take your ideas into consideration as we make our decision. Darcy do you have any further questions for Miss Abrams?"

"I do have one more question. If we made these changes you mentioned and you came to work here, would you tell us if something else came up that could be made easier for you to do your work?"

"Certainly I would bring any additional problems to your attention."

"The reason I asked was I saw you needed help negotiating our short step coming in but you never mentioned changing the step to a ramp."

"This is my first job interview, I'm nervous. I forgot about the step outside. I did notice there was room for a ramp and a larger landing area to get my wheelchair around the door to make entry much easier."

"I see, well that's it for my questions." Darcy stated. "We should be making our decision within a week. We will call, and let you know."

"Then I will be on my way, thank you for your time."

With Miss Abrams gone Darcy told Brad what he already knew. Sharon Abrams was by far the most qualified person she interviewed. "Unless you object, I think Sharon is the person I should hire." Brad sat quiet. "Are you concerned about her being in a wheelchair?"

"Changing our file cabinets to a lower style, lowering the desk and adding handicap bars in the rest room is an easy fix. How she gets to and from work is a concern. A special handicap bus brought her here today. Once she is trained and you take your time off. How often do you need to make a Bank Run or a quick trip to the Post Office?"

"We do have some people pay rent by check or money order. I run those to the bank two times after the first of the month, usually swing by the bank on my way home. I make Post Office runs on an as need basis, never more than twice a week. Set up proper, postage can be handled on the computer. The mail person can do the rest."

"I would venture to guess it would take Sharon two or three times longer to complete these errands. People say I'm a fast mover. Do you think I would have the patience to deal with her unavoidable issues?"

"There are special laws governing handicap individuals. Would we be breaking any law by asking her for a second interview? We need to discuss the concerns we have with her. We do need to know how long it takes her to get around if she were to do these outside chores"

"Call the Labor and Industries office and asking them how far we can dig into someone's personal life. We may even want to inquire if we can ask about any medication she is on."

Darcy placed the call to Labor and Industries to pose her questions. The person she spoke with informed her all final applicants must be interviewed the same. Medications and drug questions could only be asked if you had a current drug policy in place. She relayed the information to Brad along with stating she thought their rules were unfair. "If employers can't ask these questions won't they automatically shy away from hiring anyone who is handicapped?"

"I don't know, we can't change the L&I rules. We both like Sharon Abrams resume. They said all final applicants must be handled the same. Seems to me if she is the only final applicant, we can ask more questions. A second interview comes to mind. If you don't mind, I would like to conduct the interview. I can try skirting around the edge of legalities."

"The third applicant on day one would be my second choice. What did you think of her?"

"I never paid enough attention on day one to separate any of the applicants. I paid more attention to Sharon Abrams, because her wheelchair caught my attention. Don't say anything; I know her wheelchair shouldn't figure into your decision."

"Applicant three retired from the state after twenty years. She worked as a Secretary in the Criminal Justice Office. She is willing to work full or part-time, that would be a plus. My concern with her is she may retire again in a couple years."

"You are right working full or part-time would be a plus for you. You could adjust her hours as to your needs." In Brad's mind the thought of hiring the best applicant left as fast as it came.

Darcy quickly mentioned Sharon again. "I'll call Sharon and Irene both in for a second interview. Brad you conduct the interview with Sharon and I will interview Irene."

Once the appointments were set, it was time to buckle down and get some work done. Around eleven thirty Darcy suggested they order lunch in, to give Brad time to continue with his life story. "You haven't forgotten about continuing our conversation about your life have you?"

"Darcy, I'm sorry. This isn't a good time. I have a couple important errands to run. We can talk some other time. I won't make you wait too long to hear more about my personal trials as I try to do things to fast."

CHAPTER 11

The following day two interviews were on the schedule, Irene Evans interview is at ten and Sharon Abrams at one thirty. Worrying about the interviews made concentrating on my work difficult. Now would be the perfect time to tell me the rest of your life story. Once our new employee starts there won't be a good time."

Brad looked at Darcy's anxious appearance. He laughed. "I can see you won't leave me alone until I spill my guts completely. Actually I shouldn't tell you any of this."

"Oh come on don't leave me hanging. Tell me the truth, you know I'm curious, most women are. I'll hound you until you tell me. You left off telling me you were almost sued for sexual harassment. How did that come about?"

"Oh yes, now I remember. I made a modest settlement with the two women who were trying to scam my insurance for a million dollars each. After that I became smarter by hiring people through employment interviews same as you are conducting now. I needed lots of help to start the Burger Palace. My time was devoted to testing my subliminal experiments. Each day I promoted different products until I was certain my advertising skills would work. From there I wanted a business that could generate enough money to impress my father, so I quickly changed from selling burgers to selling houses. I felt more money could be made selling houses than I could make selling burgers. To speed up my plans I needed realty agencies willing to work with me. Knowing few people in the realty business I chose people I knew a little about. Judy's boyfriend Sam in Seattle and Robin Tilly here in Vegas, Robin was the lady who helped me acquire the Burger Palace. The kink in my plan was when Sam couldn't pass the State Examine to get a realty license. I decided to help him pass his examine by feeding the information to him subliminally. How to target him for a few hours without him realizing what I was doing became a challenge, until I learned Sam and Judy we sleeping together. She was getting blamed by

Sam's mother for Sam failing his examine. I had no problem convincing Judy to allow me to help Sam. I successfully targeted both Sam and Judy to help them study. In a very short time they both become the realty agents I needed in the Seattle area."

"I find that interesting."

"I incorrectly assumed Sam and Judy would marry. Judy wasn't sure she wanted to marry Sam because he probably couldn't impregnate her. He was honest with her saying he had a low sperm count. To test if she could become pregnant by Sam she went off her birth control. After a month of not becoming pregnant she decided not to marry him unless she could have children. My anxiety to get two agencies going left me vulnerable to her asking, if I could impregnate her. Presto, I had my agency in Seattle and one in Vegas, two fast growing cities. Overworked, I soon sold the Burger Palace."

"There is nothing wrong with cutting down on work when you felt overworked. Soon as we get an additional employee in this office we can again reduce your work schedule. You are looking so tired is concerning everyone. Don't let anything change your plans to go to Seattle next week. Just getting away from here you will feel better."

"My plan was working well until my father passed away and I inherited his money. I no longer have the drive in the Ad Agency I once had. Toss in Rusty spreading rumors about us, and I get angry enough to think about closing down the office completely. I had a habit of growing closer to women faster than I should. Hell, I realize my problem. That's how I became involved with Judy in a less than proper way. Thank goodness Marie forgave me. The Judy incident is behind me, unless people like Rusty keep dragging it up. He wants to throw the incident in my face time and again. It's bad enough the dipstick talks about me, but now he drags you into his accusations."

"My suggestion is to ignore people like Rusty. Let him think what he wants."

"What you say is easier said than done. Put yourself in Marie's place. You are a beautiful young lady. How many times can she hear the similar accusations, and not begin to wonder if there could be some tiny thread of truth to the rumors. She knows how fast she and I fell in love. We talked on the phone a lot but our actual dates were few. I paid her airfare to come visit me here in Vegas. My intention was for her to stay in one side of my suite, and I remain in the other side of the suite. The same way Alice and I had done to give her and me, a chance to know one another better. That plan went out the window in about three hours."

Brad paused as he drew in a few deep breaths. "Don't leave me hanging, what happened?"

"I picked Marie up at the airport. We came back to my suite to drop off her luggage. She asked if she could shower and change before we went out for the evening. Of course I said yes and to make a long story short we never made it out that evening."

Darcy gave him a huge smile. "Sounds like a relationship made in heaven to me. You fell in love instantly. Marie did what I wanted to do with you, as we stood looking up the hill at the Virgin Tree in Montana years ago."

"We shouldn't keep discussing that night. What I'm getting at is how fast my attraction to women can escalate. I was mesmerized by Marie's beauty. The Judy incident was also a whirlwind event. She shocked me by asking if I would be a sperm donor, so she could have children. Before I could think, or respond, Judy went into all the reasons she needed my help, and needed me fast. I easily fell into her way of thinking not realizing she would need my services more than once. Stupid me was thinking one and done. Clean and simple, and then I could get on with my life."

"How many times did you go to the clinic with Judy?"

"Many times, I never kept track of the exact number of times we attempted to impregnate her. We must have been together twenty or more with each child."

"What made Judy so certain Sam could never impregnate her?"

"As I said she tossed away her birth control pills. Sam had told her he wasn't sure he could impregnate her so Judy went with Sam to speak with his doctor. She saw the record of low sperm counts concerning Sam. She pressed me hard saying Sam loved children, and he deserved to have children. Only when I agreed to help with her child bearing did she agree marry Sam, and in turn as I said they could become agents for me."

"This sounds like a story straight out of a bookstore novel. What did Sam do when he discovered you were the father of his children?"

"Everyone in the universe seems to know about our story except Sam. Hopefully he never finds out, and if he does find out I hope he takes time to think before acting. He loves Carrie and Kristy and the girls love him. People like Rusty are a constant danger to our not so secret, secret."

"Wouldn't you know it. Just when your story is getting good, here comes my morning applicant to be interviewed, we can finish our talk later?"

Brad quietly worked away as he listened to Darcy interview Irene Evans a second time. In Brad's mind she had excellent skills with a nice work history. She appeared to be about fifty years old, married with two children. Her youngest child was a senior in high school, and the other a first year college student. Brad felt confident Irene would be a good employee, and could do the job with ease. He hoped Darcy would hire her.

During Darcy's afternoon interview with Sharon Abrams he studied Sharon's ability to maneuver her wheelchair around the office more than the words being said. His actions were quickly noticed by Sharon. "I see Mr. Collins has doubts about my mobility. Is there some kind of demonstration I can show you that would help prove my ability?"

"I'm not sure how you can help our thoughts, Sharon, where do you live?"

"I have an apartment in the north end of the city. I live alone."

"I saw you get off the Handicap Bus. Is that normally how you get around the city when you go places?"

"I use the Handicap Bus a great deal. It's my easiest way to get around in the city. Occasionally I scoot around in someone's private vehicle if they have room to carry my wheelchair. Smaller cars I cannot ride in. Private cars are normally difficult for me to get in and out, mini vans are great."

"How long did it take you to come from your apartment to our office today?"

"I'm not sure, I didn't come straight here. I had a doctor's appointment on my way so I'm not quite sure. Calling for a ride and taking the ride, I would estimate it might take an hour to get here." Brad nodded. "Do you have any other questions for me Mr. Collins?"

"I can't think of anything. The reason I asked about your traveling about the city is people from this office do run errands from time to time. We go to the post office or the office supply store at times."

"Most office supply stores have delivery service at little to no cost depending on what you purchase."

"That's true." Sharon was well prepared for her interview. She had good answers for his every question they had.

"The post office trip from this location might take forty minutes to an hour depending if other handicap people were using the Handicap Bus or not. Extra stops would take longer. Mr. Collins, I don't expect people to make allowances for my being handicapped. If I were to go to the post office, and for some unforeseen reason it took longer than normal. I could easily work late on my own time to get my work finished."

"That wouldn't be necessary." Brad suddenly grabbed his chest. "I don't feel well." He said in a sinking voice as he toppled forward crashing to the floor.

Darcy screamed as Sharon took charge. "Call 911." She pushed herself out of her wheelchair landing on the floor beside Brad. "He isn't breathing. You do the chest compressions while I do mouth to mouth on him. The paramedics should be here in minutes."

The girls continued CPR on Brad until the paramedics came rushing through the door. "How long has he been down?"

"Four minutes at the most. We started CPR immediately." Sharon voiced.

Paramedics ripped his shirt from his lifeless body as they prepared to shock his heart. "Alright ladies move back, clear." With each charge Brad's body violently jerked. "Again, clear." His body jerked harder as the voltage ripped through his torso. "We have a faint heartbeat, prepare for transport."

Forgetting all about Sharon's disability Darcy turned to her. "You are hired, watch the office. I'm going in the ambulance with Mr. Collins."

During the ambulance ride Darcy called Marie to explain Brad had collapsed in the office, and was being taken to the hospital by ambulance. She didn't mention his needing to be revived. Within a half hour Marie and Junior arrived at the hospital. Marie grabbed Darcy's arm. "What happened?"

"Brad said he felt funny and grabbed his chest. A second later he passed out and fell to the floor. I called 911 immediately. He wasn't doing anything unusual. We were interviewing a young woman to be my office helper. As paramedics loaded Brad in the ambulance I told the girl she was hired, and to stay at the office. I wanted her there so I could go in the ambulance with Brad as they brought him here. I haven't seen a doctor or nurse to ask any questions."

"It sounds as though Brad may have had a heart attack. Junior offered. "How could someone young as he is have a heart problem? It makes no sense."

"I know, but he was definitely was having heart issues."

Marie's mother and father came racing in together to hold their daughter's hand as she explained about Brad collapsing. "Junior, go down to the emergency admitting desk and see if they have any helpful information for us."

"I'll go with you." Darcy jumped to her feet to walk beside Ray Senior as he hurried to the admitting desk. They learned Marie was needed at the desk to fill out paperwork. "I'll go get her." Darcy volunteered.

In minutes Marie had signed the admitting paperwork along with surgical permission paperwork. "Can you tell me how my husband is, I haven't been told anything about his condition."

The stern faced nurse placed one hand on Marie's hand. "Mrs. Collins your husband is in critical condition. He has had a severe heart attack. I'm told CPR was administered to your husband at the scene before the ambulance arrived. If my information is correct. Your husband was revived twice in route to the Hospital. His condition at this time is not good."

Marie covered her face with both hands. "Oh my God you are telling me he died twice." Tears flooded her eyes. "Darcy did you perform the CPR on Brad."

"I helped perform the CPR. Sharon our new girl in the office, and I together performed CPR until the paramedics arrived. She is a wheelchair bound handicap person." All of a sudden it dawned on Darcy she had raced out of the office leaving Sharon lying on the floor. "Sharon! I left her lying on the floor. I've got to go help her up. She may not be able to get in her wheelchair on her own."

Darcy dashed off before Marie could ask further questions. She grabbed Junior's hand as she darted for the door. "Come with me I may need your help getting Sharon up." As Junior drove Darcy to the office she explained why they were racing back to the office. Much to her relief they found Sharon sitting in her wheelchair. Darcy quickly hugged her. "Thank God you are okay. I visualized you lying on the floor alone."

"I probably could have made it back in my wheelchair on my own. Before I had a chance to try one of your tenants came in to inquire about the ambulance being here. He summed other people to help pick me up."

"I'm sorry I dashed off the way I did. Mr. Collins is in critical condition and being prepared for surgery. In the bottom drawer you will find an I-9 and W-2 to fill out. Leave them on my desk and lock up when you leave. Monday I can start showing you your duties."

"Thank you Miss Burns. I'll see you Monday morning."

"Call me Darcy, oops, where are my manners? Sharon this is our main boss, Junior Richards. He is also Mr. Collins' brother-in-law."

"Nice to meet you Mr. Richards, I'm looking forward to working here."

"Nice to meet you Sharon, we owe you our gratitude for helping my brother-in-law. We are all praying for his recovery."

"Could you to stick around a minute before you leave to see if I need help in the restroom, I'll call out if I need help?"

While Sharon was in the restroom Darcy called Bob Tilly to inquire about whom she could get to make the handicap changes needed to accommodate Sharon's needs. He quickly agreed to stop by and discuss with Brad the needed changes. Bob was in the area, less than a block away. "Mr. Tilly, Brad is having some health issues today he won't be able to meet with you. If you are coming right away, I'll wait here for you to arrive. If not we need to hustle back to the hospital."

"Is Brad in the hospital?"

"Yes, Brad is in the hospital. There has been no official report on his condition."

"I'll be at your office in two minutes."

Sharon emerged from the restroom. "It wasn't easy but I managed to maneuver in there. I will be looking forward to the handicap changes to make trips to the restroom easier for me."

"Junior, you should go back to the hospital and be with Marie. I'll drive myself over soon as I finish up here. Bob should be here in a couple minutes." As Junior left Darcy turned her attention back to Sharon. "I called a man to see about making the office changes you need. He should be here in a few minutes. I'm really worried about Brad. He gets involved in way too many business dealings. I've never seen anyone stress himself to the limit as Mr. Collins does. Half the time he has dark circles under his eyes."

While waiting for Bob she called Marie to inquire if there were any changes in his condition only to learn they had been told nothing more about his condition. Is there anything I can do, should I be calling anyone for you?"

"Call the Ad Palace and tell them Brad is having some health issues. He will be out of commission for a while. You might also call Judy in Seattle for me. Its okay to tell her Brad is in critical condition. She was expecting us to fly up for a visit soon. We obviously won't be flying there for our planned visit."

"I'll make the calls for you Marie and if there is anything else you need done just tell me. I'll be coming to the hospital in a few minutes."

Bob Tilly walked in smiling. "Hi Darcy, what can I do for you ladies today?"

"Hello Bob, Sharon here is our new office girl, and she needs a few changes made to accommodate her needs."

Bob extended a hand to Sharon. "Hello Sharon, nice to meet you. Welcome to the Collins world of excitement. What can I do for you ladies?"

"We need our restroom changed enough to accommodate Sharon's needs and a ramp outside with a larger landing area for an automatic door to open without hitting her chair. Sharon can explain about her needs better than I can."

"Let's have a look and see what is involved."

Bob and Sharon discussed in length her special needs. "On down the street a couple blocks, is a business called Zack's Therapy. For someone like me in a wheelchair they have a perfect setup for a handicap restroom, complete with a call button in the restroom if a person were to need help for any reason."

"Very good Sharon, I have my notes. There is time for me to stop by Zack's for a visual look at their restroom on my way home this evening. You mentioned Brad having a health issue. I hope his problems are not serious. What kind of health problems is he having?"

"He collapsed here in the office and was taken by ambulance to the hospital. Minutes before you arrived I spoke to Marie, she has been told nothing except he is in critical condition."

"Brad is only thirty something by all accounts he is a very young man. Tell Marie we will be praying for his fast recovery. I still have my master key to these buildings so I can let my crew in to work on the restroom anytime we need. For the concrete work out front I will set up to make the pour Friday evening so we have the weekend to dry before foot traffic uses the walkway."

"A weekend pour would be perfect Bob, I thank you. If you want to do the concrete pour early Friday morning when it's cooler we can close for the day."

"Closing Friday would be a big help and my crew would love you for giving them their full weekend back. My guys work hard and they value their weekends. We could easily install a button activated door to enter the office."

"Perfect, do all you can to make this office a nice easy place for Sharon to work. I have some calls to make. You two can handle what needs done."

Darcy's next call was to a surprised Judy. "Well hello Darcy. I saw your name on my caller ID, and couldn't believe you were calling me. I thought for a second it was a different Darcy. A client I forgot about, then I saw the prefix on your number and decided it had to be you."

"Judy this isn't a social call, I'm sorry to be the bearer of bad news. Brad collapsed in the office and has been taken to the hospital. As of now he is listed in critical condition. Marie and her parents are at the hospital with him. I'm going there myself in a couple minutes. Marie wanted me to call you so you were aware of what was happening. As we learn more, someone will keep you posted."

"Hold on Darcy, don't hang up on me. What type of problem is Brad having?"

"To my knowledge his doctors have said nothing. He may have had a heart attack. He collapsed here in the office and was taken by ambulance to the hospital and listed in critical condition. He was revived in the office and twice more on the way to the hospital. We are all greatly concerned about him."

"Oh my word Marie must be beside herself, she needs me. I'll be there quick as I can get a flight."

Darcy's next call was to the Ad Palace. She spoke to Wendy telling her Brad was having health issues, and was taken to the hospital. Wendy relayed the information to Carol and Rusty, causing Rusty to burst out laughing. "Sounds to me Marie caught him with his pants down in the wrong place again. I bet she beat the crap out of him after catching him with Darcy. What a guy, I knew he couldn't leave her alone. He lets women beat the living tar out of him, but if a man looks his way in anger, Brad kills the poor devil in a split second."

"There was nothing said about Marie injuring him, or her catching him with Darcy. You have no reason to think the way you do."

"If she didn't beat him up, what do you think happened to Mr. Mighty? A drug over dose, drugs are known to take a lot of young people down?" Rusty's words were met with silence. "Hyper as he continually is he must be doing some kind of drugs."

"For God's sake Rusty, Brad is in critical condition at the hospital and you are making wild accusations again. You are spouting vile words you know nothing about. Mr. Collins is not a drug user."

"You can't possibly think Brad has that much natural energy. He could be a meth addict. Hell, he is skinny as a rail, sunken eyes with dark circles around them."

Wendy shook her head but failed to continue sparing with Rusty. "I'm going to the hospital and check on his condition."

In the apartment complex Darcy checked Sharon Abrams sign up paperwork before filing it away. "I'll see you on Monday Sharon, I'm out of here." Everyone was trying to hustle back to the hospital.

A somber mood remained in the waiting room at the hospital. Some were quietly praying to themselves for Brad's recovery. Marie keep wringing her hands as her mother continued to massage her back. Three long hours slipped by before a doctor came to speak with the family. "Mrs. Collins your husband has suffered a major heart attack. We replaced three valves to help regulate blood flow through his heart. He will remain hospitalized for several days as we monitor him. Tomorrow he will be up and moving to see how his body is accepting the work we did."

"Then my husband is going to be okay."

"We have every reason to be optimistic, but it is crucial he avoid stress of any kind for the next several months. Keep in mind if his body rejects the work we did today, step two would mean an artificial heart or a heart transplant." Marie covered her face with her hands. The young doctor eased her hands away to see her face. "Heart transplants are more common today than ever before. Great strides are being made in the area of heart transplants each and every day. His heart problem looked to be a birth defect where one of the valves didn't quite develop properly. The only other scenario is his heart may have been damaged during his chest trauma incident of some kind. We sometimes see this type of injury to a heart valve in automobile accident victims. If not detected a valve failure can cause other valves to operate improperly. Mr. Collins was lucky to have immediate help. I'm told two young ladies are responsible for saving his life. They gave our team of doctors a chance to repair the damaged valves."

"One of the young ladies would be Darcy here and the other lady, I have yet to meet. She is a new employee at one of our offices. You can bet I will be thanking her too."

"Miss you are to be commended for your CPR skills. Without your help this family would be making funeral arrangements, rather than sitting here in the waiting room. Be proud, you did well young lady."

Darcy's face turned bright pink as everyone congratulated her. "It was Sharon the new girl who is the hero. She instructed me in what I should be doing. I called 911 while she started CPR. She did the mouth to mouth while I did the chest compressions. Giving CPR was easier than I thought." Marie gave Darcy a special hug.

"Only two people at a time could enter Brad's room. After a brief visit in the recovery room Junior, Darcy, and Wendy, returned to work. In the apartment office Junior held Darcy tight. "You were wonderful today." He paused to kiss her. "Seeing Brad lying there made me realize how short life can be. I want a more a more fulfilling life, will you marry me?" Junior's words caught her by surprise. "I have little to offer but love. I do love you with all my heart."

"Yes, I will marry you. I will marry you any time any place. With Brad laid up this might not be the best time to set a date for you and me getting married. Soon as he is better I'm all for getting a wedding date set."

"How about we discuss what type of wedding we want before we choose a suitable date?"

"Our wedding may be on the small side. My mother lives here in Vegas and she is the only person from my side of the family that could attend our wedding. How about your relatives, where are they. Are there many people in your family that would attend our wedding?"

"I have a few relatives living in Oregon. Some of them might drive here for our wedding. I doubt many would come to Vegas to be at my wedding. At the most there would only be a handful, six or seven if we were lucky. What would you think about getting married at one of the Wedding Chapels here in Vegas?"

"Long as my mother can attend our wedding. I'm fine no matter where we get married." Darcy sealed her words with a passionate kiss.

"Your mother can certainly be at our wedding along with my parents, Marie, Brad, and their boys of course. All we need to do is wait a month or two for Brad to get well. Then we can be husband and wife. Marie has a lot on her mind right now. We should wait to announce our wedding plans, until Brad improves. Everyone's focus should be on him now."

"I'm not good at keeping secrets when they concern me. Waiting to tell others of our wedding plans won't be easy. Mothers are hard to keep secrets from."

"Do it for Marie's sake, you can keep our secret for a short while. It won't be that long until Brad is a strong individual again. He won't be down more than a few weeks. By week's end he may be strong enough we can tell others of our wedding plans. Soon you will become Mrs. Ray Richards Jr." He proudly kissed his bride to be. "I love you Honey, and I don't mind at all if you tell your mother of our plans immediately."

"I love you too, and my mother will be thrilled. She thinks you are great."

"I have one other question for you. This question has nothing to do with our getting married. Do you think Evan and I caused Brad's heart problems by the stress we caused him? Our making a hundred thousand dollar error and now keeping him away from the construction site couldn't be easy for him to handle. We may have caused his heart attack?"

"I wouldn't think you caused undue stress for him. Brad brings stress on himself by taking on too many projects. The doctor said something about a possible birth defect in one of his heart valves as the cause of his heart attack. There is no reason for you to blame yourself. I wouldn't advise saying any of this to Marie because she was also steering him clear, so you guys could do you work without his interference. If I was to point a finger at anyone it would be that stupid red-head Rusty."

"Rusty has given Brad fits. I need to go visit Evan at the construction site. He knows Brad was taken to the hospital by ambulance. I'm certain he must be wondering what is going on. From the construction site I will be returning to the hospital and check on Brad."

"I'll see you at the hospital later. I have a couple things to check here before going back there myself."

In Seattle Judy had filled Sam in on Brad's collapse. "I'm going to Vegas, Marie needs me. I'm talking the first flight I can get to Vegas."

Sam grabbed her arm. "Hold on Judy, who called you and what did they say?"

"I just told you Darcy called me. Brad collapsed in the office. She thinks he had a heart attack. At the time she called me they hadn't spoken to any hospital officials so his exact condition wasn't known."

"You should wait until you hear some type of doctor's report. Brad is young he can't be in critical condition from a heart attack. I'm thinking Darcy panicked about his condition before she called you. You know how excited some women can get when they think something is wrong. Call Marie before you race off to Vegas for nothing. He may have a black eye and hiding again."

"Oh alright, I'll try calling Marie." Sam smiled as she made the call. Marie's mother answered her call. "Hi Susan, Darcy Burns called me saying Brad has been hospitalized. Can you tell me what happened and how he is doing?"

"Brad has had a serious heart attack. He came through surgery reasonably well for someone who had three valves replaced. Marie is a basket case. She is in the recovery room with him as we speak. The rest of us go in one at a time to be with her, so she isn't alone. He remains listed in critical condition at this time. If he doesn't respond quickly it could mean he would need a heart transplant."

"Brad may need a heart transplant. Susan, I'm coming to Vegas on the first flight I can get." Before Susan could respond Judy ended her call. She turned to her husband. "I'm going to Vegas tonight on the first flight I can catch. Are you coming with me?"

"Honey I have work needing finished. I can't drop everything a go racing off."

"Then stay here and work, I'm going. I'll keep you posted." Sam stood silent as Judy made her plane reservation. I'll swing by the house and grab a few clothes my flight leaves in ninety minutes."

Without so much as a goodbye kiss Judy was gone. Sam cursed under his breath as he turned to his mother. "Judy is flying to Vegas to be with Marie. Brad collapsed and was taken to the hospital. The dumb goofball doesn't get enough rest. Every time we see him he has dark circles under his eyes no wonder he collapsed. I don't understand why she thinks Marie needs help to watch him sleep in the hospital. He needs to lay there until he gets caught up on his rest. It's possible he could be a heavy drug user. Some drugs cause major heart problems for young people."

"From what I understand Judy and Marie have always had a special relationship. She thinks a lot of both Brad and Marie. When she is around Brad, I don't like the looks they give one another. I know their looks are harmless, but I don't like it. Flirting is how bad things can start."

"I've noticed a few looks between Brad and Judy I didn't like either. Marie seems oblivious to their looks. I hope it's just our imagination. If he were to hit on my wife, I would take drastic action and teach him a lesson. A lesson his money couldn't buy."

"See if you can get your work finished to a point you can join Judy in Vegas. If she is still in Vegas the first of the week you need to go see her.

When you do see her, be sure she needs to return soon as possible. She has a family to care for here."

"Now there is an idea I like mother. I'll go down and keep a close eye on their flirting as he recovers. There is no reason to sit around worrying and do nothing. When I get there I'll make my presence known. I can wrap up our three sales I'm currently working on and join Judy in Vegas. It is a damn shame we have him as a working partner."

As the hours passed at the hospital Brad failed to regain consciousness. Time and time again Marie was told his vital signs were strong, and he would be waking soon. In the waiting room Ray and Susan grew weary. Junior suggested his parents go home and get some rest. "There really isn't much you can do sitting here. Darcy and I can stay with Sis. Come back in the morning. Then we can go rest."

Susan went in to speak with her daughter before leaving the hospital. With them gone Junior suggested he and Darcy slip into Brad's room with Marie. "If we are quiet the nurses won't make us leave." Junior pulled Darcy to her feet seizing the opportunity to kiss her. "You are looking tired, would you like to go home and rest?"

"No, I want to stay with you and Marie. I should call mother and tell her I may not be home tonight. It will only take a minute to call her. I'll join you in Brad's room."

Junior quietly slipped in Brad's room. "I sent mom and dad home to get some rest." He gave his sister a tender hug. "How are you holding up?"

"I'm doing okay. The last nurse to check Brad told me he may not wake for several hours. I forget what she called it but something in his IV is making him sleep. She estimated the IV to run through most of the night. Somewhere near four AM it should run out. In three to four hours after that he may wake up."

"That's positive news. We were all wondering why he wasn't waking up. Seems odd the other nurses didn't say something before about why he was sleeping this long?"

"Who knows what goes through nurse's heads, did Darcy leave?"

"No, she is calling her mother to keep her from worrying where she is. We may remain here all night with you."

"Darcy is a sweet girl you need to latch onto her before she gets away." Junior smiled at her. "You and she should go home and get your rest. Brad's hospital stay may be a lengthy ordeal."

"We are staying right here with you tonight." Darcy came walking in. "Did you get your mother?"

Darcy nodded yes, before hugging Marie. She glanced down at Brad as he lay lifeless. "How is our patient doing?"

"No change, he appears to be resting peacefully. Marie learned he is getting something in his IV that is causing him to sleep this much. The last nurse to check on him doesn't expect Brad to wake until seven or eight in the morning." Darcy gave Marie a second tender hug. "We only have two chairs Honey. You will need to sit on my lap." Junior encouraged. She eased into his lap and leaned back to snuggle as close as possible to him. Darcy's actions made Marie give them a big smile. "Why the mammoth grin Sis?"

"My dear husband said the two of you were growing close. I see love in the air. When Brad said you two were growing close, I hoped he was right. Now I'm seeing what he saw, two people in love. I think it's wonderful. Why don't I walk down to the nurse's station and see if I can get another chair in our room you can't sit on Junior's lap all night?"

"You stay put Sis, I'll go see about the chair." Junior insisted.

"No you stay put I need to go use the restroom while I'm out anyway."

As Marie exited the room Darcy turned and quickly kissed her guy. "We are not very good at hiding our affection. It doesn't seem to matter, Marie approves of our relationship."

"My complete family approves of you. I'm not letting you get away." In a playful way he touched her nose. "How many children would you like?"

"Two would be wonderful and three would be great." Their conversation was interrupted as a chair was brought into the room. "Thank you Miss."

"You may use a blanket from the closet if you need a blanket."

"Thank you again, a blanket would be nice." Darcy retrieved a blanket as Junior adjusted the chairs. He sat two chairs side by side and the third chair directly across from the two chairs. "What on earth are you doing?"

Marie returned in time to see his chair arrangement. "Marie you sit there so you can hold one of Brad's hands if you want. I'll sit here next to you. Darcy slide that chair closer to us so Marie and I can put our feet on it. That's it, now grab your blanket and sit down on my lap. Stretch your legs out on top of mine, cover all our legs and lay back against me. We are making a cuddle puddle."

Junior wound up holding Darcy on his chest with one hand and Marie's hand with the other. "This is cozy." Darcy remarked as she squirmed around to kiss him. Being after midnight all three were soon sleeping soundly.

CHAPTER 12

Throughout the remainder of the night, nurses quietly came and went as they check their patient. Marie was the first to wake in the morning as Brad moved his hand. "Good morning."

"Where am I?" He asked in a soft voice as he looked around. Hearing his voice Junior and Darcy woke. "Where am I?" He questioned as he continued to look around the room. Obviously he was confused. Marie lifted his hand enough she kissed it. "You didn't answer my question. Will someone please tell me something, why am I in the hospital?"

Marie squeezed his hand. "You are in the hospital recuperating from emergency surgery. Just relax you are going to be fine." She pushed the call button to get a nurse.

"Welcome back." Junior stated. "You gave us a bit of a scare." Brad continued to gaze about the room. "You are in a critical care recovery room at the hospital. It is standard procedure to keep patients here until they wake. You were kept medicated longer than most patients. You look confused about being here. Try not to let it bother you. Your doctor tells us you will make a full recovery."

Now standing Marie leaned over to kiss her husband on the cheek. Brad looked at all the equipment connected to him as she brushed his cheek. "The nurse will be here in a couple minutes, we pushed your call button."

"Will someone please tell me what happened to me, was I in an accident?"

"You collapsed at work, and were brought here by ambulance. You are going to be okay though. You will need lots of rest." Marie did her best to reassure him.

Judy arrived at the hospital as Ray and Susan Richards arrived. "Hi, how is Brad doing?"

"We haven't heard anything about his condition this morning. As of last night he was still listed in critical condition. Marie, Junior and Darcy stayed the night with him. Marie told us the doctors replaced some of his heart valves."

Susan urged Judy to quietly slip on down to Brad's room. "Hi Marie, how is the patient…..oh you are awake." Seeing him awake surprised her. "How is he doing?"

"Brad is resting peacefully, he just now woke up." Judy gave Marie a hug as she patted Brad's hand.

"Sis, Darcy and I are going down to the waiting room before we get tossed out. We may go down and eat breakfast before we return."

Marie hugged Judy back. "Thanks for coming, Brad is doing reasonably well. They are feeding him through IV's. The doctor said last night they would get him up walking soon as possible."

"I don't feel like getting get up. I want to go back to sleep."

"Being tired is to be expected. Close your eyes and sleep all you want. The nurse will wake you when it's time for your medication."

Marie no more than had the words out of her mouth when the nurse walked in. "Good morning Mr. Collins it's nice to see you awake. Will you ladies step out in the hall until I finish checking our patient?"

The girls walked down to join Junior and Darcy, who were talking with Marie's parents. As the six conversed Judy began to get the picture as to what happened to Brad. "This is really scary. He does look better than I would expect for someone having a serious heart problem. His color is remarkably good."

"Brad was revived three times, before getting to the hospital. Darcy and our new gal in the Collins' Enterprises office that Darcy was trying to hire performed CPR on him, until the medics could take over his care. Twice the medics restarted his heart during the short ride to the hospital." Marie's eyes filled with tears. "Last night watching him lay there lifeless was the longest night of my life. It felt like a miracle to me when he moved his hand this morning."

Mrs. Richards touched her daughter's hand. "Is he still comatose this morning?"

"He woke up a few minutes ago. Surprisingly he is somewhat alert and talking this morning. He seems confused as to what happened to him. The nurse is with him now. I'm really not sure how I should answer his questions. I'll ask the nurse when she comes out what I should say. More importantly I might ask what I shouldn't say. I don't want to get him excited."

Darcy patted Marie's hand. "Talking with the nurse is a good idea. I'm thinking it would be best to be truthful with him. Truthful as possible without telling him he was revived three times on the way to the hospital."

"I'm going to walk back down to his room, and see if I can speak with his nurse." Mrs. Richards accompanied her daughter as they walked back the room. Although one IV was still in his arm he was sitting up. "You are looking very alert."

"The nurse wasn't telling me anything. She said the doctor would be making his rounds in a few minutes. I should ask my questions to the doctor. How about you Marie, can you tell me why I am in the hospital?"

Marie touched his arm. "I told you earlier Honey, you collapsed at the office. You and Darcy were interviewing a new employee to help her in the office." Dr. Akins walked in before Marie could finish her statement. "Good morning doctor."

"How is our patient this fine morning?"

"He is slightly tired and full of questions."

"Mr. Collins you are a very lucky man. You collapsed near people who knew how to care for you until medical personnel were on the scene. You died, my friend. Two women kept your blood moving until paramedics could get you to the hospital. I'm told paramedics and the two wonderful ladies revived you three different times in route to the hospital. Once here, our fine team of doctors gave you an overhaul. We replaced three of your heart valves. You have a young strong heart that couldn't function properly because of the valve restrictions. You have been through a lot. At this point we expect a hundred percent recovery. Being young you should recover fast."

Brad continued to look confused. "Our staff will get you up walking later today. We'll continue to take good care of you. We'll monitor your vital signs, throughout the day and night. If all goes well in a few days, I expect to release you. We did considerable work in your chest cavity. You will remain sore for two or three weeks possibly longer."

"Doctor, did I hear you right, I actually died?"

"That would be correct, Mr. Collins. People liked you well enough they decided to keep you around. We gave you a new lease on life. You probably have a good seventy years of life left if you take care of yourself. Who knows, you may live longer than seventy years."

"Doctor, I'm grateful to you. I'm also grateful to the people who rescued me."

"You should be grateful to everyone. You had a lot of help before it became my turn to help you. When the nurses come to get you up later today, follow their instructions to the letter. They are trained professionals who know how to maneuver you with the least amount of discomfort to you. For the next two weeks you need to move about very cautiously. Once the stitches heal you will move about fairly normal. Be sure and listen carefully to your instructions. You are restricted from lifting anything during the next two weeks. If you drop a pencil on the floor let someone else pick it up for you."

"I'll do my best to follow your instructions."

"After two weeks you may lift five pounds. Each week you may add an additional five pounds until you pass a six months recovery time. If you experience any difficulty lifting the weight, back off a few pounds. Do you have any questions at this time?"

Brad looked at Marie before looking back at the doctor. "Why is it, I can't remember what happened to me?"

"I just told you Mr. Collins, you died. Your brain stopped functioning for a brief period. In addition the medication you were given may have blocked part of your memory. Don't worry about the memory loss. Those who helped you can fill in the blanks when you are feeling better. Your first walk this afternoon will make you extremely tired. Don't get discouraged by your weakness. Listen to your body, rest when you need rest." The nurse walked in with clean pajamas for Brad. "Unless you have more questions, I will leave you in the capable hands of Miss Ferguson. By the looks of what she brought with her. You may be getting your morning bath."

"Okay doctor, I think you covered all my questions for now."

Nurse Ferguson asked everyone to step out in the hall while she bathed the patient.

Susan walked down to the waiting room so someone else could visit Brad after his bath. Junior was quick to point out he and Darcy was going down to eat breakfast before seeing Brad. Then we need to go home and rest a while. Brad's bath took longer than his visitors expected. As the nurse left Brad's room Junior and Darcy entered. "It's nice to see you awake. We wanted to tell you to get well before we left to go rest. We have been here all night with Marie. Like you we need our rest."

"Thanks for coming. My doctor said I would be tired and sleep a lot. I can hardly keep my eyes open now."

Nurse Ferguson had other ideas. She returned to get Brad up for his first walk. Brad took three short steps and wanted to go back to bed. "Keep walking, this is good for you."

"Put that on my headstone in big bold letters. KEEP WALKING, IT'S GOOD FOR ME. If you want the truth, I don't feel well at all."

Ten more feet, and it was straight back to bed. His head barely hit the pillow before he was out like a light. Nurse Ferguson stopped by the waiting area after leaving his room. "Your husband may sleep three or four hours before he wakes again. This would be a good time for you to dash home and rest a few hours."

"I don't want to leave him alone. I slept reasonably well last night."

"I was told you dozed off a few times, but nobody saw you in a deep restful sleep. If you become ill, you will be of no value to your husband. He will be very dependent on you the next few weeks. It is important you stay well."

Judy touched Marie's arm to be sure she had her attention. "Why don't I stay with Brad while you can go home and rest? It would do you good to rest two or three hours before you come back. I have my phone. I can call you if he wakes up or stirs a little."

"A shower and change would be nice, but I'm coming right back. I don't want to be away from Brad for any length of time. I won't be gone long."

Judy felt strange sitting at Brad's bedside praying for his full recovery as he slept. Various nurses came and went as they gave her a questioning look. Eventually she walked down the hall to retrieve a cup of coffee, to help keep her awake. "Are you Mrs. Collins sister?" Nurse Ferguson asked as she passed the nursing station.

"Marie and I are not sisters. She and I have been lifelong friends. We are close as any two sisters could ever be. I came down from Seattle soon as I heard Brad had collapsed. I'm still not sure what happened to him. I'll hear the story a little at a time as people feel like talking. I'm not about to encourage anyone to relive the event completely. Only if they want to talk will I urge them to say more."

Back in the hospital room Judy began to wonder what her life would be like if she had been the girl to marry Brad. Would their life be the roller coaster life he and Marie's life has been so far? Was his being in the hospital partly her fault? She provided plenty of the stress in his life. Could that be part of his heart problems?

Judy knew he loved her children. Unfortunately he seldom could he see them. Her cell phone vibrated jarred her back to reality as Marie called to ask if he was awake. "No, Brad is sleeping sound. He hasn't moved a muscle since you left."

"Then I'm lying down for a couple hours, call me immediately if he wakes."

"Rest long as you can. I will call you soon as he stirs at all."

"Thank you Judy, I'll see you later."

Again confusing thoughts swirled in Judy's mind as time passed slow. Minutes ran into hours as she kept thinking he should soon wake. Several times Judy tapped her watch wondering if the watch had stopped. More than once she shook her head trying to stay awake as she grew drowsy. Eventually her head slumped over on the edge of Brad's bed. Although it seemed like an eternity Marie eventually returned. "Has he been awake at all?"

"Every half hour a nurse comes in and checks him but he hasn't stirred. Brad has always been so energetic. Seeing him flat on his back like this is so difficult."

"I never expected a short ten foot walk to tire him out enough he has slept almost five hours."

"Maybe the medication hasn't completely left his body. When a nurse comes in again we can ask about his sleeping all the time." Marie barely finished her sentence when a Nurse Ferguson came in. "Listening to Doctor Akins this morning we were expecting my husband to be more alert during the day. Can you tell us why he is sleeping most of the day?"

"Doctor Akins should be making his rounds in a few minutes. I'll let him explain what we thinks may be going on with your husband. In the meantime, try not to worry. Doctor Akins is a fine doctor."

Those were words Marie didn't want to hear. She watched as the nurse checked Brad's blood pressure. She quickly wrote the numbers on his chart before exiting the room. Marie grabbed Brad's chart and looked at the numbers. "Something is wrong. Brad's blood pressure is dropping. After his morning walk his blood pressure has been dropping slow but steady. I don't like the looks of this chart. I hope the doctor gets here soon. If this is why Brad is sleeping so much someone needs to do something."

A serious looking Doctor Akins entered with Nurse Ferguson trailing behind him. "Good afternoon Mrs. Collins your husband is losing blood. We expected this seepage to stop by now. It appears we need to do some touch up work. In a few minutes we will be transferring Mr. Collins back to the operating room." Tears flooded Marie's eyes. Doctor Akins touched her shoulder. "This isn't a serious situation. Left unchecked it could become serious. Try not to worry; your husband will be fine, soon as we locate and stop the bleeder."

Ray and Susan Richards came to visit as Brad was being taken back to the operating room. "Honey what is going on, where are they taking him?"

Through tear filled eyes she explained. "They are taking Brad back to the operating room for additional surgery. He has a blood seeping enough to lower his blood pressure. The doctor said his condition was not serious but left untreated it could become serious."

"I don't understand. Brad walked once today. We thought he would be walking the halls again this evening." Ray hugged his daughter. "Brad is a strong young man and given time, I'm sure he will recover."

Junior and Darcy joined the four and soon learned the disappointing news. Junior shook his head. "I was prepared to fill Brad in on how well the apartment construction was coming along. Within two weeks we should have a solid completion date so we can start signing up potential tenants. Darcy, you may as well tell Marie and my parents your news."

"I have started Sharon Abrams training. I'm proud to report she catches on fast. She will not require a lot of training. Bob Tilly remodeled the office restroom to fit her needs. He put in a taller stool, installed handicap bars, and changed the sink to a wheelchair sink. Oh, I almost forgot, we now have a ramp leading to an automatic door."

"I certainly appreciate everyone's efforts on Brad, and my behalf. Your efficient work will not go unnoticed."

Although conversation continued to flow Marie sat much of the time in a daze waiting for the nurses to bring her husband back to his room. "Won't the doctor come and talk with you before they bring him back to his room?" Susan massaged her daughter's shoulders. "Try and relax Honey. Brad is in good hands. He will be fine. I know he will."

Judy added her thoughts to Susan's statement. "Your mother is right. My concern has to do with you. Think back to when Johnnie was ill. Brad arranged a bed for you in Johnnie's room. Would it be okay if we arranged for you to have a bed in this room?"

"An extra bed in his room would be nice. See what you can do."

Junior and Darcy went with Judy as she went to see about an extra bed. The hospital knew Mr. Collins well from their previous visits. Hospital officials agreed to put a second bed in his room. Starting back to the waiting room Judy stopped Junior and Darcy. "The news about Brad isn't the best. What really concerns me is Marie seems to be off in a fog much of the time. It's as though something is eating away at her. I was thinking maybe after Ray and Susan leave this evening might be a good time to try talking with her in depth. We may be able to get her to open up."

"We noticed what you are talking about. Darcy and I can hang around for a while after the folks leave." Darcy nodded in agreement.

Rejoining Marie she continued to be in her dazed look. "Sis we have a bed ordered for you." She failed to respond to Junior's words. "You will be able to rest tonight."

Marie's eyes were locked on Doctor Akins as he came walking towards them still wearing his scrubs. "We found our problem bleeder. One of the heart valves we installed was faulty. The faulty valve was replaced and Mr. Collins is doing well. Having to change his heart valve a second time will delay his recovery a few days. Your husband will now remain in the hospital a week to ten days longer than we first expected. The next two days he will be allowed to walk to and from the restroom only. No long walks down the hall. The extra stitching we did is now a weak area requiring additional time to heal."

"Has his blood pressure stabilized?" Marie asked.

"His blood pressure has stabilized; your husband is doing well as can be expected at this time. You shouldn't worry."

As visiting hours ended Ray Sr. and Susan left the hospital. This gave Judy time to have her serious conversation with Marie. Although she refused to say anything in Brad's room she motioned they should walk out into the hall. At the end of the hall near the waiting room Marie began to talk. "I feel horrible; Brad's heart problems are likely my fault. Doctor Atkins said his problem was a birth defect or a chest cavity injury from a previous automobile accident. Brad was never in a bad automobile accident. The trauma to his chest came from me when I beat him, with the cutting board." Marie's words caused silence for several seconds. "I caused him to have this massive heart attack."

Nurse Ferguson walked near enough to hear Marie's confessional words. "Pardon my interruption Mrs. Collins. I couldn't help but overhear you saying something about you being the person to blame for your husband's condition. That's not true."

"We all heard Doctor Akins say the previous injury was probably caused by chest trauma. I'm responsible for the chest injuries. I hit him with a cutting board."

"Doctor Akins is full of his own wind. He is an excellent heart surgeon, but he has lousy bedside manners. I spoke to the operating room nurses. They saw no sign of your husband's skeletal structure ever being damaged. I don't think a full grown person being hit with a cutting board would cause a heart rhythm disruption. In my mind there is no way you are responsible for your husband's condition. It was a birth defect. Doctor Akins has a habit of using fictitious scenarios as he guesses what he might find in the operating room. Don't be lulled into his crazy thought process. I walked down here to tell you your husband is awake, you may see him now."

To everyone's surprise Brad was wide awake and feeling much better. He was laughing and happy. "Nurse Ferguson explained to me they took me back to the operating room to reconnect my veins carrying blood to my brain, now I can think better. Of course she was lying to me. Whatever the case I do feel a hundred percent better. I know what's next for me. I slept most of the day. Within the next hour some little candy stripper nurse will come walking in clicking her heels, to give me a little pink pill. Then I will sleep tonight."

Marie leaned in for a tiny kiss. "You're color looks much better. I have a bed in your room now. I can be at your side all night."

He gave her a quiet excited look before turning his attention to Darcy. "How is our work progressing?"

"Work is progressing well as can be expected. You're on hands guidance is missed. Everyone is doing the best we can in your absence." Darcy reported. "Sharon is quickly becoming a major asset in our office."

"Then you hired her as your assistant to help in your office?"

"Yes, I hired Sharon. Bob Tilly is made the changes she needed to enter and work in our office easier. The office is doing great, or I wouldn't be here visiting you. I will be going back to the office very soon to help her."

"How is your work going Junior?"

"Our construction is going great. We remain on target and under budget about two hundred thousand dollars. I'm also happy to report we are taking applications for new tenants at this point."

"If everyone is doing such a great job, I may stay here and vacation a little longer." His visitors laughed.

"We are all happy you are doing better. I think Marie and Judy can take care of you so Darcy and I will return to work. We'll check on you again this evening."

"Thank you for coming by guys. I appreciate my visitors. I also appreciate the updates on business. Judy, I'm doing great. There is a family in Seattle needing you now. It's time you tended to them. When you get there give them a hug from us."

"I'll fly home this evening."

Fourteen days later Brad was home resting. Marie was checking on their business interests for him. Life was slowly returning to normal. Judy called from Seattle each evening to check on his progress. Two months passed, and Brad still refused to leave the house. "Are you never going to work again?"

"I feel good right here. All the work is getting done. Our employees don't need me. They are working fine with you. The apartment construction is finished and filling fast. What is there for me to do?"

"You can't just sit around for the next seventy years. We could work together for a while. My next question is when will we be sleeping together again?"

"If you are talking about when we can be intimate again, I don't know. My doctor hasn't told me if my heart would take such a thrilling experience this soon." He stated in a serious tone. "I should talk to the doctor before engaging in physical activity of any kind. I sure as hell don't want to land in the hospital again."

"Even sleeping in the same bed would be nice. I like to cuddle and snuggle. I wasn't complaining about the lack of total intimacy. When are we going to discuss the Ad Palace again? Before your health problem, you were checking about the possibility of scaling back the business. Robin Tilly took your advice to heart. She is doing quite well without our total support. You may have been right. The agencies do need to see what they could do on their own. The problem is we never made it to Seattle to talk over your idea with Sam and Judy. Meaning we should be going to Seattle soon."

"I forgot all about the Anderson Agency." Brad rubbed his chin as he gave thought to her words. "You should go over to the Ad Palace and check Robin's dealings and see where we stand before speaking to the Anderson's. If the percentage is working as they should. There may be reason to speak to the Anderson's immediately."

"We could go to work together tomorrow, and see what needs to be done. If need be we could fly up to Seattle this weekend. On Monday the boys have their first baseball game and we should be back to watch them play. Children need support from their parents."

"Yes of course I want to see the boys play baseball." Brad looked out the window to see clouds starting to materialize. "It's starting to get cloudy, is it supposed to rain?"

"I haven't heard anything about the possibility of rain. I do have one last piece of news you might be interested in. Junior and Darcy are planning to get married. They want to be married soon, but they were waiting until you feel well enough to attend the ceremony. They will be getting married at the same Vegas Chapel we were married in. You were right from the beginning they are a great match."

Brad gently rubbed his chin. "It's nice to know I'm not always wrong."

"What do you mean by that statement?"

"I was wrong about watching our workers so closely. They have done well without my constant interfering. This old dog from Vegas needs to leave the hired help alone. They can do their job without my interference. I never realized how nervous I made people. My health problems have been a wake up call for me."

"You are way off base. You are talking about people who wouldn't have a job if it were not for your visions of expansion and your-on hands training. You need to continue encouraging our workers. Acknowledging the fine job they are doing. We still have the two stages of our apartment complex to think about. The way I read our figures we can start that project any time you want. Evan Thomas is waiting for your call."

Brad noticed an unusual sparkle in Marie's eyes as she mentioned Evan Thomas. "For such a young inexperienced man, he came through for us. I wonder if he might be interested in working full-time for us once we get our third apartment stage built."

"In what capacity could Evan be working for us?"

"We own a lot of buildings. We could use help in the maintenance of these buildings. We want them kept in top condition."

"Call me stupid, I thought that was Junior's job?"

"Oh no Honey, Junior is the general manager of our office buildings and apartments. If we hired Evan he would be maintenance supervisor. Evan would actually do the work or hire a crew when he needed help. Junior would locate the needed repairs, and order the supplies needed for each repair project. He would be watching all the buildings. Evan will be working where Junior tells him what repairs needed done first."

Again she smiled. "The two of them working together would be nice. Junior does have a lot on his plate. He is really busting his fanny most days."

"Another thing I was thinking is we need to think about shortening the Collins Enterprise Office name. Maybe we could say the C. E. Office, how would that sound?"

"C. E. Office sounds better to me. We should have Darcy research the name to be sure we can to use the name. I'll check the catering services about lunch tomorrow for a lunch meeting. Counting Sharon, there will be six of us. I can call Junior now and tell him of our plans. Anything special you would like to eat?"

"How about turkey sandwiches for the guys and you choose something the girls would like. It doesn't matter to me long as it's not pizza. Pizza isn't good for my heart."

"How about a Chicken Caesar Salad for everyone?"

"A Chicken Caesar Salad would be okay for me, but ask Junior anyway. He may want something different for his lunch. A working man burns more calories."

The following day at noon Brad and Marie arrive to find three anxious employees. "Our lunch should be here in a few minutes. Marie and I wanted to take time today to thank you guys for doing a great job in my absence. Every aspect of our businesses ran perfectly while I was laid up. I see our lunch arriving now. We'll talk more about business later."

After eating, Junior took the chicken salad garbage out to the dumpster to rid the office of the odor. "First order of business today is to thank you girls for saving my life. Doctor Akins made it clear without your help during my crises, I wouldn't be here today." His words of praise made the girls blush. "You had your chance to get rid of me, but you didn't. Now I'm back to pester you."

Now they were chuckling with laughter. "People say when a person dies their whole life flashes before them. That never happened to me. I lost a day or two and I had no idea what had happened to me. I was in a daze trying to figure out where I was, and why I was there. Later Doctor Akins explained my confusion was the result of low blood pressure between surgeries. So if you see me stumbling around in a daze give me a pint of blood, and send me home to rest."

Again the girls laughed. "Sorry, you can't be home resting all the time." Darcy stated. "We need you. You are the driving force behind this businesses, as employees we need your guidance."

"If my awesome presence is needed so badly let's get down to business. Sharon how long does it take for you to come and go from work?"

Brad's words startled the girls. They thought he wasn't happy to have Sharon working in the office. "Forty five minutes to an hour. Friday evening takes the longest time taking an average of well over an hour for me to return home after work. Traffic is so heavy on Fridays." She complained.

"How would it be if we cut your travel time to five minutes?"

Sharon gave him a slow grin showing her pearly white teeth. "That would be difficult unless you motorize my wheelchair with a jet engine and I drive it home."

"We have the Manager's Apartment next door sitting empty. It's a nice unit and could easily be tailored to your needs." Sharon started to say something when Brad held up his hand for her to stop. "I'm thinking you heard the same rumor I heard. Darcy is marrying a fine young man and they were probably thinking of moving into the manager's apartment. Marie and I are big believers in marriage. We would like to congratulate Junior and Darcy on their upcoming marriage. We are also prepared to give you the same deal we gave Sam and Judy when they joined our team. That deal is a no interest loan to buy a house of their choice."

Darcy's eyes sparkled as Junior's face remained rock solid. "I can easily tell Junior has questions to ask. Let me assure you this is not the time or place to discuss the details of such an arrangement. A simple call to Laura and she can have dinner for us this evening. We can discuss the intricate details of our helping you this evening."

"This is a surprise. I know the hidden details will be a benefit to Darcy and me. Plus we never turn down a free meal. Give your lovely cook a call."

"Junior, I hate to exclude anyone from a gathering, especially family. You and Darcy talk over if we should also invite your parents to eat with us this evening. I don't mind them being at the house when we talk, if you guys don't. You can call them later this afternoon if your parents should be there at dinner with us."

Marie excused herself to use the restroom. "Junior I'll leave it to you to work out the needs for Sharon to live next door. Marie and my offer is good anytime. There is no hurry for you to purchase a house. The two of you can have the manager's apartment in the other complex until you decide where you would like to live. No decisions need to be made quickly."

As Brad spoke he saw Darcy scribble a note on her scratch pad and fold it over. She stood and walked over to him. "Your pocket is wrinkled." Using her body to shield her actions she slipped the note into his shirt pocket, and wiped his shirt pocket flat. "There, now you look better."

Brad realized she had slipped the note in his pocket, but ignored the urge to pull it out and read the note instantly. He could check the note later.

"Unless someone has a question, I think we can end this little gathering."

Brad and Marie used the private office at the Ad Palace to study the results of Robin's reduction in house videos to enhance. Wendy and her crew had made up the difference by enhancing more videos for the Anderson Agency. Brad reluctantly took time to congratulate the office workers for their steady business.

From the Ad Office they went down to see Robin Tilly. She quickly confirmed what Brad suspected. If the agency used the format the Ad Palace used pointing out important details they were seventy five percent effective. "By enhancing videos for you we inadvertently trained you to do much of what we do for you. This leads me to question if we are of value to you or not."

Robin drew in a big breath before speaking. "If we are putting our cards on the table your value is shrinking. I'm not sure I want to end our partnership all together at this time."

"Same as you, Marie and I are uncertain what we should do. If we stopped enhancing videos cold turkey for you, your potential income would take a twenty five to fifty percent hit. At the same time if you hired two new agents you could cover your drop in income. I think it's clear we need to have the same talk with the Anderson Agency we are having with you. I see no reason we can't start them down the same path you are to independence. No telling how they will respond. I was prepared to have that talk with them when my heart tripped out on me. Marie and I are thinking next week we should go to Seattle. This could be the start of a two year phase out of the Ad Palace."

Leaving Robin's office they drove over so Brad could see the finished apartments. On the way Marie called Junior to see if she was supposed to invite their parents to dinner or not. "Although it might not be the best timing, we should invite our parents to keep peace in the family. We can't very well exclude mom and dad from our dinner plans and take a chance on upsetting them."

"Brad is out walking around the new apartments for a close inspection." Marie stated. "I can't ask him about inviting Darcy's mother. I think Marlina should be invited over to meet our parents. How soon should she be invited to meet them is my question. What are your thoughts towards Darcy's mother?"

"I would love for her mother to meet mom and dad. Considering we have business to discuss. Tonight might not be the best night for new introductions. I do know our wedding date is close, their introduction should be soon. I would love to show Marlina, mom and dad's setup living close to you. I don't know if she would ever consider living near Darcy and I but the joy mom and dad get from your children is amazing. I believe Marlina would love to be near our children as they grow up."

"If you think it would be best not to invite Marlina this evening we won't invite her but we better set something up next week so the introductions can take place."

"I think next week would be better."

Out of Marie's line of sight Brad slipped the note from his pocket. The note was simple it read we should talk in private soon. Darcy wrote six little words that could mean most anything. He quickly called her. "Hi, it's me. I read your note. Would you happen to be working a few minutes late tomorrow evening? I could stop by after the office closes."

"That would be perfect. I do have a pressing issue. I would like to bring to your attention, and tomorrow evening would be fine. I'll see you then."

CHAPTER 13

Laura served her short notice dinner of Tacos. "A little more notice may have gotten you a steak dinner." Darcy pointed out how great the Tacos were, and the fact they were a big hit with the boys. Johnnie and Jimmy were working on their third Taco each.

"Growing boys will eat anything and enjoy it. It's a pleasure to cook for them."

Laura commented. "They are so appreciative."

"Ray, Susan the reason for this dinner tonight is Marie and I wanted to discuss a business deal with Junior and Darcy. We didn't want to exclude you from any family dinner so you were invited. After we finish helping Laura clean the kitchen we will retire to the study and talk business. There are no secrets to discuss that you can't hear so you may join us if you wish."

Susan, Darcy, Marie, and Brad, helped Laura clean up. They made quick work of the mess. Ray and Junior sat discussing what Junior thought the meeting might be about. "Okay people grab whatever you might like to drink." Brad checked his watch. "It's later than I expected, no telling how long this meeting may take."

Once in the room Brad was quick to get to business. "In the past Marie and I have given people in our organization no interest loans when they purchased a house. We would like to offer Junior and Darcy the same deal, a no interest loan. All actions create other actions. We are not attorneys or accountants. Our first piece of advice for Junior and Darcy is to get a good local attorney, and an accountant, if you don't already have one. Your marriage needs to start off on solid ground. Make sure you have Wills in place from the get go. You two are in a position to make good money for many years to come. The opportunity for growth in personal wealth is at your fingertips. Attorneys and accountants can help guide you through life much smoother than you can maneuver by trial and error. Our offering you a no interest loan would mean you have no house interest to write off your taxes. On the plus side you have a smaller payment with more options. You can choose to pay the property off fast or drag it out making smaller payments. If you are short on cash one month for any reason, call us. You can skip a payment with no problem. Long as we know what is going on there would be no problem. If either of you became alcoholics or big time gamblers, we might frown on those activities."

Junior was smiling big. "Keep talking big guy, I like what I'm hearing so far."

"Marie and I were over at the new apartment complex earlier today. The apartment complex looks great. The manager's apartment unit is where the two of you can live until you decide on a house you would like." Junior's chin dropped. "I didn't mean to scare you Junior. What I'm getting at is a time factor. Get married and go on your honeymoon should be priority one. When you come back live in the furnished apartment while you think about the house you would like. All decisions are important, so take your time making them. Our offer has no time limit. Our vision for you is simple, have the life you want. Talk among yourselves, and learn what you want before acting. Talk about children. If you have children, how many children do you want? Will they go to public school or private school? I read somewhere the average family moves to a new house every four years. That number was on middle income people living in normal houses. You have surpassed middle income people. You may choose to purchase, or build a nicer home. If somewhere in the future you decide to upgrade what you bought keep in mind higher end houses do not sell as fast as middle income houses. Marie and my advice would be to stretch out your vision. Try looking ahead five years, ten years and so on. Think about the most comfortable way to attain your goals. If you plan ahead even twenty years, and decide to sell the property in ten years, that's okay. Certainly better than living in a house a few years and then realizing you had to move because of a bad neighborhood or something. Living in the apartment for a while will give you plenty of time to discuss and decide your future without being pressured."

"Wow Brad, in a short hour you have given us a lot to think about."

"It's time to put our boys to bed, so this would be an excellent time for a short break before we continue talking about your future."

"Darcy and I could use a break. You are confusing us more than when we came this evening." Junior stated with a laugh. "All your information is good though."

"The good thing is you have all the time in the world to make decisions. There is absolutely no pressure on either of you. Do what you want to do when you want to do it. If you want, build a new house. Bob Tilly is an excellent house builder, plus he is easy to work with."

Jimmy and Johnnie had never been put to bed by seven people before. They loved the attention. They received more hugs and kisses than ever. Happy as clams they were put to bed. "Mom can we call Darcy, Aunt Darcy now?"

"Honey, I don't think Darcy would mind if you call her your aunt."

"Yes Honey. You may call me Aunt Darcy." Both young lads received an extra kiss from their new aunt. "I'm honored to become part of your family."

"We never had a real aunt before. We call Judy our aunt, but she really isn't our aunt. She likes to be called our aunt and we like calling her our aunt but she isn't our aunt."

"I think you should continue calling Judy your aunt. Good night guys, sleep tight."

Back in the study Brad again started pointing out his thoughts. "Now we come to the part Marie and I never discussed beforehand. We didn't discuss this because it's not quite legal. I told Darcy something a few months ago. Marie and I would buy you guys a complete bedroom set with a mattress like the mattress in the suite she laid on in the suite at Caesars. I've later thought this through. When you get the house you want all your furniture can be charged to C. E. Enterprises. Your furniture will be a wedding gift from Marie and me. The Government will never know the furniture went to your house rather than an apartment. C.E. has purchased thousands of every item. All our furniture is prorated out on our tax schedule. Auditors could never prove we exceeded the thirteen thousand dollar gift limit by purchasing furniture for your home. Don't worry about the expense. Get the décor and comfort you want."

Marie finally injected her thoughts. "Keep in mind we said no decisions should be made tonight. The size of the house loan, we haven't discussed. Rather than Brad and I throwing a number at you it's more of you being comfortable with the house payment you choose."

Darcy hugged both Marie and Brad. "We don't know how to thank you."

"Then don't thank us. We may have complicated your lives more than you wanted. Any questions before we stop tonight?"

Darcy looked at both Marie and Brad. "How long do we get off for a honeymoon?"

"Sorry Darcy, I can't help you." Brad stated. "You need to speak with a gentleman named Junior, he is your boss. At least he will be your boss for a few more days. Tell him a three week honeymoon would be nice. If he gives you less than two weeks let me know. I can send his sister over to have a personal discussion with him."

"Saying thank you doesn't seem like enough, but I don't know what else to say."

"Thank you is plenty. You guys concentrate on your marriage before you put thought to what you might do. How about next week we all get together here for another dinner and include Darcy's mother in our dinner plans? I think it's time Marlina met the family."

"Mother would love to join us for dinner."

"Once you give some thought to your housing needs. Marie and I would like to hear those thoughts if you wouldn't mind. We own the property to the west of us. If by chance your housing needs and that property were a match to your plans Ray and Susan could enjoy your children as much as they see our children. There would also be room enough to build a cottage similar to what Ray and Susan lives in if your mother wanted to live nearby."

Junior's face appeared angry. "Let me assure you we are not trying to run your lives. Marie and I bought this property for security reasons. Our family can roam around any time day or night and be safe. The boys can go visit their grandparents any time they want without anyone worrying if they will be safe walking over to their house. I visualize you and Darcy becoming financially successful to the point security will be a factor in your lives as well."

"I must admit staying here with my parents has been a great place to live. I'm not familiar with the property next to you. How close would our house be?"

"The property is seventy five to a hundred yards wide and long. About the length of a football field each direction. In other words it is close but not too close."

"For tonight my brain is on overload. I think Darcy and I need to think a few days before making any commitment."

"That is why we keep telling you, take all the time you need. The school system our boys attend is one of the finest schools in the area."

"I don't know Brad. Private schools are expensive. We may not be able to afford to send our children to a private school. Not right away anyway. You are talking about financial numbers I haven't even dreamed about."

Later as Brad and Marie were turning in for the night she hugged him. "You made Junior and Darcy a happy couple tonight. At the same time you have them on mental overload."

"You are wrong, as usual Honey, we made them happy. I'm exhausted so don't squeeze me too hard, and let me sleep as long as I can in the morning." Brad slipped beneath the sheets, and stretched out on his side of the bed facing away from his beautiful wife. "Good night Honey." The silence of the night was disrupted by a strange sound. "I hear somebody rattling around in the kitchen."

"I better go check and see who is in the kitchen. Laura might be getting sick again."

The noise in the kitchen was soon identified. Two little boys were standing on a kitchen chair searching the upper cabinets looking for cookies. "Mom we forgot our milk and cookies before going to bed."

"Don't give me that boys, Laura told me you two had your snack this evening."

"Oh that's right, we ate our cookies earlier. Sorry, mom, we forgot."

"I'll sorry you, scoot to bed. Stay there and go to sleep before your father pays you a visit."

Marie left the house at nine the following morning while Brad waited until noon to drive over to the Ad Palace. He found Carol and Wendy working as usual. Rusty on the other hand was reading a technology book. "Is your computer locked up again?"

"My computer is working fine. I'm trying to read up enough so I understand more about what we are doing. This is a fascinating book. The book is written by a research team of brilliant minds."

"You are getting paid to work not read. I suggest you get busy like the girls are and carry your share of the load, or they may get tired of your face around here."

"I do my share around here. I enhanced three videos yesterday. Ask Carol how many videos she enhanced. She only did two videos yesterday."

"I spent some time with Robin Tilly yesterday discussing future needs. One thing that I wasn't able to check that needs to be checked is who enhances the house videos that sell faster. Starting today, I want each of you to make a list of the house videos and who enhanced them so we can compare your work against one another. Don't be seduced by the illusion of accomplishment when you actually do little work that sells."

Brad's words drew a glare from Rusty and no comment from the girls. He went on into his private office to make a few phone calls. Rusty took the opportunity to whisper at the girls. "Is he a grouch this morning or what?" His comment received no response. "Afraid he might hear you?" Carol turned enough to frown at Rusty, as usual she said nothing.

One of Brad's calls was to Judy in Seattle. "Good afternoon, Anderson Realty."

"Hello Judy, it's me, the lazy guy from the hospital."

"Hi Brad, it's good to hear your voice, you haven't called in forever. How are you feeling?"

"I'm doing okay. I don't have the energy level I once had, but I believe I'm getting stronger each day. These things take time. I've gained part of my weight back, so I'm doing okay. I did sleep in this morning. I just now arrived in the office."

"Be truthful with me, are you following your Doctor's Orders?"

"Of course my dear, I'm not stupid. I'm walking a mile a day on my treadmill. I'm building up to be able to walk two miles a day like the doctor wants. I see my doctor for my monthly checkup tomorrow. If that appointment is okay then I would go six months or maybe a year between checkups. I'm on the fast track to complete health."

"Are you staying relaxed like the doctor told you to, or are you becoming stressed again?"

"I exercise in the morning before I shower. I'm working half days now. When I get home, I'm too tired to exercise. Some nights I feel like going straight to bed. We had a meeting with Marie's family last night at our house that went longer than I expected so I slept in this morning. A couple nights a week we go watch the boys play baseball. It is so hot. How they can stand to play I have no idea. They love playing baseball. Watching them interact with their teammates is wonderful."

"I'm not your doctor, but if your doctor says you are doing okay you need to push yourself to exercise a touch more. Shorten your work day and eliminate the evening meetings. Why create additional work?"

"Lighten up Judy. I didn't call you to get chewed out."

"Why should those of us that care about you lighten up? We want you to make a complete recovery. You are a key component in our success. It is in our best interest to have you healthy. Is Marie near you?"

"No, Marie is over at the C.E. Office working. I'm in my private office, why all the concern if I'm alone or not?"

"Marie said something at the hospital that concerns me. She is blaming herself for your heart problems. She has it in her mind when she hit you with the cutting board in the face and chest. She damaged your heart valves. Everyone told her she was wrong, but I'm not sure she believed any of us."

"I know Marie blames herself for my heart problems. Nurse Ferguson told me she heard you and Marie talking. She also said what you said about Marie causing my problem is highly unlikely. She never said it was impossible either. I was hoping Marie would mention it to me so we could talk it out. She hasn't said one word to me. I keep hoping she will say something."

"Stop being an idiot. Stiffen up your back bone and bring the subject up to her. There is no advantage in avoiding the topic. Your heart problems were from a birth defect. The word birth defect makes me nervous. I made a doctor appointment for Carrie and Kristy. They may have a similar birth defect as you had. They need to be checked out."

"Wow, I hadn't thought about the girls. They do need to be checked out. I might take your advice and talk to Marie. At the same time I could mention you are having the girls hearts checked. You knocked me off my game plan. That isn't what I called about. This was a business call. Remember when we started enhancing house videos for the Anderson Agency and Sam was hesitant to go along with what we were trying to do for you?"

"Please don't tell me our house videos are getting bad again?"

"Oh no your videos are wonderful. So good in fact, I now question if you need the full service the Ad Palace provides. Through my urging the Robin Tilly Agency has pared down twenty five percent on the videos she sends us. The experiment looks good so far. Good enough to convince her to expand an additional ten percent cutback putting her at a full thirty five percent reduction in our services. I think what has happened is by the Ad Palace demanding excellent videos, you agents are looking at the houses in greater detail on your own. You are unknowingly doing much of what we were doing for you in the beginning. Sam is going to find this sudden turn around by me confusing. It's really very simple. You guys are becoming better professionals."

"I like your words of praise, but if we start cutting back as you suggest what becomes of the Ad Palace?"

"The Ad Palace would shrink accordingly or find new clients. No option is off the table."

Brad's words confused Judy. "If you eventually cut all business ties with our agency, our families will see less of one another. Are you saying you don't want to see the girls as much?"

"That is not the idea at all. Of course I want to see the girls. Unfortunately business is leading us in different directions. Then there is the fact I find it difficult to be near you for long periods of time. Our drifting in different directions may be best for everyone in the long run."

"From a business decision we can cut back the twenty five percent in the videos you enhance for us. I do not like the personal words towards me you just stated. I want our girls to grow up knowing you. Think about the girls for a minute they love you and Marie."

"I want to know your girls well too. Life isn't always that easy. Sometimes a person doesn't get everything they want." Brad could hear Judy crying as he started to hang up. Making her cry wasn't his intention. "This is nothing to cry about, it's life. Judy, I have another call coming in. I need to take the call. I'll be in touch soon."

His next call was to Darcy. "Hi Darcy are we still good on our appointment later this evening or have you become busy?"

In a business-like manner, she replied their appointment stood. "We have some difficult issues to discuss meaning our meeting may last longer than you might realize. Our talk needs to happen soon as you have time."

As Brad ended his call Marie walked into the office. "So this is where you are hiding today. I've been trying to call you. Your phone has been busy."

"I'm here, but I'm not hiding. I was making calls rather than going around upsetting people by visiting them personally. Unfortunately I have equal talent for upsetting people over the phone. I spoke to Judy a few minutes ago, trying to explain about the successful cutback in enhanced house videos Robin Tilly is experiencing. I suggested their agency do the same thing. Judy wigged out on me, and accused me of wanting to break all business ties with them. She even accused me of not wanting to see the girls."

"That's not good. What did you tell Judy?"

"I tried my best to tell her that wasn't my reason for calling. She started crying. I ended our conversation because we were getting nowhere. About all I can do is try talking to her another day."

"I should have told you before, but you were in the hospital with for heart problems. I didn't want to add to your stress but Sam's mother has cancer, pancreatic cancer no less. Pancreatic cancer is one of the five most deadly cancers known to mankind. Sam is spending a lot of time with his mother. Judy is trying to carry the complete load of the office herself. She didn't need the stress you put on her today."

"Well damn Honey, why did you hold things from me?" He shouted. "How am I supposed to repair the untimely damage I caused?" Brad pulled his wife close as he kissed her. "I'm sorry Honey. I don't mean to yell at you. Promise me regardless of my health, do not withhold valuable information from me in the future."

"I'll call Judy from home tonight and try calming her down. In a few days you can call her. Tell her you didn't know anything was going on with Sam's mother. When you do call her, choose your words carefully. She may be touchy for some time to come."

"Okay Honey. I have a late appointment with Darcy in a few minutes. I have no idea what she wants to talk about. She asked me to wait until after Sharon leaves the office before going to see her. I'm thinking she may not be totally comfortable with what we want to do for Junior and her. No telling how late I'll be."

As Brad arrived at the C. E. Office for his after hours meeting with Darcy she greeted him with a serious look. She offered him a chair. "You are scaring me Darcy. Where is your normal pretty smile you usually wear so well?"

"Forget my smile, this is a serious talk. No room for smiles today."

"If our talk is about last night when Marie and I offered you financial assistance on buying a house? We are not doing any more for you and Junior than we have done for other people we care about. We are not trying to control your lives. All we want to do is help make your lives easier. Marie and I have had a major amount of help in our lives. Now is the time we want to pass on help to others we care about. That includes you and Junior." She frowned at him. "Tell me what is on your mind."

"What we need to talk about has nothing to do with last night. This talk is all about you." Being nervous Darcy's words came out fast. "You had a bad heart attack. Now you have bounced back fast. Still you are refusing to lead your normal life. No longer is there anything wrong with your heart. You need to get on with life as you were before your heart problems. You can live a fruitful normal life without fear of dying any time soon."

"Easy girl, before my heart attack, everyone thought I was leading a too fast paced life. I was leading a life style that almost put me six feet under. Now you want me to go back, and do the exact same thing that put me down. I have news for you, people are supposed to learn from life's lessons. No matter what you say, or think, I'm going to live a slower paced life."

Darcy shook her head. "I knew you would respond this way. It's my fault I botched our talk already. For lack of a better way of saying it I'm going to be straight forward, and lay it on the line for you. Marie thinks your heart attack was a direct result of her clobbering you with the cutting board a few years ago. She blames herself for your heart valves failing." Brad sat silent, looking at her. "Aren't you going to say anything?"

"I'm aware of Marie's thoughts and her concerns. Others have told me the same thing. You are smart, what would you suggest I do? There are no easy words to change our past. For sure I don't need to make matters worse."

"Now that you have fully recovered you could start by being your normal self. Return to the life you had, but in a slower pace if you want. We all heard the doctor say your problem occurred because of a birth defect of some kind. Tell Marie she isn't at fault for your heart valve failing. Help Marie ease her mind, allow her to see you are okay by acting okay."

"If you remember, I was operated on a second time because one of so called new heart valves the doctors put in my body failed. If one valve failed it is possible the other heart valves could also fail. If I over-exert I might have a second heart attack, a fatal heart attack next time. You and Sharon may not always be around when I need you."

"Your heart valve failure was a fluke. You heard Doctor Akins state they had never experienced a valve replacement failure before. Why would you expect another heart valve failure, you are worrying over nothing."

"First off I have no idea if my new heart valves came from a deceased accident victim, a pig, or if they are artificial valves. I suspect they all came from the same source. The whole batch could easily be defective valves. You have no idea what my future holds."

"Doctor Akins checked the other heart valves when he replaced the faulty heart valve. I didn't want to tell you this, but it looks like I may have to tell you. I made a promise to Marie saying I would not tell you. Now I'm going to break that promise I made to her. Marie came by here the other day before going over to the construction site. This has been her daily routine each day while you were recovering. This particular day she left her purse here. I saw a stack of papers sticking out the top of her purse. I don't know what the papers were for or if they were important. I started thinking about the papers and tried to call Marie only to learn her cell phone was also in her purse. Hoping to catch her before she left the construction site I took Marie her purse."

"That was a nice gesture on your part. I'm sure she appreciated you bringing her purse to her."

"Be quiet and listen. I parked beside Marie's car and when I stepped out with her purse one of the workers told me she was in seeing Evan and they were in, I think it was apartment thirty three, I'm not sure. The door locks hadn't been installed yet so I walked in. Hearing voices I followed the sound to the bedroom. Evan and Marie were embracing until Evan saw me. They weren't having sex. What I saw left me with the impression their actions could easily escalate into improper actions rather quickly. You need to normalize your relations with Marie." Brad remained quiet as he thought over her words. "Women like attention. If you fail to give your wife the attention she deserves, bad things will happen."

"Admittedly I have neglected Marie lately, I have a bad heart. What if I expired during our normal intimate actions, how would Marie feel then? You seem to think life is simple and easy, when it is not. If Marie has a little fling, I probably deserve what I get. As you know I've not been an angel myself."

Brad's excuse angered her. "Hogwash, you don't have a bad heart anymore. You think you have a bad heart. Three months is more than enough time for your body to heal. Do you remember Jim Couch?"

"Of course I remember Jim Couch I'm not stupid. He was your mother's friend in Montana. He was the nice old guy who gave me a tour of the museum when Alice and I visited you and your mother in Montana. I enjoyed his company."

"Jim had two heart attacks during the time he and mother were seeing each other. He was something like sixty five when he had his first heart attack. He bounced back in the saddle very fast. In less than one month he was visiting mother again for her special favors. If you don't understand what special favors are, I'm talking about sex."

"I understand what you are saying. I doubt the old codger had heart valves replaced. They probably cleaned out a blockage, thinned his blood and sent him on his way to do his merry thing."

"He had a serious heart attack. Everyone in town thought Jim was a goner. In less than four weeks he had mother's bed squeaking again. Your doctor has you on blood thinner. The sooner you use your love-stem, the sooner your relationship with Marie will stabilize. "

"Are you sure about Jim's recovery time?" Brad questioned.

"I have two excellent ears, and I'm not a child. I know what the rhythm in the night is when I hear an old bed squeaking. You need to pay more attention to Marie's needs. Women need love and affection. Marie has her needs same as any woman does."

"You are not listening to me Darcy. Marie partially blames herself for my heart attack. If I had another heart attack during or right after pleasuring her. Marie would become a basket case. Our boys would have no parents. Our children could be left with only their nanny to raise them. I don't want my boys growing up the way I did. It's a lousy life. I think waiting a while longer to become intimate is the right thing to do."

"Jim Couch was living proof intimacy won't kill you. I may as well be talking to a tree outside because you are not listening to me."

"What if you are wrong? Then what would you say, oops sorry."

Darcy leaned back in her chair, and drew in a couple deep breaths. "Look in a mirror, and study your face. The chronic dark circles you had before your heart problems are gone. Blood circulation in your body has never been better. There is no reason your penis shouldn't work better than ever. Blood operates that little critter, you know. Here is my advice, if you are truly afraid to risk relations, with Marie. I suggest you go downtown or wherever men go to hire women, and test your heart while you still have a wife?"

"First off, I don't have a little critter. I have a normal critter. Second, I'm not going down to some street corner, and hire a flea bag slut to test my manhood. Those types of women could have cooties or something. After my recent health problems my immune system could be low. No telling what trouble I might get in."

"Then go home, and ease into your relationship with Marie. Pleasure her gently. While you are at it you might exercise more, and keep your mind active in business. Build yourself up emotionally and physically. Deep down you know what I am saying is for your own good. I have one other suggestion, if you are afraid to interact with Marie. Call in a favor. You did two huge favors for a woman in Seattle. Your action resulted in her having two children. It seems to me she could return one tiny little favor to you. I'm telling you, you need help. Don't bother about giving me that phony story about using a clinic to help. You were always in such a hurry. You would never have taken time to spend in a clinic. Judy might be your answer."

"Darcy, you said a lot. I don't know if I like what you said. I'll give you credit, you were brutally honest. I won't say anything to Marie about the subject of our talk. I'll not mention our discussing my lack of intimacy."

CHAPTER 14

In Seattle Sam was pacing the office from one end to the other. Judy stood up to hug him. "I know you are worried about your mother. Pacing back and forth won't help. Go to the hospital, and be with her. A visit would be comforting to you, and your mother."

Tears flooded Sam's eyes. "I can't go to the hospital. I have an appointment in a half hour. I am worried about mother, she is terminally ill. I'm also worried about you, me, and our girls. When mother dies our agency is out of business. You and I will be unemployed. Honey we are in a tough spot."

Judy smiled at her husband. "Have you considered becoming a broker so we can carry on business as usual?"

"I don't have the temperament to become a broker. Training and working with other agents is not my thing. With our girls needing part of your time you can't be a broker. We are going down in flames. There is nothing we can do about it at this time. Eventually we will need to work with a new agency to continue selling Real Estate. Real Estate is all we know. Our livelihood could disappear in a heartbeat. I don't know what we are going to do. We have some money saved but without an income our saving will disappear in a heartbeat. We may need to mortgage our house in order to have money to live on for a short time while we decide what we should do."

"We may take a temporary financial hit, but we are not stupid people. If we use our brains, we can think about what is best for us in the long run. No matter what happens, or when it happens we will survive."

"As I see it, we have no choice, but to work in another agency. Even if Brad were to allow us to hire a broker what do we know about hiring a broker. Some guy could come in here, and clean out what little we have."

"There has to be a broker somewhere we can work with. Try not to worry; we'll work things out when the time comes."

"I see my client coming this way. We need to discuss this more at home later."

Sam left with his client to show a house. He returned an hour later and kicked the door jam. "Those damn people were lookers, not buyers. It was a total waste of my time showing them a house. On my way back to the office, I stopped by the hospital to see mother. She requested no funeral services after she passes away." Judy again stood up to hug her husband. "Can you tell me why a person wouldn't want a funeral?"

"Sam, I wish I had an answer for you, but I have no idea. I'll stop by, and see your mother after work this evening."

"Judy, mother won't know you. Not always does she recognize me."

"Even if she doesn't know me, I want to see your mother."

"When I was showing the house earlier, a wild thought cross my mind. Brad has been having some kind of problem in the office at the Ad Palace. He may not want a new person coming in as a new broker in our agency. How would you feel about me flying down to Vegas and discussing our dilemma with Brad personally?"

"I think that is a good idea Sam. I can easily stay here and man our office. I also can see your mother as much as I can. My visiting her should be some comfort to her even if she doesn't always recognize me."

"Seeing Brad and discussing our dilemma could help us make a proper decision when the time comes. You can't read someone's true feelings over the phone. I'm going over and see mother again. Call Brad and tell him I want to fly down and have a business meeting with them. Because of mother being ill, it will be a fast trip. I can fly down and back the same day."

"I'll call Brad to make sure he has time to see you."

Sam ducked out the door as Judy called Brad's cell phone. Naturally he smiled when his caller ID showed her name. "Good afternoon young lady, to what do I owe the pleasure of your call?"

"Sam asked me to call you. He wants to fly down and have a meeting with you and Marie Thursday. Do you have time in your schedule to see him? He won't take up much of your valuable time. You know Sam's mother is ill. Sam and I will be facing changes in the near future."

"Marie and I always have time for you and Sam. You and the girls should fly down and visit when Sam does."

"Only Sam will be flying down to meet with you. I will be manning our office and visiting his mother. She is not doing well at all. Her cancer is getting the best of her. All signs are pointing to her body shutting down very soon. If she lives another week I'll be surprised."

"I'm so sorry to hear Carmen is slipping away. Cross your fingers and pray. Miracles do happen at times."

"With her passing our office we won't have a broker. Sam doesn't think he has the ability to be a broker. I'm too busy with our girls to be a full-time worker so I can't become the broker. He hopes you can steer us in the right direction." In deep thought Brad failed to answer Judy in a timely manner. "Did I lose you?"

"No, I'm here, I was thinking. How attached are you to living in the Northwest?"

"I'm not sure, what are you thinking?"

"I'm having internal problems in the Ad Palace office. Rusty is becoming a nonproductive entity. I now rate him as a disposable commodity. My preference would be not to replace the ignorant bastard if we boot him out. I have every reason not to replace him, that's part of the reason why we asked agents to cut back on our services. We all have options, if you and Sam were to move to Vegas. You could work with Robin. It might be a great move for everyone."

"Wow, I hadn't thought about our moving to Las Vegas someday. You would like for us to move to Las Vegas?"

"It might be worth considering. Marie would be thrilled. Our families could interact more. Give some thought to moving here."

"Have you talked this idea over with Marie?"

"No I haven't. When you said Carmen was fading away, I just now thought about you and Sam moving to Vegas. The weather conditions might concern Sam. I'm certain he could get use to our dryer warmer weather rather quickly."

"I must admit that thought never crossed our minds. Living in Vegas could be our answer, does Robin need agents?"

"Actually I believe Robin could use a couple new agents. She doesn't know it just yet. Marie's parents are getting ready to retire completely. They haven't told Robin they are planning to retire, but I'm sure they may be talking to her soon."

"Moving to Vegas sounds great to me. I'm not the person to make the final decision on moving to Vegas. Talk it over with Sam when he gets there. With Sam about to lose his mother he is emotionally at a low point in his life. He needs to feel like a man. He should make the decision about our future."

"We will have a long discussion with Sam. It's nice to hear your voice, and I appreciate your call. Not only will we discuss you moving to Vegas when he gets here, but we can discuss in detail every option for your best interest."

"Thank you for suggesting we move to Vegas. You mentioned Rusty being a problem. What is he doing that irritates you so much?"

"Every breath he draws irritate me."

"Be specific, what is he doing to upset you."

"Rusty continues to mouth off about me being the father of your girls. Everyone else is willing to let bygones be bygones. If that's not bad enough he isn't carrying his share of the workload in the Ad Palace. He has actually accused me of having an affair here in Vegas. What he saw thinking it was me, was Junior and Darcy embracing. They embrace because they are planning to get married."

"You need to do something about shutting Rusty up. Put super glue on his lips. He shouldn't be allowed to continue to meddle in something we did years ago. It's not his business. We are all moving on with our lives best we can."

"When I had my heart attack, and was rushed to the hospital he mouthed off without knowing what was wrong with me. He said Marie probably caught me having another affair. He was thinking she retaliated against me again by beating me within an inch of my life again. I've had enough of Rusty's comments. At the earliest possible moment he is history. I'll take care of Rusty soon as I can. Tell Sam whenever you get to Vegas; we'll make as much time as he needs to be certain we get his every concern covered. Marie and I can meet with him any time of day. Call us and we'll pick him up at the airport. If we are lucky we can have lunch and dinner together."

With Judy's words to use super glue on Rusty's lips he knew her words had merit. He had to silence Rusty before releasing him.

After the boys were in bed he told Marie about his conversation with Judy. "Sam is coming to Vegas in hopes of having a serious conversation with us. I'm thinking Sam might be more at ease if you join us at our meeting. If Judy is correct Sam's mother is nearing the end of her life." Brad went on to explain with the loss of Sam's mother the Anderson Realty Agency will be without a broker and soon be out of business. "Judy is busy with their girls and Sam doesn't want the responsibility of being a broker. He feels they are in a real bind. What would you think about asking them to move to Las Vegas and work under Robin Tilly?"

"To have Judy and her family living near us would be a dream of a lifetime. I would love to have Sam and Judy's family living near us. Our families could interact more. Simple things like evening barbecues together would be wonderful."

The following day Judy called to tell Brad Sam's planned meeting will be delayed. Sam had a pressing issue pop up. He has a meeting with his mother's doctors. "I understand Sam needs to do what he knows is right. Call when things settle down. We are available anytime."

Brad's thoughts turned as to how to show Marie more attention, and still be cautious about his own health. On his way home he rented a family movie to watch during the evening. He stretched a few fluffy blankets on the plush carpet. In doing so he, Marie, and the boys, could all watch the movie cuddled together. Lying behind Marie he wrapped her in his arms. The boys snuggled against her from the front side. Cozy and comfortable the family watched the movie. At the end of the movie it was the boy's bedtime. Once the boys were tucked in for the night, Brad switched the television back to the Lifetime channel. He and Marie could continue to lay cozy together. Minutes later both were sound asleep on the floor in the family room. Laura checked on them. Looking comfortable she left them sleeping where they were and went on to her room.

Sam's meeting with Brad was rescheduled for Friday. Things seemed fine except Sam failed to notify anyone about his arrival time. He arrived at the Ad Palace by taxi. Carol and Rusty were out to lunch. Wendy greeted him with a smile. "Hi Wendy, I'm meeting Brad here in the private office in a few minutes. I should have called them earlier but I didn't want them waiting on me. I spoke to Marie. They should be here in a half hour. If you don't mind me using Brad's office, I might catch a short nap?"

"Go right in and make yourself comfortable. I'm on the phone with our internet people."

"Thank you Wendy."

Wendy forgot about Sam being in the private office and unfortunately Sam left the private office door open to the point it wasn't a private office. When Carol and Rusty returned Wendy dashed out for her lunch break. "Finally your mother is gone, we can talk. Do you believe the nerve Brad has?"

"Rusty, I keep telling you this is none of our business. What happened between Brad and Judy was almost ten years ago, let it go."

"I can't believe anyone who had an affair with his wife's best friend, another man's wife no less is planning to invite them to join the Realty Staff here in Vegas. He wants those two girls he created during the affair to be near him. What a slim-ball controlling bastard Brad is."Sam couldn't believe his ears as he continued to listen.

"You know he is going to fire you if you keep talking about him helping Judy bear children. Brad impregnating Judy was an unusual situation that happened long ago, well before we knew him. He isn't the same person today. He isn't bothering Judy, the girls, or Sam. Sam is a good father to the girls. He treats them as his own. Shut your mouth and leave the past in the past or Brad will fire you."

"If he isn't the same person tell me why he wants the Anderson's to move to Vegas and work with Robin Tilly?" Carol refused to answer his question. "I'll tell you why, he wants Judy and his girls to be near him." Again Carol ignored his question. "I can't see how anyone can keep a secret that big quiet forever. I'm surprised Sam didn't ask questions when Carry came up as Johnnie's bone marrow match. For me that would have been red flag number one. I would have been checking things out."

"Let it go Rusty. Sam is coming to meet Brad and Marie this afternoon."

"It wouldn't surprise me if Brad and Judy are still fooling around when he gets a chance to be near her. I bet when they were at the Oregon Beach and he was stuck here trying to buy the medical buildings it was ripping out his guts. If you remember when Judy called and asked why he wasn't at the beach he rescinded the offer on the medical building and flew directly there. It wasn't Marie asking him to hurry to the beach it was Judy. Don't try telling me she wasn't anxious for a little action from the unfaithful bastard."

"I see mother coming back with Brad and Marie so shut your mouth while you still can. If mother or Brad hears one word you are spouting you will be fired."

Sam sat shaking inside from the news he just overheard. Anger raged in his mind he wanted to kill Brad. At the same time he needed the bastard's advice. Dealing with his personal feelings could and would occur later.

When Brad and Marie arrived Wendy informed them Sam was napping in Brad's private office. Wendy's words startled Rusty and Judy.

Brad and Marie entered the office as quiet as possible. Seeing Sam awake, Marie gave him a hug. Sam settled for a small handshake from bad-ass Brad. Both felt Sam's body quivering. They passed his actions off as nerves related to his ill mother. "Make sure the door is closed Honey. It closes rather hard."

Brad paused until Marie checked the door. "We don't need Rusty's big ears hearing our conversation." He then turned his attention back to Sam. "I had a brief conversation with Judy a few days ago. She called about your concerns for your agency's future. Marie and I are saddened to hear about your mother's failing health. Losing a parent is extremely difficult. Whatever you and Judy decide to do, Marie and I will support you a hundred percent any way we can." There was a brief mutual silence. "Sam, Marie and I have been reexamining our future. She and I spoke about cutting back in what the Ad Palace does far as enhancing house videos. Part of the reason we are considering cutting back is we have a disgruntled employee who keeps shooting his mouth off about things that doesn't concern him. He will be dismissed at the end of the month."

Sam's shaky hand wiped his face. "Everyone has problems. Judy and I won't have a brokerage much longer. The agency is all but folded now. We have two house sales to finish up and we are closing the office. If the State Licensing Office knew our situation, they would close us down now until we get a broker in the office. Our choices are limited." The more Sam looked at Brad the sicker to his stomach he became.

"I know you are upset Sam. This might not be the best time to make this offer. Here in Vegas Robin Tilly will soon have room for two new agents in her brokerage. If you moved to Vegas we could drop disgruntled Rusty and still enhance all the house videos the Tilly Agency needs. If you choose to remain in Seattle we will continue to do the best we can for your agency. We could also entertain you moving to a new agency, if the agency was not huge. We are open to any and all ideas you have."

I ought to kill your rotten ass, Sam thought as he sat dead quiet giving Marie the option she needed to say something. He tried to hide his emotion when in reality he wanted to reach out and strangle Brad with his bare hands. Then he remembered how easily Brad had killed people in the past. The intruder years ago and motorcycle gang member recently. It would take great caution and planning to dispose of Brad. Revenge could come later when Brad least expected it. His having a long standing affair with Judy and passing Carrie and Kristy off as Sam's children was too much for Sam to accept.

Marie finally touched Sam's arm. "This isn't something you need to decide today. Talk it over with Judy, and when you are ready to do something we can go from there."

Sam rotated his neck. "I'm not feeling well, I think I better go get a room somewhere and lie down for a few hours. I'm really woozy."

Marie gripped his arm tighter. "I'll run you out to our house you can lay down there until you feel better. There is no need to try flying home when you don't feel well."

"Thank you Marie. I better not go to your house. I may have picked up a flu bug on the Airplane. I don't want to get your family sick. I'll get a room and sack out for a few hours before I return to Seattle. With mother being sick, I've not been resting well so it's no wonder I picked up something. One thing for sure I don't feel well."

"Honey run Sam down to Caesars and get him a nice room I have an appointment with Evan Thomas and your brother in a half hour, or I would take him there myself. Put his room and all his needs on our credit card."

Marie was more than happy to run Sam over to Caesars and walk him to his room. "If you need anything at all don't hesitate to call my cell number." He wanted to scream at Marie to get him a pistol, a big frigging pistol to kill her husband, but he couldn't. "Rest is what I need. I don't think you can help me in that department." Marie retrieved a damp washcloth to put on Sam's forehead. "You are not used to the heat here. You may be dehydrated. I'll dash down and get you a sports drink. I'll only be gone a few minutes."

When Marie returned Sam told her he was feeling some better. "Drink this sports drink and wait until morning to fly home. If you need anything else call room service or me. I'll dash back and get what you need. You have my cellphone number."

"Thank you Marie, I'll be fine. Be sure and thank Brad for all your suggestions."

Sam waited fifteen minutes after Marie left before leaving his room. He taxied straight up to Freemont Street. From there he walked two blocks west before turning north. In a cautious manner he looked for anyone looking like a potential gang member. Fourteen blocks later the sun began to set. Sam began to worry if he was safe as he turned west again. A block and a half later he passed an alley with five young Hispanic individuals. Sam held a hundred dollar bill straight in the air. "I'm looking for information."

One young man step forward and snatched the bill from Sam's hand. "Hey man how may I be of service to you?"

"I need a hand gun, a small easy to conceal hand gun that packs a punch. I need it for a special job. A gun I can acquire that can't be traced back to me."

The young Hispanic looked at him from top to bottom. "Are you a cop?" He asked.

"I'm far from being a cop. Some slick-ass dude has been screwing my wife, he knocked her up. He needs his family jewels shot off. Can you help me or not, all I need is a simple yes or no."

"Relax man, we're cool. What kind a distance are we expecting this upcoming event to happen?"

Sam pictured in his mind the parking lot at the Ad Palace. The trash bin was fifty to seventy feet from the door and Brad's parking spot was not more than twenty five feet from the large trash dumpster. Set up proper Brad would be walking almost straight at him. "Thirty feet, thirty five feet tops."

"How soon do you need this instrument of joy?" The punk asked.

"Tonight would be best, tomorrow at the latest. I'm leaving for Seattle very soon."

"Shit man, your urgent request will cost extra, special shipping and handling charges. Urgent things cost money."

"I'm staying at Caesars." Sam gave the young man his room number. "There are five more notes like the bill I gave you if you can deliver. If I haven't heard from you by tomorrow night I'm leaving town. The weapon needs to be loaded. I'm in room three twenty one."

"Shit no man, room service could be dangerous. It's a perfect place for a police sting. I'll call and give you direction on where we'll make the exchange in the parking lot when I get what you need. No way am I going to your room, shit no."

"Alright, I'll be waiting your call." Sam turned and walked away hoping he wouldn't get mugged and lose the five hundred dollars he carried as he left. Once out of sight from the five young Hispanics Sam began to jog hoping to clear the area before total darkness set in. This was not the time to hang around and get mugged. Sweat poured from his body drenching the clothes he was wearing. Eventually he taxied back to his room. Sam was still breathing heavy when he returned to his room. Step one was complete."

Seconds later Marie knocked on his door. She was astonished at how much he had been sweating. "Oh my Lord Sam, you are really sick. I should get a doctor up here or let me take you to the emergency room at the hospital."

"I'm actually doing better, my fever broke. Could I impose on you to buy me a set of clean clothes somewhere? I don't need much."

"Certainly, I'll go see what they have in the Mall upstairs. I won't be gone long."

"I hate to impose on you, but I'll never be able to wear these sweaty clothes on the plane going home."

"Don't be silly Sam. You are not imposing on me. You are a valued friend."

Thirty minutes later Marie returned bringing Sam a casual set of clothes. He greeted her at the door wearing a thin short robe. "My shower refreshed me. Hand me the sales slip. I'll send you a check for the clothes when I get home."

"You will do no such thing Sam. Your clothes are a gift. We hope you are okay to fly home in the morning. Be sure and let us know if something happens to your mother so we can attend the services."

Sam's eyes instantly looked down. "Mother requested no services for her passing. We won't be having a formal memorial for her."

"Oh good heavens your mother's request is rather unusual." Marie stepped forward enough to give Sam a generous hug. "Keep us posted about your mother's condition. Brad and I will miss her."

"Judy or I will call when something happens. Mother always had strange ways, thanks again Marie, bye." Soon as Marie left he sat waiting for his gun call. To meet the gun guy from the ally he needed to wear his same clothes.

Two AM Sam cell phone rang. "Use the main entrance, walk towards the Strip, you will meet a friend of mine wearing a dark Tee Shirt. He will point where you go to meet me. We exchange items without stopping to talk. Your item is fully equipped. Be careful when you handle it, don't drop it. You might wake up the neighborhood. Good luck with you adventure. For a slight fee, say two thousand. I could handle your adventure for you."

Following instructions Sam was soon the owner of a 22 caliber black pistol. Back in the hotel room he checked the small revolver. He had hoped for a 38 Special or a 9mm. Still he knew at close range the 22 caliber pistol would do the job. Brad would never again fool around with his wife. Now it all came down to timing. He needed to convince Judy to move to Vegas, and for Brad to fire Rusty. His plan was to shoot Brad, and let Rusty take the heat for the killing him. Praying someone wouldn't find his pistol he hid the weapon in the alley behind a loose brick on the building. During his next visit to Vegas killing Brad should be easy. He flew home feeling happy.

A couple days later as Brad made his rounds he found Junior in the office with Darcy and Sharon. "Hi guys, how are things going today?"

"We are doing well." Junior answered.

"Sharon, how do you like your new apartment?"

"Having a nice apartment so close to my work has made my life so much easier. I'll be eternally grateful to you. My motorized wheelchair scoots back and forth with ease."

"I'm glad to hear you are comfortable living nearby. Keep in mind because you live close to work, you need to separate your off time, and your work time. If need be remind people you clock out at five. Junior, Darcy, I'm glad I caught you both. Junior your future wife gave me a lecture the other day about getting back to normal. Her words made my brain kick back in gear. You guys are getting married this weekend and going on your honeymoon. When you get back I want to start our final stage of apartment building. You might call Evan Thomas and see how old man Banister is doing and see when they are ready to start a new construction project. It's fine by me if Evan is the crew leader again."

Darcy couldn't remain quiet. "Are you sure you want Evan as the construction crew leader again? He made that hundred thousand dollar mistake pouring the floor too soon on your last project?"

"Evan is an okay guy, he learned a lot on that job. I doubt he will make the same mistake twice. One would certainly hope not anyway." Brad realized Darcy felt leaving Evan in a position Marie might be near him was an error. "He is an honest guy. I think he will do a nice job for us again."

"It's your call Brad; I was thinking you might want to try someone new to be your construction leader this time. You know a foreman with more experience, someone perhaps slightly older?"

Junior grinned. "You are not a person to sit still. What are you planning to do once the third phase of apartment building is complete and you run out of scheduled projects?"

"Funny you should ask. I do have other ideas kicking around in my head. I'm not willing to share those ideas with anyone just yet. I need to consult with my marital and business partner before sharing my future ideas. I have a call to make and then I'll be out of your hair." After making his call he placed his phone on the desk where Darcy could see him put it down.

Darcy had caught his signal as he expected, after he walked outside to leave she pretended to see his phone. "That's Brad's phone, I better run it out to him. He will need his phone a half mile down the street."

Brad played it cool. "Why thank you, how careless of me. Don't say it girl, after what you told me about Evan and Marie you think I'm a fool for keeping him around where Marie will be working near him."

"The thought did cross my mind. It could be dangerous for you and Marie, why take the chance when you don't need to?"

"This is a big city with lots of meeting places. If they are having an affair it doesn't matter where it happens. Most affairs run their course, and end before long and considering my checkered past, I have little to complain about."

"I don't understand your thoughts at all. Am I to assume you and Marie are getting along better at home? You must expect things between the two of you will smooth out soon?"

"We have a ways to go but I believe we are leaning in the right direction when it comes to our physical needs. Progress comes in small steps. I'm still being careful about what I do. I have no intention of over exerting myself."

"If that is the case I wish you luck, and I'll see you tomorrow when you make your daily rounds. It's always nice to see your smiling face."

"Darcy I've been thinking. Sharon is a good helper, why don't you take the next few days off and get ready for your wedding?"

Her eyes lit up. "Are you serious, you wouldn't mind if I take off a few extra days before my wedding?"

"Of course not, our company will continue to pay you while you take a few extra days off. Marie and I can help Sharon if she starts getting way behind."

"Count me absent. I do have a lot of things to do before I'm ready to get married. If I thought Ray wasn't watching. I would give you a big hug for giving me extra time off. You are the best boss a person could ever have. How about giving me a high five?"

She did get her high five. "I can collect a hug at your wedding. Men are allowed to hug the bride at her wedding."

After telling Junior and Sharon what Brad said about her taking time off she dashed on home. Once at home Darcy's thoughts returned to Brad and Marie. If she understood him correctly he indicated they were not yet back to a full physical relationship. With her and Ray's wedding and honeymoon there could be a three week span of time before she could question Brad on the matter again. Knowing a lot can happen in three weeks. Darcy took her cell phone outside to call Judy. "Hi, do you have a few minutes to talk."

"Certainly Darcy, I always have time for you. What is on your mind?"

"For starters Ray and I are getting married this coming weekend. We would like to invite your family to join our small wedding party. We are getting married in the same Chapel Brad and Marie was married in."

"Does your invitation include my girls?"

"Absolutely your darling little girls are invited to our wedding. Johnnie and Jimmy will be at our wedding too. Our wedding will be a very small intimate event. We can all have dinner together the night before."

"The girls and I would love to attend your wedding. With Sam's mother gravely ill he won't leave her side long enough to attend a wedding anywhere."

"I have one other reason for calling you. Are you where you can talk without others listening?" Darcy inquired.

"I'm alone in the office. You sound serious Darcy. What is it you want to ask me?"

"I'm worried about Brad and Marie's relationship." Darcy went on to relay the complete story about Brad being reluctant to pleasure Marie because of his heart problems. "I fear Marie was on the verge of having an affair.

"Are you sure Marie is considering having an affair?"

"I know Marie well. I'm almost certain. She may be having an affair as we speak."

"Wow Darcy, this could be serious." She now had Judy's full attention. "Brad and I caused enough turmoil in their marriage. They don't need their marriage rocked more than it already has been rocked."

"I believe there is someone who could help Brad and Marie."

"If you are you suggesting counseling, Brad would never go for counseling. After killing the intruder years ago he tried counseling. In fact both he and his first wife, Alice tried counseling. Counseling didn't help."

"Darcy, I'm not suggesting counseling. I'm suggesting you personally help Brad."

"What is it you think I can do?"

"His fear is he will die if he becomes intimate with Marie. As you know Marie already blames herself for his heart problems. If he were to die trying to pleasure her, he thinks it would destroy her and leave his boys alone. If you were to prove intimacy was okay for him, he would realize the danger of dying while being intimate with Marie is gone. He once did you favors. Now it's your turn to pay a favor back to Brad."

"Darcy, how can you ask me to do such a thing? The favors you are talking about were years ago when we were young and stupid. I can't do this."

"How do a few years make any difference? He needs your help now same as you needed his help all those years ago. I suggested he go downtown and pick up a girl at one of our hotels. He said no to my idea before reciting all the reasons you probably used to gain his help rather than using a stranger for your needs"

"Was this Brad's idea for you to call me?"

"Heavens no, he would kill me if he knew I was suggesting you become intimate with him again."

"You said my interaction could help them. How would I be helping Marie, an affair never helps the spouse?"

"In this case, I believe a one-time action would help. You owe these people."

"I don't use birth control. I'm sorry I just can't do what you are asking of me."

"Okay Judy, I understand, you being reluctant. I'll be looking forward to seeing you and the girls at our wedding, and tell Sam hello for us."

Failing to convince Judy she should help Brad was a setback in Darcy's way of thinking. She needed a different approach to help her friends. Junior walked in catching her lost in thought. He touched her shoulder. "Hi Honey, thinking about our wedding night?"

"I called Judy, she and the girls are coming down to join us for our wedding."

"Wonderful. What about Sam, is he coming with them?"

"Sam's mother is ill. He is unable to attend our wedding. He needs to remain near his mother and man their office while Judy and the girls are in Vegas."

"I forgot about his mother being ill."

CHAPTER 15

Sam waited until three days before Junior and Darcy's wedding to commit his family moving to Vegas. The news thrilled Judy. Before long Judy would once again live near her long-tine friend. Sam instantly called Marie. "Marie, tell Brad he can eliminate Rusty any day he chooses. We will be moving to Vegas."

"Sam, your words will be music to his ears."

"I'm sure he will be pleased. He likes people to make a decision. I've made my decision as to what I need to do to protect my family and secure our future. I'll never be able to thank you enough for giving me the opportunity to do what is best for my family."

After conversing with Sam, Marie immediately called Brad to relay Sam's information to him. "Thanks for the good news Honey, this means I will be home late this evening. I need to create a special subliminal message for my dear friend Rusty. Once he walks out the office door tomorrow he will never remember what he did while working for us. In addition he will not remember my shame I brought down on everyone. He will be a burger flipper again or looking for a hand out elsewhere. While I'm at it he may as well leave Carol. Their relationship is going nowhere. According to Wendy they fight constantly."

"Do what you have to do to rid us of Rusty, everyone will be better off. We don't need Mr. Big Mouth spilling his guts to Sam some day when we least expect it."

That weekend Sam surprised everyone when he showed up with Judy and their girls for Junior and Darcy's wedding. The wedding was flawless. Everyone cheered as the minister announced Junior could kiss his new bride. "Isn't she beautiful?" Carrie's young voice echoed in the chapel. "I'm getting married someday." She added.

The honeymooners flew off to Hawaii the following morning. Sam flew home leaving Judy and the girls in Vegas. Marie and Judy planned to go house hunting for the Anderson's. This left Brad to keep an eye on business.

Early Tuesday afternoon Sam quietly flew back to Vegas using a false ID he acquired in Seattle. In Vegas he rented a car, and parked in Caesars parking lot. Walking casually so people would not see him acting funny he strolled back to the alley behind Caesars where he hid his 22 revolver. Luck was with him, the weapon was where he left it wedged between two broken blocks. From there he drove past the Ad Palace hoping Brad's car would be there. Wintertime's short daylight hours played into Sam's hands as he found Brad's car at the Ad Palace. He parked a hundred yards away where he could observe Brad's parked car hoping Brad stayed in the office until it became full darkness.

Twenty minutes after sunset Sam began to walk towards the office. He checked to be certain other people were not around before slipping behind the dumpster where he sat on an old wood box crate. He drew the hammer back on the tiny pistol so when Brad appeared the only sound he would hear would be the blast of the muzzle fire.

Minutes seemed like hours as he waited for his prey. Brad suddenly came walking out much faster than Sam expected. He raised the weapon and fired, the bullet grazed Brad's head spinning him around and falling face down on the pavement. Fast as possible Sam pumped five additional bullets into his prone body before running off in the darkness. Not to draw attention to himself he drove exceptionally careful leaving the area. Some ten blocks away he parked long enough to strip off the dark coveralls he was wearing over his street clothes and wiped the pistol clean of his prints before ditching the weapon near where he made contact with the gang members before.

By the time Sam cruised back past the crime scene on his way to the airport he saw a massive amount of police vehicles. Seconds later he met an ambulance screaming towards the scene. "Slow down guys, you are too late. All you are getting tonight is a corpse." He said out loud as he laughed. He dashed back to the airport to catch a charter flight to Seattle. Two and a half hours later he was safe in Seattle. Rather than go home he went straight to the hospital to check on his mother. He entered the hospital through the rear door.

Sam stopped at the nurse's station to ask how his mother was doing before going into her room. "Mr. Anderson your mother slipped into a comma late today. We tried to call you."

"I popped in and out several times today. Trying to work and spend time with mother is keeping me hopping. I was tied up with business more than I expected. I'm closing our reality office."

"I'm sorry Mr. Anderson to inform you your mother may not make it through the night. Her body appears to be shutting down very quickly."

Sam lowered his head showing great concern. "May I stay with her?"

"Yes of course you may stay with your mother."

Minutes later, Sam was informed he had a phone call at the nurse's station. "Mrs. Anderson is on the phone."

"Hi Honey, how was your house hunting going?"

"Brad's been shot!" Judy screamed into the phone. "He was shot multiple times."

"What do you mean Brad's been shot, when, where, why was he shot?"

"Brad was gunned down leaving the Ad Palace Office this evening. We think Rusty Cramer shot him. Brad isn't dead but he is in critical condition. He lost a lot of blood. He was shot multiple times." She repeated.

"Did you say they think Rusty shot him, why would Rusty shoot Brad?" Sam asked trying to help bolster his own innocence. "Was anyone with Brad when he was shot?"

"They don't know for sure who shot him. He was alone and his wallet still contained money so it wasn't a robbery. Recently Brad fired Rusty. He looks to be the key suspect. The police are looking to question him. So far they have not located him."

"Geez Honey, this is terrible. I would fly straight to Vegas but mother isn't expected to live through the night, she looks bad. She slipped into a comma last night. I've been with her thirty straight hours."

"Oh geez Sam, I don't know what I should do. Should I fly home and be with you, or should I stay here in Vegas with Marie."

"There is nothing you can do here. Stay with Marie, she can use all the support she can get. If mother passes away, I'll take care of her arrangements. What little arrangements there are to do? After that I can call you and see if I need to fly to Vegas to be with you. Did Brad see who shot him?"

"He has been unconscious since being shot. It was after dark when the incident happened. Police doubt he saw anything, but we can hope he saw who shot him. One bullet grazed his head leading doctors to believe he may never remember anything about the incident."

"That's unfortunate. Then again it may be best he doesn't remember anything. I better get back to mother. I don't want her passing away when nobody is with her."

"I hate leaving you at a time when your mother is dying. Call me if anything happens with your mother. I'll call you if anything happens here in Vegas. If Brad should show improvement by morning, I may fly home tomorrow."

Sam sat beside his mother's hospital bed in the darkness wishing he wasn't alone. Judy should be with him not visiting in Vegas near her wounded soon to be dead lover. No man can live with six bullets in his body. Maybe it's just as good Judy was near him. Watching her lover die a slow agonizing death should make a big impact on his wife and make her behave in the future.

Sam realized a miracle couldn't save his mother from certain death. Life was being sucked out of her with each breath. Her body was worn out. Throughout the night each hour of darkness passed slowly. Carmen was a good woman who deserved to live. Life isn't fair; Brad was the person deserving to die. Instead he is clinging to life with a slim chance to recover. Shortly after midnight Sam heard a sound, a sound much different than any sound he ever heard before. Yet he knew the sound, it was his mother's death rattle. Without being told he knew she was gone. A slow quiver consumed his body. Tears flooded from his eyes as he pushed the call button causing two nurses to answer the call. "I think mother passed away." He said wiping tears from his eyes.

The blonde nurse confirmed what he already knew, and covered Mrs. Anderson's face with the sheet. Tears continued flooding Sam's eyes as he handed the nurse his mother's hand written note instructing a certain mortuary be called. "These are the people in charge of mother's remains. She is to be cremated and her ashes flown over Puget Sound to be spread by air. She requested no funeral services of any kind and she did not want her ashes spread from a boat."

His mother's death hit Sam hard. He went straight to the nearest bar trying to drown the sorrow before closing time. With each swallow anger grew within. After four quick drinks containing Vodka he weaved on home somewhat relieved that his mother's horrible ordeal was over. At last she was now pain free. That only left Brad for him to worry about. He wanted Brad dead as his mother.

Exhausted, he staggered into the house where Emily came to greet him. "Welcome home Mr. Anderson, it's been quiet around here with everyone gone." She realized he had been drinking. "I'm afraid to ask but how is your mother doing?"

"Ma, my mother is at peace, she, she slipped away just after midnight. I, I, I've been with her every minute this past week. She, she was in a comma the last forty eight hours. Her long ordeal and suffering are over."

As Emily hugged Sam she could smell alcohol on his breath. "I'm sorry about your mother; she was such a wonderful woman. Her passing ends her vicious pain you were describing. Will Mrs. Anderson be returning from Vegas to help with the funeral arrangements?"

"Na, no, mother requested na, no, funeral services when she passed away." He slurred his words enough Emily sat a cup of coffee before him."Ma, mother chose cremation and hired someone else to spread her ashes. The, there is nothing for Ja, Judy or me to do, I feel helpless." Sam staggered slightly as he turned to look at his coffee.

"I'm sorry Sam, how can a person go through a grieving process if there are no memorial services for the family to attend?" Emily drew in a breath before continuing her conversation. "I shouldn't say anything, but it's Mrs. Anderson's duty to be with you in a time of loss. She shouldn't be spending her time in Vegas with Mrs. Collins. Everyone needs comforting when they lose a loved one. You shouldn't be alone at a time like this. Drink your coffee, and then take a shower. You will feel better."

Sam refused to shower. Over the next hour the coffee began to sober Sam enough he could talk better. "Judy and I talked about mother getting weaker. There isn't anything Judy can do if she were here. She went down to Vegas for Darcy and Junior's wedding and now she is there comforting Marie because Butt-head Brad, was shot yesterday."

"Oh my stars, was he killed."

"Judy said he is in the hospital in critical condition, I think. She didn't call last night or today so I assume his status hasn't changed. I hate to call Judy and upset her about mother passing away in the middle of the night. I'll call her in the morning. I would rather go to bed except the idea of being alone scares me."

Again Emily hugged him. "You are still unsteady on your feet. Let me help you to your room. Shower and sleep will help you enough to call Judy later."

Sam thought about how Judy had cheated on him, and how he wished he had the nerve to take Emily to bed and ravish her body. For an older woman she remained a nice looking woman."You are very observant. I better take a quick shower before getting in bed, if I can stand."

She remained near enough that Sam pulled her close for a generous hug. "Thanks for being here. I haven't showered or changed clothes for three days I must smell terrible."

Sam finished his sentence but failed to move. She misread his alcohol stupor as mostly him being tired. "Come along, I'll help you to your room and turn down your bed. You shouldn't have stopped for a drink on your way home. Tired as you are the drink took a heavy toll on you."

"You are a mind reader. I had a few drinks on my way home. I could use help with my shower before getting into bed. I can't shower, I couldn't stand alone. I haven't showered in three days. I must smell raunchy."

She thought for a few seconds. "Forget showering, go to bed. You need to sleep off your excess drinking. Shower when you wake up. I can change your bedding tomorrow. Sleep in your clothes if you want."

"No, Judy wouldn't like me going to bed smelling like this. I better shower first."

She guided him to his bedside. "Stand there while I turn down your bed." Except for Sam's shoes she pushed him in bed fully dressed. He tried to pull her in bed with him. "No, we are not going to do what you are thinking."

Sam cursed himself after she excited his bedroom. His unfaithful wife managed to carry on an affair for years yet he couldn't get Emily to comfort him one damn night. The night his mother died. He rolled out of bed and stripped off his clothes before taking a shower.

Emily heard him showering and wondered if he was going to be okay showering alone. She returned and stood outside his bedroom door where she could hear if he were to fall. After giving him ample time to dry off and get in bed, she tapped lightly on the door as she entered his bedroom for a brief word. She found Sam sitting naked on the edge of the bed. "You should call Mrs. Anderson or let me call her. She needs to be at your side for strength. Say the word and I will call her for you."

"With mother's death we no longer have a realty agency." He mumbled. "Judy and I are no longer employed. We have no income and only four months of savings to live on while we try to rebuild our lives. We may be forced to sell this house. I've never felt so helpless in my life."

Laura stepped closer and placed her hands on his shoulders. "Try not to worry; things will work out for you and Mrs. Anderson. Lie down and I'll cover you up. Right now you need to sleep. Will you allow me to call her?"

"Judy is working on important business. Leave her alone, she is trying to salvage our careers. We need help finding another brokerage or we may need to borrow money from Dumb-ass Brad and his stupid wife. Of all times he goes and gets shot. He too may be dead by now. Without income we may wind up moving to Vegas and selling Real Estate there. We can't spend money for her to come home to comfort me and go back. You are here, you can comfort me."

She felt the rush of cool air as he opened her robe. "Mr. Anderson, get a hold of your emotions and stop groping at me. You have had too much to drink."

He ripped open her robe as he yanked her bare breasts to him for a violent kiss. A split second later she screamed before being slapped hard across the face. He angrily ripped her robe off Emily's trembling body. Women are disgraceful, you parade around in skimpy clothing, or sexy robes tantalizing men. When we react, you balk at giving us your affection."

"Stop it; you have had too much to drink. Get in bed and sleep it off." He brushed her hair back causing Emily to jerk her head back. In turn her sagging breasts began to sway before him. "Don't, you are hurting me." She tried to push his hands away. Still he grasped a breast in each hand and leaned forward to kiss them. She wanted to scream, but was afraid he would slap her harder than before. Her cheek still stung from his first violent slap. In vain she prayed he would pass out from his alcohol consumption before something serious could happen. She tried to push him away.

He continued to, mercifully nuzzle her breasts. "Mr. Anderson please let me go." She begged for her safety in place of kicking and scratching hoping to talk Sam out of his lustful ideas. Her quivering body froze in place as he ripped away her panties. "Please, I beg you don't do this to me." Her begging words were all in vain. He quickly had her naked body lying crosswise on bed. His manhood stood at attention. "Please don't rape me." She begged.

The word rape enraged him. "Shut up bitch, I'm not raping you. We are friends, good friends. I love you." He proceeded to slap the hell out of her before ravaging her body. Emily sobbed her heart out begging for him to stop. "Stop crying, you have needed a man's touch for a long time." He mumbled seconds before he passed out.

She staggered out to the hall bathroom to shower. She scrubbed her body hard trying to wash off the stench and filth of Sam. The poor girl scrubbed her skin raw as he lay sleeping. Sam woke around eleven the following day to find Emily loading the last of her belonging in her car. "What are you doing?"

She snatched a butter knife off the counter to point at him. "I'm leaving."

Sam stepped towards her. "Why are you leaving?"

She slammed the small knife down to grab a butcher knife with a twelve inch blade. "You raped me; I'll cut your throat and decapitate your manhood before you ever touch me again."

"I didn't rape you last night, we made love. You wanted me to make love to you."

"Get out of my way or I will cut you." She warned swinging the knife about. "Move, get out of my way."

"Emily please, I never meant to hurt you. Let me give you some money."

"I don't want money or anything else from you. All I want is out of this house. You are an animal. You will never touch me again."

Sam eased back a step. "Don't go telling people I raped you. We both know I didn't rape you. A rumor saying I raped you could destroy my life. Saying I raped you would label me a sex predator when I have done nothing except what you wanted. Don't destroy me. I'll not let you do that to me. I only responded to your actions."

Flashing the butcher knife back and forth she slowly backed out the front door. "Don't try stopping me. I'm serious I will cut you to ribbons. I should kill you for hurting me." As he stepped closer she slashed the big knife through the air. "Get back!"

"Put that knife down before the neighbors see you. Think about what you are saying. Rapists don't leave their victims alive to testify against them. I never raped you, or you would be dead. Please don't go. Give me a chance. I'll make it up to you."

Try as he might Sam could not persuade Emily to stay. He stood in the doorway wondering what he should do."

To be safe he called the police and reporting he fired Emily for stealing and she vowed to get even. Two detectives came to interview him. Sam's story was simple. He told them Emily had stolen cash from his billfold. He wasn't sure how much she took. "She took a couple hundred dollars at least."

"Unless you charted the serial numbers before the money is stolen. The court would view this as a he said she said situation. If we found money on her, we have no way to prove the money was your money. We can't arrest this woman without more evidence."

"She threatened to harm me. She had that butcher knife after me. Her fingerprints are on the knife."

"As your nanny, her fingerprints would be on everything in this house. Her fingerprints on the knife could not be used as evidence against her."

"Calling you was a waste of time. You may as well leave."

With the police gone his mind returned to Brad, he was cursing for screwing up on trying to kill him. He shouldn't be lying in a hospital bed in serious condition. Had the job been done properly Brad would be dead. Now it's probably too late and too dangerous to make a second attempt on Brad's life. For one thing, Sam had tossed his weapon away. Had his mother not been ill he could have gone to the hospital in Vegas with Judy. There may have been a slim chance to be in his room alone with him. A simple pillow across his face may have finished the job and cleaned up the botched attempt on Brad's life."

In Vegas, Marie sat at her husband's bedside praying he would heal quickly and live a full productive life. She breathed a sigh of relief as he opened his eyes for the first time after the incident. In response she instantly grasped his hand. "Welcome back, you gave everyone quite a scare. A lot of people have been here at the hospital to comfort me and pray for you. Junior and Darcy are making plans to return home." She stood and leaned over to kiss him. "You were shot, someone tried to kill you."

"Why would anyone want to shoot me? I've done nothing wrong."

"We don't know who shot you. The police were hoping you might be able to tell us something. It could have been Rusty who shot you. You were leaving the Ad Palace Office after dark when you were shot. You were shot next to your car in the parking lot and left for dead."

"I don't remember anything about being shot. What was it you said about Junior and Darcy ending their honeymoon early?"

"They are making arrangements to return from Hawaii. When you were shot they became worried about you so they are returning home."

"That's not right Honey. I may feel like a truck ran over me, but I'll be okay. Call Junior and tell him I'm going to be fine. Don't have them come home just because I had another hospital stay.I won't be laid up more than a few days. There is no need for them to return home, and listen to me grumble about my pain."

"Brad, you were fortunate. Somebody wanted you dead. We are not sure who or why, they want you dead. Lucky for you the shooter was a lousy shot and only grazed your head knocking you down. The other five bullets were fired into your thigh while you were down. Not one bullet in your thigh hit a bone. The police think the shooter was an amateur because he used steel jacket bullets in place of shooting you with hollow point shells that would flair out in your body, and do far more damage. Rusty could be the amateur shooter."

"I know they have great doctors here. I hope they are right about me being fine. Honey, try calling Junior, we can talk more about my ordeal later. There is no reason the newlywed honeymooners should return early."

Marie was unable to contact her brother. She surmised they were in the air flying back from Hawaii. Her second call was to the police informing them Brad was awake. Two police officers came straight to the hospital to question him. Officers Dan Fuller and Ann Alder officially introduced themselves. "Mr. Collins someone dislikes you a great deal. They want you dead. Do you know any reason why anyone would want to kill you?"

"I don't have any hardcore enemies that I know about."

"We doubt it was a case of mistaken identity. There was money in your wallet, so robbery can be ruled out. Can you tell us if you saw anything?"

"I saw a brief flash of light slightly off center to my right, but I didn't see anyone. I fired a skinny little red headed kid recently. Marie thinks he could be the shooter, but I doubt he would have the courage to try ending my life. Most generally, I spend nothing but routine days working."

"You may have seen a muzzle flash of the weapon when the person shot you. We found one cartridge for the weapon used at the crime scene. Other cartridges were found ten blocks away. We found no actual weapon. Our lab has nothing to go on except the empty shell casings and they may be of little help. So far our investigation indicates the shooter was an amateur."

"Sorry I can't help you more. I have no idea who would want me dead. Why do you say an amateur shot me, Marie said I was shot several times."

"No professional shooter would leave even one shell casing lying around anywhere to be used as evidence against them later, nor would they use such a small caliber weapon. The 22 caliber bullet that grazed your head did little damage. A 44 caliber bullet would have taken a huge chunk out of your skull killing you instantly."

"If you are trying to convince me I was lucky forget it. Lucky people do not get shot by accident or on purpose. You don't think so, but maybe my getting shot was a case of mistaken identity? Maybe someone screwed up and shot the wrong person?"

"It is not likely you were shot by accident. You getting shot may have been a gang initiation of some kind. We do have gang initiation shootings, so there is a possibility you getting shot may have been a random target. Mrs. Collins, will you please step out of the room for a few minutes. We need to talk with your husband alone?" The officers requested.

Marie joined her parents and Judy in the waiting room. "The police chased me out of the room. Apparently they want to ask my husband personal questions."

"How is Brad doing?" Susan asked.

"He is awake, and alert more than I expected he would be this evening. He does have a headache and his thigh hurts. I hope the police don't take too long questioning him. He may tire out fast. Brad and I talked before the police arrived he doesn't remembers anything about the incident other than seeing a flash of light. Police suggested the light may have been the muzzle flash of the first shot. According to them by the angle the bullets penetrated his body the five additional shots were fired after he was down on the pavement. The officers further stated the shooter more than likely was amateur because the caliber of the gun used was too small to be certain of a kill."

Marie's father leaned back in his chair. "Makes me shudder just to think about him getting shot, and it confirms my thoughts. All signs point to Rusty, the employee he fired recently." Marie's father was convinced Rusty was guilty of shooting Brad.

Although Brad was offering little useful information to the police they continued to ask questions. "Mr. Collin how is your relationship with your wife?"

"Marie and I have a good marriage. We have two wonderful children and a comfortable lifestyle."

"Could you be stretching the truth just a little? We know your marriage wasn't always great. We saw your hospital records. Somebody worked you over on one occasion. My partner and I have been in the police business to know everyone has someone that does not like them. Have your been seeing other women?"

"Officer, you are barking up the wrong tree. This dog doesn't hunt anymore. I'm not seeing any other women, and I haven't for several years. Try a different theory. That theory doesn't work."

"With your history, how do we know you are telling us the truth or not. We believe you have been subject to straying affection in the past. You were beat up once enough to cause you to be hospitalized. You needed facial reconstruction on your face during that stay. Although officials were never certain who worked you over, the result of your beating paralleled the actions of a jealous husband, or your wife, if she were the jealous type. Because their first attempt failed could that person have made a second try at killing you?"

"You are talking ancient history my friend. There is no connection between my getting shot and the previous incident. That I'm certain of."

"Our point is if you want to live a long happy life you better level with us. Someone deliberately tried to drill you between the eyes with a small caliber pistol. I'll say it one more time. This looks to be the work of an amateur who pulled the gun slightly to the right each time they pulled the trigger, nearly missing you all together. This person could be someone you know very well. Had this person waited for you to take two more steps closer to them, you would be dead."

"Are you thinking this person may try to kill me again?"

"If the attempt on your life was by someone that knows you well, they may well try killing you again. You haven't given us any reason to think they won't try to kill you again. Let's talk about this employee you dismissed earlier this week."

"Rusty was an unhappy employee. He didn't like the routine boring job he was doing. In a nut shell he was wasting our valuable time, and looking on line for a better job during work hours. His actions were disrupting other employees. We had a talk and he realized it was time he moved on to greener pastures. I gave him a three month severance check to help with his transition to a new job. I don't believe there was a lot of hard feeling over his dismissal. I think he was expecting to be let go."

"Then let's go back and discuss your indiscretions further. Since you admit to having past indiscretions is it possible your wife might be having an affair now?"

Brad paused a few seconds before answering the officer's question giving them a chance to doubt his forthcoming words. "I'm certain Marie is not having an affair. Feel free to ask her if you want. She has been covering much of my work since my heart attack. In doing so she is very busy and works with several individuals of the opposite gender. That is no reason to believe she is having an affair. In most cases working together with people of the opposite gender does not automatically mean illicit activities are going on."

"When it comes to affairs, things sometimes happen unexpectedly. Sometimes they happen faster than most people believe things could happen."

"I suppose a person might make that assumption. You and Officer Alder are of the opposite gender and working together, probably have been working together for some time. People may point a finger at the two of you and say you are having an affair, does that make what they might say true?"

Phrasing his words as he did led the officers to believe there may have been rumors about Mrs. Collins. "Mr. Collins people with your type of family money draw all types of individuals to them. If you think of anything or anyone that might be of help in our investigation, call us immediately. You appear to be getting tired. We'll let you rest for now. I'm sure we will have additional questions for you as we move along in our investigation."

Officers Fuller and Alder stopped at the visitors lounge to speak with Marie before leaving. "We will need to question each of you on an individual basis and give each of you a simple test. At this time we would like to suggest this questioning be done in our office soon as possible. Your cooperation would be greatly appreciated; if necessary we can get court orders. We have so little information or evidence as to who may have shot Mr. Collins. Any tiny tidbit of information might help tie something together so we can get a break in this case."

Marie stood up. "Give me a couple minutes to see Brad and then I'll drive down to the police station and meet with you."

"Very good Mrs. Collins, we'll go back to the police station and await your arrival. Please don't make us hunt you up, and drag you to the police station."

The officers also requested Judy and Marie's parents make an appearance at the police station. Without visiting their son-in-law Ray Sr. and Susan went straight to the police station.

Powder residue tests were taken of their hands. Few questions were asked of them. "You live on the same property as your daughter and son-in-law. Have you noticed anything unusual going on between your daughter and son-in-law? Things like arguments or loud voices?"

"No absolutely not, Brad and Marie are working together and getting along well. Their businesses are operating perfect. Together they have a loving family." Susan stated. "They do live extremely busy lives."

Ray leaned forward as he spoke. "Recently, we never saw nor heard anything out of the ordinary. Brad recently had some unfortunate heart problems. They obviously shifted work around to help relieve stress on Brad to allow him to get the rest he needed. Marie covered his work as best she could. Other than that nothing unusual was going on that we know of." Ray Sr. commented.

"Has Marie been working late inconsistent hours?"

"Marie was home before six each evening. She loves her husband, and values their family time in the evenings. They have two wonderful boys."

"Do you know if Mr. Collins is currently having an affair with anyone?"

The officer's blunt question startled Marie's parents. "We just told you they are a very happy couple now with two young boys they dearly love. I doubt either of them would risk losing what they have by fooling around with other people." Ray insisted.

"You mentioned now they are a happy couple. Earlier you mentioned nothing recently. It sounds as though you are holding something from us. The reasons behind why people fool around as you put it are many. It could be boredom, stress, or just because they can. In many cases I doubt they know reason why they become involved with someone else. What you are trying to hold back could get your son-in-law killed."

"I don't believe what you are saying, or what you are insinuating is correct." Susan argued back. "Nothing is going on."

Ray Senior leaned forward again. "Eight or ten years ago, Brad did become involved in an affair. That resulted in him fathering two children for a friend of theirs, by the name of Judy Anderson. All was forgiven long ago."

"Thank you, now we have another direction to investigate. I think that covers everything for now. We appreciate you coming in. If you think of anything that might help us find who tried to kill your son-in-law, please don't hesitate to call us. It may take lots of small pieces to solve this crime."

"Come to think of it there may be one other person you might look at as a suspect. A young man about thirty years old, Steve Avery is his name.

He and Brad were locked in a realty battle not long ago. Young Avery's father owned four medical buildings when he passed away. The boy inherited his father's estate, but he had no money to pay the inheritance tax. They struggled about Brad's takeover offer. In the end, Steve Avery wasn't dealing straight forward. He was no match for Brad. The kid gained little of nothing."

"Thank you for the additional information Mr. Roberts. In the coming days write down any little thing you remember about any incident, concerning your daughter and son-in-law. We may be meeting with you again."

Judy and Marie arrived as the Richards interview ended. Judy was brought in first. Her hands too were tested for power residue. "Our back ground check on you revealed quite a bit. You and Mr. Collins have quite a history resulting in two children. It's hard to believe that went well when others learned of your adulteress affair, and who fathered your children."

"You are correct to assume our secret disrupted a lot of lives. I damaged several lives. That was several years ago. Fortunately those near Brad and me have forgiven our actions and that is all history. It happened ten years ago to be exact. "

"It is possible your forgiveness idea is not as complete as you think. Our preliminary investigation indicates your husband does not know he isn't the father of your children."

"Sam hasn't been told he isn't the biological father of our girls. He is very much the father of our children. If he were told he wasn't their biological father he wouldn't try killing Brad. If he finds out about what Brad and I did all those years ago he might divorce me, but Sam is not a killer, he is a passive man. I see doubt in your eyes. No matter what you think my husband, Sam, would never try killing anyone."

Over the next three hours Judy and Marie told the complete story of their lives and how they intertwined. Questions were asked about Sam, and why he wasn't with his family in Vegas. The women were questioned why he wasn't told about Brad being the father of his children when Marie learned of the ongoing affair. "We had our reasons is all Marie or Judy would say."

Sam was in Seattle caring for his ill mother. Her passing away seemed like an alibi enough to satisfy the investigating officers for the time being.

Tired and hungry the girls were allowed to leave and went straight back to visit Brad again. "Hi there, I thought everyone deserted me."

"The police had questions for us. We were busy trying to help with their investigation." Marie shook her head. "Unfortunately the police have little evidence to work with. Officer Alder suggested you need to wear a bullet proof vest when you return to work. Oh, I almost forgot. The police believe they picked up a burglary suspect carrying the pistol you were shot with. The punk claims to have found the weapon in the trash."

"Is this police woman stupid, I was shot in the head how is a bulletproof vest going to help me? I need a frigging helmet?"

Marie smiled at her husband. "I can tell by your comment you are feeling better."

"I am feeling better, and tomorrow after lunch I'm going home. I haven't told the doctor yet but I'm tired of his accommodations. I can get better rest and care at home."

"You can't go home tomorrow. The doctor has you scheduled for another surgery tomorrow to remove the deepest bullet in your thigh. You must remain patient until the doctor releases you. When you are able to go home, you will get great care. We know four youngsters dying to care for you."

"You ladies look as tired as I feel. You need to go home tonight and get proper sleep. Since they are carving on me again in the morning, tomorrow may be another long day. Proper rest tonight will do each of us good."

Judy gave him a serious look. "You seem very relaxed for a person who was shot. I hope someone is guarding you tonight. You might be a target for another attempt on your life. I'm not sure I would want to walk down the street beside you any time soon."

Although nervous on the inside he managed to fool people into believing he wasn't scared. "If you were the shooter would you have tossed your weapon away before you knew the results of your actions? I'm thinking the shooter made one try and high-tailed it out of the city. Carol was here while you ladies were at the police station. She mentioned Rusty moved to Arizona rather fast. I find that very interesting."

"Did you tell the police about Rusty's sudden departure?" Brad shook his head no. "You must call the police."

"I have no desire to spend months in a courthouse trying to convict someone with so little evidence. His moving to Arizona is not a Crime.

My case may never be solved because there is no witness, no fingerprints and no weapon. The kid's gone and I'll be okay. He won't dare show his face around Vegas again for a very long time. Who knows he may believe I'm dead. One other thing we don't need is the police nosing around the Ad Palace investigating our business in depth."

Junior and Darcy came charging in all excited. "What happened, who shot you, why did they shoot you, did they catch the guy who shot you?"

Brad groaned as he moved slightly to look at Junior and Darcy. "More importantly why are you here? You are supposed be in Hawaii enjoying your honeymoon?"

Junior touched Brad's good shoulder. "Mother called saying you had been shot and was in serious condition, who shot you?"

Marie touched her brother. "I tried calling you guys to say it wasn't necessary to come home. Brad has improved much faster than any of us expected. He is scheduled for a second surgery tomorrow. There is bullet lodged in a difficult area." Her words didn't matter. Junior and Darcy wanted to hear every detail of the incident. "Why don't we talk at home, our patient needs his rest."

Shortly after his visitors left, two other visitors arrived. Detectives Dan Fuller and Ann Alder came walking in. Brad wrinkled up his nose at them. "Geez guys, don't you ever sleep. I have a big day coming up tomorrow my doctor is probing for the bullet deep in my thigh. He claims it must be removed, I hope he is gentle with me."

"We have a few questions we need to ask while others are not around. Our street patrol picked up a young gang member carrying a 22 caliber weapon. After tests were performed we matched this weapon to be the weapon, and possibly the person who shot you." Brad was shown a picture.

"Someone mention earlier the police thought they found the weapon. Now it is confirmed. I don't know the person in this picture. Why would he shoot me?"

"I've been a police detective for twenty years and I have no idea why gang members do what they do. This young kid claims to have found the weapon near where we found the spent shell casings. When was the last time you saw Sam Anderson?"

"Sam and Judy are somewhat business partners of Marie and me. They were here in Vegas a few weeks ago checking out a possible move to work with our organization here in Vegas. Sam's wife Judy and my wife

Marie have been best friends since childhood. A move to Vegas might be good for Sam and Judy. I think they are seriously considering moving here. Judy came down for a wedding. She was planning to hang around a few days and scope out the area more. She mentioned checking out schools and housing while she was here. Sam stayed in Seattle to man their office, and keep an eye on his mother. The poor lady has cancer."

"Did you see Sam the day you were shot?"

"No, weren't you listening to me. I just told you Sam's mother was gravely ill he couldn't leave her alone very long, so he flew back to Seattle before I was shot. Sam couldn't have shot me, he was in Seattle. When he was here last, Judy was in Seattle keeping an eye on his mother. They trade off watching his mother. The medicine these people gave me is making me sleepy. It's hard to remember things but I think someone mentioned earlier today Carmen Anderson passed away last night. Sleeping so much I get my days mixed up. I'm sure Sam never left his mother's side these last few days. He was very close to his mother. You may want to check dates with Judy. My memory is foggy."

"It might be helpful for us to speak with Mr. Anderson too. It's part of our routine investigation. Ann and I feel that somewhere in your circle of friends, relatives, or employees is the key that might give us a break in this case. It's important we find the person who tried to murder you."

"Sam will be staying at our house when he gets here. If you want to investigate him, you may do so when he comes down."

"Do not tell anyone we want to speak with Mr. Anderson. We don't need him repeating what others have already told us. Part of any investigation is listening for a different slant on issues, and facts, from all sources."

"You asked a favor of me, may I ask a favor of you?"

"What favor are you asking for?"

"Sam lives life in a fog. He has no clue I'm the father of Judy's children. He has a medical condition rendering him unable to have children. He has a low sperm count. Judy wouldn't marry him until she was certain they could have a family. In a moment of weakness, I fulfilled her desire to have children by donating sperm. Only then did she agree to marry Sam. Judy and I were both young, and stupid. Our first indiscretion was before Marie and I were officially married. When Marie and my son Johnnie became ill with leukemia Judy and Sam's daughter Carrie was the person to provide the bone marrow needed to save Marie and my son's life."

"What an interesting story."

"Everyone except Sam quickly knew I was Carrie's biological father. For his own good, its best he continues as he has the last ten years, to live in the land of fantasy. He loves those girls. I would hate for anything to separate them."

"Where was your meeting with Mr. Anderson on his last visit to Vegas?"

"We met at our business office at the Ad Palace. Marie was at the meeting with Sam and me. The meeting was cut short when he became ill. He checked into a hotel room for the night. Feeling better the next morning he returned to Seattle."

"Is it possible Mr. Anderson learned you were the girl's biological father during his brief visit for your meeting?"

"I don't see how he could have found out. We meet in my private office. He was there such a short time before getting sick."

"Could he have delayed returning to Seattle until after you were shot?"

"No it's not possible. Sam flew back to Seattle the next day. That was several days before I was shot. Judy would be the person who could vouch for his return to Seattle. It's fine for you to check Sam out but he didn't shoot me. In addition you could check with hospital officials as to when Sam was with his mother."

"Thank you Mr. Collins, your information may be helpful." The two officers started to leave but stopped. "I have one last question, had your assailant been successful what would have happened to your business operation?"

Brad thought for a few seconds. "Little of nothing I suppose. Marie would have become president of our corporation, and business would have continued as usual without me. We have one last apartment building project about to be started, other than that we have no further business expansion plans. I have a few ideas floating around in my head but no solid plans. Marie could easily keep Collins Enterprises operating in a normal manor. Once our next apartment complex was complete we will probably kick back and take life easy for a while. Sam and my family often vacation together. Everyone gets along well. The kids squabble occasionally but nothing serious. Sam can get a little testy at times because he doesn't like me tending to business by phone while I'm on vacation."

"Thank you again, Mr. Collins, get a good night of sleep, you look exhausted."

Officer Dan Fuller and Ann Alder stopped at a coffee shop to discuss the findings over a cup of coffee. "Mr. Anderson is looking like a possible suspect. He has motive and that is a start. One of us will be going to Seattle and checking on his whereabouts at the time Mr. Collins was shot. Ann, I think you should be the person to fly to Seattle tomorrow and check up on him there. Check on his mother at the hospital. Talk to doctors, nurses, neighbors, or anyone else you can find who knows Sam Anderson. If he should happen to return here in Vegas, I'll question him here. Be sure and pick up a set of Sam's fingerprints from the State Real Estate Licensing Office. Check with anyone who can vouch for his being in Seattle in recent days. Check his credit card and phone records they might tell you something."

"Give me a break Dan. I know what to look for when I get to Seattle." Officer Fuller's advice irritated Ann. "I've been an officer long as you have."

Dan ignored Officer Alder's irritation. "We also have two other suspects to take more serious."

"Who are you referring to?"

"I'm referring to Mrs. Collins, and Mrs. Anderson. It strikes me strange these two women wanted, and do have children about the same age, by the same man. A scenario both women wanted at a very young age. With little effort they may have accomplished their goal. These women were in college together. Could this be a premeditated Lesbian conspiracy they pulled so each woman could have children closely related as possible? Half-brother and half-sister would make the children close as possible. If so, now might be the time to dispose of the men in their lives."

"You have a vivid imagination. Of course that is a trait in a lot of men."

"What better way could there be for these women to rid themselves of the men they dislike, than to allowing Mr. Anderson to find out about Mr. Collins fathering all the children. In anger he might shoot the man who has killed two people in self-defense before. Then when we charge Mr. Anderson he would be sent to prison. There may have been one hitch in their plan. Mr. Collins didn't die."

"Now I understand what you are getting at. You could be right saying if the women's plan was successful they would only have one man to deal with, and he could be charged with the crime of murder, thus eliminating both men from their lives. What I don't understand is both these women appear to love their husbands."

"It could be the Black Widow theory. Show them enough love to keep them near long enough to bear the children they want and create the wealth they desired before they love their men to death. Money and power can do strange things to people. Do you ever watch that forensic show on television narrated by Dominick Dunn?"

"I have seen the program you are referring to. They profile old crimes cases involving rich people."

"Then you know people surrounded by money are sometimes capable of anything. We'll leave no stone unturned during our investigation. While in the Northwest check the college these individuals attended. Talk to anyone who knew these women."

CHAPTER 16

Brad's second surgery the following day went well. Seven days later he arrived home appearing nervous. Marie saw his uneasiness while his two boys noticed nothing beyond their father was home. The boys were thrilled to have him home and were willing with the help of Carrie and Kristy to wait on his every need. Judy remained at a distance.

Brad enjoyed the attention given him but continued to think about all the questions the police asked about Sam. The police had placed a cloud of suspicion in Brad's mind. It was possible during Sam's recent visit to Vegas he somehow found out he was not the biological father of the girls, and he was."

Marie offered to get Brad a glass of water. "No thank you, Honey, all I need is a nap." Together Marie and Judy took the four children off to play in their bedroom.

Brad found napping difficult as he thought about Darcy's warning about Evan Thomas and Marie possibly having an affair. Many thoughts raced through Brad's mind. Evan may have designs on Marie, and a shortcut to wealth. He is a young aggressive person. Could he have been the shooter?

While Brad napped, and the children were playing in their room, the women were sitting in the kitchen discussing his situation. "Brad put up a good front in the hospital. Here at home he acts fearful of what might happen if there is another attempt on his life. If you ask me he is aware his shooter is still out there somewhere. He knows full well that person could be looking for a second chance to kill him."

Judy nodded her head in agreement. "If he is nervous sitting here in his house how will he ever handle going off to work?"

"Good point, Judy, wish I had an answer for him. I am ordering a bulletproof vest for him. He won't like wearing the vest but I will see to it he wears it."

Ray, Susan, Junior and Darcy all stopped by for a brief visit later in the evening. Although Brad was awake, he wasn't the old out-going Brad.

They saw exactly what the girls saw earlier. Out in the yard as they left, Ray Sr. was quick to point out you couldn't blame Brad for being scared. "If I had someone shoot me six times I would be scared too."

"I know, dad. He is a lucky man. I doubt anyone getting shot could go on living a normal life. Since the shooter failed, he may try getting a larger caliber weapon for his next try at Brad."

All of a sudden Darcy jumped slightly. "I've got it! Let's go back in and speak to Brad again." The others followed her inside. "Will you kids please excuse the grownups for a few minutes we have business to discuss?"

Once the young people went off to the family room Darcy shared her idea. "We all believe Rusty shot you. Actually there is little doubt about it. He supposedly left the city so you should be safe. To be sure you are safe we should hire a detective agency to track Rusty down. You can find out if he is working in Arizona or roaming around the country elsewhere. Getting a good detective shouldn't be hard."

Marie was quick to get on board with Darcy's idea. "What a great idea, we'll do it tomorrow, first thing in the morning. We can track Rusty's every movement. "While others were pleased with the idea Brad showed little emotion."What's wrong with Darcy's idea, you don't look pleased?"

"We could be wrong. Furthermore we have no legal right to harass Rusty if we are not sure. All we know is the guy who shot me wasn't a professional hit man. If the shooter's first shot knocked me down, as the police are certain it did. Why didn't the shooter step up close and finished killing me by placing the next five shots in the back of my skull?"

"The shooter was scared of being caught. He fired quick and left the scene fast as possible without checking to be certain you were dead. Be thankful he did leave quickly."

"It was a disturbing incident, but I feel the threat has passed. If the person was that scared he will be too scared to come near me again. I'll be looking in the eyes of everyone I meet for a long time. The authorities may eventually figure out who took the pot shots at me, but for now, we can't be sure it was Rusty. If you hire a detective, tell him to be discrete."

Marie looked her husband square in the eyes. "I haven't mentioned this before but could the shooter be one of your father's old cronies?"

"That thought crossed my mind, but I doubt it. The police insist it was no professional hit-man firing at me. They feel it was someone I know well. I should say thought I knew well."

"That seals it for me. I'm certain we should track Rusty. There would be no harassing going on. We are only interested in knowing if Rusty is staying away from Vegas. He won't have the slightest idea we are checking up on him."

"Alright call someone tomorrow if you want. You have my permission to track Rusty, if you think it's the right thing to do." As Brad spoke he never looked up as he used one finger to trace the pattern design on the end table.

"Statistics say most murders are committed by someone near a person on a regular basis. People like a close friend, a coworker or a neighbor." Darcy stated.

Her comment drew a quick look from Brad. "Who cares about statistics? Statistics are like a woman in a bikini, they show a lot, but still hide vital information."

Marie sat down next to her husband. She placed one hand on his leg. "I have one other idea you won't like, but you should consider doing at least for a while. You should hire a bodyguard."

"You are correct Marie. I do not like your idea. I grew up hating my father. I saw him only a few times. I remember creepy bodyguards hanging around him. They stood out by the car he rode in wearing sunglasses and smoking cigarettes. They were no doubt his bodyguards. I don't think my father had a peaceful moment in his life with people watching his every move. I do not want any bodyguards. We'll move to a new city, before I hire a bodyguard."

"It was only an idea. We could go away for an extended period of time, Hawaii, Europe, or anywhere. We could stay away until the shooter forgets about trying to shoot you again."

"People, I know you mean well, but I have a plan of my own. I will carry out my plan my way in my own time." To everyone's amazement Brad struggled to his feet. "I'm getting dressed now. Marie I may need your help getting my pants on. I have some work to do at the office."

"You don't have strength enough to go to the office and work tonight. If you are going to the office, I'm going with you."

"No Marie, you are not going with me to the office. I'll fill you in later, but not now. I need to check my facts first. I'll be okay because no one will expect me to be out and about this soon."

"Brad, you are too weak to be sneaking out at night. Going to the office alone makes no sense. Someone needs to be with you."

Everyone's eyes were glued to his unsteady body as he went to get dressed. Darcy said what everyone was thinking. "Marie is right. He should not be going anywhere especially alone."

He continued walking away. "How are we going to talk him out of going to the office?" Susan commented.

Judy shook her head. "He seems determined to go to the office tonight. I don't know if anyone can discourage his going there or not." Brad returned on his way out when Marie stopped him. "For your own sake, if you must go, please let someone go with you."

"Sorry people, I'm going to the office alone. Don't get excited, Honey. I'll explain everything to you later."

"Can my brother go with you? He can drive and remain in the car as your lookout while you go inside the office?"

Brad studied Junior's face before agreeing to allow Ray to drive him over to the office. "Okay, he can drive me over to the office. He must remain in the car. You can park directly in front of the office and if anyone comes around snooping you start the car and leave. When I see the car lights come on I'll take appropriate action to protect myself inside the building. You just get the hell out of there."

Junior looked about the room. "Call me a coward if to want, but I'm not driving Brad to the office unless I have my big pistol with me. I'm ex-military. My comfort zone is to take a weapon with me. A weapon I know how to use."

Brad looked directly into Junior's eyes. Could Junior be the shooter, just as quickly the answer came to Brad, Junior couldn't be the shooter. He was in Hawaii with Darcy when he was shot. "Get your pistol and let's go. I'm taking my pistol too. Hustle up, Junior, I need to get back home and get my rest."

On the way to the office Brad thought more about Sam waiting in the office when he and Marie arrived for their meeting two weeks ago. There was a slim chance he may have overheard Rusty mouthing off about his less than honorable actions with Judy years before. If he did hear something, it could easily irritate Sam enough for him to react violently without thinking. He had no way of knowing for certain if Sam could have made a quick trip to Vegas, and shot him. Brad decided to play it safe by making a subliminal message and have it playing when Sam joins Judy at the house in a day or two. One vital part of his plan was to keep Judy clueless as to why music is being played at home.

Judy knew a little about his subliminal messages because she used his system to pass her State Real Estate Exam. Somehow he must convince her he was playing the subliminal message music for himself, to make him less fearful of leading a normal life after being shot. She wouldn't be aware of the special subliminal message instructions were actually targeting Sam. Several times while creating his message Brad paused to regain his strength. Evan Thomas was another gentleman of interest, if Darcy was correct saying he and Marie were growing close during the last stage of apartment building, she may need a subliminal message too. He could put two messages on the same CD. A properly worded subliminal message for Marie would diminish her interest in Evan if there were any interest.

It took twenty minutes to complete the CD and marked it MS for Marie and Sam, to identify the CD. Proud of his work he pocketed the CD and turned towards the door. The last thing he remembered was the room getting dark until he woke up in the hospital again surrounded by family. "Where am I?"

"Easy Honey, you are in the hospital. You collapsed in the office. We knew you were too weak to go there. When you didn't return in a short time Ray went looking for you and found you unconscious on the office floor. You were brought by ambulance to the hospital."

"I had a CD with me when I started to leave the office what happened to the CD."

"Junior wasn't concerned about a CD he was concerned about you."

In a wild manner Brad looked about the room. "Damn, they have an IV in my arm, where is Judy?"

"Judy is at the airport picking up Sam."

"Shit, listen to me Honey. Don't ask questions, go straight to the office fast as you can, and find the CD I made. The last I remember is I had it in my hand. It should be on the floor near where they found me. When you find the CD start it playing at our house before I go home."

"I don't have a car."

"Take a frigging taxi, just go!" Brad shouted. "I made the CD to help me relax and not be afraid of everyone I meet. Fear of the unknown is eating away at me. I need that CD playing at home when I get there."

With Marie gone his panic slowly subsided. The duty nurse came by to check on Brad. "My word, sweat is pouring off of your forehead." She felt his pulse. "Mr. Collins, we better take your temperature."

"Relax nurse, I was upset earlier but now I'm settling down."

I need to take your temperature anyway."

"I had a little problem at the office but things are being taken care of. Half hour from now I'll be fine. I could use a washcloth and a pan of warm water."

"Your slow drip IV will run another hour and a half. Since you smell none too great from sweating I think we better give you a sponge bath and change your gown. I'll be right back and clean you up."

The nurse no more than left when Detectives Dan Fuller and Ann Alder entered his room. "We called your house, and were told you were hospitalized again, what happened this time?"

"Nothing serious, I went home a little early. I came back to the hospital to rest a bit longer." Brad looked up at his IV. "That little bottle is supposed to pep me up enough I can go home in a couple days. Hospital stays are not my thing."

"We stopped by today to give you an update on our investigation. All our leads are coming up cold. We are unable at this time to tie any clues together. No partial fingerprint match, basically we have nothing. One puzzling area is Sam Anderson. There is a brief time window we cannot find one person to account for Sam's where-a-bouts. He claims the time was spent in the waiting room near his mother. According to him he alternated between visiting his mother, sleeping in the waiting room, eating at the hospital buffet, and using the restroom. The unaccounted time window is so short it is extremely doubtful anyone could fly from Seattle, shoot you, and return home in that time frame."

"That is good to know. I wasn't worried about Sam, he is an okay guy. Thank you for the update."

After the two police officers left, the nurse gave Brad his sponge bath. Feeling clean and refreshed he relaxed enough to go into a deep sleep.

Sam flew down to Las Vegas to look at three different houses Judy had been looking at. Her joy and fascination about moving to Vegas overshadowed her ability to read her husband's serious face. Back at the house the children's laughter was infectious to everyone, except Sam. "Would it be okay if I went to the bedroom and saw Brad?" He asked.

Judy touched Sam's arm. "Brad isn't in the bedroom. He is in the hospital tonight. Marie hopes the doctors will keep him a few days. He is living proof irresponsible actions can come back to haunt a person.

He insisted he needed to return to the office and do some secret thing. He collapsed while he was there."

"We are going to give him a new nickname, The Connoisseur of Chaos. He rejects every idea given him." Junior stated.

"How stupid can he be?" Sam remarked. "You said they never caught anyone for trying to shoot him. He should be nervous. Someone could be watching his every move through the scope of a rifle. We all know someone wanted him dead. Doesn't that scare Brad at all?"

"Marie hired two security guards for him at the hospital. To answer your question, he is scared. That is how he landed in the hospital again."

Judy leaned over close to whisper. "Marie called a bit ago and told me he went to the office to create a subliminal message so he could relax and get more rest. Why else would he want to make a subliminal message if he were not scared? Don't say anything about the music playing in the house when he gets home."

Sam's head bobbed up and down as he tried to understand what Judy was telling him. "Are people allowed to visit Brad at the hospital?"

"No one but Marie can visit him this time of night. I would expect her to return home any time. With two bodyguards watching over Brad he will be safe. Everyone should be able to come home to sleep and get the rest they need."

Marie searched high and low looking for the subliminal CD Brad made. Try as she might there was nothing to be found near where she thought he was found lying on the floor. If only she could find the CD. She spent a full hour searching for the CD without any luck. Marie called the house for a brief conversation with Judy. "Brad was making a CD so he could rest better. I can't find the CD he made. I'll make a new relaxation CD before I come home. You will see me in about an hour."

"I agree with your assessment, he probably was making a subliminal message CD for himself. We were all bothering him with questions. He was so nervous, sleep wouldn't have come any time soon, and our words were not helping him at all."

"I'm thinking he was unable to create the subliminal message CD, but thought he made it. About all I can do is to make a message for him to rest and have it playing when he gets home."

"Good idea, Brad certainly needs rest. We'll see you in a short while."

To keep Brad resting in place of worrying, Marie ducked by the hospital long enough to tell him she found the CD. The CD will be playing when you arrive home." She kissed him goodbye before leaving. "Get your rest Honey. I'll see you in the morning."

Brad took Marie's words to have it playing when you arrive to mean Sam would be targeted prior to his release from the hospital. He also knew Sam was likely to be at the house before he went home. "Thanks, Honey, you are an angel."

"Your eyes are looking heavy. I better go home and let you rest." She gave him a kiss before departing. "You have two security guards in the hall so sleep tight."

At home Marie shook her head. "Poor Brad, they have him so bombed with medication he can't think straight. I did make a CD encouraging him to rest more when he gets home. Hopefully this time when he gets home he can relax and get rest enough his body will heal up. For his own good he needs to return to work."

Sam looked at Marie. "Do you know if that red-head kid, Rusty checked out okay, or is he the number one suspect?"

"The authorities haven't been able to locate Rusty. He left the area in a hurry. Rather than waiting for the police to locate him. We hired a detective firm to track him down. In a few days we should know about his every move. Then we'll have a better idea how to proceed when it comes to protecting Brad."

"If Rusty left the area hiring a private detective seems unnecessary. Maybe it's good you are proactive in locating Rusty. Sitting around expecting the Police to do everything may not be of much help. Brad is a tough business man who steps on people's toes now and then. He may well have enemies we do not know about."

"He doesn't harm anyone that is fair to him."

"Try telling that to Karen Moore or her parents. They felt Brad's wrath when he was trying to get his first business off the ground. When they got in the way there was hell to pay. Possibly someone from his father's past acquaintances could have been involved in the attempt on Brad's life. That Avery kid Brad pushed to the limit wasn't a happy camper either. He might be holding a grudge against Brad. You don't pull the stuff Brad pulls without making enemies along the way."

By now Marie's face turned white as a sheet. "I haven't thought of any of those people you mentioned as suspects. We better call the police and give them the names you mentioned before Brad comes home from the hospital. Kathy Moore could be the person holding a grudge. She would be capable of shooting him. She is one certified flake. They need checked out before Brad comes home. I'm sure he will be home in a day or two. I dearly wish he would stay in the hospital longer. The problem is the hospital won't want to keep him very long, and he won't want to be there long."

"I don't envy the Police, there are two and a half million people living in the Vegas area and literally thousands of so called tourists coming and going each day. Finding Brad's shooter with so few clues is like looking for a needle in a hay stack."

Marie called and reported the Moore family to the police. Minutes later Sam cornered her. "You didn't tell the police about Brad's father having ties to the Mexican Drug Cartel."

"If a solid connection were ever proven between the Collins family name and the Mexican Drug Cartel our entire estate could be seized. At the time Brad inherited his father's money we had some interesting characters come looking for handouts claiming to be a loyal employees of his father. They tried to convince Brad they deserved a portion of the estate. We paid them nothing. One guy Brad roughed up because he wouldn't take no for an answer. Those were troubling days in our lives. I don't want to open that can of worms again. All that business was settled ten years ago." By the expression on Sam's face Marie realized she had said too much. "Brad didn't break the guy's leg or anything. He manhandled the man by slamming him against the wall and taking his gun away from him. Brad told him if he ever came back he wouldn't be so kind. We never saw the guy again."

"I would think all that business was far too long ago to be connected to this shooting." Judy said.

Sam sat stroking his face with his left hand wondering if he had stirred up enough old memories in Brad's past, to lessen the chance anyone would zero in on him as the shooter.

Judy had said little for some time, but now she stepped into the conversation. "When I see the things you and Brad are able to do, and the people you help along the way. I can't help but envy your lifestyle, but I don't need the side effects that come with having money. Years ago I remember Brad said something to the effect trouble follows money. How right his statement was."

The following day, Marie received a detective report. She read the report twice. "This report isn't much help. Everyone pretty much thinks

Rusty was the shooter, and according to our detective report he has moved from Arizona to Florida to be near his parents so any future threat from him seems unlikely. I made the relaxation subliminal message CD for Brad so he can relax once he gets home. Hopefully our lives will settle down to a normal pace."

Marie's words were music to Sam's ears. He wanted Brad and Marie's lives to settle down in hopes of getting a second chance at killing Brad. "Wouldn't it be nice vacationing together on the Oregon beach again next year or a Mexico Beach perhaps?" He suggested. "I always wanted to go deep-sea fishing. I wonder if Brad would like to go fishing." In Sam's mind, he visualized when the other people weren't looking he could nudge Brad overboard as the charter boat sped out to the fishing area.

Marie smiled at Sam. "I don't know if he would like ocean fishing or not. He needs to do relaxing things, people claim fishing is relaxing. I wouldn't ask him right away, but maybe next summer you could ask him to go fishing."

Soon Marie dashed off to visit her husband in the hospital. She found him awake, alert and sitting in a chair looking out the window. "Hi Honey, I saw you turn into the parking lot."

She gave him a quick kiss before speaking. "You look great. How are you feeling this morning?"

"I feel fully rested. I'm ready to go home provided you started my CD playing."

She nodded and smiled. "Your CD is playing. With all the people at the house you may want to stay here and extra day or two, to get the rest you need. It's like a zoo at home. Do you think the doctor will allow you to have other visitors today, Sam and Judy were planning to stop by later and visit you if it's okay?"

"How long has Sam been at our house?"

"He arrived late afternoon yesterday. Once he was at the house he hasn't gone anywhere. I'm hoping Judy takes him house hunting sometime today. They committed to moving to Vegas. The sooner Sam and Judy get a place of their own the sooner we'll have peace and quiet at home. It is amazing what four extra people in a household do to peace and harmony."

"That's good, but there is no need for them to come by the hospital because I'm going home later today, soon as I talk the doctor into cutting me loose." His real reason for not wanting Sam to visit was he wanted all the time possible for what he thought to be his subliminal message to affect Sam.

"Are you being released to go home for sure?" Marie questioned. "You look good but that might not be enough to convince the doctor to release you?"

"Honey, I'm paying the bills. I'll leave the hospital when I please. I feel great so why shouldn't I go home. With the CD playing at home I can get my rest there." Marie gave him a look of are you sure? "Honest, Honey, I feel great." Brad's doctor walked in before Marie could inquire about the CD further. "Good morning doctor. I'm feeling great, and I'm going home this morning."

"The nurses at the nurse's station warned me you were feeling your oats this morning. You sound anxious to go home." The doctor studied his chart at the foot of the bed. "Let's have a listen to your heart." The chilly stethoscope caused him to jump slightly. "You sound fine. To my knowledge they haven't caught the person who shot you. How much rest will you get at home?"

"I doubt they will ever catch the person responsible for shooting me. The police have no evidence. Whatever happens, I can't live in this hospital forever. I may as well go home, and move about in a cautious manner. I have a lot of safety and protection at home. Only our friends can get in to visit."

"Considering I have no reason to keep you hospitalized. I have little choice but to sign your release if you are sure you want to go home. I do wish you luck."

"Doctor, luck is for gamblers. I plan on taking no unnecessary chances. I love life, and I'm not through living yet." He turned to Marie. "You heard the man Honey, take me home. You and the boys can shower me with love when we get there."

Feeling confident he was safe around Sam, Brad was anxious to get home. Being a Saturday he was also welcomed by four happy children. "I love you guys, give me a hug, but then I need to lie down and rest. I still get tired easy from my accident." He preferred using the word accident rather than attempted murder in front of the kids.

Watching his girls hug Brad same as his boys, angered Sam. Their affection towards him created more hidden anger in Sam's brain. He never received a welcome from his girls like Brad was receiving when he arrived in Vegas. Brad is not a God; he is a philandering fool with more money than brains. People like him, because of his money. Without money he would be nothing. Anger continued to build within.

"Sam, are you feeling okay, you seem quiet." Brad inquired.

"I had momentary flashback about mother lying in a comma. She went through hell before she passed away. Why do good people die so young, mother wasn't old."

"It's true Sam. Only the good die young."

"I've heard that saying many times. Over and over that thought rolls through my mind. Then our decision to move from beautiful Seattle to the arid desert of Las Vegas was a hard choice. Judy and the girls are excited about the move, I'm nervous. Other than your family we don't know anyone here. We don't know the city at all. How are we supposed to sell houses we can't find?"

"You and your family will do fine here in Vegas. A GPS will allow you to go anywhere and show houses. Marie and I are sorry about your mother passing away. She was a lovely woman. We enjoyed working with her. No one should have to go through the months of pain she endured. You are absolutely right, life can be so unfair."

"My mother was a faithful woman to everyone around her. Complete honesty was her motto. She was a straight forward no nonsense lady, someone who loved life."

"I didn't see your mother often, but I certainly will miss talking to her on the phone. I loved her positive outlook on life. Her entire life was devoted to Real Estate. She enjoyed matching people to the right house. I often thought about her style of selling houses. Unless I'm crazy your mother sold people houses she thought they could be happy in for a number of years, but not the rest of their lives."

"What is wrong with having repeat customers?" Sam fired back.

"Easy Sam, don't misunderstand me. There is nothing wrong with repeat customers long as the customers income increases so they can afford a nicer place. If you over-sell a customer to the point they struggle to keep the house. Never again will they buy another house at any price from you, or anyone else."

"You are splitting hairs and talking bullshit. You don't know a damn thing about selling real estate. Why are you trying to tell me my business?"

Considering the subliminal message CD Brad had made for Sam his argumentative words were confusing to Brad. He realized something was amiss. "Good point Sam, I apologize. You are the expert in selling houses. I know very little about selling houses."

"Are you mocking me?" Marie saw Sam's anger growing and become concerned. "You were born with a silver spoon in your mouth. Some of us have to rely on hard work to make our living. Your money creates shortcuts for you. When you want something you get it while the rest of us work our ass off scraping up pennies."

Sam marched off to the guest bedroom with Judy trailing behind him. Marie immediately turned to her husband. "What was that all about?"

"Don't worry about it Honey. Sam is stressed by his mother's death. I tried to imply she was a nice woman. He took my building her up as my tearing him down. I was only talking about his mother not him. If you get a chance to speak with him, encourage him to work on getting his mother's estate settled quickly. He needs something to concentrate on besides her death to get over his anger."

In the guest bedroom Judy was trying to calm Sam telling him similar words as Brad told Marie. "Brad was only complimenting your mother. He wasn't making a derogatory statement against you or her. You took his words wrong."

Sam's body quivered with anger. "If people didn't need that jerk he wouldn't have a friend in the world. Being so high and uppity he makes me sick. It will be hard working here in Vegas with him."

"Sam, how many mixed drinks have you had this evening?" Sam failed to answer his wife. "I think your alcohol intake may be clouding your brain. You are not your usual self tonight. Get some sleep. I'll go apologize to Brad and Marie for you."

"You do that. Go kiss his lily-white butt on the left side. The right side of his fanny where he was shot is probably still tender. While you are at it, ask for another handout. Pick up all the crumbs you want because we are unemployed. If we don't get a little Collins luck, we may wind up in the poorhouse."

Totally embarrassed by her husband's actions Judy went to apologized to Brad and Marie. "Sam is upset about his mother dying, and stressed about our future. In addition he had too much to drink this evening, he is talking nonsense. I'm sure he is passed out by now. I'm sorry this happened. Normally Sam doesn't drink this heavy. I've never seen him like this except our first New Year's Eve together. We are facing great changes. I think moving to Vegas makes the most sense but he isn't sure."

"Tomorrow when Sam is thinking clear again, tell him there is no rush to make a decision. He will have plenty to deal with to settle his mother's estate. If necessary take six months or a year to decide. It's important you both come to the same conclusion on where to live, and what you want to do. If you need additional financial help to get you over this difficult time, all you need to do is ask."

The following morning Sam stopped to gaze out the window at Marie, Judy, Brad, and Laura before joining them on the patio. Brad sat quiet as Marie said good morning to Sam. Laura rose to her feet. "I have a breakfast pizza in the oven. I need to check if it is ready to eat."

During Laura's absence Sam was very fidgety. While the girls chatted Brad studied Sam's actions and began to worry. It became clear he wasn't being influenced by the special subliminal message he made for him. Laura brought out plates and forks to the patio table before serving the breakfast pizza. "I forgot to get a knife to cut the pizza."

Sam bounced to his feet. "You guys stay put, I'll get a knife."

Everyone was distracted by the Pizza's smell. "I've never had a breakfast pizza but this smells great." Judy voiced her excitement about breakfast on the patio. "You can't eat breakfast outside in Seattle very often, one day a year if we are lucky."

Sam returned with a huge butcher knife. "Will this knife work?"

Everyone looked up in surprise. "The knife you choose is a little big but it should work." Laura commented. "Hand it here."

"I guess the knife is a little big. I could probably cut Brad's head off with a knife this large." He slightly swiped the knife in Brad's direction.

Judy slapped him arm. "Stop clowning around. Do you want the children seeing you horsing around with a sharp knife, I don't. Sit down and behave yourself."

"Give me the knife." Laura took the knife away from Sam to cut the pizza."

He seemed a little more jovial as people started eating. Marie turned to her husband. "What are you guys planning to do today, Judy and I are going to the kid's school so she can check it out? Laura has grocery shopping so you guys are free to do as you please?"

Sam immediately leaned forward. "I've been eyeing the hot tub since I arrived. I think a good soak might help me relax and clear my foggy head. Mother's death has taken a toll on me. One thing for certain I'm not ready to look for a house today."

At last, Brad smiled thinking his special subliminal message for Sam was beginning to work. Evidentially the alcohol intake yesterday blocked his attention span so Brad's message was not affecting Sam. "A morning hot tub session does sound nice this morning. Relaxation never hurt anyone. I have waterproof bandages on my injuries so I'll join you Sam, but I can't stay in the water long. Twenty minutes is about it."

Sam's plan was to hot tub as usual until he and Brad were getting out of the water. With a slippery wet body he would push Brad while pretending to catch him as he stepped out of the hot tub. He could guide his head to the concrete of the sidewalk in hopes of killing him and making it look like an innocent accident. Over and over he rehearsed the scenario in his head. There could be no mistake this time. While Brad was changing into his swimsuit as insurance Sam grabbed a hammer from the shed to lie beside the hot tub. If necessary he would smash Brad's skull to kill him and finish the job once, and for all this very morning. The thought of killing Brad made Sam smile.

Brad returned apologizing. "Sorry I took so long changing, I had a couple phone calls to make. I also directed the music out to the patio."

"No problem Brad, the ladies are gone. We have all morning and then some. We can hot tub long as our hearts desire." Sam climbed in first and slipped down in the soothing water. "If I can make enough money. I'm having a hot tub when we move to Vegas."

"I'm glad to hear you made up your mind to move here. Marie and I were telling Judy last night you actually have lots of time to make up your mind about where to live. We told her to take long as you want. We understand you will need time to settle your mother's estate. July and August are miserable hot months to do much outside in Vegas. The other ten months of the year in Vegas are great. At first I questioned if we wanted a hot tub living here. I thought it would be too hot to enjoy. During July and August we drain the hot tub and do other inside things early in the mornings. Even at midnight it's too warm to enjoy a hot tub during those months. Once we had children, Marie and I no longer skinny dip. With Laura, our boys and Marie's parent so near there are too many people around. We can't get careless, so we never hot tub in the nude anymore. If we feel like a little horse play, we use the Jacuzzi in our private bath area."

"If Marie were here now in place of me, you could safely skinny dip unless someone I don't know about is coming to visit. The kids are at school, her parents are at work and Laura is off shopping. We are alone, buddy."

"You are right to say I need to watch for opportunities like this when Marie is here and others are gone. I wouldn't advise shucking your suit, Laura just may return early. The women I don't expect to see until mid-afternoon. Marie wanted to show Judy some of the better streets to use during heavy traffic times to avoid gridlock on the Vegas Strip. Getting caught in gridlock and missing an appointment can be disastrous."

"Damn it Brad, just stop. You keep referring to business when I don't want to discuss business today. I want to relax and enjoy a break from the constant worry about work." Feeling confident no other people were around Sam thought this was the perfect time to make his move. "Are you about ready to get out of the hot tub, I'm getting waterlogged faster than I expected." He really wanted to act before Laura returned. "The water is too warm anyway. I'm not sure how you can stand this. My body is starting to itch. I must get out."

"Sam, I'm just starting to relax. I'm not ready to get out just yet." In hopes of getting Sam to relax more he needed to stay in the water longer. "Is Emily moving to Las Vegas with your family?"

"No, now that Judy and I are not working I let Emily go. Having a nanny was great, but these are tough times. We lost a lot of work time while mother was ill. Mother doesn't have much of an estate to settle. Her cancer treatment wiped out most of her money."

"What about her house and office. You will be selling those."

"Both the house and the office were recently remortgaged to help pay her medical bills. She didn't have any insurance. Brad, we have been in here over a half hour. I don't want you tiring out too much. Since getting shot you are not the most steady person on your feet. I may need to help you steady yourself when you get out. I was thinking if you feel like it maybe you can show me around the city after lunch."

Before Brad could answer Sam, Brad's cell phone rang. "I've got to take this call." After saying hello he listened carefully. "He returned last night! Why didn't you call me last night, what the hell kind of detective are you?" Brad shook his head as he ended his call. "Damn, that was our private detective. He just informed me Rusty is back in Vegas, but they are not sure where. I better hurry inside and close the security gate. The girls left it open when they left."

Sam opted to play dumb. "Why is Rusty returning important to you?"

"I fired Rusty a few days before I was shot. He is the most likely suspect in my getting shot. He may have come back for another try. I didn't think he had the guts to try killing me again. Underestimating people may be the death of me yet."

"I take back what I said about you showing me around the city this afternoon. I'm not riding around in the city with you if you think Rusty may make another attempt on your life. You are on your own. I'm also getting out of the hot tub and going in the house where it's safer." Sam quickly bailed out of the hot tub. "Come on hurry up Brad." He reached over as if to help Brad get out of the hot tub only to hook him under the arm and behind the head. Sam jerked him over and down towards the sidewalk. Brad caught the edge of the hot tub enough to break his fall. Sam grabbed the hammer drawing it high above his head for a powerful swing at Brad's head. "Wealth does not give you the privilege of screwing my wife."

A shot rang out striking Sam square in the back. The sudden force caused him to fall over face first into the hot tub. Brad rolled over to look around for Rusty only to see Emily standing at the corner of the house. As if in slow motion she lowered the big revolver in her hands and dropped it to the ground. Brad scrambled to his feet to fish Sam out of the water. Through the gaping hole where the bullet exited his chest he could see part of Sam's heart missing. The single bullet hit him dead center in the heart. Looking back he saw Emily walking towards him. "Is he dead?" Brad nodded yes. "Good, the bastard will never rape me again." She slumped to sit down in one of the patio chairs. "You better call the police."

"Sam was going to kill me with that hammer." He studied Emily's bruised face. "What happened to you?"

"Sam raped me, and he threatened to kill me if I told anyone. I didn't tell a sole about being raped until now. I wanted him dead first. He will never rape a woman. He got what he deserved."

"Just relax, while I call the Police. You shouldn't be in any trouble, you saved my life. Sam was going to kill me with that hammer." Brad hugged her.

Turning towards home Marie saw a sea of emergency vehicles filling the street by their house. She screamed and covered her face with both hands completely releasing the steering wheel. The car swerved to the left before Judy could grab the steering wheel to correct their direction.

"Stop the car!" Judy yelled. Braking hard Marie slid to a stop. Judy raced around the car. "Kill the engine and scoot over I'll drive."

Trembling in fear Marie slid to the right allowing Judy to drive. Her face was ghost white as tears streamed down her face. "He's dead, I know he is dead, I can feel it. Look at all the police cars and the ambulance, no one is hustling around. I know he's dead this time."

Although the police tried waving them on by Judy stopped blocking the street. "The keys are in the car. Move it if you want." Marie and Judy ran towards the house fast as they could.

"Come back here, you can't park here and you can't go back there. Other officer's blocked their path by grabbing them. "Sorry ladies. That area is being investigated as a crime scene."

Marie fainted and collapsed in a heap on the ground. Judy knelt beside her to straighten her prone body before looking up at the officers. "Our husbands were here alone. Can you tell me what happened?"

"Our investigation is currently in progress. We cannot give out sketchy information." As Marie stirred Laura came running up to the ladies. Judy looked up at her. "I think Brad has been shot again, maybe Sam too. They won't give us any information."

Laura joined Judy as she knelt beside Marie. All three women were visibly shaking. "Take those women inside out of the heat!" Someone yelled from a distance.

"I'll call Junior." Laura stated. He answered her call immediately. "Junior, you need to come home. There has been some kind of trouble at the house. The police are here but they won't tell us anything. Brad may have been shot again."

Judy, Marie, and Laura were herded inside the house by one officer. "Stay in this section of the house. Someone will be talking with you as soon as possible."

"Please tell us what you know." Marie's words fell on deaf ears as officers ignored her. "Damn you guys!" She cursed. The minutes ticked by slowly creating the illusion time was standing still. "Why did I leave Brad today?" Junior and Darcy soon joined the three girls. "They won't tell us anything. I'm certain Brad is dead and Sam may have been shot too. We haven't seen either one of them."

Darcy massaged Marie's shoulders. "Why did any of us leave today?"

Detective Ann Alder entered the room as Marie remembered the children. "The kids are due from school soon!"

"Mrs. Collins, your children are fine. Your parents have been contacted and gone to pick up the children, they are safe. Mrs. Collins your husband is okay."

Marie gave a sigh of relief. "Where is he, may I see him?"

"It will be a while before you can see your husband. He is still being questioned about what happened out by the hot tub."

Judy touched the detectives arm. "Is my husband okay, are they questioning him too?"

"Mrs. Anderson, your husband tried to kill Mr. Collins." The detective's words put Judy in the stage of disbelief. "He tried to smash Mr. Collins head with a claw hammer. He was shot in the back. Your husband was shot by a woman we tried to interview in Seattle but we couldn't find. Her name is Emily Parsons. She is sitting out by the hot tub in the state of shock. Emily has said very little as to why she shot your husband since we arrived."

"Emily is our nanny. We left her in Seattle at our home. She wouldn't be here. You must be confused about who shot my husband?" Judy couldn't believe her ears.

"Mr. Collins identified her as Emily Parsons, your nanny. Apparently she followed Mr. Anderson here. So far she has spoken only three words. She keeps pointing at your husband's body and saying he raped me. You ladies need to be patient. The security videos are being studied now. The Coroner arrived a few minutes ago. It will still take considerable time to wrap up our investigation. As we were certain years ago keeping secrets is a bad idea. Once again we have proof love triangles seldom work forever. Sins of the past can easily rear their ugly heads on any given day. We warned you people of such danger. You wouldn't listen and now things turned deadly."

Judy's head hung in disbelief as tears flowed from her eyes.

As police questioned Emily, she came forward with additional information. "During the last couple weeks of Sam's life, he changed. When Judy wasn't home Sam exposed himself to her and his daughters. From the hall bathroom he would step out and get a towel from the hall closet. Prior to the last couple weeks he had always showered in the master bath of their bedroom. He would say oops sorry as if our seeing him was an accident. After he raped me, I started thinking about Carrie and Kristy. Had someone not stopped him, I believe he would have soon molested them. After not reporting him raping me immediately, the police might not have believed me. Someone had to stop him before he hurt the girls."

In the end, Emily' case was dismissed as justifiable homicide. A term no longer used today, today's term is temporary insanity."

With Sam gone, it was up to Judy to return to Seattle to wrap up Sam's mother's estate. Among her things, Judy found two insurance policies totaling over a million dollars. Apparently, Sam didn't know about the policies.

Over time, Junior and Darcy had Bob Tilly build them a new house and a guest house for Darcy's mother, Marlina, on property given to them by Brad and Marie. The houses were near but not next to the Collins House. Beyond Junior and Darcy's home Bob Tilly also built a home for Judy and her girls. All the houses were surrounded by the same security type fence as the Collins had. It wasn't over a quarter of a mile to any of the houses. The neighbors saw the houses as a compound.

Early one morning, Marie sat across the kitchen table from Brad, drinking coffee. She smiled at him big. He couldn't help but smile back at her. "What are you smiling about this early in the morning?"

"I'm smiling because I love you and life in general. Our lives have settled into a wonderful relaxing lifestyle. Something we both have wanted for a long time. I believe we have finally matured enough to enjoy life more. I also have news for you. Marlina is thinking about getting married to Tom, the guy she has been seeing since moving to Las Vegas."

"I like the sound of them getting married. Marlina is a wonderful woman. She should not be living totally alone."

"And then there is Judy." Brad looked straight up at Marie as if to say what about Judy? "She and Evan Thomas are seeing a lot of one another. With Emily still being her nanny, she and Evan date on a regular basis. I can easily see them getting married in maybe a year. Carrie and Kristy think Evan is wonderful."

"Everything you are telling me is wonderful. I, too, have news. Carol is getting married and moving to Denver." Marie gave him a quick look of concern. "Hold on Honey, don't get too excited. Wendy is ready to retire. I spoke to Robin Tilly. She feels they are a good enough agency now they can do fine without our help enhancing videos. I think it is time to close down the Ad Palace."

"With the Ad Palace gone life would be much easier for us."

"I absolutely agree. How would you feel about keeping the office as our personal office, and hiring a personal secretary to handle most of our personal business?"

"We could benefit greatly from have a good personal secretary. It would mean hiring a new person." Her words made him smile. "Okay, spring it on me. Who do you have in mind as our personal secretary?"

"We know a wonderful middle aged lady who is currently working in a restaurant as manager and bookkeeper that might be interested in joining our group."

"Are you planning to keep me in suspense all day or are you going to tell me who you are talking about. No wait, I know who you are thinking about, Darcy's mother Marlina." He nodded she was correct. "Marlina is trustworthy; I'm all for offering her our new position if she wants it. When are you planning to speak to her?"

"We could buzz over to the restaurant she manages and have lunch today. While we are there we could ask her to walk over to our house this evening. It would not be proper for us to make our offer while she is at work."

"Then we have a dinner date today."

The result of their dinner date and evening conversation Marlina did become the personal secretary for Brad and Marie. This led to the Collins wanting to celebrate. A catered barbecue was held in honor of Marlina joining the team. The people living in the Collins compound enjoyed the evening. Judy brought Evan Thomas as her guest, just to keep the numbers even she said with a smile.

Finally Brad was living the life he always wanted, with family and friends, surrounding him. "Someday, in the not too distant future, we are going to have a block party, and invite some of our neighbors over for a catered dinner. It's time we grew our circle of friends."

Made in the USA
San Bernardino, CA
08 June 2016